THE WINGS OF MORNING

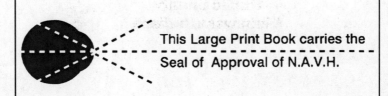

THE WINGS OF MORNING

MURRAY PURA

KENNEBEC LARGE PRINT
A part of Gale, Cengage Learning

GALE
CENGAGE Learning·

Detroit • New York • San Francisco • New Haven, Conn • Waterville, Maine • London

GALE
CENGAGE Learning®

LIBRARY OF CONGRESS CATALOGING-IN-PUBLICATION DATA

Pura, Murray, 1954–
    The wings of morning / by Murray Pura.
        pages ; cm. — (Kennebec Large Print superior collection)
    (Snapshot in history series ; #1)
    ISBN 978-1-4104-4968-9 (softcover) — ISBN 1-4104-4968-8 (softcover) 1.
Amish—Fiction. 2. World War, 1914-1918—Participation, Amish—Fiction.
3. World War ,1914-1918—Pennsylvania—Fiction. 4. Large type books. I.
Title.
PR9199.4.P87W56 2012b
813'.6—dc23   2012017088

Published in 2012 by arrangement with Harvest House Publishers

Printed in the United States of America
1 2 3 4 5   16 15 14 13 12
FD201

For my brother Bill, always
with his heart in the skies,
and his wife, Talia, who has kept to
the best of her Mennonite roots —
compassion, grace, faith, and peace.

If I take the wings of the morning, and dwell in the uttermost parts of the sea; even there shall thy hand lead me, and thy right hand shall hold me.

PSALM 139:9–10

ONE

Lyyndaya Kurtz straightened her back and looked up at the blue and bronze evening sky. It was that strange sound again, like a large swarm of bees at their hive, and it grew louder and louder. She leaned the hoe against the picket fence her father had built around the garden. Her mother, whose hearing was no longer very good, continued to chop at weeds between the rows of radishes and lettuce. She glanced at her daughter as Lyyndaya shielded her eyes from the slowly setting sun.

"Was ist los?" she asked, using Pennsylvania Dutch.

"Can't you hear them, Mama?" Lyyndaya responded. "There are aeroplanes coming."

Her mother stood up, still holding the hoe in her brown hands, and squinted at the sun and sky. "I don't see anything. Is it a small one?"

"No, it's too loud for just one aeroplane.

Do you see, Mama?" Lyyndaya pointed. "Coming out of the west. Coming out of the sun."

Now her mother shielded her eyes. "All I am seeing is spots in front of my eyes from looking into the light."

"Look higher. There are — three, four, six — there are half a dozen of them."

The planes were not that far from the ground, Lyyndaya thought, only a thousand feet, not much more. Each with two wings, the top wing longer than the bottom one, each plane painted a yellow that gleamed in the sunlight. As she watched, one of them broke away from the others and dropped toward them. It came so low that the roar of the engine filled the air and children ran from their houses and yards into the dirt road and the hay fields. They were soon followed by their mothers and fathers and older brothers and sisters.

Lyyndaya laughed as the plane flew over their house. A hand waved at her from the plane's open cockpit and she waved back with all her might. "Can you see the plane now, Mama?" she teased.

Her mother had crouched among the heads of lettuce as the plane flashed past. "Ach," she exclaimed with a cross look on her face, "this must be your crazy boy, Jude

Whetstone."

"He's coming back!"

The plane had banked to the left over Jacob Miller's wheat field and was heading back over the farmhouses while the other five planes carried on to the east. Its yellow wings dipped lower and lower. Lyyndaya's green eyes widened.

"He's going to land in Papa's field!" she cried. "Where the hay was cut on Monday!"

She lifted the hem of her dress in both hands and began to run. The black *kaap* that covered her hair at the back, left untied, flew off her head.

"Lyyndaya! This is not seemly!" her mother called after her.

But the young woman had reached the old gray fence around the hay field, gathered the bottom of her navy blue dress in one hand, and climbed over, and with strands of sand-colored hair unraveling from their pins, she was racing over the stubble to where the plane's wheels were just touching the earth. Others were running toward the plane from all directions, jumping the fence if they were spry enough, opening the gate to the field if they were not.

The aeroplane came to a stop in the middle of the field and when the propeller stopped spinning a young man in a brown

11

leather jacket and helmet pushed his goggles from his eyes and jumped from the cockpit to the ground. He was immediately surrounded by the several boys and girls who had outrun the adults in their rush toward the craft. He mussed the hair of two of the boys who came up to him and tugged the pigtail of a red-headed girl.

"Jude!" Lyyndaya exclaimed as she ran up to him, the tan on her face flushed. "What are you doing here?"

"Hello, Lyyndy," the young man smiled, lifting one of the boys up on his shoulders. "The whole flying club went up and I convinced them to come this way to Paradise. I wanted to see you."

"To see me? You fly a plane from Philadelphia just to see me?"

"Why not?"

"But you were coming back on the train in a few days."

"A few days. I couldn't wait that long."

Lyyndaya could feel the heat in her face as neighbors looked on. She saw one or two frown, but most of the men and women smiled. A very tall man in a maroon shirt wearing a straw hat laughed. She dropped her eyes.

"Bishop Zook," she murmured, "how are you?"

"Gute, gute," he responded. "Well, Jude, what is all this? Why has a pigeon dropped out of the sky?"

Bishop Zook was not only tall, at least six-foot-nine, but broad-shouldered and strong. He shook Jude's hand with a grip like rock. The young man pulled his leather helmet off his head so that his dark brown hair tumbled loose. Lyyndaya fought down an overwhelming urge to take Jude and hug him as she had done so many times when they were nine and ten.

"I wanted the children to see the plane, Bishop Zook," said Jude.

"Only the children?"

"Well —" Jude stumbled. "I thought perhaps — I might ask Miss Kurtz —"

"Ah," smiled the bishop. "You want to *take her up,* as you flying men say?"

"I thought —"

"Are you two courting?"

"Courting?"

"You remember what is courting, my boy — you have not been among the *English* in Philadelphia that long, eh?"

Everyone laughed, and Lyyndaya thought the heat in her face and hands would make her hair and skin catch on fire.

Bishop Zook put an arm like a plank around Jude's slender shoulders. "You know

13

when there is the courting here, we let the boy take the girl home in the buggy after the Sunday singing. You remember that much after a week away?"

"Yes —"

"So your horse and buggy are where?" the bishop said.

Jude continued to hunt desperately for his words. "In the barn, but I wanted —" He stopped, his tongue failing him as the whole colony stood watching and listening.

The bishop waited a moment and then walked over and touched the top wing of the plane. He ran his hand over the coated fabric and nodded. "A beautiful buggy. Pulled by horses with wings, eh? How many, Master Whetstone?"

Jude was trying not to look at Lyyndaya for help, but did anyway, and she was making sure she did not look at him or offer any by keeping her eyes on the stubble directly in front of the toes of her boots.

"There are —" Jude stepped away from the crowd pressing in on him and Lyyndaya and turned around to look at the plane behind him as if he were seeing it for the first time — "there are —" He stood utterly still and stared at the engine as if it did not belong there. Then he looked at Bishop Zook's thick black beard and broad face.

14

"Ninety. Ninety horses."

The bishop nodded again and kept running his hand over the wing. "More than enough. There is the problem however — if God had meant us to fly, Master Whetstone, wouldn't he have given us wings, hm?"

He took his hand from the plane and looked at Jude directly. Several of the men and women murmured their agreement with the bishop's question and nodded their heads. Most remained silent, waiting for Jude's answer. Jude stared at the bishop, trying to gauge the look in the tall man's blue eyes. He thought he saw a flash of humor so he went ahead with the answer he had used a hundred times in their own Amish colony as well as in dozens of the ones around it.

"Bishop Zook," he responded, "if God had meant us to ride a buggy he would have given us wheels and four legs."

"Ah ha!" shouted the bishop, slapping his huge hand against his leg and making most of the people jump, including Lyyndaya. "You have it, Master Whetstone, you have it." He clapped his hands lightly in appreciation and a smattering of relieved laughter came from the small crowd. "So now take me up."

"What?"

15

"As bishop, I must make sure it is safe for Miss Kurtz, *ja?* After all, who has ever had such a horse and buggy in our colony, eh?" He gave his hat to one of the men and climbed into the front of the two cockpits.

"I only have a little time before I must head back to Philadelphia —" Jude began, again glancing at Lyyndaya for help, who had gone so far as to raise her gaze to stare fixedly at the bishop and the plane, but still refused to make eye contact with the young man.

"Five minutes," said the bishop with a gleam in his eye. "That is all I ask. I am not the one you are courting, eh?"

The people laughed again. The thought passed through Jude's head that the bishop was enjoying a lot of laughter at his expense. Then he shrugged and climbed into the rear cockpit. He saw his father in the crowd and gestured with his hand.

"Papa, will you give the propeller a turn?" he asked.

"Of course, my boy."

As Jude's father, a tall, slender man with a short beard and warm brown eyes, walked toward the plane, Bishop Zook leaned his head back and asked, "Now, before the engine noise, tell me, what is the name of this aeroplane and where do they make such things?"

Jude handed the bishop a leather helmet and goggles. "It's a Curtiss JN-4, the Jenny, and they're usually made in Buffalo, New York. But our flying club outside of Philadelphia was able to purchase these at a very good price from our Canadian friends just across the border. They are built there by Curtiss's Canadian associate, the Canadian Aeroplane Company, so we call them the Canuck."

"But they are the same as the New York ones?"

"Almost. They have one great advantage. I use a stick, a joystick, to control the aeroplane in these. The old American ones have a wheel that is not as good."

"Why don't we put the stick in ours then?"

"We will. The next model has the stick, the JN-4D. But they have only brought it out this month. There are not enough of them. Besides, it's 1917 and they are all going to the army. Civilian clubs will not be able to purchase them while the war is on."

Jude's father, in his brown summer shirt and straw hat, was standing in front of the plane and smiling. Jude played with a switch on the control panel in his cockpit. Then he pulled down his goggles and smiled back at his father and made a circle in the air with his hand. His father nodded, put both hands on the top blade of the wooden propeller, and swung it downward. The engine coughed twice and roared. His father's hat went spinning into the sky with the prop wash.

"Contact," Jude said loudly. "Please buckle on your harness, Bishop Zook."

"Ah. So we truly do have something in common with the horses."

Jude's father had caught up with his hat. He looked back at his son and pointed east. Jude turned the plane in that direction.

"What is your father telling us?" shouted Bishop Zook.

"The direction the wind or breeze is coming from. We take off into the wind."

"Why?"

"It gives us lift to help get the aeroplane off the ground."

The craft moved ahead, slowly bouncing over the field, then gathering speed and rising into the air. Jude took it to a thousand feet and made sure he flew over the entire town of Paradise and especially the bishop's dairy farm on the west end. The sun was still an hour or two over the horizon and covered the plane in light. The bishop began to laugh and slapped one of his hands against the side of the Jenny.

"Too beautiful, too beautiful," Jude heard him call out. "*Mein Gott,* what a gift you have given the birds, such a gift, such a world."

When they landed again and the propeller had spun down to a stop, Bishop Zook climbed out, pumped Jude's hand like an excited boy, and then beckoned to Lyyndaya.

"Come, come, my dear," he smiled, "your buggy awaits."

Feeling every eye on her, the skin of her face burning, she stepped up to the plane and the bishop helped her into the front cockpit. She used one hand to manage her dress and the other to grab onto parts of the plane. When she was finally in her seat, the bishop gave her the helmet and goggles and showed her how to tighten the buckles of the shoulder harnesses. Then he walked to the front of the plane and bent his head at Jude's father.

"May I?"

Jude's father stood back from the propeller. "Of course."

"I just pull it downward?"

"*Ja,* just a sharp tug and then let it go. Do not hold on."

"Yes, yes, all right — when?"

"My son will tell you."

Lyyndaya sat in her cockpit feeling an odd mixture of embarrassment, excitement, and fear. Suddenly Jude's hand squeezed her left shoulder from behind.

"You will be all right, Lyyndy Lyyndy Lou," he said.

She could not turn all the way around to see him, but she knew he would be smiling just as his use of the childhood nickname had made her smile as well. Now, ten years later, without having had a chance to discuss it between themselves, the plane ride had become a buggy ride and they were courting, thanks to Bishop Zook. Well, it would give them something to talk about besides the weather and the crops when he came back to Lancaster County from Philadelphia in a few days.

She could not see what Jude was doing, but the bishop all of a sudden nodded, swung down on the propeller with his enormous hands and arms, and the engine burst into life. They began to roll across the ground faster than she had ever traveled in anything before, faster than galloping her mare, Anna, bareback. She felt her heart hammering and her mouth go dry.

"Hang on!" shouted Jude.

The wind was rushing against her face and body. The earth streamed past brown and green. The sky was a streak of blue and silver. Then the plane lifted into the air and her stomach seemed to turn inside out and upside down. She looked down and the men and women and children were like dolls and the wagons like toys and the houses like tiny boxes. Suddenly the plane banked to the right and she felt herself falling out of her seat. The leather flying helmet, unfastened, was torn from her head, her hair exploded in the rush of air, and as her arms dropped over the side into empty space she could not stop herself and started to scream.

TWO

"What is it?" shouted Jude, straining his head forward as far as he could. "What's wrong?"

She had grabbed onto both sides of the cockpit. "I feel like . . . I'm falling out of my seat . . ."

"You are strapped in, aren't you?"

"Yes — but they are very loose —"

"Because Bishop Zook was sitting there. Pull on them. Tighten them."

"He showed me, but I'm not sure how he held the straps."

"Grab the open ends."

Jude leveled the plane out while Lyyndaya struggled. She tugged and tugged and finally they snugged up against her shoulders. Closing her eyes, she whispered a prayer of thanks.

"Do you want to go back down?" Jude asked in a loud voice.

Lyyndaya opened her eyes. They were flying right into a sunset of crimson and amber. It was as if they were going toward a huge bright flower in the air. The green land spread underneath them for hundreds of miles. She could see the rivers, the forests, the villages, all as if they were part of some miniature play set. Her lips parted. This was what it was like to be a robin or a lark or a dove. She closed her eyes again. *God,* she prayed, *calm me so that I can take in more of this, enjoy what you have created, celebrate a gift of wings.*

"Shall I land?" Jude asked again.

He couldn't see her face, of course, but when she opened her eyes again they were narrow and emerald and sharp — what her brothers and sisters called "Lyyndy's cat eyes" and which usually meant trouble.

"No, I don't want to land, Jude Whetstone," she called back, "I want you to take me right into the sun."

"What?"

"Fly me into the greatest amount of light possible."

Lyyndaya could feel him grinning in the irresistible way he had, feel it the way she could sense it when his eyes rested on her during a Sunday meal.

"How fast are we going?" she asked above the sound of the rushing air and the engine.

"About 60 miles per hour."

"How fast can we go?"

"Oh — 73 or 75."

"Do that."

"Do what?"

"Go as fast as you can."

"Are you serious?"

Lyyndaya took a deep breath and blurted out the very thing she was most frightened of. "Go into the sun as fast as you can and do a barrel roll."

"A barrel roll? I've only done a barrel roll two or three times."

"Do a barrel roll for me — please."

She leaned her head back and heard the engine take on an aggressive snarl, like a wild animal pouncing. Red and purple light swooped into her eyes as Jude hurled the plane west. *Like a smooth yellow stone,* she thought, *from his boyhood slingshot.* The light came on and on and filled her vision and filled up everything that was inside her, heart and soul. *I have wings,* she repeated to herself over and over again to fight down her fear of the speed and the roll Jude would do at any moment, *I have wings like a swallow, like a hawk, like an archangel.*

The plane flipped upside down. Lyyndaya's breath burst out of her. She might have screamed again, but she pressed a hand over her mouth and bit into a finger. Her whole body was hanging down toward the ground, held in place only by the seat harness. The hair on her head, completely free of any pins now, fell loose and thick and golden like a flame burning out of the cockpit. Both hands gripped the sides of the plane until they were white as bone. She arched her neck, saw the streams and barns and farm fields below, wrong side up, thought it looked ridiculous, as if she were walking on her hands, began to laugh, and then Jude flipped the plane to the side for a few moments so that her hair streaked out from the plane as if a wing were on fire, and she laughed even harder. When the biplane swung right side up once again, completing the roll, Lyyndaya thought, *Why, it's like doing a cartwheel, or riding the Chicago Ferris wheel, only we're doing it in thin air.*

"How was that?" Jude called.

"Wonderful!" she shouted, and she did feel wonderful.

"Shall I do it once more?"

"Yes, please, yes!" she almost screamed.

She heard him laugh out of his chest. "What a crazy girl you are. You should be hollering for me to land."

"Why should I?"

"Because that's what the girls do who we

take up for rides at a dollar apiece in Philadelphia. We no sooner get them up than they scream they want to go down again. What a waste of a dollar. At least you should try to get your money's worth."

"Is that how much this will cost me? A dollar?"

"I had something else in mind."

She smiled and shouted, "Oh, yes? And what was that?"

He yelled something at her, a single word, she wanted it to be *kiss,* but she wasn't sure if it was kiss or hug or what it was, because just as he said it he flipped the plane upside down again, let her hang by the straps and feel her hair almost touch the earth once more, then swung her upright — *Almost,* she thought, *as if he swung me in his strong beautiful arms.*

Now the sunset was all around them — the sky was red above, below, in front, and behind. They were flying in vermilion. She pulled the red into herself in great big lungfuls, opening her mouth as wide as she could, opening it as wide as a tomboy, not an Amish woman. Her fingers and toes tingled. She let one arm dangle out of the side of the cockpit as if she were in a boat and trailing her hand in the water.

"Still doing well?" Jude called.

"Very well."

"Aren't you cold with just that little dress on?"

"No."

The dress was short-sleeved and goose bumps ran up and down each arm.

"We have to head back."

"Yes, I was afraid of that."

"I think well of you, Lyyndy."

"Think well of me? Whatever for? All I did was sit here like a sack of oats."

"I think well of you because whatever you're afraid of you face head-on and conquer."

"I'm not —" Lyyndaya began, and she was going to finish the sentence with "afraid of anything to do with flying," but she knew that was a lie, and knew Jude would know it too. So she decided to let his sentence stand, unchallenged, not only because it was the truth, but also because she liked the idea of brave and wild and beautiful Jude Whetstone thinking well of Lyyndaya Kurtz.

The plane banked to the left as Jude headed the Curtiss Jenny east. The movement felt as normal to Lyyndaya now as a sailing vessel heeling to port in a stiff breeze or a cart full of vegetables for market leaning heavily to one side as it took a sharp turn in the road. The town and the people

27

who stood watching rushed back at them. The green corn, the green hay, the black fields, and the earth jumped up. They hit and bounced and the engine cried and the propeller spun like the Chicago Ferris wheel and stopped.

Her mother was at her side immediately, face creased with lines of worry. "Lyyndaya Kurtz, just look at you. You are as red as a beet. Your hair is a mess. Pin it back up. Where is your *kapp?*"

"Oh, Mama, I feel fine, it was —"

"And your arms. Like ice."

"I'm fine, honestly, it was wonderful."

"And what have you done to your finger? How did you cut it?"

Lyyndaya looked down at the finger she had bitten till it bled. "Just a scratch. A grass cut."

"A grass cut? Where is the grass when you are a hundred miles in the air where man was never meant to go?"

Lyyndaya's mother began pulling pins from a pocket under her apron and hurriedly tidying her daughter's windblown hair.

Her father loomed up, dark and stocky and frowning in his beard. Lyyndaya thought he looked like a papa bear robbed of its cubs. "That wild boy will be the death of you," he rumbled.

"Oh, Papa, he was a perfect gentleman."

"Upside down," her father continued to growl, "sideways, spinning like a top. This is a circus? You are on the trapeze? What is to keep the plane from falling? What if God stops holding you up?"

"Papa, the wings and the engine and the air hold us up —"

His hands were grasped tightly behind his back. "We are the laughing stock of Paradise. You could not hear what the people of the colony said while you fooled around up there as if you were in your own little world, but we could hear them. Oh, *ja.*"

"Papa —"

He clenched and unclenched his teeth and his beard moved up and down with his jaw. "We are converts to this community. Only ten years we are here. It is important that we be accepted." He lowered his voice as the engine noise died and people crowded around the plane to touch it and talk to Jude about the barrel rolls. "This idea of you courting that — young man — you can put that from your head. It is out of the question."

"Papa, that was just something Bishop Zook said —"

"I do not care what Bishop Zook said. You

29

will not see that boy again. There will be no buggy rides. And there will certainly be no more aeroplane rides."

Now everyone was pressing in, laughing, asking Lyyndaya questions, and her father and mother withdrew. Lyyndaya smiled and answered the children and adults as warmly as she could, but inside her a heavy stone of darkness dropped and took all her good spirits with it. She felt like bursting into tears. *Jude's family are converts too,* she wanted to shout after her parents' receding backs as they walked stiffly home, *and he has lost his mother, but look how the colony loves him.* Of course, she said nothing. An older woman was wiping Lyyndaya's finger clean with a damp cloth she had pulled out from under her apron. Lyyndaya took her eyes from her mother and father and thanked the woman, Mrs. Stoltzfus, whose husband, Samuel, was one of the colony's ministers.

"So, so!" boomed Bishop Zook, smiling and patting her on the arm. "How was the buggy ride?"

She burrowed around inside her misery to try and find a quip. "Ah, Bishop Zook," she finally said, "it was as if the horses flew."

"Ha, yes, so young love makes you feel, eh?" He leaned in closely to her and said quickly and quietly, "I see this is a difficult thing for your mother and father. Respect their wishes. Pray. Wait. You and young Jude, love, aeroplanes, this is still unfolding like a summer rose for our colony. Let us see how God will surprise us. It is necessary to have some rain before we can see the bud open."

Then he clapped his hands gently. "The night comes. It is time our young aviator was up and away to Philadelphia. You may speak with him when he returns by train in three or four days. In the meantime, we send him on his way in God's mercy." The bishop and the other men doffed their hats, the bishop prayed, the hats returned to their heads.

"Let me try that propeller one more time," the bishop smiled as soon as he had lifted his head and planted his hat firmly back on his head. "You have enough of the fuel, yes?"

"Just enough, thanks," said Jude.

The sun was still above the horizon in the west, but only just. Jude would be flying east to the Atlantic and Philadelphia where a purple darkness was already rising from the trees and crops and ponds. It was eighty miles by train or horse and would take Jude over an hour. Lyyndaya gave Jude a crooked smile, feeling a new fear, of him going it alone into the black night. He saw her worry

31

and shook his head.

"I have flown under the stars before," he said. "I'll be all right."

But it was not just the night of stars Lyyndaya was troubled about, it was the night of a future without him, without any possibility of being at his side to help move the stick and guide the flight. She gave a small smile she knew he would misunderstand as a nagging concern for the night flying. He winked and tugged the goggles over his eyes. She felt cold and alone as the bishop swung the propeller downward and the prop wash blew his hat off and the colony laughed.

When Jude was in the air and gone, her two sisters and three brothers gathered around her, jabbering and asking her things she did not feel like answering. Her quiet and unease quickly communicated itself to her siblings as they all walked back to the house together. Everyone grew silent. The oldest, Ruth, as always, hit the nail on the head and linked her arm through Lyyndaya's.

"It is Mama and Papa," she said in a sad way. "They do not approve of Jude Whetstone or of aeroplanes and now they will give our sister *the talk*."

As they came up the walk to the house

the lamp in the kitchen was burning brightly. In the square of window, Lyyndaya could see her mother and father sitting at the table drinking coffee.

"Mama and Papa are waiting for us," chirped Daniel, who was nine.

"They are not waiting up for us," said Ruth softly, and she gave her sister's arm a squeeze. "They are waiting for Lyyndaya."

THREE

After milk and cookies had been consumed in silence, Mama shooed everyone to their rooms and came back to sit down with Papa and their second oldest daughter, Lyyndaya. Mama poured her daughter a cup of coffee and added the cream she knew Lyyndaya liked, but the girl did not drink from the cup. Her father picked up on her mood.

"It is not the end of the world, my Lyyndy," he said forcing himself to smile. "You are a beauty, our blessing, and many young men, good young men, will be asking for your hand. Why, only last week, wasn't it, Mother, the Hostetler boy, young David, he was asking after you."

"He is a child," Lyyndaya said quickly, in a voice like a pair of scissors snipping fabric.

"He's only one. There was the Beiler boy as well, Jacob, and Jonathan Harshberger —"

"Hush, Father," said Lyyndaya's mother,

putting a hand on her husband's arm. "I know you mean well, but a young woman does not want to hear about other young men when she has her heart set on a particular one."

Lyyndaya's father bristled, losing his good temper immediately and completely. "Heart set? Heart set? How can her heart be set? The two scarcely know each other."

"They grew up together, Father."

"Children's games, childish antics. Now it is time to be an adult and put aside the toys of infanthood."

"He is very kind —" Lyyndaya started to say, but her father interrupted.

"We are converts and we are trying to make a good impression," he snapped.

"So is he," Lyyndaya responded, "and he is already making a good impression."

"What? By jumping around in the air like some sort of — balloon?"

Lyyndaya shook her head and sat straighter in the chair. "Didn't you see the way they crowded around his aeroplane? How they smiled at him? Yes, I know not everyone is sure about flying, just as we are not sure about telephones and electricity and motorcars and photography. But the decision has not been made to exclude flying from the Amish, Papa. And even if some

35

are not sure about flying machines they are sure about Jude. He is one of them. One of *us*. All the pastors agreed he should be allowed to learn to fly last year. All the pastors agreed he should be permitted to belong to a flying club provided he did not purchase an aeroplane and park it in his field like an object of pride."

Her father pointed a finger at her. "The colony may like him the way all parents like all their children. But he is still considered a wild one. Look at the stunts he pulled tonight, dangerous stunts, *ja?* If the engine had failed . . ."

"I asked him to do the stunts." Lyyndaya sat even straighter. She knew her green eyes were on fire by the way her mother looked at her.

"No — not just the flying," her father went on, "I mean these stunts, upside down, around and around —"

"*Ja,* I asked him to do all of that. Otherwise he would have flown straight and level like an arrow."

"You did?" Her father struggled to grasp this. "You asked him?"

"*Ja.*"

He sat back in his chair a moment and stared at her. Then he began to nod, glanced at his wife, and looked back at Lyyndaya,

36

still nodding.

"It is his influence that changes you," he finally said. "I should have put a stop to this years ago, when you were fifteen, sixteen. May God forgive me for being such a poor father."

"You are not a poor father," Lyyndaya protested.

"Too soft. I am always too soft." He rapped his knuckles on the table. "No more. There he is, off in Philadelphia, when he should be hard at work at the forge —"

"Papa!" Lyyndaya exclaimed. "That is not fair. You know how he worked night and day to get plows ready for spring planting, to shoe horses, fix buggy wheels and suspensions, all so he could spend a few days developing his flying skills —"

"A few days!" her father almost shouted. "Weeks among the English! Weeks!"

"— and go to Philadelphia, something the bishop and the leadership approved of and gave their consent to. You make it sound like — like — he is some lazy gadabout with his head in the clouds —"

Her father snorted like a horse. "What else would a flyboy be?"

"— when he has always done his duty by this colony, always worked hard as our blacksmith. Don't you remember the Widow

Borkholder, her iron bed, she could not sleep on any other, and he was up twenty-four hours mending the frame so that she could rest. He took no sleep for himself for more than a day so he could —" Lyyndaya felt the tightness in her throat and the burning on her face and stumbled for words. Looking like a twelve-year-old again, she appealed to her mother. "Mama, you know that what Papa says about Jude is not true —"

Her mother waved a hand in the air. "The pair of you. I should have locked you both up in the corncrib years ago until you settled matters. You are too much alike — headstrong, determined, independent, clever with the tongue." She looked at her husband. "You know, Papa, that we have said we will abide by the rules of the colony and the decisions of the bishop and elders."

He averted his eyes and looked at the wall on the other side of the kitchen. *"Ja, ja."*

"So then there is no argument when Jude is permitted to take flying lessons or go to the aerodrome in Philadelphia if the colony's leadership have agreed to allow it, is there?"

Lyyndaya's father said nothing, but she could see his jaw working under his beard. Then her mother turned two tired but very dark eyes on her.

"And daughter, I know you like this boy, this man, this Jude Whetstone. No, he is not old family, they came at the same time we did thanks to Bishop Lapp's ministrations, may he rest with the Lord. But — perhaps — you are not right for each other. Perhaps —" She hesitated, gazing at her daughter's broken face and the broken spirit it expressed, then bit her lower lip and plunged ahead "— perhaps it is like striking a match by a barrel of gasoline. The two should not mix. Not unless you want to blow something up. Or burn down a house."

"Mama —" Lyyndaya began.

Her mother waved her hand again. "Let me finish. You are very young. So is he. *Ja,* some girls here marry at sixteen or seventeen, but that is not for everybody. Who knows what you will yet grow into? Who knows what you will become? Who knows how he will change, how the both of you will change? It is enough now that you respect our wishes and not spend time with him and certainly not let him court you. Your father and I are unsure about flying, but that is a debate the whole colony is having and it is not for us to decide for the colony what is right and what is wrong. But you are our daughter, and when it comes to you and your future then it is for us to decide what is right and what is wrong. We feel this young man is wrong for you and that what is best for you is a future that does not have him in it."

Lyyndaya sat very still, then began slowly to speak. "Very well. I will do as you wish. May I meet with him again to tell him what we have discussed, or should I write a note?"

Her mother smiled in a sad, lopsided way and nodded. "I think a note would be best, dear. Ruthie can deliver it."

Lyyndaya pushed back her chair and stood up. "May I go to my room now?"

"Of course, dear," her mother responded. "Are you sure you don't want your coffee?"

"No, thank you. Good night, Mama. Good night, Papa."

She avoided looking at her father as she went up the stairs to the room she shared with Ruth. When she opened the door a lamp was lit on a table, but Ruth was not there. Often she read Bible stories to the younger ones at bedtime and prayed with them before Mother and Father came up to tuck them in. Lyyndaya wanted Ruth's company with one part of herself, and wanted to be alone with another part, so she accepted her sister's absence with a sense of what was meant to be, flopped down on her bed, and cried as quietly as she could manage into her pillow.

When all her tears were exhausted, she rolled over on her back and stared up at the ceiling of plain boards. How could an evening that had begun so beautifully, in an aeroplane flying through the sunset, end so badly, with her parents telling her she could not see Jude again? *Oh, God,* she prayed, *what am I going to do? How can I tell Jude? He just lost his mother in February and now he will lose our friendship as well.* She sat up on her bed, opened the drawer of her night table, took out a fresh white handkerchief, and blew her nose into it. On top of the small table was a thick black Bible and another book bound in red leather. She took the red book and lay on her stomach.

This dear book was the most precious possession she had. Great-grandmother Kurtz, who loved playing with words and had given her the unusual name of Lyyndaya, had also written a devotional book for her great-granddaughter. The book, bound by hand by her great-grandmother's husband, Grandpapa Moses, contained Grandmother's own ideas about various scriptures, which were combined with her vast store of life experiences so that she was able to produce unique day-by-day readings for the whole year. Lyyndaya had been using the red book since she was ten, a month before her great-grandmother died, and had been reading it through every year since then. It had inspired and encouraged her more than once, and now she turned to it again, her heart a stone in her chest.

She opened it to June twenty-seventh.

The Bible verse her great-grandmother based the day's passage on was from Philemon 15: *For perhaps he therefore departed for a season, that thou shouldest receive him for ever.* Lyyndaya was startled and read the verse twice. Then she looked over what her great-grandmother had written in her neat, precise hand. It was about the goodbyes and farewells of life.

Sometimes you see the person again on earth, sometimes in heaven. If it is on earth, the separation may be due to war or employment or illness. It might be, if the person is meant to be a close friend, that neither of you are quite ready to be close friends yet. Or it might be, if you feel the person is destined to be your husband, God has more work to do in each of your lives before he entrusts you to one another forever. One must rely on God above all. One must learn not only patience and perseverance, but a deeper faith in him, in his goodness, and in his ways.

Her great-grandmother had underlined the word *rely* three times.

Suddenly Lyyndaya felt light as air. A warmth and a freedom swept through her mind and body and she felt like God was in the room with her, granting her joy in the midst of sadness. The Bible's words ran through her thoughts over and over again: *for a season, that thou shouldest receive him for ever.* She went to a corner of the room, where there stood a fold-down writing desk with three drawers and two glass sides for books. Her favorites were on one side, Ruth's on the other. She lowered the writing surface and sat in the chair. Taking a sheet of paper from one of the small shelves within the desk, she began to copy what her great-grandmother had written. When she was finished, she took another sheet of paper and penned,

Dear Jude Whetstone,
We cannot court as we might have wished for Mother and Father do not approve of aeroplanes nor of my spending time with a man who flies them. Their disapproval is exactly the opposite of my own feelings, for I approve of you very much, and if I could have things my way, we would be taking the one-

horse buggy or the ninety-horse buggy home from Sunday singing together every week.

Please read over what my great-grandmother Kurtz wrote so many years ago. The verse for today, the day we flew into the sun, was Philemon 15, and it is about letting someone depart for a short amount of time, so that they can come back to you later, when everything and everyone is ready, and then stay forever. I believe the verse is meant to speak to you and me.

I will see you at the Sunday gatherings or barn raisings or picnics. I will say hello, but that is all I may do — for this season. If you fly over the settlement and you wave to me, I will wave back — but only once. If I pass you on the road, whether I am walking or there is a buggy, and you doff your hat to me, I will incline my head — but only briefly. I must obey my parents. But I pray and believe that one day, in God's time, I will be able to put my arms about you and ask you to put your arms about me.

Your friend, and someday much more,
as God wills,
Lyyndaya Kurtz

When Ruth came softly into the room a half an hour later, Lyyndaya had brushed her teeth, combed out the snarls in her hair, put on her white summer nightgown of cotton, crawled under the covers, and was asleep. A letter in an envelope lay on Ruth's bed with the name *Jude Whetstone* on it. Ruth had been told it was her task to take her sister's note to Jude and bring back any reply, whether verbal or written — but only once — for her mother had spoken to her about it. By common consent, they had agreed it was best to give Lyyndaya more time to herself, so Ruth had sipped a cup of tea in the kitchen and listened to her parents tell her why they had to do what they were doing to Lyyndaya and Jude.

She took the envelope in her hand and sat on her bed and thought about purposely losing it or destroying it. Then Jude would be none the wiser and would show up at the door or at the Sunday singing with a horse and buggy for Lyyndaya. Mother and Father would have to explain themselves to Jude at the house or in front of the whole colony at the singing instead of hiding behind the letter.

Ruth sighed. Of course, she would not do that. She was a good daughter and tried very hard to be a good Christian. The day

45

Jude returned on the train, hoping to see her sister, she would be the bearer of bad tidings that would crush his spirit. Oh, she liked him — she thought he was perfect for Lyyndaya. Her younger sister needed someone as strong-willed and adventurous as she was. Why couldn't Mother and Father see past aeroplanes and propellers and focus on the young man at the smithy who worked hard, sang the hymns like an angel, and who had wept unashamedly at his mother's funeral? He was a man with heart and soul.

She looked over at Lyyndaya, fast asleep, bright hair fanning across her pillow like a bird's wing.

"Oh, my little Lyyndy," she whispered, "what Jude wouldn't give to be sitting where I am right now and looking at your beauty. Will there ever be such a day for him or you? I fear that before there is even the remotest chance of that happening you will both have to go through waters that are too deep, too dark, and too chill. I will never stop praying. But may God have mercy on you both."

FOUR

The train whistle blew twice, long urgent notes, telling Paradise it had arrived. Lyyndaya stopped milking her cow a minute and looked out the open barn door to the main road. There were still buggies, carts, and wagons moving along toward the station — some to pick up supplies or tools, others to meet family or visitors or bring members of the colony back to their homes. Ruth would be there, ready to greet Jude and give him the letter at the train or follow him back to his house. Perhaps he would give her sister a note to bring back, the last exchange of messages Mother and Father would permit.

She went back to milking and tried, unsuccessfully, to put the matter from her mind. A few cows down from her, her younger sister, Sarah, who was fourteen, struggled to get Primrose to cooperate and muttered away in Pennsylvania Dutch. Daniel, who was nine, and Harley, who was twelve, were helping their mother at the butter churn in an adjoining shed. Luke, at fifteen, was with Papa examining their second hay field to determine when it should have its first cut. Lyyndaya leaned her head gently against Cynthia and kept working, holding the teat in one hand and expressing the milk with the strong slender fingers of her other hand. One of the fingers had a small white bandage. Lyyndaya looked at it and thought of the aeroplane ride and that first thrilling barrel roll. She smiled at the memory and prayed, *Please, God, I hope you do not see this as a frivolous request, but may there be many, many more aeroplane rides with Jude.* Yet once she had finished her short prayer a part of her felt sorrow at something that she feared might never be again.

Her pail full, she carried it to the nearest milk can sitting in the cool shadows. After pouring her pail into the can she moved on to Vivianne, who always made such a fuss. She continued to milk down the row of cows, now and then stopping to help Daniel or Harley — Sarah always refused help of any kind. After more than an hour she began to fret about Ruth's absence. Was it a good thing or a bad thing that her sister was gone so long? She had no sooner begun to wonder than she heard Trillium's smart step in the drive and the sound of buggy wheels. Luke and Papa had returned and she could hear them talking to the horse and to Ruth. Then she heard her mother's voice. She hurried with her milking of the second to the last cow. Just then Papa appeared in the barn doorway.

"Lyyndy?"

"Yes, Papa."

She looked up. He was smiling at her.

"Come, have some fresh buttermilk. We will talk in the kitchen."

"I just have Bella here to finish and then Trinket."

"All right. Join us when you are done. Are the children still in here?"

"No, they finished about ten minutes ago. I think they went to check on the robin's nest by the stable."

Her father lingered in the doorway. He removed his straw hat and held it in his hands, turning it. "My girl. You know I have a temper. May God forgive me. I know that Jude Whetstone is not a wicked boy. He is just young and full of dreams."

Surprised, Lyyndaya watched as her father sat down on a milking stool nearby.

"I build up steam like a locomotive," he went on. "It drives me forward too quickly.

49

Then I am out of steam and I sit on my tracks and I go nowhere. I think what it is for me, when it comes to Jude, is that I once thought as he does now. Oh, yes. When I heard that the Wright brothers had made a plane back in 1903 I knew the whole thing would get much bigger. And I myself wished to soar among the hawks. But there was the question of whether to join the Amish faith or not. I was certain then, just as I am certain now, that the Amish will not permit their people to fly the planes. They are still considering the matter, but that is what they will come to in the end. So I turned my back on my dreams of flying so that we could be a good Amish family. I suppose that's what irritates me about Jude, my girl. He is living what I forsook for the gospel's sake and I resent it. God forgive me, I resent it."

He stood up and put his hat back on his head. "He is not a bad boy. Forgive me for treating him as such. But he has no future with the Amish people if he continues to fly. He is not a man who can ever be a husband for you." His face was sad as he walked out of the barn.

Lyyndaya rushed through milking Bella and Trinket, emptied her pail, then half ran to the house, taking her apron off her dress as she did so and wiping her hands on it. The kitchen table was crowded and noisy, Daniel and Harley half-shouting about the robins and Sarah scowling and arguing with them, disagreeing about everything they said. Ruth sat beside Mama and had been talking to her when Lyyndaya came in, but then she abruptly stopped. Papa and Luke were speaking about mowing the second hay field in a week if it did not rain. Ruth beckoned with her hand and Lyyndaya took the empty seat by her sister. A glass of cool buttermilk was waiting for her.

She sat and sipped the fresh buttermilk and tried to decipher her sister's mood. Ruth's blue eyes, framed by her oval face and raven black hair, flashed with annoyance as she told Sarah to calm down. Then she asked Lyyndaya how the cows had been, especially Vivianne, and her blue eyes softened. She patted Lyyndaya's arm gently.

"All right, good," Papa finally said. "Everyone outside. Luke, we will go to our third hay field after I am finished in here. Please get the horse ready. We'll take the gelding."

Luke quickly got up from the table and took his glass to the sink. "Yes, Papa."

The kitchen soon emptied, leaving Ruth and Lyyndaya and their parents. Papa did not waste any time. He lifted his thick

51

eyebrows at Ruth.

"So, my girl, what did we find out?"

"I said hello to Jude at the station," Ruth replied, "and told him I had a letter to give him. He asked where Lyyndaya was, and I told him the letter was from her and that it would explain. That worried him a little, I could see, but he had no time to think about it for so many wanted to talk to him."

Father's brow creased sharply. "What do you mean so many?"

"Well, a good number of the colony were there to welcome him back. All the leadership and the bishop as well. The children were all over him."

Lyyndaya felt a pang. So many there to greet her young man, to touch his hand, make him laugh, but not her. Papa was rubbing his hand over his mouth and beard at this news, no doubt worried that the Kurtz family might be looked upon in a bad light for not being there with the old families.

"Well, but then you followed him back to the house?" Mama spoke up.

"Yes, I followed him and his father. They invited me in and we chatted a bit about the warm weather and how hot that made the work at the forge. They asked after our dairy herd."

"Ja, ja," said Papa impatiently, his rough,

squat hands playing with the empty buttermilk glass.

Ruth's blue eyes snapped with an inner
light. "I gave him the letter and he got up
from the table and walked to the window to
read it."

"And what did he say?" pressed Father.

"He said —"

"Did he write a note?" asked Mama looking worried, glancing at Lyyndaya.

Ruth shook her head. "There is no note.
He simply came to me, thanked me for
bringing the letter, wished our family well,
said he was making up several dozen horseshoes, if we needed any now was a good
time to let him know, he'd be happy to serve
us, and then —"

Ruth hesitated and in a gesture just like
Mama, bit on her lower lip.

"And then what?" demanded Father.

Ruth closed her eyes and let her words
out with a deep rush of air. "And then he
said, 'Tell your father and mother, and
Lyyndaya, that I am very sorry to have been
a burden and a trouble to them. It was not
my wish.' "

Father spread his hands as Lyyndaya felt
her throat and eyes burn. "That is all he
said? Nothing more?"

Ruth's eyes flew open and the blue in

them flamed. "What did you expect him to say? His mother is in the grave, we cut him out of our lives, cut him off from the girl he loves, all because he flies an aeroplane — you'd think he were a murderer the way we treat him!"

Father rapped his knuckles on the table-top. "That is enough, young lady — more than enough."

Ruth dropped her head and closed her eyes again. "I'm sorry, Papa. What's done is done." She looked at her mother. "It does not matter anyway. The women are all around him like hummingbirds at a flower. He will be courting one of them in no time. Anna Lapp, Katie Fisher, even Bishop Zook's daughter, Emma —"

"Emma?" asked Lyyndaya in a weak voice. Despite her faith of a few days before, she suddenly felt she had lost Jude forever, lost him to Emma and all the other young girls who had been dying to get their hands on him — all because her father and mother thought flying was a sin, an unholiness, a wrong in the eyes of God. The tears erupted. She pushed herself away from the table and fled up the stairs.

"Lyyndy, please, wait!" called Papa. "We are not finished."

"Papa, she has heard enough," Mama

said. "Let her be."

"I wished to say I care for the young man. I do not hate him, Rebecca."

She placed a hand gently on his. "That is very good. That is very kind. But try to understand that your daughter is eighteen and a woman and in love and in great pain because of a decision we made, Amos."

Lyyndaya could hear them talking even with her face buried in her pillow. Then it was quiet and soon afterward the door to the room opened and Ruth sat on the bed beside her. She began to smooth Lyyndaya's hair with her hand.

"I'm sorry," Ruth said, "I didn't mean for it to be so rough. I didn't want to see you hurt more than you already are. I just wanted Mama and Papa to realize how wonderful everyone in the colony thinks Jude is — everyone except them — and that it is you he loves. I know he does. But if they will not let you have him then a dozen other girls are eager to take your place — with their parents' good favor. Mama and Papa are wrong. I feel in my soul they are wrong, that this is not God's will — but what can you and I do?"

Lyyndaya groaned in her misery and burrowed her face even deeper into her pillow. "You make it sound like the colony already knows Papa and Mama have forbidden me . . . to court him —"

"They do know. Whether Father said something among the men, or Mother among the women, or Luke or Sarah among the youth — who knows? I'm sorry, Lyyndy. We can only pray Mother and Father change their minds."

"They'll never change their minds."

Ruth rubbed Lyyndaya's back and then added, "Lyyndy, I have more to tell you. Are you listening?"

"What is it?" came a muffled voice from the pillow. "More glad tidings?"

"Actually, yes. Jude said more than I told downstairs. But, God forgive me, it is not for Mother and Father's ears."

Lyyndaya sat bolt upright on the bed. "What? What did he say you have not told me?"

Ruth looked at her sister's unraveling hair, the redness and puffiness around her eyes, smiled, and shook her head. "Of course, no one could fault Jude if he changed his mind after taking one look at you now."

Lyyndaya grabbed her sister by the shoulders. "Tell me! What did he say?"

Ruth brought a sheet of paper folded in half from under her apron. "Read for yourself."

Lyyndaya snatched the note and, sitting cross-legged on the bed in her dress, read it with her mouth partly open.

My dear Lyyndy Lyyndy Lou,
Do you really think I will give you up without a fight? Do you think the other girls matter to me when you are the one I flew into the sun with? The one who asked me to go faster? The one who demanded I do barrel rolls?
    The Holy Bible says love is as strong as death.
    Well, mine is even stronger.

                                    Jude

"Oh!" cried Lyyndaya as she flung her arms about her sister's neck. "Does he love me then? Is he telling me he loves me?"

"The words are fairly clear, my dear sister."

"Is it true? That he won't give up? That he doesn't care about Emma or any of the other girls?"

"It sounds to me like he cares for only one woman — a golden-haired beauty named Lyyndaya Kurtz."

Lyyndaya started to cry and laugh at the same time. "But can I believe it? How long will it take for us to be together? How can

God make everything perfect?"

Ruth put her arms around her sister and they hugged each other and rocked back and forth. "I don't know the hows and whens. I only know the Who. God is in love with love, I'm sure of it, and looks for every opportunity of cultivating it like a green field on this often barren earth."

She patted Lyyndaya on the back. "I promised Mama we would see to the laundry before lunch. We should get on with it. At the clothesline we can talk some more."

It was while they were hanging up Father's shirts and pants, as well as the ones belonging to Luke, Harley, and Daniel, with wooden clothespins in their mouths, that Ruth asked, "Lyyndy, would you ever consider leaving the colony?"

Lyyndaya glanced over at her sister while she pinned up a large white shirt. "You mean, leave the Amish?"

"Well, something like that, yes."

"No, never. I love this way of life."

"More than you love Jude?"

"Why would I have to choose?"

Ruth shook out a pair of Daniel's black pants. "Because we still don't know what the colony will eventually decide about aeroplanes and flying. What if they forbid it like they forbid telephones? What will Jude do?"

"He would accept it."

But Lyyndaya had stopped hanging clothes and stood still, thinking about Jude Whetstone and the clouds and the tall blue sky.

"Would he?" challenged Ruth. "Would he, really, Lyyndy? If you flew as much as he did and you saw it as a gift of God, would you give it up just like that?"

Lyyndaya looked down at the ground. "You give me hope and then you take it away again."

"I'm sorry." Ruth came over and held her. "I don't mean to. I guess I'm asking these questions because I also wonder — would I leave the colony if I thought they were withholding a good thing that God meant for me to have? Would I leave if the man I love was forced to leave and I had to choose a husband among those I considered less than the right man?"

Lyyndaya leaned her head into her sister's shoulder. "Why are you bringing up all this now?"

"So that you can pray about tomorrow."

"What about tomorrow?"

Ruth pulled out of the hug and ran her hand down her sister's suntanned face. "I overheard Bishop Zook telling Jude that he and the leadership wished to have a talk with him in the afternoon. That there were some concerns about flying and aeroplanes. Jude agreed to meet with them, of course."

"Tomorrow." Lyyndaya looked confused. "Would they really have decided about the aeroplanes and the Amish so soon?"

Ruth shrugged her broad shoulders. "I don't know. I just know this — tomorrow at one o'clock, you and I, no matter what we are doing, need to be praying for Jude, for the colony, for the bishop and the ministers — and for everything that is to come."

FIVE

"Jude."

"Yes, Papa?"

"It is time."

"Just this one last shoe — could you pump the bellows for me?"

"All right."

Jude, stripped to what was once a brown work shirt, but which now was streaked with black and grey, hammered at a red-hot horseshoe, pinning it to an anvil with iron tongs. His father, in black pants and jacket and straw hat, came and stood near him. Removing his hat and jacket, he worked the bellows with his slender arms, vigorously, so that the forge suddenly glowed orange. Jude thrust the shoe into the heat for half a minute, placed the shoe on the anvil, banged at it again, put it back in the fire, returned it to the large anvil, hit it three or four more times, grunted and nodded as he examined the shoe, then plunged it into a large tub of cold water so that steam hissed and spurted into the air.

"Done," he announced.

"I'm sure Mr. Fisher will be pleased," said his father. "We can drop the set off when I take you to the Zooks'."

"I'll wash up quickly."

"The buggy is in the drive and ready. I'll pack up the shoes after this one cools off. Go ahead. We are still early." Then Jude's father added, "Son, are you prepared for what might come of this meeting?"

Jude looked his father in the eye. "God has prepared me, Papa. I'm ready."

Mr. Whetstone nodded in silent satisfaction in his boy's confidence and headed out to wait in the buggy.

At a washbasin at the back of the smithy Jude took off his shirt and scrubbed his chest and arms with a bar of soap and a rough brush. Then he cleaned his face and neck and hands. By the time he had gone into the house for a fresh shirt and pants, his skin was tingling, making him feel alive and hopeful, no longer apprehensive. It was amazing how God could use hard work to clear a man's mind and heart.

When they arrived at the Zooks', the bishop stood on the porch with his hands in his pockets, his suspenders' black strips over his white summer shirt, a large pipe slowly smoking at one side of his mouth. He greeted the Whetstones warmly, taking the pipe from between his lips, and waving as Jude's father drove off. Once Jude had walked up the steps, he said hello to Mrs. Zook who, round and sturdy as an apple, sat in a rocking chair at the far corner of the porch.

"The others are inside," explained the bishop, putting one arm around Jude.

Just as they walked through the front door Emma Zook was coming out.

"Why, hello, Master Whetstone," she said brightly, her green eyes lighting up at his presence. Jude took off his straw hat. He was not used to having a woman's eyes at the same level as his own and it took a moment to untwist his tongue.

"Good afternoon, Miss Zook. How are you?"

"Perfect. God's in his heaven and all's right with the world. Wouldn't you agree?"

Jude couldn't help but return the smile as she stood there, tanned and cheerful in a light green dress that went with her eyes.

"I would, Miss —"

"Oh, stop," she laughed. "Haven't we known each other since we were ten? You know my name. Make him use my name, Papa."

Bishop Zook took his pipe from his mouth and nodded. "It's quite all right to call her by her Christian name, Master Whetstone."

"All right, then," Jude said. "I'm glad you're feeling on top of the world — Emma —"

She lightly swatted his arm. "Oh, the great aviator. You may be on top of the world when you're up in your aeroplane — I'm just content to be on top of my day." She started down the steps and then looked back at him. "Would you like to join Mother and myself for a nice long walk? We are heading in the direction that has the most shade trees."

"Emma —" her father began.

Emma pouted. "Oh, yes, of course, you men have such serious business to discuss."

Her father frowned. "Emma —"

"Never mind." Her mother had joined Emma on the bottom step and they linked arms. "Perhaps another day — Jude." Smiling, Emma glanced up at her father. "Papa, couldn't we have Jude and Mr. Whetstone for supper sometime?"

"Of course, we could, my dear —"

"Tonight?"

"Well, tonight —"

"Please, Papa?" She was looking at Jude as she pleaded.

Bishop Zook nodded. "Very well. Is that acceptable to you, Master Whetstone?"

"I'm sure my father and I would be most happy to share your table this evening, if it's not too much trouble, Mrs. Zook —"

"Trouble? Nonsense." Mrs. Zook patted her daughter's arm. "You will make our day."

Emma's eyes were at their brightest and greenest. "We will see you tonight — my pilot."

"Hush, Emma," said her mother as they began to walk out to the road. "How you carry on sometimes."

Bishop Zook brought Jude into the parlor and closed the door behind them. Seeing the three pastors seated at a table and nodding their welcomes as he sat down, a twinge of the old apprehension sought to reassert itself in Jude's mind. He rebuffed the fear and glanced out a window facing the road and saw Emma and her mother making their way at a good pace.

"You know, of course, Pastor King, Pastor Stoltzfus, Pastor Miller," the bishop said, taking a seat across the table from Jude.

Jude had his hat in his hands and inclined his head. "Hello."

"Good afternoon, young man," responded Pastor Stoltzfus. "Thank you for coming."

The other two smiled and murmured their greetings, They all wore summer vests instead of jackets. Bishop Zook rubbed his hands together.

"I like a good talk," he said. "Pastor King, would you get us started, please?"

Pastor King got to his feet and began to pray in High German. After about five minutes, he sat down and without a pause, Pastor Miller asked Jude, "How have you liked living with the people in Paradise?"

"My father and I like living among the families here very much," Jude replied.

"You like the work you do?"

"Yes. I enjoy making things of iron, useful things."

"It is hot, dirty work," Pastor Stoltzfus spoke up, "eh?"

"The work makes me feel good," Jude said. "I like the heat and I like to use my muscles."

Pastor Miller leaned forward. "Your handiwork is good, *ja. Danke* for repairing my carriage so promptly last month."

"*Bitte,* Pastor Miller."

"You approve of our way of life, then, Master Whetstone?"

"Very much."

"There are perhaps some — young ladies — who catch your eye, huh?" asked Pastor Stoltzfus. "You hope to marry, settle in, raise children among us?"

"I do."

"I will not ask which young ladies."

The men laughed. Then Bishop Zook stood up, loosened his suspenders, and, still standing, asked, "Are you old enough to remember when we had telephones?"

"Yes," Jude replied. "My mother used one all the time when we were first accepted into the church and the colony."

"We had them from, I think — 1893 — until 1908. You are twenty, am I correct in saying this?"

"Just twenty."

"You were eleven when we take them out. It took us that long to discuss and debate the matter. All seemed well . . . until some of the women were caught gossiping with the invention, hm?" The bishop sat back down. "Those who mock our way of life say we are against change and innovation. This is not true. When my youngest, John, took sick last winter, you may recall we traveled by train to Philadelphia because we could do nothing for him here. We use modern medicines and modern surgeries and hospitals if we need to. What we are concerned about is preserving community, relationships, family — the Amish way, the God-given way. After all, we have never refused a ride on the railroad, whether we are eight or eighty."

The pastors smiled. Pastor King tapped his fingers on the table. Then he flicked his head toward the window to the road. Jude looked too, expecting to see Emma. The road was empty. Pastor King only said, "They will put up poles to carry electricity to us in a few years."

"It is doubtful we will hook up to the wires," the bishop carried on, picking up from Pastor King. "All the Amish are talking about it. I will be meeting with the other bishops in August or September and we must go over the arguments for and against. It is not because it is electricity. After all, God made electricity — hm? Every thunderstorm we see it. But — if it makes things happen too quickly, if it brings in devices and contrivances that complicate life, that force our lives to speed up, things that chop our community into small, isolated little parts — it is not a good thing if it makes our world hectic and — divided. Do you understand?"

Jude nodded. "I think so."

"So we say, yes, get into someone's motorcar, one of our neighbors who isn't Amish, get into their Ford and go to Harrisburg if you must — but we do not allow the Amish to own one because then some have, some don't have, and there is division, disunity, haves and have-nots, *ja?*"

Jude began turning his straw hat about in his hands. "I understand."

Pastor King made a circle in the air with his finger. "This is a roundabout way to get to the gate. But we wanted to see how the crops and fields were faring first. You know we must talk about the aeroplane."

"Yes," said Jude, turning his hat a bit faster.

"Most in the colony like it, huh?" blurted Pastor Stoltzfus. "Sure, some ask: Are we angels? Are we birds? But the people like to see the flying —"

"Yet there is the same problem as with the motorcar," interrupted Pastor Miller. "Shall people buy planes and put them in their hay fields? So two or three have them, and what about everyone else?"

Pastor King shrugged. "And really, what are they good for? Yes, yes, they are fun, and there is a place for good fun, but what do you do with them except play around in the sky?"

"What do they use them for?" frowned

Pastor Miller, lines crossing his face. "We hear they are used to kill, to make war, all over Europe they shoot one another down, that is all they do with them."

"But —" Jude suddenly spoke up, "it's the same as the train, isn't it? It gets you from one place to another more swiftly. One day they will be flying dozens of people from Pittsburgh to New York and from Boston to Chicago —"

"One day, one day," mocked Pastor Miller, "but today they are only killing people. Railroads don't kill people."

"Railroads take troops to the front lines to fight," responded Jude.

"That is not the same thing —"

"Now, now," Bishop Zook broke in, "we are not talking about war. Young Jude is below the conscription age and, in any case, our young men are exempt from serving in the American army. We do not take up arms. You agree with this stance, do you not, Master Whetstone?"

"I do."

"So it is not a problem, this war, it is not a problem for our young man. We are talking about flying, about aeroplanes without guns, about machines that bring delight and wonder — and believe me, if you men found yourselves up there with the swallows, you

70

would see God's creation in such a marvelous way as would bring you to worship, to prayer, to praise. And I don't doubt Master Whetstone is right, someday there will be aeroplanes going back and forth across the country the way trains do now."

"But you are opposed to the conflict?" Pastor Miller pressed, his eyes fastened tightly on Jude.

"Yes."

"You would not go over there to fly, to fight in an aeroplane, even if the government insisted?"

"No."

"And you are sure of this?"

"I will not fly an aeroplane to kill."

"How many no's from the boy do you want, Jacob, huh?" demanded Pastor Stoltzfus.

"I am only —" began Pastor Miller, but Bishop Zook raised a large hand and the men were quiet.

"We see the young man is one of us," the bishop said, "that his family is one of us, just as his dear mother, God bless her, was one of us. The matter of flying has not been settled among the Amish. It is not our place to settle it today. But it is clear, is it not, where this young man's heart is? That is all we needed to know. Am I right?"

No one spoke. Pastor Miller sat with a dark face and tight lips.

"Am I right?" the bishop repeated himself.

"Ja, ja," sighed Pastor King. "We do not take out on him what the kings and Kaisers and presidents do with flying machines."

"Let him fly," grunted Pastor Stoltzfus. "If a decision is made among the Amish against the machines, the young man's delight will be taken away quickly enough. Today let him fly."

The bishop looked at Pastor Miller. "Jacob?"

The pastor ran a hand over his face and closed his eyes. "Let him fly, let him fly."

Bishop Zook nodded slowly and stroked his dark beard. "And we remain committed to what we discussed about the July picnic? About the aeroplane and the picnic?"

The pastors all nodded, Jacob Miller more hesitantly than the others.

"What is this about?" asked Jude, surprised.

Bishop Zook turned to him, still stroking his beard, but smiling now. "We had wondered if it were possible to bring the flying machine here for our July picnic. The colony would pay for the fuel used, of course. Despite our own debate among the leadership, we recognize that many of our people, especially the children and the youth, find the aeroplane amusing, and we believe a good number would like to have you take them up. It is not just something we do for a family holiday. Those who go up with you will see the world God has made in a beautiful way, a holy way — so I cannot believe God did not intend for us to build a flying invention like this. But time enough in the days ahead to speculate about that. Now, my boy, what are the realistic prospects of you being able to bring an aeroplane to us on the seventh of July, hm?"

"Why —" Jude thought a moment. "I know some of our members take our planes to all sorts of state fairs or other summer celebrations — the army makes requests for the planes for Independence Day —"

The bishop held up a hand. "You know the Amish people do not do anything for July Fourth. They dislike the military parades, they see the flag waving as a pride in military might. We only wish for a peaceful summer gathering of families to thank God for the freedoms we have in America. No flags. No marches. No soldiers. No fireworks. Just a thanking of God. For if the Lord had not brought our people to this country, where would we be today? None of this freedom did we have in the places our forefathers left. So we do not ask for the aeroplane as the military men ask for the aeroplane. We ask for it because it flies, and because it flies, it is a symbol to us of being cut loose from the earth, yes? A symbol to us of the freedom God gives us when we obey him — freedom here —" he placed his hand over his heart "— and here —" he tapped his boot on the floor.

"I'm sure I can do this," said Jude. "I will talk the club into lending me a Jenny."

"Wonderful. Then we are done. Pastor Miller, please pray for us."

Pastor Miller made as if to get up, then hesitated, looking at Jude. Suddenly he leaned forward, his hands on the table.

"Forgive me, young man, forgive," he said, in an anguished voice, his face broken up with his pain. "I do not mean to put this war on your shoulders because you fly an aeroplane."

"It's all right, Pastor Miller —"

"No, no, it is not all right. It is never all right to condemn another. I feel so much about the war and I feel it so strongly that sometimes I cannot rein in my emotions. It is like I am a runaway horse." The pastor looked down at the table, took a deep breath, shook his head, and looked Jude in the eye once more. "So again, I apologize, I repent of my behavior, and I ask you to forgive me. Then I can pray."

"I understand what you are saying and what you are feeling, Pastor Miller," Jude assured the distraught man. "I'm sorry you're upset and I do forgive you."

"Thank you, thank you." The pastor extended his hand. Jude shook it and the pastor stood up. He prayed for ten minutes in High German, just as Pastor King had done. With his *amen* the others got to their feet, shook hands, and began to leave by the front door. Jude followed them out.

"So, then," Bishop Zook said, taking Jude's hand on the porch, "tonight, hm? At eight. You and your father will be most welcome."

"We'll be here," Jude promised and started down the steps just as Emma and her mother walked in off the road, their faces flushed from their walk under the summer sun.

"Why, Jude Whetstone," Emma said, "where on earth are you going?"

Jude took his straw hat off. "Back home, Miss Zook. I have some work at the forge to take care of before we return here for the evening meal with your family."

"Well, I don't wish to keep a man from his employment, but I was hoping for a few

75

minutes of your help in the garden —"

"Emma," her mother interrupted, "let the boy alone, you know he will have his hands full at the smithy."

"It won't take but twenty minutes." Emma's eyes glittered in the bright July light, small drops of perspiration collecting on her fair skin.

Jude shrugged. "How can I say no? Lead the way."

Emma went ahead of him and up the front steps. "Please go around to the garden. I'll meet you there after I get some bowls."

Minutes later Emma handed Jude a bowl and they began by picking strawberries. "I'm always looking for the dark overripe ones that Mama doesn't want anyway," Emma said, crouching among the small green plants. "They taste like jam and are even better when they have been heated up by the sun. Ah, here's one!"

She stood with a large dark berry in her fingers. "Open up," she said to Jude.

"Oh, no, I'm fine —"

"Here." She pushed it against his lips and he had to open his mouth and take it.

"How was that?"

"Very good," Jude responded, still chewing.

"Now me."

Jude knelt and bent back leaves and searched while she waited. He finally found one that was so soft it was almost jelly. Getting back to his feet, he offered it to her with an outstretched palm. "Here you go."

"Oh, no, Jude Whetstone. You have to give it to me properly."

Awkward, hesitating, Jude put the berry to her mouth and she took it with her perfect white teeth. "Mmm. Good choice. Delicious!"

After they had filled their bowls Emma dropped into a white chair near the bean-poles, exclaiming, "My goodness, it's warm."

"Shall I fetch you some cool water, Miss Zook?"

"You don't need to fetch Miss Zook anything. Remember, you must call me Emma now. Just take a seat beside me here." She patted another chair.

"Well — I should be getting back —"

"Only five minutes. I have something for you."

Jude took the seat and she pulled a card out of a pocket in her light green dress. It was covered with lines and her neat hand printing. She gave it to him.

"What's this?" he asked, turning the card over.

"Among the English, the girls have a card when they attend a dance," she explained, "and the boys fill in their names so they are sure to have the opportunity to dance with the girls they like the best. So this is your card for your dance — in the clouds."

"My dance? You mean taking people up in the aeroplane?"

He looked so surprised she laughed. "Of course."

"How did you know about that?"

"Oh, my goodness, I live in the same house as my father."

"But we only just discussed it. How did you know I'd say yes?"

"Why wouldn't you say yes? You love to fly, don't you?"

"Sure, but suppose there were no planes available?"

"My Jude would find a way, he'd always find a way."

Jude was quiet.

"I'm sorry, Jude," she said. "Am I being forward?"

"It's all right. I should go."

"How are things with you and the Kurtz family?" she said teasingly. "Is it true you're not able to see Lyyndaya anymore?"

Jude stared at her, his lips in a straight line.

"Well," he answered, "the whole colony knows her mother and father do not approve of flying, so she is forbidden to meet with me."

"It must be very difficult."

"Yes, and confusing. Lyyndaya is a pleasant young woman."

"Of course, a very pleasant girl, we were great friends when we were younger."

"But we cannot be together, we cannot exchange notes, so — so I don't know what will happen now."

Emma nodded. "God will open a door."

"Do you think so?"

"He always opens a door. It's just we don't always recognize right away which door it is he has opened." She touched him gently on the arm. "Do you pray up there?"

Jude half-smiled. "No one's ever asked me that."

"My father said it made him feel closer to God to be so high in the sky with the wind in his face."

Jude had been making the motions to rise, but now he sat back. "I do pray. Yes, I do." He gave a small laugh and his eyes fastened on the horizon between sky and earth. "Sometimes it's in my head. Then I might mumble out loud. Or just move my lips."

"What do you pray about?"

"Well — it's not prayer like when you're asking for things or for help. I guess it's mostly — happiness. It's too big and bright and beautiful up there to be thinking of any problems you might have on earth."

Emma gave Jude a slow, gentle smile. "I like to listen to you talk."

Jude felt a warmth in his face and chest. She touched him on the arm and got up. "I suppose your father will be wondering what happened to you. He'll think the pastors had you for dinner. Which reminds me. Don't be late for supper. I look forward to seeing you tonight and chatting some more."

Jude stood. "So do I."

"Would you like a ride?"

"No, no. It's not far. I'd like to stretch my legs."

She walked with him as far as the road. "Don't lose the July seventh 'dance' card. I spent a half hour getting it just right."

"I won't."

"I hope you don't mind, but my father was so enthusiastic, I had to make sure I got up at least twice. So I signed myself in at the top and at the bottom. The first and the last."

She was at his eye-level again. He still couldn't get used to it. Smiling, he planted his hat firmly on his head. "Sounds like a great idea to me. So long."

He started along the dirt road baked hard and dry from the sun. Glancing back once, he saw she was still standing, watching him go. He gave a small wave and she waved back. As he continued on he saw the Kurtz home far to the east and a stab went through him. Slowing his pace, he gazed at it and wondered if he might catch a glimpse of Lyyndaya. Her hair would give her away. But he only noticed two children playing with a dog.

All sorts of feelings streamed through him. Emma's eyes, Lyyndaya's face, the note he'd written to Lyyndaya, the words he'd spoken to Emma. He shook his head to clear it, but that didn't help much. He'd as much as told Lyyndaya that he loved her. And he did. But he doubted her parents would ever change their minds. Whereas Emma had a way of getting into his thoughts and sticking there, like a rose's thorn, and Emma's parents believed in him and what he was doing with his aeroplane. It was as if a new path had suddenly opened for him in the forest and the way forward was obvious.

He put his hands in his pockets. The old path had looked so good too . . . until it had become blocked by vines and brambles and deadfall.

SIX

Lyyndaya was milking Vivianne as she listened to the sound of the aeroplane passing by the house for the third time. The cow began to fidget and moan and Lyyndaya leaned her head against the Holstein's flank and closed her eyes.

"Yes, go ahead, Viv, kick up a fuss," she murmured in a weary voice. "I don't mind. I feel the same way."

For a few minutes it was quiet, though Lyyndaya was certain she could hear the Curtiss Jenny's engine higher up and farther east. Then the drone came back, growing louder and louder, until it snarled over their rooftop once again. A streak of pain shot through her. A week ago she would have been running to the field where Jude was landing. Now she wanted to avoid him at all costs.

"Are you not finished yet?"

Ruth stood in the doorway.

Lyyndaya quickly brushed the back of her hand against both cheeks. "I'm just done." But she did not stand up.

Ruth waited a moment and then picked up a milk stool and came over and sat beside her sister. Then she took one of Lyyndaya's hands and held it tightly.

"Listen," she said in a quiet voice, "you and I and Mother and Sarah are in charge of slicing and serving the pies in an hour. Father and the boys are helping with the games. Everyone in our family is at the Stoltzfus meadow already. As we planned, I have come back for you. The table of pies is under a big tree and far from the Stoltzfus hay field, where Jude is taking off and landing. You will not see him very much."

"How do you not see an aeroplane buzzing over your head?"

"By keeping your head down — and praying."

"Where is Emma Zook?"

"She'll be helping people line up for the plane rides. So she is also far away."

"What happens when she comes for her piece of pie?"

"I will serve her."

"*Ja?* You will serve her? Will it be strawberry pie?"

Ruth sighed and closed her eyes a moment. Then she kissed her sister on the head and pulled her against her side.

"Is it that again? People exaggerate. Emma gave Jude one strawberry and Jude gave Emma one strawberry. That was it. No one fed anyone a bowlful of strawberries and there certainly wasn't any sugar or cream. Emma's little sister, Annie, told Sarah that her mother would have thrown a fit if Emma hadn't brought all the strawberries they'd picked into the house."

"No doubt," responded Lyyndaya, biting out each word. "After all, Mrs. Zook had *two* suppers to prepare for."

Ruth exhaled a long and noisy rush of air. "Oh, my dear, what do you expect? If Mama and Papa felt all right about flying then we'd be the ones having Jude and his father in. You can't ask Jude to become a hermit."

"I thought he loved me."

"So that means he should be rude to Emma and her parents?"

"He doesn't —" Lyyndaya took in a sharp breath and struggled not to begin crying again. "He doesn't have to enjoy it so much."

"We don't know what he enjoys and what he doesn't, Lyyndy. How could he tell you? He's forbidden to talk to you or even send a note."

"I wish — he loved me enough — to break the rules —"

"I know, but that's asking a lot for an Amish convert who wants to stay on the good side of the colony just as much as Papa does."

"It is not the colony's rules I want him to break."

"No, but the *Ordnung* demands that the wishes of the parents with regard to their children be respected."

"Then maybe I should leave the colony, maybe Jude and I should both up and leave the colony and live in Philadelphia."

"Hush. That's quite enough. I have brought your red book." Ruth took it out of a pocket in her dress and put it in Lyyndaya's hand. "You can read it in the buggy if you feel inclined to hearken to your great-grandmother's words. Now take off your apron and leave it here. Mother has fresh ones for us at the table. We must go." She pinched Lyyndaya's cheek. "And last I looked there were no strawberry pies."

Minutes later, the gelding, Old Oak, trotted happily along the road toward the celebration. Lyyndaya could see ahead that Jude's plane was on the ground; she could see it turning into the light summer breeze blowing from the south. She put her head down so she wouldn't have to watch. Her eyes fell on the red book on the seat between her and Ruth and she picked it up, opening it to the page labeled July seventh.

Where the Spirit of the Lord is, there is liberty. The handwriting flowed like water across the page. Lyyndaya gently moved a black-eyed Susan she had pressed when she was twelve. She read,

I am not thinking about the liberty wrought by armies or frigates, but that which is brought about by God's Spirit. It has nothing to do with soldiers and guns and killing and death. Instead, it has everything to do with peace and life: the freedom to love thy neighbor as thyself; the freedom to forgive and be liberated from hate; the freedom to come to the Lord in any mood or state of despair and find acceptance, reconciliation, and a new beginning; the freedom to find light in the darkness, hope in hopelessness, one promise kept when a hundred others are broken; the freedom to have God even when you have no one and nothing else.

Find something on this summer day that sets you free to believe in God's ways and God's plan and thank him for it. Such liberation is the great road to happiness and a deep, unending joy. Oh, but so few find their way to it. Do not count thyself among the numbers who miss the signposts and spend a lifetime meandering in the wilderness or charging along, pigheaded, in the wrong direction. Find God's way, take it, and secure thy emancipation in Christ. Have faith, trust in God, love and forgive; oh, forever forgive; and in return you will never lack the sweetness of God's own forgiveness and will receive complete and utter liberty to rise above all life's tangles and snares and pitfalls. You will never be less, you will always be more.

Lyyndaya closed the book. She could make out Emma waving as Jude took off yet again with, it looked like, Pastor Miller of all people in the front cockpit.

"Well?" asked Ruth, glancing over at Lyyndaya.

"Well, what?"

"Did Great-grandmother Kurtz help you out today?"

"What will help me out today," replied Lyyndaya, looking straight ahead, "is not to wait for Emma Zook to come for her piece of pie —"

"Lyyndaya —"

"— but to bring it to her instead. Do you have any idea what her favorite kind is?"

Ruth stared at her and then turned back to the road and flicked the reins. "I don't, but her mother will, and she is standing and talking at the pie table right now."

Ten minutes later, with Jude still flying south and west with Jacob Miller, Lyyndaya approached Emma, simple and elegant in her light yellow dress, where she was chatting with the next person in line, a boy named Peter King, a good friend of Lynndaya's brother Luke.

"Emma," she called cheerfully.

Emma looked toward her with surprise, and even, Lyyndaya noticed, a dash of guilt. "Oh, hello, Lyyndaya," she said, working up a smile that didn't include her eyes.

"How are you?" asked Lyyndaya.

"Perfect," she chirped, widening her smile. "And you?"

"I'm perfect also." She extended the slice of pie she was carrying on a white plate. "This is for you."

Emma flushed and stammered. "For *me?* I thought — I thought surely you had brought it for young Peter —"

"Oh, no," Lyyndaya said with a smile, reaching over and giving Peter a playful shove, "he'll have to come down to the table himself and bring me some daisies if he wants a piece of pie."

Peter grinned. "But after my aeroplane ride."

"If there's any pie left by then," Lyyndaya teased.

"I don't see why —" Emma was still struggling. "You — didn't need to go to this trouble."

"It was my pleasure." Lyyndaya plucked a fork from a pocket under her large white apron. "Here you go. It's cherry, your favorite."

"Yes." Emma still looked bewildered. "My favorite."

"Not just any cherry pie either. This is from Mrs. Beachy's oven."

"Oh, Mrs. Beachy — do you mean this is from one of those big ones she makes?"

"Twenty-nine inches across."

Emma laughed and began to regain her composure. "I don't know how she does it."

"Neither do I," said Lyyndaya. "If I tried to bake a pie that size I'm sure one side would be raw and the other side burnt."

"Yes," Emma said, plunging her fork through the crust, "that would be me also. Do you and Peter mind? I haven't had anything all day and I'm starved."

"Go ahead," coaxed Lyyndaya. "How many people have gone flying so far?"

Cherry juice stained one side of Emma's mouth. "Oh, I have the card here — people write their names in — six, seven, *ja,* Pastor Miller is number eight. Jude is stopping at twenty. But if you wanted to go up, we could squeeze you in right after Peter."

Lyyndaya shook her head and forced herself to laugh. "No, no, I've had my flying adventures. How about yourself?"

"Oh, I've been up already, it was *marvelous.*"

Lyyndaya felt the stab of pain again, but was determined to push on with the conversation and the forgiveness. "Did you — did you do anything different?"

Emma was chewing smoothly as she finished the pie. "What do you mean — different?"

"Well, did you do any crazy things, like go faster or — do a barrel roll?" Lyyndaya hated herself for asking, bracing for the added pain of finding out what she did not want to know.

"Heavens, no. I'm not like you, Lyyndy. You were always the tomboy, I was always the lady. Remember our games? You ran through the mud puddles, I went around them. You jumped into the creek to swim, I waded at the edge." She handed the now empty plate and fork back to Lyyndy. "Thank you so much for the pie, that was so sweet of you. Would you like to say hello to Jude? He'll be landing in a few minutes." She pointed toward the sun where Lyyndaya noticed the Canuck was fast approaching the hay field, dropping lower and lower.

Lyyndaya began to move away. "No, I have to get back — I've left Mother and my sisters alone long enough."

"Perhaps someone should bring Jude some pie," Emma suggested. "Do you know what he likes, Lyyndaya?"

"I'm not sure. I'll send Sarah over with one apple and one blueberry," Lyyndaya said over her shoulder.

"What if he likes what I like?" smiled Emma.

"I'll send cherry and peach too. Our aviator can have a feast."

"He'll get too fat to fit in the cockpit."

When Jude landed with Pastor Miller a couple of minutes later, Sarah was arriving with the four slices of pie.

"That seems too much for one man," Mrs. Kurtz grumbled, watching Sarah from the pie stand. "Even a healthy strapping one."

"Mama," said Lyyndaya, "he's been flying for hours with only the time to swallow a mouthful of coffee. It's the least we can do."

Her mother waved a hand in the air as if her daughter were a fly. *"Ja, ja."*

Ruth was cutting a raisin pie for Annie Zook. "There you are, you little drop of sunshine. Large enough?"

Annie grinned. "So large. I will have to find someone to share it with."

"Sharing, yes, that is something you love to do, Annie. Try and save a bite for yourself."

Annie spun and danced away. "All right. But no one likes to eat alone."

Ruth glanced up at Lyyndaya. "So, how was your chat with Emma?"

"Perfect."

"Perfect? Speaking with Emma Zook was perfect?"

"It couldn't have been better."

"What does that mean?" Ruth had her hands on her hips.

Lyyndaya poked at a slice of rhubarb pie, licked her finger, then picked up a fork and began to eat the whole slice. "It means," she said between mouthfuls, "that I will let Emma be Emma, and Lyyndaya will be Lyyndaya, and God can determine the outcome."

"Don't talk nonsense," muttered her mother as she set out three new pies at the approach of one of the Fisher families, with twelve children in tow.

But Ruth would not let go of it. "Is this something Great-grandmother said?"

"And something Emma Zook said." She laughed and changed the subject. "This pie is so good!"

"Come, sister," Ruth ordered. "No more games. Out with it."

"Emma Zook is not half so bad a soul. And Emma Zook does not do barrel rolls."

Ruth thought about this and then her blue eyes smiled. Their mother busied herself at the table between them with a knife in her hand. "All the crazy talk. Emma Zook. Barrel rolls. I thank God you are done with that flying boy. Am I the only one serving the pie? Can you two not find something to do besides stand around and make wild talk?"

Young John Zook stood quietly in front of Lyyndaya. "May I have apple?"

Lyyndaya smoothed back his hair. "Oh, of course, Johnny." She cut him a generous slice of apple pie. "How's that?"

"Danke."

"Didn't I see you under a tree reading a book a little while ago?"

A tiny smile came to John's serious face. "*Ja.* About Moses and that Exodus."

"Are you going to go up in the aeroplane?"

93

"Well — that is why I am reading about that Exodus. To get up the courage."

"Truly?"

He nodded as he thrust a fork into his pie. "I read so much about brave people trusting in God, Miss Kurtz. Always I am reading about them. Today I would like to be one of them. If I could only trust God enough to go up like the others. Well, I have asked my sister Emma to hold a place for me."

"Do you think you would take a book up there?" teased Lyyndaya.

He gave a small laugh. "I might if I thought reading a chapter helped me forget I was a mile high."

The aeroplane roared past and at a glance, Lyyndaya realized no one was in the front cockpit. Just then Sarah arrived with Peter King, who asked for his promised pie.

"Peter!" exclaimed Lyyndaya. "Why aren't you up with Mr. Whetstone?"

Peter had his hands in his pockets and kicked at a stone. "He said he thought the engine didn't sound right at five thousand feet. So he went out alone to test it."

"Well, isn't that the right thing to do? Mr. Whetstone doesn't want you to get hurt."

"I guess so."

"You didn't lose your place in line, did

you? Of course not. I'm sure Miss Zook will make sure you get on the next ride."

"If there is a next ride."

"There must be a next ride," said John Zook. "I think it is God's will that I go up."

"Well, maybe not," grumbled Peter.

"Stop being so impossible," Sarah scolded Peter. "Now, look here. Isn't this what you always go on about when you want something sweet?"

She held a lemon pie in her hands. Peter whistled and took off his straw hat. "May I eat it here?"

"What?" Sarah laughed. "The whole pie?"

"Oh, no," the boy said quickly, "just as many pieces as others don't want."

"Start with two," Sarah said, cutting the slices for him, "and tell me what you think."

Peter sat on the grass and dived into the lemon pie with a fork while Sarah watched, half-smiling and half-frowning. "Do you even taste it?" she asked.

"It's very good."

"Oh, so how good?"

"Only my mother's and my nana's are better."

"Then this pie is a third-place pie?"

Peter smiled with his mouth full. "Well, outside of my family, it is a first-place pie."

Sarah clapped her hands. "So a good

answer. It's my pie. I baked it."

"No." Peter stopped eating.

"Ja."

"What is this happening now?" Benjamin Kauffman, holding one of his little boy's hands, jerked his beard at the sky and the buzz of engines. "Part of the show?"

Lyyndaya glanced up from cutting apple pie for him and his boy. "What do you mean?"

"Those other aeroplanes."

From the north three Curtiss Jennys were flying close together, fairly high, yellow like Jude's plane, but with stars on their wings. Jude was a few hundred feet below and slightly ahead of them, slowly banking to the left. It appeared the three Jennys were going to continue south and, as everyone watched, Jude began dropping in elevation and heading toward the Stoltzfus hay field. Lyyndaya glanced away and back to the Kauffman boy, handing him his slice with a wink, when she heard people gasp and shout. She spun around and looked back in time to see, one after another, the three Jennys with starred wings dropping down and diving straight at Jude so steeply that their engines screamed.

SEVEN

As the planes dived upon Jude he continued toward the hay field as if nothing were amiss.

He doesn't see them, Lyyndaya thought in a panic, *but why should he be looking for them? Why should he expect to be attacked?* As he drew closer to the hay field, the other planes were almost upon him. If they weren't careful they could make him crash into the ground. And it didn't look as if they were being careful.

My Lord, open his eyes, she prayed, *make him look up and back, make him look behind.* She continued to pray with her eyes open and, because she didn't know what else to do to help him, she reached as high as she could and pointed. *Oh, this is ridiculous,* she thought, *why would he be looking over here? Why would he be looking for me?* Nevertheless, she half-ran from the pie table and the large oak it was under and, standing on her toes and stretching, pointed behind his plane with every fiber of her being. *I know it's a crazy prayer, but please, God, please, something is not right about those other planes.*

Suddenly Jude's aeroplane put on a burst of speed. He flew over the hay field and headed north and away from the picnic and the crowd of women, children, and men. The three Jennys sped over the field in hot pursuit. Jude threw his Canuck into a steep climb. The Jennys matched the feat. Then, as everyone watched, Jude looped quickly and neatly back over the Jennys and was on their tails. People clapped.

"Oh, ho!" cried Bishop Zook, standing beside his daughter Emma. "Such a stunt!"

The three planes were now being chased by Jude. They swerved left and right, dove and climbed, but they couldn't shake him. Finally two of them put on speed and kept heading higher and further north, with no obvious intention of grappling any further with Jude and his Canuck.

The third plane seemed to stall, but that caused Jude to fly past him, and the other pilot then resumed the pursuit of Jude's Canuck, opening the throttle and racing after him from behind and below. Yet it almost seemed to Lyyndaya as if Jude had anticipated this. He immediately dove to the right and banked at the same time. When the other Jenny went after him, Jude in his turn stalled the plane deliberately so the Jenny with starred wings overflew him, and he swiftly gunned the engine and pounced on his back.

From then on, no matter what the other pilot did, up and down, using the stall again or putting on speed, he could not shake the Canuck. It was as if a rope had been tied from one plane to another, and nothing either one did could sever it. Even when the other Jenny did a barrel roll, hoping to confuse the Canuck, Jude simply matched the roll and then did a second one so that he was suddenly right on top of the other plane.

Unable to lose Jude, the Jenny waggled its wings and slowed down, and the pilot made indications with his hands that he intended to land on the Stoltzfus hay field. Jude waggled his wings in return, but remained above and in a position of advantage, obviously not trusting the other aviator. He let the man's Jenny drop slowly. When its wheels had touched grass he came in behind it and landed a couple of hundred feet away. The colony ran toward the planes and swarmed over them once the propellers had stopped turning. Lyyndaya lifted the hem of her dress and ran with them, racing past Emma, who had never been fast, even as a thin, skinny teenager.

She saw Jude working his way through the crowd to get to the other pilot, who was similarly surrounded. Jude finally got up to the man. When Lyyndaya looked at his face, it was a thundercloud, and for a moment she thought Jude was going to throw a punch. Instead she heard him snap, "Who are you and what was all that about?"

The pilot, shorter than Jude and sporting a mustache, dressed in a uniform under his leather flying jacket, extended a hand through the crush of bodies. "Cook, Lieutenant Brendan Cook, old boy, His Majesty's Royal Flying Corps. Sorry about that. I had some of you Yanks on a training flight and there was a decoy we were supposed to attack. Thought it was you."

Jude did not immediately take the hand. "You staged a mock attack over an Amish colony during a summer picnic? Suppose one of the planes had been forced down or crashed? Look at all these women and children —"

"No chance of that, we keep our Jennys in tip-top shape — as you do, obviously. Sorry again. The chaps I was leading will be going to France in the fall. That's why the mock combat. I expect we missed our target aeroplane some miles north of here."

The pilot's hand was still extended. Jude got his emotions under control, thought briefly about what the man had said, then shook his hand. Lynndaya could see that many of the people thought this was all part of the act. They smiled and clapped their hands softly.

"What about the American pilots?" asked Jude.

"I indicated they should head back to base. That I'd finish you off. Well, that didn't happen, did it? Where did you learn to fly like that, may I ask?"

"I took lessons in Philadelphia. I'm a member of a flying club there."

"And you stage mock aerial attacks?"

"No, we don't. But we — I — like to do loops and dives and — I've read some of the aviators' accounts of the flying in France and Germany in the New York newspapers —"

The Royal Flying Corps officer raised his eyebrows. "What? You mean you're self-taught in your aerial combat skills?"

"Well —" Jude hesitated. "I have no desire to be a combat pilot. But I do like the exciting maneuvers."

"No desire to be a combat pilot?"

"No."

"Then you're not registered for the U.S. Selective Service?"

"I'm twenty."

"And when you turn twenty-one?"

"I'll register. And I'll be exempted."

"Exempted?" The officer put his hands on his hips. "A healthy lad like you? On what grounds?"

"Religion."

"Religion?" Lt. Brendan Cook laughed and looked about him as if expecting support. "Plenty of the lads who are flying are religious — Catholics, Church of England, Church of Scotland, Methodists —"

"The Amish are conscientious objectors. We don't take up arms."

"Is that what you are —" Cook glanced about him again. "Is that what these — oddly dressed people are?"

"We're Amish. Our people came here from Europe over two hundred years ago, looking for freedom to live our Christian beliefs. Not long after the *Mayflower* brought Pilgrims here for the same reason."

"I see. I see. So — you will not fight — even though thousands of people are being slaughtered — the Huns are bayoneting babies and violating Christian women —

towns and villages are going up in flames —
your own American boys are being machine-
gunned in the trenches —"

"There is no need for a war."

"No?"

"The Germans are Christians too."

"Are they?" Cook stood facing Jude like
someone who was not used to having his
arguments turned aside. It was Bishop
Zook, unaware of the tension between Jude
and the British officer, who arrived and
unwittingly defused the situation.

"Ah, sir," he boomed, shaking Lt. Cook's
hand, "*Willkommen, willkommen,* that was
quite a show you put on for us. Such stunts.
So what do you think of our young man
Jude Whetstone? Can he fly, hm?"

"Oh, he can fly, sir," Cook responded, still
not sure what to make of this part of
America he had landed in. "The question
is, *will* he?"

"What?" The bishop did not understand.
"Are you going up again so soon?"

"I don't know —" Cook began.

"*Nein, nein,* it is a picnic, we celebrate our
freedom to live and follow our Lord Jesus
Christ in America, you must stay a while,
we are just about to eat — well, we eat all
day —" he said with a laugh. "Come, sit
with us for an hour, why not?"

"Are you speaking German, sir?" the startled officer asked Bishop Zook.

"Some German, some English, if one doesn't work I use the other, come, come."

The bishop managed to coax the English pilot to a blanket under a cluster of shade trees. He introduced the man to Emma, who gave the officer her brightest smile — and a plate of food. Meanwhile, the crowd dispersed back to their own blankets and picnic lunches.

Lyyndaya had to smile at the scene. *Soon the pilot will be eating cold chicken and potatoes and Emma will be feeding him fresh strawberries for dessert.* Her thoughts were interrupted as she was suddenly aware that she was not alone. She turned her head to see Jude standing beside her.

"Do you think your mother will notice?" he asked.

She dropped her eyes from his intense gaze and mumbled, "Not right away."

"I wanted to thank you for letting me know about the aeroplanes. I saw you pointing."

She looked up in surprise. "You couldn't have possibly seen me."

"I saw you all right."

"How could you know it was me amongst the scores of people?"

"Well, not all of them wear a navy-blue dress. Not all of them have blonde hair and such beautiful green eyes."

"Oh —" She couldn't stop herself from laughing and giving him a shove. "As if you have eyes that could see all that from so far up."

"Then how did I know, Lyyndaya?"

"From what I've heard, I would have thought you'd be looking for Emma Zook."

"Is that what you really think?" He took the risk of tipping up her chin with his finger so her eyes were looking directly into his. She didn't push away his hand or glance in a different direction. "Because I gave her a strawberry? Because my father and I had supper at her house?"

"Twice, I heard," added Lyyndaya.

"Because she was helping people get into the aeroplane today?"

"You didn't look like you were suffering." She gently moved his hand aside.

Jude nodded. "Yes, she is tenacious. I admit she has caused me some confusion."

"Oh, has she?"

"So have you."

"I?" Lyyndaya pointed to herself. "Little short me? From a million miles away?"

"Yes, little blonde green-eyed *you.* Do you think you are so easily forgotten?"

She shrugged. "I suppose you don't have much choice. My parents won't permit us to see one another. So what are you waiting around for? Go put Emma Zook in your buggy and court her. She's dying to be courted."

"And you? Do you wish to be courted?" Jude asked. He reached out to touch her face, but she shook her head and stepped back.

"It doesn't matter what I wish. You're not the one who can court me. So you should move on to the next in line."

"The next in line? Are you and Emma my customers then? Am I to make each of you a set of horseshoes for your feet? A bit for each of your mouths?"

Lyyndaya laughed and pushed on his chest. "Stop it. I shouldn't be laughing. I shouldn't be enjoying your company."

"Why not?"

"My mother and father — we have no future —"

"Is that really what you think?"

"Yes . . . but . . . I . . ." She stopped and looked helplessly at him.

"Is this what God tells you?"

"I don't know what God tells me."

"You don't? Are you sure?"

She felt heat in her face and looked

toward the people picnicking in the meadow. "My parents will notice us."

"Very well. Then I am telling you about the fuel. What the British pilot would call petrol."

Lyyndaya stared at him, confused, her eyebrows coming together. "What?"

"You see the wagon by the side of the fence? The fuel drums on it? My two mechanics eating the sandwiches and drinking the lemonade Mrs. Kauffman brought them?"

"Yes."

"They came on the train with the fuel, and Bishop Zook's son Hosea brought the men and the drums to the field with his wagon. I am going to go over to them now and ask them to top up the British officer's tank. And mine. After all, the King's boy has to have his moment in the sky, doesn't he? And little John Zook, the reader of entire libraries."

Lyyndaya smiled. "Shall I call it — 'petrol'?"

"Yes. Why not? And if your parents ask, we were talking about aeroplanes and fuel drums — and horseshoes — among other things."

She inclined her head. "So we were."

Jude began to walk toward the mechanics.

"The truth is, I miss you, Lyyndy," he said.

Later in the afternoon, with Lt. Cook gone and Jude taking Peter King up to five thousand feet and down again, Lyyndaya wondered if Jude had really meant that, or whether he'd said it just to make her feel good. After all, hadn't he confessed that he was confused about both Emma and herself? How did he really know what he felt about either of them? If she could see him every day, talk with him, listen to his words, watch his actions, then she might see the truth and, if he honestly felt something for her, she might become convinced of it. Since that was not possible, she would always be in doubt and never have a sense of security about their relationship, whatever that relationship might be. She prayed, but prayer didn't make anything clearer in her mind about the two of them. Lyyndaya only knew she must obey her parents and could only hope that something might happen one day to change their minds about Jude.

But at breakfast the next morning Lyyndaya's father began to grumble about what had happened with the planes the day before.

"Flying with those planes over the heads

of our children and livestock, diving, rolling, so dangerous, he does not even think about what he is doing —"

Lyyndaya couldn't stop herself from bursting out, "Papa, that's not true. As soon as those planes came after him he flew as fast as he could away from us because he didn't want anyone to be endangered."

Her father shook his head and put a fork and knife to his eggs. "All part of the act, Daughter."

"No, Papa, it was not. He didn't know those planes were coming. He didn't even know who they were. He was as surprised as anyone else."

Her father kept shaking his head. "This is what you want to believe because you still harbor feelings for that boy."

"When they landed he marched right over to the British officer and demanded to know what the man thought he was doing by flying over the heads of the crowd. I have not seen him angry like that before. I thought he might . . . but he reined in his temper."

Her father leaned back again in his chair. "So — how do you know this happened? This anger?"

Lyyndaya didn't look away from his hard gaze. "Many people ran up to the aeroplanes when they landed in the Stoltzfus field. I was close enough to hear what was going on. Jude had words for him."

Her father shrugged and twisted his mouth. "Words."

Lyyndaya pushed aside her plate of toast, reached out across the tabletop, and gripped both her father's hands. Everyone at the table, including her father, was surprised.

"Papa, when the officer asked Jude if he would fly for the army when he was of age, what do you think he said? He said, no, he would not fight, he would not use a plane to kill. 'We are Amish,' he said. 'We do not bear arms against our fellow man.' "

Her father narrowed his eyes. "He said this?"

Lyyndaya's green eyes were burning in her face. "Yes. And more, Papa. He told the officer our people had come to this land to find a place to worship God in peace, just as the Pilgrims had come on their ship from Britain to find the same sort of freedom. He said our people did not come here so they could go back to Europe and slaughter others in a war."

She released her grip.

Amos Kurtz sat still. Then he looked at his wife. "Well, Mother. If our daughter heard all this, so did others. It is Thursday. No doubt we will hear more about it long before we meet for worship on Sunday." He turned to his oldest son. "Luke, hitch up Trillium. Bring the old shoes from the Percherons. Jude made them anyhow. Let us see what he can do for us today." He smiled at Lyyndaya. "My girl, I told you I did not think he was a wicked boy. Just someone who thought he was more bird than man. Now that he is more of a man again, well, let us see what we can do to help him keep his feet on the ground."

Lyyndaya felt like she was flying inside while she stood on the porch watching Luke and her father pull out of the yard in the carriage and head for the Whetstone house. Ruth caught her mood perfectly, coming up and linking her arm through her younger sister's and asking, "Are you coming down for a landing anytime soon, Lyyndy?"

Lyyndaya laughed and hugged Ruth. "It is too good to be true. Papa is going to give his work to Jude. Oh, I pray something wonderful will come out of this."

"So do I. And while we're praying, Mama wants us to help with the baking for the Sunday meeting. You and I have the bread to take care of. Come. It will help the time pass quickly. Before we know it there will be Trillium stepping smartly up to the barn."

The sisters went to the kitchen and set to work on the dough. Lyyndaya thought she would hear the buggy turning into the drive in an hour, but after two hours her father and brother had still not returned.

"What can have happened?" she asked Ruth as they pulled a half-dozen loaves from the oven, their faces red in the heat.

"They are talking."

"Is it a good thing that they talk this long?"

"It can't be a fight. No one could argue with Papa for two hours. He would just walk out."

Another hour went by, and they were cooling loaves by the open window and putting more bread in the oven, when they both heard the crack of a horse's hooves on stones. They quickly closed the door on the bread and raced to the door. Mama was already at the buggy and her hand was on her husband's arm as he spoke. Her forehead was creased and her lips tight. Lyyndaya felt a coldness rush through her. Her father looked up at her and shook his head.

"My daughter," he said, "the news is not good."

EIGHT

Lyyndaya walked as quickly as she could along the dirt road, the sun and her stride bringing a fine film of sweat out upon her arms and hands. Father had said she could take the buggy to the Whetstone home, but she found she needed to work off the strain and restlessness she felt. Letting a horse pull her would not do that. It wasn't so far to Jude's smithy anyway, two miles at most. The Kauff mans drove past in a large wagon loaded to the brim with children and offered her a ride, but she forced a smile of thanks and waved them on.

When she reached the Whetstones' she went immediately around back without once slackening her pace.

He may not even be at the smithy. If it were me I'd be out somewhere by myself, praying and trying to think everything through.

But Jude was at the forge in a work shirt and suspenders, banging at a glowing orange-black horseshoe with one hand while pinning it to a huge anvil with a long pair of tongs. He did not look up as she stood in front of him. Only when he put the shoe over the coals again and pumped the bellows with his free hand did he finally look up and realize Lyyndaya was there. He stopped hammering.

"I'm just making your shoes," he said.

"Not *my* shoes."

He smiled. "But how is it you're here? What will your father say?"

"It was my father who suggested I come."

"Why?"

"You know why."

"What has he told you?"

"That the army arrived here at your house while you were discussing the shoes for our Percherons. They will be extending the ages for those that can be drafted into the military — as young as eighteen and as old as forty-five. You will have to register. And there is no guarantee you'll be exempted on religious grounds if your number is chosen."

"One minute." Jude worked on the large horseshoe a bit longer and then thrust it into the water. After that he laid it on a cooling rack. He wore a heavy leather apron that he began to unknot from behind his back. Hanging it up on a peg he went to a washbasin and soaped his face and hands and arms vigorously. Then he rinsed himself and rubbed himself with a clean blue towel. He turned back to Lyyndaya and said, "Come sit with me on the bench under the tree. Father set out a pitcher of lemonade and glasses about fifteen minutes ago. The ice has not altogether melted. You look like you could use a drink as much as me."

"I walked here."

"In this heat? Did no one want to lend you the buggy?"

"It was my choice."

"Sit down, please."

Lyyndaya sat with him on the wooden bench under the shade tree. She was glad to be away from the heat of the forge and was sure Jude felt the same way. He downed one glass of lemonade, then another, and another. Finally, with the fourth glass, he began to sip. She had drunk about half her glass.

"Do you want more, Lyyndy?"

She shook her head. "Thank you, not yet."

Jude leaned his head back and closed his eyes. "Your father would also have told you he was gone so long because Bishop Zook asked him to meet with my father and himself in our parlor. Just after the officers and the sheriff left."

"Yes. He said the three of them had decided they must send several men from the colony to the governor to protest this idea that some of our people might not be exempted from military service on religious grounds. Perhaps the pastors would go as well as the bishop. Even bishops from some of the other settlements might make the trip."

"Are you worried, Lyyndy?"

"Of course I'm worried. This is because you fly so well. The British officer is behind this. He's trying to force our government into making you a pilot for their war in France. Why, it was only a few Sundays ago Bishop Zook prayed for some of the Amish and Old Order Mennonites east of us. They have been persecuted by the communities near to them for not sending their young men to fight and not supporting the war by purchasing war bonds."

"I remember, Lyyndy."

"Even the U.S. Army was making life difficult for them. Six Amish men were forced into uniform and made to carry rifles and drill with a battalion —"

"And Hosea stood up and said we should not only pray for the Amish and Mennonites but for those who persecuted them as well, including the army."

She nodded. "I did pray in that manner. But even with the prayers I'm still worried and my spirit is troubled. The army could persecute you for refusing to fight."

"Well, you know, I'm not so worried."

"Why not?"

Jude stood up and stretched and looked down at her. "This is a good country. America has always been kind to the Amish. We have many freedoms. Our nation will not hurt us."

He poured himself more lemonade and gestured with the pitcher. She nodded and he filled her glass. Then he began to pace.

"Still, I don't know what a few of the officers may try to do in secret. It's important to me that my father be safe. The whole colony, all our people, all the Amish and Mennonite people who have chosen to follow Jesus Christ without taking up the sword. So even though I believe our country will protect us, there may be schemes hatched in the shadows that Washington and the president will not know about."

Lyyndaya saw a glint of uncertainty in his brown eyes. She was holding her fresh glass of lemonade in both hands in her lap, untouched. "I can pray for you."

"Yes? You would like to do that? Here? Now?"

"Yes."

"I must ask this one thing if you pray."

"What is that?"

"I would like it if you hold my hand as you do so."

Lyyndaya smiled up at him. "Really, I'm not afraid to do that. But only while we pray."

"Of course."

He sat beside her and bowed his head. She rested her right hand lightly on his left. The skin was surprisingly soft at the back of his hand, but she also felt the roughness and strength of fingers that were curled into a loose fist. She put all this from her mind and began to speak to God in High German as she'd been taught since she was a girl. The war concerned her, flying freely in a tall blue sky being turned from a joy into a curse. Freedoms lost concerned her, freedoms that had always been part of the promise of America, freedom that would be dishonored if their faith in Christ was now ignored or trampled on.

Oh, Lord, help us, oh, Lord, do not desert us, do not desert this country, help us bring peace and forgiveness into this clash of nations, not more violence and harshness. Tell us what to do, tell us what to say, and when it comes time to decide may our decisions be

118

your decisions, may they be the right deci-sions, the ones that make life abundant on this earth. We would not be a plague to this nation that has blessed us so much, we would not be locusts that devour. We would be light as Jesus is light, strength as Jesus is strength, love as God is love.

Im Namen des Vaters, des Sohnes, und des Heiligen Geistes.

Amen.

She gave Jude's fingers a squeeze and then removed her hand.

"Danke," he said.

"Bitte."

He leaned forward, his hands knotted together, his arms resting on his knees. "So now tell me something. Why have your father and mother let you come to see me?"

"I'm not sure. Papa knows the people like you and he doesn't want the church to think he's against you."

"Isn't he?"

"Oh, I don't know, it is all mixed up with the flying." Lyyndaya put her head back and looked up at the leaves of the tree they were sitting under. "But the moment I told him you had stood up to the British officer when it came to the war, that you had made your case for not bearing arms, for peace, some-thing lit up in his face. He decided then

119

and there to come to you to have our horseshoes done. After he returned with the news you might not be exempted from military service, I think he felt a great deal of sympathy for you. He insisted I visit. You must understand he lost his grandfather in the war to save the Union, and not just his grandfather, but many other family members as well."

"I see. Then does this mean —" He looked at her, but did not finish his sentence.

He had such a hopeful puppy-dog look in his face that Lyyndaya realized he truly did care for her. She felt warmth inside her as well as a sudden ache to gather him into her arms and kiss the top of his head and his beautiful brown hair. Instead, she only smiled sadly.

"Courting remains out of the question. Papa made that very clear. But we are permitted to visit each other at our homes and at worship gatherings. And we can walk together anytime we like — so long as we keep walking and do not hide away somewhere."

"Walking? Is that why you came here on foot?"

Lyyndaya felt the blood come to her face. "Maybe."

He got to his feet. "Then let's walk."

"Walk to where?"

"Philadelphia. New York. Los Angeles in California. What do I care where we go so long as it's you I am walking with?"

He extended his hand and helped her up from the bench.

"Well," she said with a sly smile, "what will Emma Zook think?"

"Probably the same thing David Hostetler will think, and Jacob Beiler, Jonathan Harshberger, Samuel Miller, Hosea Zook —"

She laughed and slapped him lightly on the shoulder as they walked slowly out to the road. "All those boys never come to the house."

"They will now, if we're seen together."

"Why is that?"

"They all thought the two of us had no chance. Now they'll be worried. So they will begin to pester you, bringing flowers and chocolates like the English do."

"Stop, Jude — no Amish boy is going to do that to win a proper Amish girl."

"And you are the proper Amish girl?"

"Yes."

"I do not think of you that way."

"No?" Lyyndaya looked at him as they went along the dirt road under the July sun. "How do you think of me then?"

121

"As Barrel Roll Kurtz. That is my new nickname for you."

He anticipated another swat from her hand and ran ahead, laughing. "Catch me if you can."

"It's not seemly," she called after him.

"Is it that . . . or is it that my Lyyndy Lyyndy Lou has become old and fat?"

Lyyndaya drew a sharp breath and said, "So that's what you think?" She began to run and caught him almost immediately and gave him a firm slap on the back. "Who is old and fat now, Jude Whetstone? You're it!"

The two laughed and took delight in playing again as they had done as children. A teasing game of "chase," then a run to the small grove of willow trees . . . and back again.

It was summer and it was the perfect time to be in love.

NINE

It became, Lyyndaya thought as the days rolled on in sunshine and in thunder, raindrops dripping from barns and oak trees, sun ripening the green tobacco leaves and the golden corn, the perfect summer of long walks with Jude, visits after church, long talks at picnics and in each other's homes. They were able to spend so much time together that she found she didn't mind it when on occasion she saw him with Emma Zook or Katie Fisher because she had seen, again and again, the way his brown eyes softened and warmed when he looked at her.

"I think he just might love me," she said to Ruth one August evening while they were brushing out each other's hair and watching the sun set from their window like the ball of a brass bedpost.

Ruth snorted. "I do not think it. I know it."

"Truly?"

"How can you ask? You're a woman just as I am, aren't you? If I can feel it from the other side of the room, how can you not feel it when you are two feet away from him at the kitchen table?"

"I don't know — what if I'm simply imagining it?"

"Do you never look into his eyes?"

"Of course I look at his eyes."

"Or are you always staring down oh-so-modestly at the salt and pepper shakers?"

"I look at his eyes!"

"And you read nothing there?"

Lyyndaya stopped pulling the brush down the gleaming length of her sister's dark hair. "What if I read what I want to read? The way some people go to the Holy Bible and tell us it says what they want it to say when it doesn't say anything like that at all?"

Ruth glanced back at her. "Are you finished?"

"With your hair or my questions?"

"I think with both." She turned around and took the brush from Lyyndaya's hands. "Honestly, Lyyndy, if you can't tell that man is crazy about you, I worry about your eyesight — and your intuition."

"Why? I'm just trying to approach this with humility."

"Humility is one thing. Discernment is something else. Turn around." She began to brush Lyyndaya's long blonde hair. "You need both. Don't deny the one to exalt the other. What good is a humble farmer who can't plow a straight furrow or a humble milkmaid who keeps missing the pail?"

"Then I shall exercise both," Lyyndaya said. "I shall not miss the pail!"

It was the very next morning that the two sisters found themselves walking in the direction of the Whetstone house. It had been days since Lyyndaya had heard from Jude — she knew he was busy at the smithy — but there was something more. She just felt it. Something was amiss, and she and Ruth would simply take a walk past Jude's house and see what, if anything, might come of it.

As they approached the house, Ruth was the first to speak. "Isn't that the Zooks' buggy in the drive?"

Lyyndaya squinted. "Yes, I think so."

"Emma is visiting, trying to undo Jude's affection for you," said Ruth.

"No, I don't think so," said Lyyndaya. "Besides, let her try if she must. What will be, will be. I can only stand in front of Jude as who I am — Lyyndaya Kurtz. I don't have Emma Zook's eyes. My skin is not the color of cream. I'm not so tall and slender. My father is not the bishop."

As they walked closer to the house strong male voices came to them from inside. Then they noticed the army truck parked on the other side of the house and a cluster of soldiers at the bottom of the front steps.

Before they could speak, Emma Zook came running down the drive — her cheeks shone with her crying. She seized onto Lyyndaya's hands and sobbed, "Please, Lyyndy, you care for him as much as I do. Can you not help? Didn't your father work for the government in Philadelphia before he joined the Amish people?"

Lyyndaya and Ruth stared at her in surprise.

"What is it, Emma?" asked Lyyndaya. "What's happening?"

"The soldiers have come to take him. They will not recognize his exemption."

"How can they not recognize his exemption?" demanded Ruth. "He is Amish. It has always been so for our people in America."

"They say he's hasn't been Amish long enough, ten years is a small amount of time," Emma said through her tears. "And the Lapp Amish have only been a group since 1890, they say that also is not enough to excuse him."

"Nonsense," snapped Ruth. "They can't get away with this. That's your carriage by the forge, isn't it?"

"Yes. Father is trying to reason with them. They came to our house first to fetch Hosea. I insisted on driving here with Papa."

Ruth's eyes took on dark fire. "They think to take Hosea as well?"

"Because the Lapp Amish are not one of the old Amish groups."

"Since when does this matter? Amish are Amish. Where is your brother?"

"In the truck — under guard — along with Jude." Emma broke down and collapsed into Lyyndaya's arms. "They will take them to the base after they have collected the other young boys — Samuel Miller, Jonathan Harshberger, Jacob —"

"Come." Ruth took Emma's hand. "We'll take your buggy to our house and tell my father. He will have words with them. Quickly. Come, Lyyndy."

Lyyndaya hadn't spoken, but now said, "No, I want to wait here. I . . ."

Ruth hurried Emma up to the smithy and the buggy and the two were gone in a whirl of dust.

Lyyndaya went around to the front of the house where Emma's father was pleading

127

with the officer in charge of the squad of soldiers armed with rifles.

"These are my orders, sir," the captain was saying. Lyyndaya noticed a soldier nudge a companion in the side and how they both began to stare at her, but she ignored them.

"I ask you to wait until we've had a chance to get a message to the governor," the bishop replied. "There is a mistake. It will be rectified."

"There is no error on our part, sir. The young men's names have been selected for service. If they will not comply, I must take them into detention. The religious exemption does not apply."

"It has always applied."

"This is a world war, sir. There has never been such a war before. The exemption does not extend to a new group such as yourselves."

"We are Amish."

"Lapp Amish."

"We are no less Amish than any other group."

"I have my orders, sir. Now, we have a long drive ahead of us. I must collect the others. Will you assist me by pointing out the various homes or must I go door-to-door with my men?"

The bishop closed his eyes briefly and shook his head. "No, no, there is no need for that. I will go with you. I will direct you."

"Thank you, sir. Please step up into the cab of the truck with me and indicate to my driver the home of Samuel Miller."

Lyyndaya rushed to the back of the truck, which was covered with dark green canvas, and saw Jude and Hosea sitting side-by-side.

"Lyyndy!" Jude reached out his hand and she grasped it without a further thought. "How is it you are here?"

"Ruth and I were out for a walk when Emma ran up to us and told us —"

"Poor Emma. She is so upset. Be kind to her, Lyyndy."

Lyyndaya gripped his hand tightly. "Of course I will be kind."

"You are both rivals for my affections, it seems. But it would please me if you became friends again, if you treated each other as sisters."

"No, Jude," Lyyndaya protested. "Emma is not my rival. We both care about you, but what happens is up to you . . . and God."

"Do you mean that?"

"Of course I mean it."

"And where is she?"

"They took the Zooks' buggy — she and

129

Ruth — and went to fetch my father."

Jude squeezed her fingers. "That's good of them, but I don't think it will help."

Lyyndaya reached out and took one of Hosea's hands that rested in his lap. "And you, Hosea? How is it with you?"

Hosea gave his usual sleepy and peaceful smile. "I'm more than fine. God is in his heaven. It will turn out all right."

"How calm you are."

"Our people have been persecuted for their faith much worse than a little inconvenience like this. I suppose I will be home in a week or less. I may miss a cutting of the hay."

"But it could be longer."

Hosea shrugged. "As God wills. There are already blessings from this mix-up. A beautiful woman is holding my hand."

He and Jude laughed. Lyyndaya swatted Hosea, breaking her grip.

"You are always the one for mischief!" she said.

"A merry heart doeth good like a medicine," responded Hosea, his green eyes and freckles dancing.

"Step back." A soldier with corporal's stripes jostled Lyyndaya. "My men have to get into the truck."

"Hey!" exclaimed Jude. "Go easy with the lady."

"You can shut your mouth anytime, coward," growled the corporal, "or I'll shut it for you."

"Whatever you're upset about has nothing to do with her."

"You are all birds from the same nest."

"Yes, we are all Americans."

The corporal struck Jude across the face with his fist. "Don't put yourself in the same camp as our soldiers. They are fighting for the freedoms you enjoy. You do nothing but hide behind your women's skirts."

"How dare you say that!" Lyyndaya flared. "He's as much a man as you. No, he's more of a man! He doesn't need to act the bully to prove his manhood."

The corporal's face darkened and he was about to reply when the captain appeared and barked a command. "As you were, Corporal. We do not make war on women and children. We are not the Hun. Get your men in the back of the truck." He noticed Jude's bleeding lip. "What happened here?"

The corporal snarled. "He banged his head climbing in, Sir. Clumsy oafs, these German farmers."

The captain cut him with his eyes. "See to it that it doesn't happen again. As he told you, he is still an American citizen."

The truck lurched forward, turned onto the road, and headed for the Miller's farm. Jude's father took Lyyndaya by the arm. "Come, my dear, we will follow them. And pray. Nothing good can come of this if we don't pray."

Lyyndaya bent her head as the buggy rattled toward the Millers'. At first she prayed silently, but Mr. Whetstone asked that she speak out loud so he could follow along and join her with his own words. So she prayed in a quiet but firm voice and now and then, when she paused, Mr. Whetstone interjected his own High German. Ahead of them, the truck had already parked at the Miller farm. Lyyndaya could see the family crowding onto the porch as soldiers led Samuel down the steps and into the back of the green truck.

As they drew up, Pastor Miller was remonstrating forcefully with them, trying to hold back his anger, refusing to let the young captain leave.

"We pay our taxes," he was saying. "We thank God for this country, *our* country."

"This is a time of war and we need your sons," the captain responded.

"We are farmers, that is what we do. It is not for us to bear arms. We bear the scythe.

132

We grow the food you eat."

"I come from a farming family myself, sir," said the captain climbing up beside the driver and the bishop. "Four brothers. All of us are in uniform. One is even a pilot."

Lyyndaya saw the bishop turn to him at this. "So, that's what this is about? You need more pilots? And young Master Whetstone is a good flier?"

"I don't know anything about Mr. Whetstone and his flying abilities. I just have orders to bring in the young men selected for military service who refuse to take up arms in defense of their country."

Pastor Miller stopped talking and looked at the captain more sharply than before. "What other young men? Which others besides these three?"

"I have six names. Now we must proceed to the house of David Hostetler."

"Who else?"

The captain consulted a sheet of paper typed with a column of names. "Besides this Hostetler, one Jacob Beiler and one Jonathan Harshberger."

"All six of them? All of their numbers were drawn? From the same settlement? At the same time? I don't believe it. You are trying to punish us."

"I have my orders. I do not have reasons.

133

But I can assure you this is not a punitive exercise."

Pastor Miller's face was grim. He spoke softly. "You lie to us. We all of us are Americans together and you lie to us."

"I'm not lying," retorted the captain. "Each of their numbers was drawn. It sometimes happens."

"Where and when? Where else and when has it happened?" demanded the pastor.

The Zooks' buggy, driven by Ruth, stopped in front of the truck, the harness on the mare jangling. Lyyndaya's father stepped down and removed his straw hat.

"Captain," he said, "I once held a job with the governor's office in Philadelphia. Not this administration. But the rules have not changed. You know the Amish are permitted to refuse military service. This right has been guaranteed to them under dozens of governors and presidents."

The captain nodded. "I am aware of that, sir."

"It's guaranteed in the Constitution. Freedom of religion. Our faith will not allow us to take human life."

"The Amish are protected, sir."

"But not the Lapp Amish?"

"The Lapp Amish are considered a new sect. Apparently it's not clear, sir, that the

Lapp Amish are sufficiently connected to the Old Order Amish and have the same rights and privileges. It will take some time to sort out."

"We will send our people to Philadelphia."

"By all means, send your people to Philadelphia," the captain said. "Send them to Washington. But until then, I have my orders. These men of yours must be brought to a military detention center for refusing to bear arms in defense of the Republic. They will be given adequate shelter and provision. No harm will come to them. They will be released upon the cessation of hostilities between the United States and Germany. Or at such a time as your ministrations obtain their release."

The captain leaned from his seat through the open door of the truck, his demeanor like that of a hawk. "Just remember," he added, "it was your people who brought this on. It was Germans who torpedoed our ships. It was they who drowned American sailors and merchantmen. You were warned when you sank the *Lusitania* in 1915. But you began sinking our ships again this spring. The *Vigilancia*, fifteen killed. The *Healdton,* eighteen or twenty killed. The *Aztec,* almost thirty killed. So we declared war on you. And your response? To kill more of our people by sinking more of our ships. Just the other day your U-boats torpedoed the *Platuria* tanker and took at least ten more American lives. You can thank God we don't line the bunch of you up in front of a barn and shoot you on the spot."

He pointed forward with his hand and the driver steered the truck around the Zooks' buggy and back down to the main road. Lyyndaya heard the captain almost shout at the bishop, "Where is the Hostetler home?"

Lyyndaya's father gestured with his hand to Pastor Miller. "Get in, Jacob. It's important we follow them. That we see everything they do and hear everything they say."

The pastor didn't move. "We have done all that we can. It's in God's hands now."

"God works through men and women of faith, Pastor. We are the instruments of his peace, are we not? The ones who hammer swords into plowshares."

"Very well. But this captain has no authority to do anything but carry out the orders given to him. He cannot change a thing."

He clambered up beside Lyyndaya's father. Ruth and Emma sat behind the men.

"Nevertheless," said Lyyndaya's father, snapping the reins, "we will keep them honest. At least while they are here in Paradise."

Lyyndaya looked at Mr. Whetstone. He

was already clicking his tongue and turning their buggy around to the left. "I will talk to my son once more before they take him away. We must stay with him, with all of our young men, until the truck is gone."

"I agree with you."

He looked up at Mrs. Miller standing with her children on the porch and a newborn in her arms. "Will you come, Rachel?"

Her face looked swollen and red. "No, Adam, my place is with my children and the baby. But you go. Yes, go, please, and keep our young men from evil. Guard them, please, guard them."

What, thought Lyyndaya as the carriage bounced down to the road, *could they possibly do that would quell the hatred and contempt she had seen in the eyes of both the corporal and the captain? How could they turn the key in the lock that would set their Amish men free from the wrath of the United States Army?*

TEN

A month passed as they prayed and fretted over the fate of the young men from their colony. Finally word came that the men were to be allowed a visit. Everyone thanked God and began to prepare food to take to them. Lyyndaya was still packing items away the day of the train ride to the camp.

Her father called up the stairs to her. "Lyyndaya, you must hurry, we'll miss the train."

"Yes, yes, Papa, I'm coming." How could she not be ready? She had looked forward to this day since it was announced through the colony that family members could travel to the army base to see the six young men who were still under detention until the matter of their enlistment was settled.

Lyyndaya opened the screen door and ran down the front steps to the buggy where her father waited, holding the reins. Her mother kissed her on the cheek. Ruth stepped from the barn as they swept down the drive and waved, calling out, *"Geht mit Gott."* Lyyndaya settled the wicker picnic basket, covered by a green checkered table-cloth, into her lap of black apron, navy-blue dress, and long black coat.

As they approached the railway station she saw the locomotive taking on water and coal and building up a head of steam. The other families were already there standing in a cluster on the depot platform. From the Zook family, Emma would be there, not the bishop as everyone had expected. He had expressed his contentment that Pastor Miller would be traveling with the group. His presence was, then, unnecessary. The fathers of David Hostetler and Jacob Beiler would be going as well. The mother of Jonathan Harshberger would join them.

Lyyndaya had no business going on this trip, not having family at the army base where the Amish men were detained. But Jude's father had said he felt poorly and asked her to go in his stead, telegraphing this change in plans to the military — they were permitting only one family member to visit each of the young men. Mr. Whetstone stood on the platform with the others and turned and smiled as the buggy approached, Old Oak tossing his head and whinnying at the other horses. *Mr. Whetstone does not look ill,* Lyyndaya thought as she smiled back, *but then who believed he was truly badly off to begin with?*

When Lyyndaya approached Jude's father, he pressed a wooden object into her hands and said, "Give my son this." It was a model of an aeroplane.

Lyyndaya turned the model over in her hand. "It's not like the plane Jude flies."

"No, this is the 1903 *Flyer,* the plane the Wright brothers managed to get aloft near Kitty Hawk. I will say it is a copy of the first real plane. Do you know about that?"

Lyyndaya shook her head. "Was it you who made this for him?"

"*Ja.* When he was eight. After he had seen an aeroplane for the first time. He just calls it 'Kitty Hawk' or 'Kitty.' "

She tucked it carefully under the checkered cloth of her picnic basket. "He will love it." She touched his arm. "Thank you — Mr. Whetstone — for allowing me this opportunity to see Jude."

He nodded. "Tell him I am praying for him. He will be all right." Then he shrugged. "He doesn't need to see an old broken down plow horse like me. Not when he has the two Amish beauties of Paradise to preoccupy him."

140

"Emma and I shall do our best to cheer him up."

"For him to see you, Lyyndaya, you alone, would be enough."

Just then the conductor announced, "All aboard!" and there were last-minute good-byes and hugs all around as the travelers made their way onto the train.

Lyyndaya and Emma found seats facing one another and settled in for the two-hour trip.

"Will he have lost weight, do you think?" asked Emma. "It's been over a month and I never hear good things about army food."

"I hope he's just the same. He has nothing extra to lose."

"Yes, I know, he is perfect, thank God." Emma lifted her own wicker basket that was covered by a solid yellow cloth and almost twice as large as Lyyndaya's. "Between the pair of us we can fatten him up, if necessary."

"What do you have in there? A roast ox?"

Emma laughed. "Remember, I'm packing for two — Hosea and Jude."

Lyyndaya let out a puff of air in a quiet sigh. "Let's just hope the army will permit us to give him all of it. I've heard stories about them confiscating food meant for prisoners."

Emma's eyes became a dark jade color and her lips formed a line as straight as a ruler. Her good humor had instantly vanished as if in a gust of cold November wind. "He will have all of it. He is an American citizen. They cannot deny him our help."

Lyyndaya smiled with her eyes. "I like your spirit. It brings to mind the time we had the acorn war with the boys. You threw handfuls so fast they all scattered."

"Oh, that." Emma looked out the window at black beef cattle grazing near a patch of golden pumpkins. Her lips curved upward slightly. "I was mostly mad at my brother for getting mud on my dress."

"Well, I think you'll need that same strength at the army base. Remember how the soldiers acted in Paradise? All their swagger and rudeness? The country is in a fight with Germany, and for some it seems to excuse all the rough behavior they wish to indulge in."

"God will direct our steps."

Lyyndaya nodded. "Yes. But who is directing theirs?"

As promised, two military cars met the train at the depot. Lyyndaya, Emma, and Mrs. Harshberger rode together in one vehicle while the three men took the other. The officer who had greeted them, a lieutenant, had been polite and friendly. Lyyndaya could see his head turned toward the men in the car ahead as they moved quickly over the dirt roads. Their own driver, a young man like Jude and Hosea, said nothing as he steered and shifted gears. Lyyndaya suddenly felt cold and too far from Paradise and wished she had not come. But she needed to see Jude — that was all there was to it. She thought about him, worried about him, and prayed for him day and night. Perhaps it was important he see her too, or if not just her, to see her and Emma both. At this point, thinking of him under guard, treated like a criminal, she cared less about who Jude liked most and more about what was good for him. And if two women picked up his spirits, she didn't mind sharing him with Emma Zook.

Soldiers opened the gate to the camp and saluted the officer in the first car. Their driver followed closely behind. Lyyndaya saw men in brown uniforms marching back and forth in front of wooden buildings and rows of tents in the sharp October sunshine. Some were shouting. Many of them held rifles to their shoulders. After a few minutes of driving they left the main part of the base and came to a corner where there was hardly any activity. They had to go through another gate into an area surrounded by tall barbed-wire fences. Soldiers with guns stood by buildings with bars in the windows. The two cars parked and the lieutenant walked over to their motor vehicle and leaned in.

"Here we are, ladies," he said. "We'll just step into this main barracks here, look over your baskets to make sure everything is in the pink, then we'll escort you to the dining room, where you can meet your brothers and sons."

Inside, the six of them stood quietly by as two soldiers lifted the cloth coverings from the baskets and dug deeply into the contents, examining everything they put their hands on. Four jars of preserves were lifted from Emma's basket and set aside. The officer, who was standing back and watching, stepped forward as Emma began to protest.

"I'm sorry, miss," he apologized, "but we can't give them anything that might be used as a weapon."

"A weapon?" Emma bristled. "You think my brother will throw jars of peaches at you?"

"I was thinking more along the lines of broken glass being used like a knife blade."

"Hosea? Jude? Jacob?" Emma's eyes

flamed a bright green. "Our men wouldn't harm a kitten. Don't you know we're Amish? Don't you know what we believe?"

"Well —" The officer paused, surprised by Emma's ferocity. "I suppose I don't know much, miss. There are no Amish in Idaho, where I'm from. All I know is, these men of yours will not fight, they will not join our troops in France and do battle for our country's freedoms."

An edge had come into his voice. Lyyndaya put her hand on Emma's arm. "Is it only the glass jars you are worried about, Lieutenant?"

"And any knives or forks."

"How do you expect them to eat then?"

"They have their hands." Ice came into the officer's eyes. "Permit us to finish our work."

When the soldiers were done Lyyndaya counted over two dozen jars of fruit and jams and vegetables lined up on the table. There were three large glass containers of fresh apple cider as well and five pints of milk. The lieutenant had the privates remove the jars from the room and then led the group through another door into what he called the mess hall. It was a small room with an odor that made Lyyndaya put a hand briefly to her nose and mouth. Rough wooden tables were lined with equally rough wooden benches. She heard Mr. Beiler mutter, "Shoddy workmanship. The boys will get splinters from those."

There was only one small window with iron bars. Some light made its way into the room, but it felt to Lyyndaya as if it were dusk, even though she knew it was just ten o'clock in the morning. Everyone in the group whispered as though somewhere people were sleeping. The officer had left through another door but soon returned, followed by a tall, heavy guard who carried what looked like a club, and then right behind him came Jonathan Harshberger. Lyyndaya heard his mother let out a small cry.

His hair was shaved off and one eye was swollen and purple. An old shirt with holes and old pants almost worn through at the knees hung from his body as he shuffled toward them, limping. Lyyndaya looked on in shock. Where once his baby face had been round as an orange, now it reminded her of a plank of wood.

"My boy, my boy!" Mrs. Harshberger rushed to her son and took him in her arms, hugging him fiercely.

Behind him was Jacob Beiler and after him Samuel Miller. Each of them had bruises on their cheeks and the same shaven heads and tattered clothing as Jonathan. Jacob burst into tears the moment he saw everyone. But Sam Miller kept his face tight and his emotions under control as his father shook his hand and gave him a swift hug. David Hostetler, when he appeared, wore bandages on both hands. Yet he marched steadily across the room and greeted them all as if he were arriving at church meal after the Sunday service. The moment Hosea walked into the room Lyyndaya saw Emma put her fist to her mouth. His sleepy, easy smile was gone, dark rings were under his eyes, and large scabs festered at each side of his mouth. Beginning to cry, Emma ran to him. Pastor Miller turned from embracing his son to glare at the lieutenant. "What is this you have done to our young men?"

The lieutenant returned the glare with one of his own. "Clumsy men, you Amish types, once you're away from your barns and draft horses. Perhaps it's just as well you aren't in France. Probably shoot more of our own than you would the enemy."

For a long time Jude didn't enter the room. Lyyndaya was about to ask the officer where he was when he made his way slowly through the doorway. She thought she might faint, he looked so unlike himself

— no hair, a cut above his left eye, a whiteness in his face, hardly more than skin and bones. He had lost so much weight, his body sagged.

"Jude!" she said, coming quickly and holding him up.

"I'm so weak, so tired," he answered in a rasp. "Never seem to get enough sleep, can't manage to keep all my food down."

"What do they do to you here?"

"I must sit."

She helped him onto a bench.

"Have you brought any milk with you?" he asked.

"No, they took it all."

"Any cream?"

"They wouldn't let us keep our glass containers. What do they give you to drink?"

"Water. Very bad water. Not like our own wells."

"I have some soft cheese."

He shook his head. Lyyndaya scrabbled through her basket, looking for something that might appeal to him. She came upon fruit wrapped in a towel.

"I have cherries, old cherries, but they are still —"

"Yes, please. I would like that."

She gave him the cherries and he began to pop them into his mouth and slowly spit out the pits.

"Very nice," he said with his first smile. "Thank you, it's so good to taste something."

"And there are apples. The Jonathan, the McIntosh, and that new Cortland you like so much."

"Ah. You're wonderful. A Cortland would be —" He closed his eyes and his head fell sideways. Lyyndaya thought he was going to pass out. Then he sat up and blinked. "I'm sorry, I probably needed a few more hours sleep."

"What time were you up?"

"Two or three."

"Why?"

"They needed the latrines cleaned out — all of them — so they got Hosea and Jacob and me out of bed —"

"Why couldn't the others help?"

Jude laughed quietly, turning the idea over in his mind. "Because — they had David and Samuel and Jonathan digging new ones at midnight —"

Lyyndaya felt the familiar tingling of blood rising to her face. "They can't treat you like this. You're not cowards. It's our faith, our beliefs, we do not take a human life, do not go to war —"

She turned on the officer, who was watching Pastor Miller offer his son honey from a small wooden box.

"You can't treat them like this," she almost shouted. "They are Americans. You should be proud of them."

The officer looked at her in amazement. "Proud of them? For *what?*"

Lyyndaya clenched her fists. "The rest of you go like sheep to the slaughter. These are the ones with the courage to have minds of their own. To think for themselves. Not to blindly follow the pack. Isn't that American, yes? To make your own path, follow your own vision, to do what is different? Why do you punish them for being what you say you fight to preserve?"

The lieutenant was caught without words. "I — we — do not punish anyone here. They are merely detained. We ask them to help us keep the camp clean —"

"If they were the cowards you take them to be," Lyyndaya continued, walking toward him, "then why haven't they caved in to your demands? Why haven't they told you, *Yes, enough, give us a rifle, send us on the boat to Europe, we will do your dirty work in France for you?* If they are so craven as you imagine, why haven't they given in to you long ago?"

"I don't know what you're talking about."

"Of course you do!" She stood directly in front of him. "You've been trying to break them and you find they are not so easily broken, yes? Doesn't that indicate manhood to you? Is it not the very expression of bravery?"

The tall weighty man with the club laughed and began to clap his hands. "My lady, you have a golden tongue."

The lieutenant shot the soldier an angry glance. "That will do, Sergeant."

"You must admit, sir, that she gives a good account of herself and the Amish."

The lieutenant fumbled in one of his pants pockets for a watch. He showed it to Lyyndaya. "I said an hour. No more. You have thirty-five minutes left." He placed the watch back in a different pocket. "Don't waste it arguing with me. Your men are not mistreated."

Lyyndaya stalked back to Jude's side where Emma was now fussing over him with Hosea at her other side. Her brother tried to smile his slow lopsided grin at her, but he couldn't turn up the corners of his mouth. She put a hand briefly on his cheek.

"Don't smile to please me, Hosea," she said quietly. "I can see how it hurts. How is it with you?"

"I pray for our return to Paradise."

"As we all do."

"Do you happen to have a bit of — soft cheese?"

She smiled. "I do." She reached over into her basket that sat near them on the long table. "Here. Have it all."

"What about Jude?"

"No, he's not interested. His stomach is upset."

Hosea sat chewing carefully, trying to move his mouth as little as possible. "Yes, it is always that way with him since we've come here."

"Don't they ever bring a doctor in to see any of you?"

"Twice. He always says we need more fresh air and exercise."

"Do they give you that?"

Hosea laughed and winced, putting a hand to one of the cuts near his lips. "Don't do that, Lyyndy. I can't afford to hear a joke. It hurts too much."

She looked at him with wide green eyes. "What did I say that was funny?"

"Fresh air. Exercise. We're always outside cleaning up latrines or digging ditches or burning garbage. Or mucking out the stables. It's rare to see four walls around us except for meals and a few hours of sleep."

Upon hearing this, Lyyndaya glared at the

lieutenant again. The officer deliberately turned his back on her. The sergeant with the club winked. She kept staring at the officer, knowing he continued to feel her eyes on him, like hot pins.

"So am I to believe the lieutenant," she asked Hosea, "when he says you are not treated poorly?"

"Oh," Hosea gasped, pushing another piece of yellow cheese cautiously into his mouth, "he doesn't know a thing that goes on with us. He's just here for show. Remember that corporal who was with the group that picked us up in Paradise? He's the one who cracks the whip."

"Where is he?"

"You won't see him. He'll drop out of the sky the moment you're gone."

"Lyyndy." Emma turned to her. "Don't you think Jude's looking better already? I can't get enough of Mother's yogurt into him."

Lyyndaya looked over Emma's tall shoulder at Jude. He was spooning the fresh white yogurt into his mouth like someone who hadn't eaten in days.

"I did not know you favored the yogurt so much, Master Whetstone," Lyyndaya said.

"I can't describe how it cools my stomach," he offered.

"I'm glad to see it. Emma is right. At least now you have some color in your cheeks. You could do with a good night's rest as well and a long draught of well water."

"That will not happen anytime soon."

Lyyndaya turned to glare again at the lieutenant's back.

In what seemed like only a few more minutes, the officer announced, "Your time is up. Say your goodbyes and we'll transport you to the depot for your return trip. First, you must pack up any remaining food. Anything left will draw rats to the barracks."

"Oh, I almost forgot this!" Lyyndaya dug down to the bottom of her basket and pulled out the wooden aeroplane. "Your father wanted you to have it. He misses you very much and is praying for you."

Jude smiled as much as she'd seen him smile at any time during the visit. " 'Kitty Hawk.' Look at that." He admired the model as he held it in his hand. "I've had this for over ten years." He looked up at Lyyndaya. "I see the Jennys here, you know. There's an aerodrome nearby. It's quite beautiful how they go by in formation. Makes me feel good. Even when I'm up to my ears in mud and shovels."

Lyyndaya had not felt like crying once since they had arrived, but now she sensed she was about to come apart completely. "They must look like birds to you."

"Better, Lyyndy, better. I can't fly like a bird. But I can fly like them." He shrugged. "Maybe again, one day, you and I —" But he did not finish his sentence.

"Time to move on, folks. Sergeant, get these men back to their work."

"A moment, Lieutenant." Pastor Miller approached the officer, his black hat in his hands. "We are grateful for the opportunity to visit our sons. There are some concerns and some questions, but these we will take up with others in higher places than you occupy. I would like to pray before we leave."

"Pray?" The officer stared at him.

"Are you yourself not part of any religious group?"

"Uh —" The lieutenant glanced at the sergeant. "My parents — I was raised Methodist —"

"Then you will welcome our request to pray for our boys here. And not just our boys, but all who are at this camp, all who are already across the ocean in Europe."

The officer inclined his head. "Of course. If you will go ahead."

"Thank you."

Pastor Miller refrained from praying in German. Instead, after a moment's silence, he spoke slowly in English. "Protect, our Father who art in heaven, the women, the children, the men. Safeguard, our Lord, the horses and cattle, the farms, the crops. Bless in such a way as removes the sting of the curse man brings upon your earth. May the warring countries come gladly to the table of peace. Heal the land. Heal the human heart. We ask in Jesus Christ our Savior."

When he closed with an "amen," the lieutenant nodded at the sergeant, who began to move the six young men toward the door. But he did it gently, Lyyndaya noticed, pushing no one, barking no commands, taking his time, letting Mrs. Harshberger kiss her son a final time, allowing Mr. Hostetler to finish placing fresh bandages on his son's wounded hands and hug him goodbye. He saw the plane in Jude's hand, but only looked at it and said nothing, nor did he force Jude to move any more quickly than he could through the doorway. Jude glanced back at Lyyndaya and Emma and offered them a small wave. Then the door shut behind the sergeant.

The officer accompanied them to the second gate and then jumped out of the car that carried the men and waved both vehicles on. He would not meet Lyyndaya's eyes.

At the station, Pastor Miller patted her on the shoulder and said, "You have fire and I do not say it is wrong. Plenty of people in the Holy Bible had this fire. But you must keep a tight rein on it, *ja?* Just as we keep a spirited horse from bolting with a firm grip. By no means do we wish to break the horse's spirit. Yet if we do not have control it will run wild and injure itself and others."

Emma cried off and on as they traveled back to Paradise. Eventually, tall as she was, she curled herself up like a small pretzel and fell asleep at Lyyndaya's side. Lyyndaya put one arm around her as she began to breathe deeply. *Poor sweet thing,* thought Lyyndaya. *God bless you, God bless us both. There is no rivalry for Jude here. We are sisters in the Lord.*

She leaned her head against Emma's. The rocking of the train had a lulling effect. An image of the tall sergeant's stern face filled her mind. She began to pray for him just before she dropped off.

ELEVEN

Something had awakened Jude. He lay in the dark and listened to Jonathan Harshberger snoring. That was Jonathan's way — he could ignore pain and humiliation and drop to sleep in an oven or on a cake of ice and awake again in a kind of innocence that forgot and forgave the abuses of the day before. There were no other sounds. It was still too early for the corporal to come raging into the barracks and tell them to grab their shovels and run to the latrines. Or to get down on the floor and do fifty push-ups. Or march back and forth in the cold dawn without their shirts. The one barred window brought only blackness into the room.

Then a hand went over his mouth and a rough voice whispered in his ear. "Say nothing. Do not wake the others. Throw on your clothes and follow me."

It was the tall sergeant. *What devilry does*

he have in store for me? worried Jude as he got out of his bunk and pulled on his pants and shirt. He followed the large figure out of the barracks and across to the mess hall, the stars sharp over their heads. Inside the mess a lantern had been placed on one of the tables. The sergeant sat there and gestured with his hand for Jude to do the same.

"The corporal will be waking you all in an hour," the sergeant said, his face yellow in the light of the lantern's flame. "It will go hard with you. Sometimes, as you know, I have ordered him to let up."

Jude nodded. "Yes, thank you."

"But I am being transferred to another base. The others who outrank the corporal will not be so . . . lenient. They'll look the other way like most of them have been doing since you were brought here in September." He leaned forward across the table. "We were taught to despise you before you even arrived, you and all the others who will not fight — Mennonites, Quakers, whichever group. But those of you with a German background we were told to deal with using an especially heavy hand. Most of the army not only think of you as traitors, but likely spies. I thought that way too."

Jude didn't know how to respond. The

159

Amish had lived peaceably in America for centuries. Now, overnight, they were suspected spies and traitors just because they spoke with a German accent and refused to kill other men.

"Your sister, lady friend, whoever she was," the sergeant went on, "she really made me think. Sure, I'd like to see you men fight. You all have the hearts of lions and you'd be great soldiers. But what makes our country great is that persons like you can be different and safe here and, I guess, give America the kind of color and character and, I don't know, flavor that makes us special. I've turned this over in my head a lot, Whetstone. Here's what I have to say — it's a privilege to have you Amish as American citizens, the courage of your faith and convictions is as American to me as apple pie, and it's an honor to preserve a way of life that permits people like you to flourish."

Jude felt a warmth go through him at this unexpected friendship. "Thank you — but shouldn't you be telling the others as well? It would mean a great deal to them."

The sergeant shook his head. "Let them sleep. They'll need it. Once I'm gone they'll be treated even more severely and there'll be no one around to say, *Stop, enough.*"

"So — is that why they're transferring you out?"

"They won't say as much. My orders state that my skills are needed elsewhere to prepare American soldiers for combat. But I suspect the real reason is to give the corporal and others like him free rein to do as they see fit with you. The nation is in no mood to quibble about how you and other war objectors are treated. They don't care. Their sons and fathers and brothers are being killed in France. For all your treatment here, you're alive and safe and have food — such as it is — and you have a roof over your heads. The soldiers being killed in Europe sleep in the mud under an open sky and eat cold beans. To tell you the truth, I worry about what will happen to you. I don't know where they'll draw the line. Whenever we get a report of heavy casualties over there, they take it out on you."

The sergeant got to his feet and picked up the lantern. "President Wilson was concerned that getting into the war would make America thicker-skinned and cruel. I thought he was wrong. Now I see he was right to be worried."

Jude made no reply.

"You'd better get back under your blanket before the corporal shows up or it will go

161

from bad to worse for you."

They walked outside. There was still no light in the east. As they went toward the barracks Jude thought about everything the sergeant had told him. Why had the man taken Jude into his confidence?

"I still don't understand why you're telling me all this," he said.

The sergeant stopped walking and turned the lantern so it shone fully in Jude's eyes. Jude blinked and squinted in the glare.

"Because you're the only one who can stop it."

"How can I stop it? What is it I can do?"

"This British officer Cook convinced the brass you're ace material. That you can fly as good or better than any of the German pilots he's faced at the front. That you can be America's hero. The day you say you'll fly for the United States in France is the day the others from your church go home."

Jude gently pushed the lantern down so he could see the sergeant's face. "Are you serious when you tell me this?"

"You remember how they tried to get you signed up and you refused? This goes on until you change your mind."

"I fly and the others go free — is that it? Is this official?"

"Yeah. After they soften you all up some

162

more an officer will be along to pop the question." Then the sergeant shook his head. "But it's a lot to ask of a man to go back on what makes him what he is. You cross that line and suddenly you're someone else and it makes you less, no matter how good the reasons are. Oh, I guess you could argue in your head that you have better reasons than most for selling your soul to the devil. But I wouldn't go back on what I am. And I'd never tell another man to do it either."

He began to move toward the barracks again, holding the lantern in front of him. "You'd all probably be better off dying here together. Like a squad of soldiers in the trenches. At least you wouldn't risk losing the best part of yourselves."

"Surely they're not going to kill us off, Sergeant."

"Accidents happen. Or someone goes too far and a man collapses and never gets up. Believe me, Whetstone, we've sent Mennonites home in pine coffins with no apologies or regrets. War changes a nation's heart. Sometimes for the better. But, and now I can see for myself, sometimes for the worse."

They were at the barracks' door. The sergeant extended his hand. "It's been an honor knowing you and your men. Good luck. And — God bless."

Jude took his strong hand. "Thank you."

He watched the lantern move away into the blackness until it seemed as far away as a star. He remained standing in his shirtsleeves with his hands in his pockets, feeling the November chill, but unwilling to go inside and crawl back under his warm blanket, looking at the sliver of moon slowly setting in the west and thinking of his friends asleep, their bodies aching and bruised, eyes swollen, fingers broken. *God, what shall I do? How can I say I will fly with machine guns on my plane? How can I say I will kill so my friends may go safely home to Paradise? If I asked them, none of them would want me to take up arms, even to save their lives.*

Jude returned to his bunk, but sleep would not come. And only an hour later, the corporal and a group of men with truncheons descended on the barracks. As the sergeant had warned Jude, it was a worse day than any that had preceded it. It was as if someone in higher authority had given the corporal orders to literally kill the Lapp Amish from Paradise and be done with it.

They were ordered outside, naked, and made to line up in the dark. Pails of water were thrown on them until everyone was shaking from the cold. Then the corporal ordered them to go back inside and get dressed. When they returned he told them to run to get their hearts pumping and warm their bodies up. At the end of the run he had every one of them beaten harshly with the truncheons.

"You're traitors to your country!" shouted the corporal while this went on. It seemed to anger him more that the young Amish men scarcely cried out as the blows fell again and again. "You don't deserve to be called Americans! You're nothing but German spies, Huns, *Boche,* devils! You send reports back to Kaiser Wilhelm about our troop preparations. You tell him about our training methods and equipment. You slip notes to your mothers and sisters and they give them to enemy agents in Philadelphia and New York. You think we don't know? You think we're fools? This beating is nothing compared to what I have in store for you swine."

The corporal had his men put their boots on the Amish men's heads and press their faces into the muck and stench of the latrines. Had them carry one another on their backs and run back and forth carrying cans of garbage. Made them pick leftover food from the cans and eat it for their breakfast — and then their lunch. Ordered them to crawl back and forth under barbed wire strung so low it tore their shirts and pants to pieces. Then had them beaten again for destroying military equipment.

Each of them handled it according to the sort of person they were. Jonathan absorbed the punishment, only the eyes in his child-like face showing the struggle, then slept it off and began anew each morning. Sam was dark and grim, ready to argue and protest, ready to fight, it seemed to the guards, so they beat him more severely than the others because they perceived him to be a threat. Jacob was the opposite — he couldn't control himself from crying out — "yelp-ing" the soldiers called it mockingly — or stop the tears from bursting down his face so that he was beaten as much or more than Sam. It took all of Jude's self-control to stop from attacking the guards whenever they knocked a sobbing Jacob Beiler to the ground.

Despite the agony of watching his friends get hurt and of taking his own blows, Hosea somehow managed to stay the best-natured of any of them, maintaining his easygoing smile and sense of humor and his faith, encouraging the others to stand up under the harsh treatment and not lash out. He was, Jude thought, so much like his father Bishop Zook.

Though most of them looked to Jude as the leader of the group, he knew they would gravitate to Hosea if anything happened to him. And should anything, God forbid, happen to Hosea, it would be David Hostetler they would turn to — tall, strong, always thinking, always working out a plan, kind to everyone, a man who prayed constantly and who always had a Bible verse on his lips. The only one who might not fall into line under David's leadership was Sam Miller. But then Sam didn't like anyone's leadership, whether in the camp or back in Paradise. He would go along with things as far as he needed to, yet he always preferred to go his own way. After particularly difficult times, while the others came together at night to lift each other's spirits, he often chose to sit apart and stare into space.

For three days the harsh treatment went on with hardly any variation except the fourth time the Amish men crawled back and forth under the wire in their ragged clothing the corporal blasted the air over their heads with a semi-automatic pistol. Several of the men were coughing uncontrollably by the second day, but no doctor was brought in. They began to sleep in pairs for warmth on the second night, but made sure they woke early enough to return to their own beds before the corporal's arrival each morning.

When the third day was over, Jude listened to Hosea Zook struggling for breath next to him. He turned and whispered, "Perhaps we should do what they want and enlist."

Hosea turned over and looked at him in surprise with bleak, swollen eyes. "How can you say that? We know what God expects of us. How can we help the world if we are just like them? Weren't our ancestors persecuted for following Jesus? Don't we sing the hymns about their suffering every time we gather for worship?"

"But several of us are sick. You yourself are not well."

"I'm as strong as a draft horse." Somewhere inside himself Hosea found his lopsided smile. "I could pull a plow for our corporal if only he would ask."

"Our corporal?"

"Yes. Our corporal to pray for. Who knows what God will do to change his heart?" Hosea put a hand on Jude's arm. It was ice-cold. "We can do nothing for America if we do not remain true to our beliefs. If we stay faithful to Jesus, we can do the nation much good. But if we break off following Jesus and his teachings, America will wind up the poorer for it, and we should lose our own souls in the bargain."

Jude estimated it was around midnight when he saw a part of the thin moon through the barred window. Now and then someone coughed for a long time before returning to sleep. Next to him, Hosea had taken most of the blanket and was lying on his side, breathing through his mouth because his nose was plugged. Jude felt the chill on a leg and arm that were not covered. But he had no intention of taking any portion of the blanket from Hosea.

The wooden aeroplane was under his bunk, tucked behind one of the iron legs. The corporal had never bent down and looked there and so he had never found it. Jude reached for the model and held it up to the white moon. *Should I fly again, Lord? Is it possible to go up in the air once more and feel the rush of your wind, the color of your blue? Is there a way to fly and not shoot, a way to go into combat and never kill?*

He did a barrel roll with the plane and smiled. Barrel Roll Kurtz. He saw again her bun falling loose, the pins scattering into the air like startled blackbirds, the color of the hair a sudden and welcome burst of light. He thought about both Emma and Lyyndaya often during the hard, cruel days at the army base and the images of their beauty warmed his mind and body and helped him endure. That and the strength and presence of God in an environment that appeared utterly forsaken by Father, Son, and Holy Spirit. All the men lived only to see their loved ones again and to thank God. A Thanksgiving visit had been denied, so now they could only wait another month until Christmas, hopeful but tormented by the nagging thought that even on that solemn day they might be denied a visit from the home folk. *Unless . . .*

Unless I tell the army I will fly.

Jude pictured himself in a uniform standing by a fighter plane. The thought repulsed him. He had been taught since he was ten that war was wrong, that the Amish did not embrace a military solution to conflict though they did pray for the souls of the soldiers on both sides. Other young men might dream of flying at high speeds and shooting down enemy planes and being called an ace. He simply dreamed of doing cartwheels in the sky and calling upon God to enjoy the tumult and exuberance of flight with him.

For a few moments he drifted off with the

aeroplane on his chest. Words from the Bible entered his sleep — *the Son of Man came to give himself as a ransom for many.* It seemed as if the phrase was addressed to him. He protested, *But I am not the Son of Man.* Immediately, more words clustered in his mind — *He that taketh not his cross, and followeth after me, is not worthy of me.* Then Lyyndaya was smiling and touching his hand and telling him, *Even if others turn their backs, I will always believe the best of you, and God himself will never reject or shun you. That's two of us.* His eyes opened and everything was suddenly crystal clear. He placed the plane carefully back under his bunk and waited for the corporal's arrival.

Soon enough the door to the barracks flew open and once again the shouts of "traitors!" "spies!" and "Huns!" were hurled at them as they were ordered out of their bunks and onto the floor to do fifty push-ups.

Jude tumbled out of bed with the others and lowered himself to the floor. David Hostetler and Samuel Miller could scarcely move. They each did one or two push-ups and collapsed. The corporal ordered men forward, who poured buckets of cold water over them. Jude could see the chunks of ice.

Samuel and David gasped and each produced three more push-ups before their arms gave out again. The corporal kicked both men in the ribs.

"Get up!" he roared. "It's important you have your breakfast. It's waiting for you at the officer's mess and it's piping hot. We don't want it to cool off, do we? So we must run for our breakfast and make sure we get to it in time."

The corporal's men hustled them out of the barracks and into the dark morning and made them run half a mile to the officer's mess hall. Then he took them around to the back and ordered them to fish through the garbage cans for something to eat.

"It's cold, it's cold!" he raged. "I warned you. None of you ran fast enough. Swallow what you can — it's more than you filth deserve, and it's better than what our real American boys are eating in the trenches right now."

Jude took in mouthfuls of cold porridge with his hand. He noticed several officers walking past after leaving the mess hall by the front doors. They ignored the knot of men bending over the trash cans scraping bits of food from among the ashes of cigarettes, coffee grounds, and brown apple cores. He made up his mind and suddenly ran toward them.

The corporal was hot on his heels. "Get back here, Whetstone!"

But Jude reached the officers first, stood at attention, and saluted. Their lips curled at the condition of his clothing and the stains of rubbish on his hands. He spoke quickly, "I am a friend of Lt. Brendan Cook. He is a British flying officer. He —"

One of the men, a captain, was startled by Jude's words. "I know Cook," he interrupted. "How is it a prisoner like you knows him?"

"I flew with him."

The corporal hit Jude from behind with a truncheon, using all the force he could muster. Jude fell to his knees. Face purple with anger and embarrassment at his prisoner's actions, the corporal was about to swing at his head when the captain snapped, "That will do, Corporal. I want to hear what the man has to say."

"Sir, I apologize for this insubordination. Rest assured —"

But the captain waved his hand impatiently. "Stand down, Corporal. Let him get to his feet."

"But, sir —"

The officer's eyes turned the color of gray iron. "Stand *down.*"

The corporal saluted awkwardly and backed away. Jude got to his feet and returned to attention, a thin line of blood trickling from his nose in the silver dawn light.

"How do you know Cook?" the captain demanded.

"I was flying over the field where we were holding our church picnic in July — the lieutenant and his men engaged in mock combat with me."

"Really?" The officer looked at him with doubt glazing his eyes. "What were you flying?"

"A Canuck."

"Stick or wheel?"

"All Canucks have joysticks, sir."

The captain gave a small smile. "So they do. What is your name?"

"Jude Whetstone, sir."

"Whetstone. That's not a name easily forgotten. Are you one of the Amish prisoners? The ones who refuse to fight?"

"It's against our religion, sir."

"Yes. Would to God it was against the religion of more of the Germans." He stared at Jude with eyes that cut. "You Amish are supposed to be over at the other end of the camp. Not at our end. What do you want?"

"I want to fly, sir."

"What?"

"I want to fly for our country, sir. I see that I have been mistaken in refusing to join our boys in Europe. I long to take up a plane against the Hun, sir. I want to *fight*."

"Do you?" The captain turned to his companion. "Major, does his name ring any bells?"

The other officer shook his head. "No, but I can get to the bottom of this quickly enough. I'll get a motor over to the general and ask him here to clear this up. Meanwhile, we should get this whole crew to stand down."

"All right." As the major hurried off, the captain glanced over to where the corporal was venting his frustration on the other Amish men, having them empty the garbage cans on the ground and then return the contents to the metal barrels using their hands. "That's enough, Corporal. We're going to figure out what's going on with this Whetstone and the other prisoners, and until we do, I want you to leave them be."

The corporal shook his head. "Sir, I can't do that. I'm authorized to make sure —"

"You're authorized to obey the orders of a superior officer. No more of this. You men — you prisoners — step back from those trash cans. You must be freezing. Corporal, get them some coats."

"There are no cold-weather coats authorized for the prisoners."

"Give them your own."

"Excuse me, sir?"

"There are six of you and six of them. Give up your coats and then go get some more for yourselves. Tell the quartermaster that Captain Peterson and Major O'Shea need your old ones."

"I can't, sir."

"Right now, Corporal. Or the next thing you know you won't be giving your coats to the prisoners. You'll be trading places."

Swallowing his bewilderment and fury at the sudden shift in the prisoners' fortunes, the corporal indicated to his men to do as the officer had ordered. He did not remove his own coat as they handed theirs over to the Amish men.

"Give yours to Whetstone here," the captain said.

The corporal saw the superior's dark eyes and didn't bother arguing. He peeled off his long brown coat and walked over. Then he threw the coat on the ground by Jude's feet.

The captain narrowed his eyes. "Thank you, Corporal — you're relieved."

"But I have to take care of these prisoners, sir."

"I'm in charge of them now. Take your men and do your nasty little business somewhere else." Then his voice dropped to a harsh whisper that only Jude and the corporal heard. "America may not like men who won't bear arms in this conflict. But it likes men like you who bully them even less. Get out of my sight."

Jude slowly bent down to pick up the coat as the corporal and his men, visibly shivering in the icy dawn air, shuffled around the corner of the mess hall and away. He pulled the coat on over his shirt. It covered him to his knees.

"How's that?" the captain asked.

"I haven't felt this warm in weeks, sir."

"I don't know your whole story, Whetstone, but Cook did talk about it and bits and pieces are coming back to me. The coat is the least I can do on Uncle Sam's behalf." He looked around as a pale sun rose in the east. "Imprisonment for refusing to serve in this conflict is one thing. Torture is something else. Cook would not believe what we've done to his prize American."

A car raced up with an officer and a driver but no Major O'Shea. The long, unsmiling man in a trench coat and uniform unfolded himself from his seat and came towards them with purposeful strides, stones crunching under his shoes. They both caught the glint of the star on his collar.

"Captain Peterson?" the man snapped.

Peterson saluted. "Yes, General."

The general saluted in return. "You are dismissed."

"But, sir —"

"You can wait for me in the car."

Peterson shot a look at Jude, hesitated, then walked to the motorcar. The general stared at Jude.

"Are you Whetstone?"

"Yes, sir."

"The flier?"

"Yes, sir."

"I'm told you want to enlist."

"I do."

"You think you are ready to take a plane up in combat?"

"Yes, sir, I am," replied Jude, meeting the general's gaze.

"To *kill?*"

Jude hesitated a moment and then decided to salute. "I want to fly, sir. Please let these other men return to their families. Let them grow corn and wheat and feed America. They're a waste to you in the trenches."

The general put his hands on his hips. "As are you, Whetstone." They continued to stare at each other for several long moments. Then the one star said, "The others can go home now. But you stay."

Jude nodded. "Thank you, sir. I should go and tell the boys what I've decided. Even though they won't understand."

"I suppose they'll think you've turned your back on your faith."

"Yes. It will be like that."

"If it helps, you may tell them a truck will be taking them to the train depot within the hour. They will be given new clothes and fed and their wounds looked after."

"Yes, sir," Jude responded.

Jude turned toward his friends who had been sitting out of earshot. Hosea came up to him anxiously before he reached the group.

"What is going on, Jude?" Hosea asked.

"A truck is coming to take you all to the train station, and the train will take you home."

Hosea frowned. "Just like that? Months of this and suddenly we're going home?"

"Yes, that's all there is to it."

"No, there's more to it than that. What were you talking about all that time?"

"I'm not going with you," Jude said.

"What do you mean? Why not?"

"I'm — I joined up — I'm going to fly —"

179

"You're going to *fly?* You mean — in the war?"

Jude met Hosea's shock with a steady gaze. "I will try not to hurt anyone."

"You can't do this, Jude." Hosea tripped over his tongue. "I don't — I don't believe it. You negotiated something. You worked out some scheme for our release, didn't you?"

"Just go home to your father and mother. Tell Emma I will write."

"From *where?* England? France?" Tears started in Hosea's eyes. "You don't need to do this, Jude, we would have survived."

He followed Jude's glance to the young men behind him, some too weak to even lift their heads.

"No," Jude responded, "you wouldn't have."

"And if we didn't we would have died for Christ, we would have died for the gospel."

Jude put a hand on his shoulder. "Why not *live* for Christ and the gospel instead?"

"Don't do this, Jude. No one at home will accept it. Such a sacrifice on your part is not needed." Hosea's young face was streaked where the tears cut through the grime. "The boys love you."

The general in the trench coat had walked up to the two of them and was listening. He

180

coughed to get their attention and looked directly at Hosea. Jude was reminded of a bird of prey.

"It's necessary that your people back home understand that Whetstone did this of his own free will," the general said in a low voice, his eyes dark. "It would not do to suggest otherwise. It would not do to mention that you think he might have been forced into enlisting in the army. In a time of war the country needs to be united. This unfortunate episode of you and your Amish brothers is over — please do not consider speaking in a reckless manner that may cause something like it to reoccur. Your friend has freely chosen this course of action. Whetstone puts on the uniform of an American military pilot in response to his country's call to arms. He is a patriot."

Hosea stared at the officer. "You're asking me to lie?"

The general set his lips tightly. They had no blood in them. "Tell your church exactly what Whetstone has told you. Don't offer your own perspective on the affair. He has said he wants to fly for our country. It happens to coincide with your release from this camp on time served. Let it go at that." His features sharpened. "You don't want to be arrested and detained again, do you? Risk

181

being sent to Leavenworth? Have your homes vandalized? Your crops set on fire?" He leaned down to Hosea in a kind of swoop. "You and your people are German-speaking. You don't fly the flag and you don't buy war bonds. You don't fight. It would be easy to convince a mob you want Germany to win the war. No one would come running to rescue a pack of Krauts if certain persons took matters into their own hands. It's already happened to Mennonites and Hutterites. So seal your lips and keep your mouth shut."

Hosea's face had gone white. He thought a moment and suddenly put a hand on Jude's arm. "Is that what it is? You have not negotiated our release? No one has twisted your arm? You really want to get back into an aeroplane so badly you will shoot other men out of the sky to do it?"

Jude shrugged and went along with Hosea for the general's benefit. "God has put it in me to be a good aviator. There is nothing more to it than that. I want to fly as God intended."

"As God intended?"

"Yes, my brother. God gave me wings and I am going to use them."

Hosea turned away from him and the trench-coated general with a broken look

182

and headed back to the other four, who were slumped on the grass. The sky was a mixture of dawn and darkness as he walked. "May God have mercy on us all," Hosea whispered, closing his eyes.

The five men returned to Paradise with a military police escort. Their families and friends were waiting, and the men had hardly stepped down onto the train platform before people swarmed over them, hugging and kissing. They were in new clothes and their wounds and bruises had been cared for. Yet it immediately became obvious that someone was missing.

"Where is Jude?" asked Mr. Whetstone. "Where is my son?"

"What has happened to him?" Lyyndaya demanded of Hosea.

Hosea had one arm around his young brother, John, who clutched one of his precious books, and his sister Annie, who had knitted a woolen scarf he wound about his neck. The easygoing smile dropped from Hosea's face as he explained. "Jude enlisted in the army. He's going to fly in France."

"What?" Bishop Zook's face crisscrossed with lines. "Impossible."

"I'm sorry, Father, but it's true. He's in training camp right now and soon he will be going overseas."

The bishop stood rooted while others swirled around him, laughing and praising God, unaware of what Hosea was saying, overjoyed to see the young men safely back.

Bishop Zook's lips scarcely moved. "I cannot believe it. I cannot believe Jude would do this." He looked sharply at his son. "There must be an explanation. What is the explanation?"

Hosea shrugged unhappily. "He wanted to fly, Father. That's all. He wanted to fly."

Lyyndaya found she could no longer enjoy the joyous occasion and returned to her buggy. What on earth had happened? Had Jude's love for flying now become more important than his faith?

TWELVE

Weeks and months passed until 1917 became 1918. No one heard from Jude or the army — not his father, not the bishop, not Emma, and not Lyyndaya Kurtz. The snows of January and February swept over Pennsylvania and the Lapp Amish prayed, unwilling to believe one of their own had gone off to war, hopeful they would soon receive news to the contrary, that somehow Hosea had misunderstood what had happened at the camp. Then it was March, and still not a word. Until one gray morning found Emma and Lyyndaya moving rapidly along the road in a carriage, heading toward town.

"And Mrs. Stoltzfus said there were two letters from Jude?" asked Emma.

Lyyndaya flicked the traces for Old Oak and nodded. *"Ja."*

"A letter for each of us?" Emma's eyebrows had come together in a dark line of anxiety.

"No. He wrote both letters to me." Lyyn-daya glanced at Emma's troubled face and laughed. "Oh, you silly girl, of course he wrote you a letter. You know he has feelings for both of us. He has said so many times."

Emma leaned her head back and closed her eyes as the buggy bounced and swayed down the road. A few snowflakes, like thin snips of paper, spun down out of the March clouds. "Men change their minds."

"So do women."

"Well, not these two women. Not yet, at any rate." Emma opened her almond-shaped green eyes and looked at Lyyndaya. "If this were the time of King Solomon then Jude could marry both of us. We'd be like sisters."

"We're already sisters."

"But not just Christian sisters. Oh well, it wouldn't work, I'm sure. We both want Jude to ourselves, don't we? Whichever one of us wins his heart, she's the one who gets him all to herself. And that's the way it should be."

Both girls turned silently to their own thoughts about what might be in their futures.

As they passed another buggy headed in the opposite direction, Lyyndaya came out of her thoughts and asked, "Have you heard anything lately? Maybe through your father?"

Emma rubbed her temples with her hands. "Oh, nothing, really. There has been talk, meetings, but no decision has been made, if that's what you mean."

"What about your brother? What does he say?"

"Hosea says that Jude wanted to fly so badly he decided to enlist. Last night there was a meeting and I could hear their voices through the floor. Pastor Miller and Pastor King are very angry with Jude. They say he has not only betrayed the Lapp Amish but has also turned his back on God."

Lyyndaya felt a stab of pain. "But he has done nothing more than enlist. As far as we know he is not even in France. Has not even fired a shot."

"But he will."

"Perhaps not."

"How can he not?" Emma's usually smooth brown face was creased with deep lines. "Or does he think the army will just let him fly one of those aeroplanes that takes pictures?"

"Reconnaissance aircraft?"

"*Ja.*"

"They may permit that."

Emma made fists. "No, they won't,

Lyyndy, you know they won't. He's too good for that. He can do circles around robins and starlings and hawks. They won't waste him flying a plane in a straight line. And what makes you think he would want to fly a plane in a straight line anyway?"

Lyyndaya had no answer.

Emma struck a fist against the side of the buggy. "Why did he join the army? Why is it in him to be so crazy about flying? If he had waited until the war was over he could have just flown a plane for somebody without having to shoot a gun. You can see there will be plenty of things to do with planes once the war has ended."

"And when will the war end, Emma?"

Emma shot Lyyndaya a dark look. "How should I know?"

"It could be years yet. How can we be sure the Lapp Amish will still allow him to fly in 1919 or 1920?"

"You think that's why he signed up? It might be one of his last chances to really fly?"

Lyyndaya shrugged. "Put yourself in his shoes. You know how these things turn out. Electricity, telephones, the new motorcars . . . I can't imagine it will be decided that aeroplanes are permissible. If aeroplanes, then why not motorcars?"

"But I don't want to put myself in his shoes!" Emma almost shouted, startling Old Oak, who broke into a faster trot. "I want him to put himself in mine. He knew the trouble this would cause me — cause the two of us. It's only a matter of time before they pronounce the *Streng Meidung*. Once he's flying in France against German aeroplanes, that will be the end of it. My father will not be able to stave off Pastor Miller and Pastor King and others in the colony any further. The strictest shunning will begin. Jude *knew* this would happen. He *knew* it would hurt me, hurt our chance to have an Amish marriage and be an Amish couple. Yet he is so *verruckt,* so crazy in the head about being up in the air like a bird, he is thinking like one now."

Lyyndaya reined Old Oak in and stared at the anger in Emma's face. Her long hands, large for a woman, were still balled into fists, and strands of her dark hair had unraveled against her cheeks. She was glaring straight ahead.

"I doubt we know the whole story of why he enlisted," Lyyndaya said in a soft voice.

"Of course we know." Emma's voice was harsh. "He got tired of cleaning latrines. He wanted out of the camp. He could have returned to Paradise and me — us — along with the others when they were released, but he wanted to fly more than he wanted to court either of us."

Lyyndaya shook her head. "I know he loves to fly, but it still doesn't sit right with me. There's something, I think, that we do not know. It's not like Jude to make a decision that flies in the face of everything that's Amish and not even come home first to explain himself. Or at least write it in a letter."

Emma leaned forward with her face in her hands. "The army changed him. Hosea says some of the soldiers were very cruel to them. He doesn't go into details. But it was hard on all of them. Maybe something inside of Jude snapped and broke — like frayed leather."

"It may be that he will tell us what made him do this in his letters."

Emma's voice came through her fingers. "If Mrs. Stoltzfus was correct. If there are letters at the post office."

"Why would she not be correct? She is not that old."

Emma sat up, her eyes a pale, washed-out green. "I feel old. Like I am forty! When the shunning begins we can't even eat at the same table with Jude, or take rides with him, or accept gifts, or receive mail. We certainly can't court." She blew out a lung-ful of air. "Oh, well. There are handsome men in some of the other Lapp Amish settlements."

Lyyndaya was surprised. "As handsome as Jude? Like who?"

"Benjamin Fisher over by Intercourse. He's good-looking. And Noah Raber at Bird-in-Hand. He is very tall and manly."

"Are you serious?"

"Well, I must pray and ask for God's guidance, of course. But I don't intend to become an old maid waiting for the war to end and Jude to confess and repent."

"Are you giving up so easily?" teased Lyyndaya. "Aren't you afraid I'll run away with him?"

"The only way you'll run away with him is if you both run away from the Amish altogether. Are you prepared to do that? To separate yourself from your mother and father and sister? From your people? Your God?"

Lyyndaya kept her eyes on the road. "I suppose not," she replied.

"So I'm not worried about you running off with Jude. Or even flying off."

Lyyndaya clucked to Old Oak and the buggy began to move again. After a long silence, she spoke up as they came into

Paradise's small downtown. "Perhaps his letters will tell us why he did what he did."

Emma had worked herself up and didn't smile. "It's a long time coming if he does so. Why couldn't he have written one of us right away before he boarded the steamer in New York? It is over three months now."

"I don't think the mail travels quickly between Europe and America. Sometimes I worry we have never received letters he wrote because they were on ships the Germans sank."

Emma flipped a hand in the air. "*Ja, ja,* anything is possible. Now the U-boats are after us."

"Well, he's written us now. That's what's important."

Minutes later, they were in the post office, where Mrs. Stoltzfus placed a single letter in each girl's hand. The gesture seemed to calm Emma down.

As they headed back to their farms in the buggy the two young women agreed the right time to read their letters would be alone in their rooms or alone by the wood-stoves in their kitchens. Or even in the barn or the attic, just so long as they were not being pestered by their brothers and sisters and parents. Yet as Old Oak jogged along and the snow began to fall thicker and thicker from fresh gray clouds banked against the sky, they both began to change their minds.

"My little sister will follow me around like a cat waiting for me to open the envelope," complained Emma. "How can I concentrate on what Jude is telling me with her on the prowl?"

Lyyndaya nodded. "For me it will be my mother. She doesn't want Jude and me to write back and forth anyway, but since a letter has come she will want to know how he crosses his x's and rounds his o's. Even if I hid with the cows in the barn she would come looking."

"It's exasperating."

After another few minutes of quiet driving the two glanced at each other.

"Why not pull over here?" suggested Emma.

"All right."

The top of the carriage protected them from the snowfall, and they tore at the envelopes as if the letters within had caught fire and needed to be rescued. Emma pulled out three pages and held each one up in dismay before reading them.

"Look at the holes!" she exclaimed. "Who does this?"

"The military censors," said Lyyndaya.

"Papa told me it would be so. In case Germans get their hands on the letters."

"Ha. Well, two German girls did."

Lyyndaya had spread out her own two pages in her lap. Where Emma's letter had dozens of small rectangular cuts that had eliminated words, phrases, or sometimes whole sentences, she saw only three or four in hers. As they began to read, often speaking lines out loud to each other, it became clear why, at least to Lyyndaya. Emma was constantly being told about units of the American Expeditionary Force that Jude had spent time with, where and when he had met other Americans from Pennsylvania and what units they belonged to, the sorts of planes he had been able to train on, and all kinds of information about the soldiers and sailors and aviators where they were training in Britain. To Lyyndaya, he went on and on about what he was thinking and feeling, only mentioning aeroplanes or when they might be sent over the Channel to France in a few places. She had no intention of reading his long intimate meanderings to Emma, who was more than pleased that her entire first page was taken up with his apologies for not writing sooner and for not discussing joining the Aviation Section, U.S. Signal Corps, with her.

"So he *is* thinking reconnaissance," Emma breezed, "and look, his postmark is for early January — he wasn't so late writing to me, after all. It's just the steamer that was late. And he tells me he misses me and fresh strawberries."

"That's wonderful," said Lyyndaya. And it *was* wonderful because while he had kept his letter to Emma light and charming, the letter he had written to her almost smoldered in her hands. *I can't stop thinking about you. I dream about us flying together again and again. Now and then we get a sunrise green as jade here and whenever we do it is as if my plane takes me into the color of your eyes.*

She noticed where his thumb or finger had smudged the ink and left a print. In another place there was a dark ring from a cup of tea or coffee. She longed to get home and read his words over and over again while she lay in her bed, her covers snugged up to her chin. Or to pick up a pen of her own and respond.

"I want to write him now, tonight — no, this minute," laughed Emma. "Is it possible to ride in a buggy and use a pen?"

"Come on, Oak," called Lyyndaya taking up the traces, "let's go home and get some oats. Or ink."

"Of course my father will want to know everything."

"What will you tell him?"

"That Jude will be flying reconnaissance and not fighting."

"We don't know that for sure."

"Close enough."

"Pastor Miller won't give up."

Emma's face grew stony. "That man. God forgive him. No, he won't. Let us write and post our letters to Jude quickly before we're told that is no longer permitted."

Lyyndaya didn't find the privacy she craved for hours, not until the house was asleep, including Ruth in the bed beside her. Then, her candle still lit — something that did not bother her sister, who loved to fall asleep to firelight or candlelight — she read the letter three more times as she sat up in bed. She pressed her hands, one after the other, onto the ink smear of his fingerprint, then brought the hands to her lips and gently kissed them. *How foolish I am,* she thought, *but God must be relieved to have a silly girl's foolishness to gaze down upon now and then.*

From under her bed she brought out a small oak lap desk fashioned in the shape of a heart. Inside were pen, paper, envelopes, and a bottle of ink. There was a round hole to secure the bottle on the lid of the small desk.

Dear Jude, she began to write, then thought better of it and placed the sheet of paper on the floor to clear away later. She began again. *My dear Jude.* She paused. Then decided to push on. He was her dear Jude even though Emma thought he was her dear Jude too. But suppose Emma began her letter *My dearest Jude?* Or *My one and only Jude?* Lyyndaya decided to lay this sheet of paper on the wooden floor as well. She penned, *My dearest Jude,* hesitated, thought about *My dearest and truest Jude,* heard the clock downstairs strike twelve and forced herself to press on.

But there were greater obstacles ahead. He had mentioned her eyes. Should she mention his? *Your warm brown eyes are like the spring earth.* Or was that forward on her part? Too much, too soon? *Is your hair still the thick curly mop I liked to pull on when I was ten?* She laid this sheet on the floor and started once more. *I miss you. I also long to fly again with you over Lancaster County and count the toy horses.* She made up her mind to keep this phrase. *It sounds like you have gained your weight and your strength back. Have you been eating well? Peas? Corn?*

197

Beef? How about sleep — are you getting enough of it? No, no, she sounded like an Amish mother nagging her boy at the kitchen table: *Eat, eat, grow big and strong as a horse.* This sheet of paper joined the others on the floor. *My friend Jude, I miss you too. I wish you were here — everyone goes to Intercourse to get their smithing work done now.* What a stupid sentence! Her letter was getting worse instead of better! Onto the floor it went.

The clock struck one. *Dear dear Jude.* No. She let the paper drop. Her pen needed to be cleaned. Once that was done she tried again. *I remember resting my hand on yours when I prayed that day. I always think of it. I am glad you asked me to pray.* She was going to let this one fall onto the pile too, but another part of her argued that she had not made this up, it was true, why not say it and let Jude decide how to respond? After all, what sweet delicacies was Emma Zook cooking up? So she kept it in and continued to fill the page with her smooth looping cursive. Now and then another sheet made its way to the floor.

When Ruth awoke at half past four for the milking, she placed her feet on a carpet of white paper. She picked up a few of the sheets, looked at Lyyndaya sleeping with the lap desk still on her bed, read the half-finished sentences, and began to giggle like a twelve-year-old, quickly covering her mouth with her hand.

Oh, sister, you are smitten.

Lyyndaya mailed the letter in town after finishing her morning chores. Somehow completing four pages and handing them to the postal clerk in Paradise gave her an extra boost of energy that compensated for her lack of sleep. She was able to clean up alongside her mother in the kitchen following lunch and smile at various barbed comments about Jude instead of snapping back in response. Surprisingly, it was her father, sitting and drinking a second cup of coffee at the table, who kept sticking up for Jude and coming up with reasons why he might have felt it was important to enlist in the Aviation Section of the Signal Corps.

"You astonish me, Amos," said Lyyndaya's mother, turning from the sink with her arms up to their elbows in soapsuds. "You're the one who has been against Jude and his flying all along."

He ran his fingers through his beard. "I'm not thinking so much about the flying, but about the boy himself. Our young men went through terrible persecution at that army base. How can I blame him for seeking a way out? Even a way out that offends the Amish faith?"

"The others saw no need to join the army as a means out of the camp," she retorted, still staring at him while she was scrubbing a pot.

"Yes, and that's what bothers me. He joins the army. The others are released. This happens at the same time. Why didn't he just leave with his friends?"

"He didn't want to come back," she said sourly. "Flying was more important to him than the Amish way, more important to him than following Christ."

"That's just it." Lyyndaya's father rapped his knuckles on the table. "That's not the way he acted here. *Ja,* I was annoyed with the flying. But he respected our wishes with regard to our daughter, he made no fuss, he did not complain, he followed the *Ordnung,* remained true to the Amish faith. The horseshoes he crafted for me were impeccable, the finest I have ever seen — *ach,* I hate to put them on my horses' feet."

"So what are you saying, Amos?"

"That I'm not content with the explanation young Hosea Zook has given us. Jude up and enlists even though they are being released? He doesn't want to come back to Paradise? He doesn't want to see our daughter even though he could be killed in Europe? He expressed no desire to go and fight while he lived among us. In fact, he defended our position on war. And when did he ever speak to us of winning medals or shooting down planes or killing other men? Did he ever speak like that around you, Lyyndy?"

Lyyndaya, still surprised by her father's vehement defense of Jude, shook her head. "No, Papa. He had no interest in going to war, no desire for any sort of — military glory."

Her mother handed Lynndaya another pot to dry. "They say the cruelty in the camp broke him. Changed him."

Father raised his dark eyebrows. "Only *he* is broken? No one else? Yet he is one of the strongest of the bunch?"

"Not everything in this life makes sense."

"*Ja*, and this makes no sense at all." He stood up from the table. "I think there is a connection between our young men's release and Jude's enlistment. I don't know what it is. But there is something there."

Mother kept her back to him as she drained the sink and wiped her hands on a cloth. "Hosea Zook says not, Father."

He grunted. "Hosea may have his reasons."

"So? You are saying he is lying? That all of them are lying? That crazy Jude Whetstone had a gun held to his head and had to say yes to the American army?"

"I'm saying I do not know. I will pray, I will read the Holy Word, I will think. I may talk to some of my old colleagues in Philadelphia. But I tell you what it is, Rebecca. I do not like to see a man bullied. And this young man, this Jude Whetstone, no matter what you think, he has been bullied."

When her father left the kitchen, Lyyndaya's mother sighed and opened a container of flour.

"Do you want some help with the bread, Mama?" Lyyndaya asked.

"I have no idea what's come over your father." Her mother was looking out a window at the gray skies and the falling snow. "I have no idea what he thinks he knows that no one else knows." She stared at her daughter with tired, dark eyes. "The shunning will come. He cannot stop it. This will hurt you and I'm sorry for that. But remember, my dear, your boy brought this on himself. He has wings and propellers on the brain. He forgets about everything else."

She reached over and stroked Lyyndaya's cheek. "You must stop thinking about him. Yes, it is hard to do. But he is bad for our family, bad for the Lapp Amish. He brings us only trouble. Write a goodbye letter. Be gracious, be kind, but be firm. End it before the shunning prevents you from saying farewell in a decent, God-fearing manner." She turned back to the small bin of flour. "I am baking alone today. Go and do what needs to be done."

Lyyndaya walked slowly up the stairs to her room. Ruth was not there. She sat on her bed and tried to think clearly, tried to pray. Across the hall she could hear the children laughing and a door slamming. Outside, Papa was calling Trillium with his distinctive whistle. He would never tell her to write the letter her mother wanted her to mail before the *Meidung* was put into force. But perhaps her mother was right. Perhaps it was better to say some last words to Jude than to be left unable to say anything at all.

She pulled the lap desk out from under her bed and lifted the lid. Inside were the sheets of paper, the ink, the pen, the envelopes. She picked the pen up, dipped it into the ink, pressed the back of her hand against her eyes, and began to move the nib across a clean piece of paper.

THIRTEEN

"Mail call!"

Jude had been lying on the bunk in his room with his hands folded under his head, alternately thinking of Paradise, Emma Zook, Lyyndaya Kurtz, and flying, when he heard the voice in the hallway. He got up quickly just before there was a knock on his door. Opening it, he saw Mitch Jones grinning at him and holding out a handful of envelopes.

"You lucked out today, Whetstone. A pile of letters, and I'm pretty certain I can smell perfume."

Several other fliers had come out into the hall when Mitch had shouted and they began to give Jude a hard time, one whistling, another chanting, "Hubba hubba," still another crying, "Oh, please, Mr. Aviator, won't you make an honest woman out of me?" Jude laughed, waved, and vanished back into his room.

He sat on the edge of his bed and went through the stack he'd been given: one from his father, one from Bishop Zook, three from Emma, one from someone named Deborah King and, at the bottom, a letter from Lyyndaya. He read his father's first.

It was a sad letter, his father obviously lonely and missing him and still wondering why Jude had just up and enlisted without talking things over. Bishop Zook's was not as sad, but it ran along the same lines: Why had a Lapp Amish boy joined the military, why had he gone to war, did flying matter so much to him that he had to go against his church and his faith? What could he, as bishop, do to protect Jude from the *Meidung* once Jude was flying aeroplanes over the battlefields of France?

The letter from Deborah King was a request from a young woman at Bird-in-Hand for Jude to locate her brother Matt, who had left the Amish faith years before and was now a combat pilot with an American squadron. Could Jude write back and tell her if Matt was all right? He had been shunned for years so they could not receive correspondence from him, nor could the family send him mail.

Then Jude opened one of Emma's letters. It was her envelopes and pages that were scented, not with perfume — not from a good Amish girl and the bishop's daughter — but from the soaps she used on her skin and her hair. It immediately took him back home and filled his mind with her eyes and smile. The feeling was so strong that Jude had to shake his head to clear it. Her letters were funny and witty, and line after line she teased him about when he was coming back to court her by buggy and aeroplane. He lay back and closed his eyes after he had opened all three, listening to the English rain rattle on his windowpane.

In his right hand he held the envelope with Lyyndaya's flowing script on it.

Why did I open Emma's first? Why did I save Lyyndaya's to open last?

There was a loud knock on his door. He sat up and Mitch poked his head in. "Hey, lover boy, the old man wants to see you *tout de suite.*"

"Major Jackson? What for?"

Mitch shrugged. "Beats me. I just deliver the news. And the mail." He grinned his freckled grin again. "Maybe perfumed envelopes violate military protocol. Which puts you in hot water and absolutely no one else."

Jude threw on a coat and walked from their barracks to the command hut, slog-

206

ging through grass and pools of water. To his left, the biplanes sat stoically in the gray rain, looking undefeated and strong and as ready to take to the air as if it were a sunny day. He stepped into the hut, spoke to Jackson's aide, and was ushered into his commanding officer's room without any delay.

He saluted. "Sir."

The salute was returned. "Stand easy, Lieutenant."

Major Jackson was in a brown uniform shirt and pants like Jude. Tall and lean with a perpetual tan. His hair was silver and cut short for the warm Arizona days he had ranched in until America entered the war. The pilots said he was making a fortune with his beef contracts to the army and could have stayed in southern Arizona without any danger of being drafted. But Jackson had volunteered. Behind his back they called him "Ironwood" after the desert ironwood tree that grew in America's Sonora Desert.

He stood up and went to the window that looked out on the aerodrome and the planes neatly lined up on the green grass.

"What do you think of the English climate, Whetstone?"

"I can live with it, sir. Our Pennsylvania

springs are pretty wet too."

"But warmer."

"Yes sir, warmer."

"I can't stand the constant rain myself. I feel like I'm on Noah's ark. The desert suits me better."

"Yes, sir."

Jackson put his hands in his pockets and turned to face Jude, his gray eyes sharp, but not unkind.

"I was reading up on your — church — and it made me wonder about a few things. For instance, if the Amish won't bear arms, what are you doing here?"

Jude had not expected this. He cleared his throat and went back to attention. "Well, sir —"

"Stand easy, I said."

Jude tried to relax. "It was something I had to do."

"Why?"

"To save lives."

"*Save* them? Most airmen talk about taking lives and becoming aces."

"Well, sir, I suppose they and I come at this conflict from different perspectives."

Jackson came slowly toward him, hands still in his pockets. "Your people are exempt from serving in the military. You could be at home chatting up a pretty girl with perfumed hair and plowing your land for spring planting."

"Well, sir —" Jude wondered briefly if Jackson knew about Emma's letters and then plunged ahead. "I mean no offense, but you could be on your ranch in Pima County riding at the head of your spring roundup."

The major thought about this, smiled in a small way like a dry, curved stick, and jingled some change in his pocket. "You have horses, Whetstone?"

"Yes, sir."

"You like 'em?"

"Yes, sir. I got my first pony when I was twelve. An Appaloosa."

Jackson's eyes widened and changed color to an almost bright blue. "Appaloosa! You like that breed?"

"Grit's always been a great horse."

"I had a bunch of Appies once that near drove me around the bend. Stubborn, knot-headed, you say left, they go right. As for me, I have a fondness for paints. All the horses on my ranch are paints."

"Beautiful horse, sir."

"Darn right. And they know how to take orders."

"Yes, sir."

Jackson walked back to his desk and

209

picked up a sheet of paper. "Your gunnery has improved. You couldn't hit the broad side of a barn last month and now you're shooting ticks off a flea's back. What happened?"

Jude lifted one shoulder in a shrug. "Don't know, sir. Got the hang of it, I guess."

Jackson stared at him. "I think you always had the hang of it. I think you were holding back on us. Not sure why." He sat on the edge of his desk, still holding the piece of paper. "Eyes like a carbine sight. Reflexes sharp as a razor blade. Mind as cool as a blue norther. I believe you always could shoot like Wyatt Earp. What's going on, Lieutenant?"

"Not sure, sir."

"Oh, I'm pretty sure you know." Jackson looked back at the paper and ran a hand through his close-cropped silver hair. "You've requested reconnaissance duty. The observer has the guns on reconnaissance. Not the pilot. Is that what you were thinking?"

Jude stumbled. "I'm not . . . I suppose I was hoping —"

Jackson put the paper down and folded his arms over his chest. "Have you given much thought to what it's like in the air during a war?"

"Of course —"

"Well, whatever you think, change your mind. It's *worse*. Even up in the air and away from the trenches, it's worse."

"Yes, sir."

"It's not about flying, Whetstone. It's not pretty like that. Not a hop over the Grand Canyon. Or a cruise over Lancaster County. It's about killing men. It's about sending planes down in flames. We want twisted wreckage on the ground, Lieutenant. *Their* wreckage, German and Austrian wreckage. Their pilots getting the glorious military funerals."

Jude felt a coldness working its way through his body from his head to his stomach and legs. "Yes, sir."

Now Jackson's gaze on him was like rock. Or, Jude thought, a rattler.

"Can you do that? Can an Amish boy shoot men? Not just Fokkers and Albatros fighters?"

Jude didn't respond. Jackson sat gazing at him, arms still over his chest.

"I have a faith too, Whetstone. Born and raised Baptist. Got dunked at fourteen and I darn well meant it too. Still mean it." He tapped a black leather book on his desktop. "Keep my Bible with me at all times. Read it morning and night and a lot of times in between. *Blessed be the Lord my strength, which teacheth my hands to war, and my fingers to fight: My goodness, and my fortress; my high tower, and my deliverer; my shield, and he in whom I trust; who subdueth my people under me.* A psalm of David, number one hundred forty-four, verses one and two."

"Yes, sir."

"*The Lord is a man of war: the Lord is his name.* Exodus chapter fifteen and verse three."

Jude nodded. "I know, sir."

"Then *live* it. Live your faith in God and honor his Word." Jackson stood up. "Your request to fly reconnaissance is denied. You are much too good of an aviator. We need you at the front bringing the enemy's planes down. In the name of God."

Jude looked straight ahead.

"You are on your way to France in the morning. We've kept you here far too long as it is. There's no need to put you in our advanced schools at Issoudun or Clermont-Ferrand. You were already ace material when you arrived. But we needed your help teaching the prairie boys and the mountain men and the city slickers. You did a good job. Got them to love flying as much as you love it, as much as I love it. However, now

that your shooting eye is what it needs to be
— well, we've taken casualties, Whetstone.
We've lost a lot of good boys. And we want
to prove to our allies that an American flier
can be just as tough and resourceful as a
French or British one. America wants her
best pilots at the front. It'll mean a lot to
our doughboys down below in the muck
and poison gas. And it'll mean a lot to the
American public back home."

Jude came to attention. "Of course, sir."

"The transport will pick you up at 0300
hours. Take everything you need. You won't
be coming back."

Jackson drew himself up as rigid as a
flagpole. He saluted. "I hope to join you in
due course, Lieutenant. Good luck. And
God bless you."

Jude returned the salute. "Thank you, sir."

That night, Jude did not sleep well. When
the motor vehicle arrived with a British
driver he threw his duffle bag in the back
and climbed in. Neither of them had anything to say. A fine mist was drifting over
everything.

Later, on board the ship that took him
across the Channel, he leaned against the
rail and finally opened Lyyndaya's letter
Mitch had given him the day before. Tiny

droplets of water formed a film over the paper and made some of the ink run, but Jude kept reading as the sun whitened the sky.

Do I love you? I don't know. I pray about you, think about you, care about you, but deep, deep love, the love a woman has for her man, the love that lasts a lifetime — do I have that for you? I don't know. I suppose if I don't know, then I don't have it, do I? Because I don't think I would have to guess. But I care for you so much — oh, so much — can it be far away?

Jude smiled, the Channel spray and slowly lifting fog making his face shine with water droplets. Emma would say, *Oh, I'm sure it's love, I'm certain I'm in love with you,* over and over again in her letters. Lyyndaya would express her doubts, her hesitations, her uncertainties, knowing she took the risk of losing out to her rival when she did so. There really was no one like her. Though he wished she would dab her envelopes with the soap she used on her hair and hands — yet he knew she was not the kind of woman who would ever do that.

Of course you created a little bit of a

thunderstorm among the colony by joining the military. I don't understand why you did it and I can't believe it was just so you could fly. After all, you could still fly your Jenny here, couldn't you? You don't really explain yourself well in your letter, it all sounds mysterious and — forgive me — evasive and not to the point. What are you not telling us? What are you not telling me? Oh, I suppose that eventually the truth will come out. God will always make sure the truth comes out. Except I have no idea when that will be. You could change all this with a pen stroke. But will you? You are hiding something from me, it is like one of our childhood games, only it's not so much fun, it's too serious, war is too serious to be fun.

A French driver was looking for him at the dock and they began the long morning's drive to Paris.

"Is that where I'll be stationed?" asked Jude.

The driver had been chosen for his facility with the English language. He smiled at Jude's naivete. "Wouldn't that be nice, *monsieur?* All the charms of Paris and the war far away."

Jude felt his face flush with embarrassment. He surprised himself by saying, "I don't wish the war to be far away, *monsieur,* and I do not wish to remain and partake of the city's charms if it is. It's just that I have no idea where the front is."

The driver stopped smiling. He felt the *americain* was almost ready to come to blows with him. They were a rough and ready bunch, always looking for a fight. He changed his tone of voice. "*Pardonnez-moi, monsieur.* You will need to transfer to another transport in Paris. I am not sure where you are heading exactly, but the front is hours away from our great city and many of the *americain* squadrons are south of us."

Jude was humiliated by his burst of temper. *I am still Amish and a Christian,* he reminded himself, *whether I am heading into a war zone or to a café in Paris.* The two men did not speak for the rest of the trip. The mist from England and the channel was gone and a blue April sky had been spread over them by the sun. Birds swooped in front of their vehicle. Green fields and hedges gleamed in the light. It was beautiful, and except for an occasional military convoy or group of soldiers Jude would have had no idea he was getting closer to the battle lines.

The driver dropped him off at some sort

of gathering point for Americans in Paris. He was told by a young man with an accent as thick as creamed honey that he would have to wait. Did he want a book? A coffee? Jude said no to the book and yes to the coffee, taking it outside and settling down on the steps to watch the Paris traffic as well as the men, women, and soldiers cramming the streets. After a while he began to reread Lyyndaya's letter. He smiled again as he read the part where she said, *And if I did fall in love with you, how would it be any different from the way I feel about you now? Would my heart race a little faster? Would I get goose bumps when I heard you call my name? Would I have trouble keeping myself from taking you and your mop of brown hair into my arms? Well, all those things are happening now anyway, so what will be the difference — can you tell me?*

Jude heard his name called, and he quickly folded the letter and tucked it back in his pocket. He was quickly herded into a truck with five other fliers and two American drivers. The truck banged and snorted east, the drivers warning the pilots they would not get to their aerodromes anytime soon. Jude pulled out Lyyndaya's letter and began to read it again.

"Where are we headed?" asked a youth

with flaming red hair sitting beside Jude. "Is it a state secret or something?"

"Nope. A placed called Nancy." A pilot facing them yawned. "It's a couple of hundred miles away. Betcha they pull over and snooze for the night once it's dark." He glanced at Jude. "Whatcha got there, sport? Letter from your girl?"

"Are you talking to me?" Jude looked up from the pages.

"Don't see no one else with a letter."

"She's — a friend."

"Sure. A friend. We all like gals that are friends."

The others laughed.

Jude felt the heat in his face. "Well, I'm telling you the truth. No one is talking about marriage yet. I like the wisdom in her letters."

The man stared at Jude in mock disbelief, his mouth open in an exaggerated way, his eyes popping. "You like her *wisdom?* Are you kidding me?"

"Look, she is a friend, nothing more than that."

"Nothing more, huh? Say, you got a funny accent. Where you from? Berlin?"

"Knock it off," growled an older and muscular man with a thick black mustache. "He's an American. That's all that matters.

Where's home, kid?"

"Pennsylvania," Jude responded, as if he were speaking with one of the Amish elders.

"A good place. The North won the war in Pennsylvania. You ever been down to Gettysburg?"

"Once when I was seven or eight."

"I got to get to it after this French fracas. Granddaddy fought there. Lost a lung, but he never regretted the wound. Said the United States was made there more than it was made at Lexington or Concord."

As rough as the ride was, as the day dragged on and night fell, each of them dropped off. Jude thought he never slept, but over and over again he kept jerking awake and snapping his head up, Lyyndaya's letter still clutched in his fingers as if it were diamonds or gold. Once he sat straight quickly and stared about him in a bewildered way, his mind racing. The older man with the thick mustache grunted.

"That got your attention. See out the back?"

Jude saw only blackness. Then it lit up as if it was on fire. After several moments it went dark. Then flared up again. A loud grumbling reached his ears.

"Looks like a lightning storm is coming this way," he said.

The older man grunted again. "There's a storm all right, but it's not coming to us, we're going to it. An artillery barrage, kid. Ours, theirs, who knows? But I been watching us get closer and closer. That's to the west and north of us, that's why we can see it even though we're looking out the back of the truck. We must be right on top of the lines by now."

"What time is it?" someone asked.

"Three," answered another voice.

The next flash made the backs of Jude's hands yellow. The pages of Lyyndaya's letter were sharp and clear.

"You could read by that," said the man with the mustache. "Why don't you give us something, kid? Nothing that's personal, keep that to yourself. Just something to cheer a fellow up that's a long way from home."

The flashes were getting stronger and brighter and the roar of the explosions coming to their ears sooner. Jude glanced at the men around him in the glare and all of them were looking at him with faces that were tired, lonely and, meeting his gaze, hopeful. Then it went black.

"All right," he said.

The next burst of light lasted fifteen or twenty seconds. His eyes fell on the page in his hand, the ink smeared by the Channel spray from the day before.

"This is what I pray," he read out loud, *"that you may be safe, that you may be well, that no harm may come to you or those you call your friends, that the war may end soon, that by this Christmas of 1918 you will be home among those who love you and standing at the table, carving the roast goose, laughing and thanking God for every breath you take."*

FOURTEEN

Lyyndaya heard Bishop Zook's voice calling to his horse — "whoa" — and came down the stairs to open the door with her mother and father. The April sun was setting in purples and reds behind him.

"Guten Abend," the bishop said. "I'm sorry it's so late. May I come in?"

"Ja, ja," Lyyndaya's father said. "Come."

They all took seats around the kitchen table as Mama brought coffee with milk and sugar and placed it by the bishop's hand.

"Danke," the large man said with a nod. "So is Ruth here as well?"

"I have put her to bed early with a fever," replied her mother. "She has not been well since breakfast."

"I'm sorry to hear it. I will pray for her before I leave." He sipped at his coffee and his eyes fell on Lyyndaya. "But Lyyndy is here. That is good." He looked at her father. "The Holsteins are fine?"

"*Ja.*"

Then he met her mother's eyes. "And the other children? The boys? The girl?"

Her nodded. "*Gute, danke.* Luke is in the barn rubbing down the horses. I can fetch him."

The bishop lifted a hand. "Luke need not be here." He took more of his coffee then set the cup down and looked around at them, his eyes sad but firm.

Lyyndaya knew what was coming.

"Sometimes we make such an announcement at the church gathering," he began. "This time I felt it best to speak with each family in turn. I have been to see Mr. Whetstone. Next, after him, I knew I must come here." He looked down at his coffee cup a moment. "The *English* do not understand these things. Our neighbors think us harsh and cruel when we pronounce the *Meidung.* Yet they quarrel and have lawsuits and will break off friendships, even with family members, for a lifetime. They have their own *Meidungs,* hm? Only they turn a cold shoulder, as they say, for years even, without ever giving the person who has been cut off an opportunity to say they are sorry, to come back. Sometimes, even if these persons say they are sorry, they still are not permitted to a return to a church or a business or even their family."

He lifted his eyes to Lyyndaya. "It is not that way with us. We ask a person to repent. If they do, if they stop the wrongful behavior, that is enough. So far as the east is from the west, so far is the taint of sin removed from them by the cross of Jesus Christ. For us, and for God, it is as if it has never been. We bring it up no more and do not permit it to be held against them in the church or among the Lapp Amish. This the *English* rarely do."

He quietly asked for a refill of his cup. Once Lyyndaya's mother had poured the coffee and returned to her seat, he resumed his talk.

"I promised the leadership we would deal with this after Easter. Well, Easter, as you know, was at the end of March and more than two weeks have gone by. *Who knows?* I thought. Perhaps Jude would send us a letter. Perhaps he would show up at the door. Maybe we would hear he has been arrested by the army for refusing to fly an aeroplane and shoot down other men. But there has been nothing. When I made inquiries as to his whereabouts, military officials told me he had left England and been assigned to an aerodrome in eastern France, right at the front. 'What sort of squadron,' I asked.

'Reconnaissance?' " He shook his head. "They stared at me as if I had grown a horse's head and said, 'Of course it is a fighter squadron, sir. A pursuit squadron. Americans are anxious to see their boys perform well in aerial combat like the great French and British and German aces.' " The bishop lifted his cup to his lips and drank. "Even our good Canadian neighbors have many men who fly and kill. So of course we cannot be seen as second-best."

"Jude is to be shunned," Lyyndaya blurted, suddenly tired of the long buildup to the inevitable.

The bishop nodded.

"But what if he repents?" she asked, almost desperately. "What if he returns from the war and says he is sorry?"

"I have told you. We welcome him back. He is forgiven as we are all forgiven in Christ."

"What about Pastor Miller? Or Pastor King? They are very angry with Jude. What if they do not forgive?"

"They must forgive. *Forgive us our debts, as we forgive our debtors.*"

"But if they do not —"

"Hush, daughter," soothed her mother, putting a hand over her daughter's. "They are good Christian men. They know what it means to live the life of following Jesus."

Bishop Zook nodded. "*Ja,* they know. But there is something I must explain. You came here after the Spanish–American war. It was in 1898. Lyyndaya, you were not even born. Twenty years have gone by. Yet the Kings and Millers cannot forget they lost family in that terrible war. America brags about her great victories. The Millers and Kings lost sons and brothers. They have nothing to brag about."

Lyyndaya's father sat up. "I knew nothing of this."

"It is not spoken about. As I say, it has been twenty years."

"But were these family members not part of the Amish faith?"

"Some were — but they left us and chose to fight. Others had struck out on their own. A few were living in Philadelphia. A few in Pittsburgh. One of Pastor King's brothers was in Florida, very close to Cuba. Patriotic fervor was running very high at the time. As it is now."

"So they —" Lyyndaya began and stopped.

"The pain is always with the Kings and Millers," the bishop said to her.

Her father cleared his throat. "Do you not think it strange, Bishop Zook, that Jude

Whetstone should do this? Enlist? Go to war?"

The bishop's eyes seemed to droop. "I do."

"Does it not sometimes occur to you that we do not know the whole story?"

The bishop shrugged. "I have spoken with my son. And not just my son, but all the other young men. It is the same. They believe the harsh treatment altered his thinking. Hardened him. So that suddenly he felt the way to follow God was to fight for America's freedom. Though what a European war has to do with our country's liberty has never been satisfactorily explained to me."

"Don't you — sometimes wonder — if there is something we do not know?" pressed Lyyndaya's father hesitantly.

The bishop sat back in his chair and hooked his thumbs in the suspenders under his dark jacket. He glanced up at the ceiling. "*Ja, ja,*" he seemed to say to himself. "But what?"

No one spoke.

Finally he rose to his feet. "I must go to other families yet this evening. The rest I must visit tomorrow. Let me pray for all of this and for Ruth's illness."

He stood with his head bowed for several minutes without speaking out loud. Lyyndaya could clearly hear the clicking of their grandfather clock as if it were three times louder than normal. She struggled to pray, but her thoughts were confused. She imagined she saw her last letter to Jude stuffed in a mailbag on a steamer heading to England. The steamer was torpedoed and the bag sank to the bottom of the sea, her letter lost forever, Jude never knowing she had written a final time, never knowing how she felt, and he himself was in an aeroplane that was burning and falling to the ground.

She gasped and jerked in her chair, and this time both her father and mother placed their hands gently on her shoulders. Now Bishop Zook began to pray in High German and after a few minutes it calmed her and filled her mind with an image of Jude flying and smiling and waving at her, the clouds tinged rose and copper. She was grateful when he closed his prayer with, *Let him give no harm, let him receive no harm, in the name of our Lord Jesus Christ.*

At the door the bishop held her hand briefly. "You are no happier with this than my daughter Emma. But then who takes pleasure in the shunning? It is only a means to something better, like an ill-tasting medicine. I pray he will return to us, just as the prodigal did, and that all shall be well once more. Meanwhile, I want you to know what I told my daughter and Master Whetstone's father — I have instructed the postmaster to collect all letters that come from young Jude and keep them in a safe place. He said he would use a special drawer he can lock. When Jude returns to us and if he confesses and repents, the letters will go to those they belong to. Nothing will be lost, my dear. *Gute Nacht. Gottes Segen.*"

When the door closed, her father said, "Have courage, my daughter. Pray to our God day and night. We will see him back at Paradise before the year is out."

"*Ach,* Amos," moaned Lyyndaya's mother, "how can you say that? How can you get the girl's hopes up? Jude back by Christmas? Repentant? Received back into the church? In hardly more than six months? You must have the faith that moves mountains."

Lyyndaya had already turned toward the stairs, her hand on the bannister. "I'm going to pray alone. Is that all right?"

"But I have made a bed up for you in the spare room," her mother said. "You must not catch Ruth's illness."

"Did you place my Bible or red book there?"

"*Nein, nein.* Very well, fetch them from your room, but please do not wake Ruth.

She needs her sleep."

"What if she is awake?"

"Then say good night and God bless. I do not want you upsetting her with talk of the shunning. She can hear about it in the morning."

But Ruth was standing in her white nightgown at the head of the stairs. "Mother, the shunning hardly comes as a surprise. I want to speak with Lyyndy about it."

"What are you doing out of bed?" Mama said. "Please, back under the covers, Ruth. You are sick enough as it is."

"I want Lyyndy to come to my room."

"*Ja, ja,* just get back into bed. I will bring you up some hot tea with lemon and honey."

In their room Ruth sat up under her covers and Lyyndy perched on the edge of her own bed.

"You're not even crying." Ruth said gently. "Is it because you've already shed your tears over this?"

"I've cried many times," Lyyndaya said. "*Ja,* I knew it was coming. We all did. So I suppose I've run out of tears. For now. But there will be fresh ones."

"Was the bishop kind?"

"*Ja.* He says all Jude's letters will be saved at the post office until he returns to us. Nevertheless, I fret."

"That he will not confess and repent?"

"No, I don't worry about that. I have no idea why he's done what he's done, but somehow I believe when he returns he'll have no trouble telling the people he's sorry. I fret that he may not get my last letter —"

"Why shouldn't he? You mailed it a week ago."

"Well," Lyyndaya sighed, "I keep thinking about those U-boats —"

"Oh!" Ruth flung her head back onto her pillow. "Those U-boats of yours are everywhere. I expect to see one coming along the road in the morning pulled by a team of draft horses."

"A lot of ships do go down, Ruth."

"And a lot of ships make it to England and France. If the mail gets past the German submarines will it be worth it?"

"What do you mean?"

"I mean — did you write him a good letter, knowing it might be your last for months or —" She did not finish her sentence and wished she had not started it.

But Lyyndaya wasn't listening. She was thinking to herself, practically rereading the letter in her mind. Out loud, she said, "There will have to be two boats, one to get it from New York to England and another to get it from England to France. He will be at his aerodrome near the front lines when he receives it. I put my heart and soul into that letter. Perhaps I said too much, perhaps I said it too strongly. But what was I to do? What if I can't write him or see him for another six months? A year? How can I be cautious when so much is at stake? And what if . . . if he is . . ." She stopped.

"Let's think the best and hope for the best," urged Ruth softly. "To live in any other manner makes a person go through their days like a ghost."

Her sister clasped her hands together tightly. "I know you're right, but —"

"No, Lyyndaya, we must not walk there. That part of the garden is *verboten* to everyone but the Chief Gardener himself. So you must tell me this — will the letter drive him crazy so that he can't think straight?"

Lyyndaya felt her face redden. "What do you mean?"

Ruth laughed. "My proper Amish sister. Did you say things that will make his heart beat faster?"

Lyyndaya grabbed her pillow without thinking and threw it at her sister's head.

Ruth gave a mock cry as the pillow struck. "How can you be so mean to your dear sister? Don't you realize how sick I am?"

"Oh, *ja,* you are sick."

"So you just talked to him about the weather, is that it? Jude, the crops are planted, the rain is wet, when the sun comes out it makes the soil warm, we are sure the barley will grow, and the cows, well, the cows —"

Lyyndaya pounced on her sister's bed. "I have the cure for your fever. I discovered it in an old Amish book last week. First you tickle the ribs, *ja?* Then you twist the arm. Like this."

Ruth shrieked at her sister's attack and then began to giggle. "Which of them will cure me?"

"Both, of course! You must have both together to get the cure."

Ruth shrieked again and began to fight back, wrestling with her younger sister. "And where did the good Amish book get this idea from?"

Lyyndaya pinned Ruth's arms with one of her own and began to tickle again. "The Bible."

"Ruthie! Lyyndy! What is this?" Their mother was in the doorway holding a cup of tea. "Stop this nonsense. You are not children anymore. Lyyndy, I must ask you to leave your sister alone. She has to get her sleep. Get your book and Bible and go."

"Oh, Mama —" began Ruth, but was cut off.

"Never mind this 'Oh, Mama.' Back under the covers. And you, Lyyndy, quickly, *schnell, schnell.*"

Ruth and Lyyndaya smirked at one another as their mother marched in with the tea, set it down, and began to straighten Ruth's blankets, tucking the quilt up around her ears. Lyyndaya hurried out the door with her Bible, red book, and nightgown, managing a small wave to her sister while their mother's back was turned.

The spare bedroom was cold, so she got under her covers as soon as she had put on her gown and brushed out her hair. In the red book, her great-grandmother was writing about Isaiah chapter seven and verse nine — *If ye will not believe, surely ye shall not be established.* Great-grandmother said it was not only a matter of believing in God himself, but believing in his promises despite difficult circumstances. It was also about believing in what God was performing in your life, even if he appeared to be going about it in a roundabout way.

Lyyndaya wondered how this might apply to her and Jude. She couldn't write him anymore. He might write her, but after months went by with no letters from Pennsylvania he would stop. What then? Would he have a French girlfriend like she had heard other American pilots did? Someone in Paris he went to visit when he was on leave? That didn't sound like Jude. But then, the Jude she had known before he was taken to the military camp with the others would not have signed up to fight in the United States Army either.

Lord, what can I do now?

The answer seemed to come to mind immediately: *Keep writing letters to Jude.*

She was astonished. This was not an idea she would have come up with. She wouldn't disobey the *Meidung* and risk being shunned herself. Yet the Holy Spirit was making a distinct impression on her mind: *Keep writing letters to Jude.* She laid her head back and tried to sleep after blowing out her lamp, but the inner voice persisted. After several minutes she realized she wouldn't be able to rest until she acted upon what she felt she was being told to do.

Coming out of her room quietly, she saw that the hallway was empty and that no light appeared under her sister's door. She tiptoed over the wooden floor, went into her sister's room, stood still a moment and listened to Ruth breathing deeply, then knelt and drew her lap desk out from under her

235

bed, and slipped back into the hall.

Back in the spare room, the lamp relit, she took out paper, pen, and ink and sat on the bed with the heart-shaped desk on her crossed legs. Without hesitating, she began to tell Jude how difficult it was for her that he had been shunned and that she didn't even know when he would be permitted to read what she was writing now. But it was important that he know the shunning did nothing to change her feelings for him. She still cared for him: *Despite the* Meidung, *I can say that I am more inclined to believe we could be husband and wife than ever before. Every day I am more sure of myself when it comes to you, and every day I think of you more often and care more deeply.*

She finished the letter, placed it an envelope, and blew out her lamp for the second time that night. This time she could feel sleep rushing in upon her with swift feet. Just before she began to dream she said to herself and God, *I will go to the post office in the morning. I shall ask to speak to the postmaster. Whatever the stamps cost to send the letter to England or France I will pay. I will ask him to place my letters in the same locked drawer he intends to place Jude's in once they come from France. Then when the day comes and the postmaster is permitted to give Jude's letters to me I shall have all my letters sent overseas to him. Whether he chooses me or Emma or some girl from France, I want him to know I never stopped thinking about him, never stopped praying, never stopped myself from loving him.*

FIFTEEN

France was spread out below Jude through the broken clouds just as England had been and, before that, Pennsylvania. In so many places the land was April green, and the rapidly moving streams were either silver or a muddy brown from the heavy rains. He smiled as the wind passed over his face. He began to imagine that Lyyndaya was seated in the cockpit with him, an impossibility in the compact pursuit plane, but not an impossibility in his large imagination.

What is this we are flying in? Lyyndaya asked.

A Nieuport 28, he answered. *French-built. We can go 122 miles per hour if we want to.*

I want to.

All right, Lyyndy Lyyndy Lou, I'll open 'er up.

Bishop Zook would want to know how many horses this buggy has you are courting me in, she teased.

The last buggy had 97, but this one has 160,

how's that?

My goodness. Lyyndaya laughed. *No wonder I feel like I'm in a windstorm in Pennsylvania. What city is that below us?*

Nancy.

And the place that looks like it has toy planes?

That's our field. That's where my Aero Squadron is located.

Are the other pilots nice? she asked.

Most of them, he responded.

Oh, the green grass is all gone, she said in a surprised voice. *Now everything is gray and black.*

That's because we're right over the front now, he explained. *This is what four years of artillery bombardments and trench fighting have done to the earth.*

It's terrible. It looks like a place where only the devil could be comfortable.

Shall I turn around? he asked.

Yes, turn around, she agreed, *but first I want to dive.*

Now? Here?

Yes, now, here, she insisted. *I have missed the dives and loops and rolls so much. Will you not take us down into a dive? Please?*

All right, he told her. *Hang on, Lyyndy.*

Jude's squadron leader was repeatedly

thrusting his arm downward, trying to get his attention. Jude looked below and recognized four German Pfalz D.IIIs flying in formation and protecting a German two-seater observation aircraft. It was taking photographs of the Allied lines. Jude glanced back at Lt. Frank Sharples and nodded in an exaggerated way so that the squadron leader could see it. Sharples put his plane into a dive. Jude and Billy Skipp, the young man with flaming red hair Jude had met in the truck that first night, put their Nieuports into dives right after him.

How's this? Jude asked the imaginary Lyyndaya.

She had closed her eyes and leaned her head back. Blonde hair was tugging loose from her leather flying helmet and streaming backward like streaks of light. She smiled. *Perfect,* she said.

It was Jude's sixth time up in almost two weeks. Bad weather had prevented any more sorties than that. He had been over the lines before, faced antiaircraft fire that had exploded in angry blackness all around him, had seen different formations of German aeroplanes, but this was the first time he was being directed to attack. He had dreaded this moment. He could not let the Germans kill his friends without intervening. Yet he had no desire to kill Germans for being in the sky at the same time and in the same place for the same bad reasons.

Sharples had opened fire on one of the Pfalz D.IIIs. It had not seen him and tried to pull out of his sights. But another burst from the squadron leader's guns and flame sprang up over its engine cowling. The Pfalz began to spin and fall. Sharples followed the stricken plane down to see if it would crash and he could claim it as a victory. The first American claims had taken place only a few weeks before on April fourteenth at another squadron. Jude had heard Sharples say many times in the mess hall that he wanted to be the first American ace.

Billy was on the tail of another Pfalz and blazing away. Bits of wood and fabric flew into the air. Jude saw that the observation plane had turned tail and was heading east for the German lines. One Pfalz was shadowing it and shielding it from attack. *Where was the other German fighter?* Jude wondered. Then he saw it latch onto Sharples from behind and begin to shoot at the American pilot.

For an instant Jude felt like asking Lyyndaya what he should do. But he couldn't imagine her being with him during aerial combat so he found it no longer possible to conjure up her presence. It didn't matter. There was only one thing he could do. Try to save Frank Sharples' life.

Jude placed his Nieuport into a steep dive and swooped in on the Pfalz. Perhaps his attack would frighten the pilot into breaking away. But the German was intent on blasting Sharples out of existence and didn't pay any attention to Jude's approach. Even when he closed the distance to the point where his propeller could have chewed off the Pfalz's tail rudder the German didn't budge, but kept maneuvering and firing bursts at Sharples.

I'm going to have to use my guns, Lyyndy.

But she didn't reply.

I will shoot under him and over him. Perhaps that will be enough.

Jude prayed and triggered his twin .303 Vickers machine guns. He deliberately aimed high. The German didn't even seem to notice. He pressed his attack on Sharples, who was twisting and turning frantically. The German was finally rewarded with a trail of black smoke.

I don't have any choice, Lyyndy. Blood is on my hands either way.

He fired at the Pfalz practically point-blank and shattered the rudder. The German plane suddenly skewed to the left and

242

began to fall in a spinning motion like a dead leaf.

You still have your ailerons, Jude said to the pilot. *Use them. Get to your lines and put your plane down.*

As if they could communicate, Jude saw the hinged wooden ailerons move on the back edges of the Pfalz's wings as the German fought to stabilize his aircraft. He managed to pull out of the spin and, in a rolling and wobbly fashion, his wings dipping down to the left and then down to the right, only a few thousand feet above the ground, head toward the German trenches and a patch of level ground. Satisfied he would make it, Jude turned away to check on Sharples and Billy Skipp.

Sharples was erratically moving west toward Nancy and their aerodrome, still trailing gray and black smoke. Jude quickly got into position above and behind him to make sure he was shielded from any further attacks. Then he craned his neck and scanned the sky for Skipp. He finally spotted him miles away in the direction of St. Mihiel, still tangling with his Pfalz, refusing to break off the engagement even though he was dangerously close to the German trenches and might tempt other enemy fighters to climb up after him.

Again, it was as if the German pilots could read Jude's mind. One, two, three — Jude spotted a trio of Pfalzes rising from below in such a way as to get behind Billy and swing the odds in the dogfight. *What am I supposed to do?* Jude asked himself anxiously. This time his imaginary Lyyndaya was in the cockpit with him. *Why are you looking to me for help, Jude Whetstone?* she demanded, her eyes sparking. *You are here now, aren't you? Then make a difference. You have saved Frank Sharples' life. Now save Billy Skipp's.*

Sharples had his craft under control, though he and Jude both knew it could explode into flame at any moment. Jude felt the lieutenant ought to put down somewhere near Nancy, or even Toul, which was closer, but obviously the squadron leader was intent on getting back to his aerodrome. The sky was empty of aircraft — all the excitement was taking place behind them where Billy Skipp was about to take on half a *Jagdstaffel* of German fighters single-handed. Jude swooped alongside Sharples and signaled that he was heading back, shouting as loudly as he could, *Billy Skipp, Billy Skipp,* though he knew he couldn't be heard above their engines and the wind

244

scream. Finally Sharples nodded and waved Jude back. Jude could distinctly see his lips forming the name in reply — *Billy Skipp.* He banked his Nieuport left and raced north and east, leaving Sharples to carry on alone.

The three Pfalzes were still climbing, but Jude wouldn't arrive on the scene before they had engaged Billy. The boy, not even seventeen, who had admitted to the other pilots weeks ago he had lied about his age and forged his documents, was stuck to his Pfalz like an iron shoe to a hoof, and minutes before Jude showed up he saw the German plane suddenly flash like a lit match and tumble in black and orange smoke from the sky.

Now run for home, Billy.

But Billy, in following the burning Pfalz down for a short distance, had run right into the Germans rising up to engage him, and instead of trying to disentangle himself, had decided his best course of action was to attack these planes as well. He quickly drew one into his sights, for Jude could see tracers leaving the front of Billy's Nieuport. He could also see that two of the Pfalzes had swiftly pounced on Billy's tail while he was firing on the third. At top speed, his Gnome rotary engine howling, Jude still might not get there in time. Both of the planes on Billy's back were firing, the one stacked above the other and shooting from a few hundred feet farther up, straight into the top of Billy's aircraft.

Twist and turn, Billy. Forget your target.

It was actually the Pfalz that Billy had targeted that saved his life. It went into a steep dive and banked hard to the right, closely followed by Billy, and this rapid maneuvering caused the other Pfalzes to overshoot the American pilot. By the time they had pulled up and were hunting for the Nieuport again, Jude was upon them in a screaming dive, firing purposely over their heads but bearing down in such a way as to ensure a midair collision if either he or the Pfalzes did not break off. Unnerved by the sudden appearance and hard assault of another Nieuport, guns blazing, the Pfalzes split away to the east and to the west and left the airspace to Jude.

Coming out of his dive, he saw the two heading after Billy again and climbed quickly after them, triggering his guns before he was close enough to be accurate, yet clearly seeing his tracers arcing over the tops of their wings and falling in front of their propellers. The Germans saw them too. When by sheer chance several tracers tore into a wing and a large strip of fabric ripped loose and began to flap in the wind, they decided enough was enough. With Billy's Pfalz trailing sparks and now another Pfalz dropping rapidly in elevation and weaving wildly from side to side, it was time to head for German territory. The Pfalz that had lost its wing cover was shielded by his companion, who kept twisting his neck and looking back and above at Jude, obviously expecting a fresh attack at any moment. Jude knew that a plane could be flown with fabric gone, for American aviators had already done this with damaged Nieuports. He prayed the German would make it back safely and turned away to see what Billy was up to.

The youth was either out of ammunition or had, for whatever reason, chosen to stop firing at the Pfalz in front of him that had also turned toward the German trenches. Every few moments it spurted thick black smoke from its engine, and white sparks continued to spray the air in its wake. Billy followed closely behind, probably willing it to blow up or go into a death spin, whereas Jude was praying that the enemy plane would make it back and land within the German lines. After all, how did he know there wasn't a red-haired youth like Billy in the Pfalz cockpit, someone who ought to still be in school or working a plow horse on a farm in the Rhine valley? A boy too young to be out sparring with death in the sky over France, as if all the nonsense about knights jousting in the spring air really were true.

Jude came alongside Billy and kept pointing at the cockpit controls with large hand movements, trying to get him to look at his gas gauge. There was barely enough to get back to their aerodrome. At first the boy did nothing. Then, finally, as the German plane showed no signs of crashing and was still sputtering east toward Chateau-Salins and the German lines, Billy, quite obviously out of shells, waved to Jude and began to turn his Nieuport. Flying virtually side by side, the two finally sped back over Nancy at five thousand feet and began to descend to their Aero Squadron's field near the Moselle River.

They got a hero's welcome. Pilots and ground crew ran across the landing field to welcome them back. Men vigorously pumped Jude's hand, grinned, and slapped him on the back.

"Well done, Lieutenant!"

"Bravo, sir!"

"That's showing the Hun who's boss!"

Jude smiled awkwardly as he shook hands.

"What's all this about?"

One of his mechanics thumped him on the shoulder. "British troops have confirmed Sharples' kill. They've also confirmed Billy's first plane and that his second Pfalz crashed in no-man's-land."

Jude felt a coldness in his chest. "Crashed?"

"You bet. Kaput. The pilot 'chuted down and he's a POW now."

Jude put his hands in his pockets, struggling to keep the smile on his face. "I'm glad to hear that. But what does this have to do with me?"

"Are you kidding?" It was Billy, throwing his arm over Jude's shoulders. "You saved my life. You saved Sharples' life. The Huns were all over us. You fought them off."

"They would have left soon anyway," Jude argued. "They were low on gas."

Billy shook his head. "They wouldn't have left before shooting me and Sharples down. You saved our necks."

Jude let them lead him off to a celebratory meal of steak and potatoes in the mess. He could hardly avoid it. But while others shouted back and forth and raised their knives as if they were swords in their excitement, he picked at his food. He kept asking himself, *What am I doing here in Europe?*

What is an Amish boy doing fighting in a war in Europe? What blood have I helped shed today?

"Why didn't you finish that German off?" asked Sharples, taking a chair next to Jude in the mess.

"Which one?" Jude asked.

"The one that almost got me."

"I took off his rudder and he headed for home. I had to choose between helping out you and Billy or chasing him toward Pont-à-Moussan. It was an easy choice to make, sir."

"But you're the only one of us who didn't get a German."

"I have no regrets, sir. I'm glad you're sitting here now and that Billy is plunked down over there stuffing himself with T-bones."

Sharples clapped him on the shoulder. "You're too good for this war, kid."

Alone in his room, Jude sat on the edge of the bed and looked at his hands, the hands with which he flew. He had enlisted to save lives, the lives of his friends and Amish brothers at the army base in Pennsylvania. He didn't blame Hosea for choosing not to make that clear to the Lapp Amish of Paradise — the one-star general had been serious about further arrests and detentions, perhaps even dire consequences for the church, if it ever got out that Jude had been coerced into flying for the U.S. army. It was a time of war. It didn't pay to tweak Uncle Sam's nose when his blood was up and he was in a fighting mood. No, he had done what he felt he had to do to save the other men.

The result, though, was that he was now in combat and doing what he had to do to save both Germans and Americans. But he wondered how long he could get away with it. Suppose the bursts of Vickers machine-gun fire that had ripped up one Pfalz's rudder and torn the covering off another's wing . . . suppose those bullets had happened to strike differently . . . what if both planes had simply blown apart instead? Jude let out a breath and rubbed both hands over his face. It made him sick to think about it.

There was that verse he had read in the Bible the other day, a verse people in Paradise quoted all the time. Jude closed his eyes and it came to mind — *And we know that all things work together for good to them that love God, to them who are the called according to his purpose.* He knew he loved God. God had mattered to him long before the Whetstones became Amish. It was the last part of the verse that troubled him. How could he believe he was one of *the called* according to God's purpose? How could he claim this verse as his own, sitting in his room in France, his pursuit aircraft perched on the grass not two hundred yards away and ready to take to the skies in the morning to hunt and kill Germans? It was against everything he believed in as an Amish man. He had only wanted to turn and tumble and twist in the air far above the earth. He had only wanted to fly into sunrises and sunsets. And it had led to this. The army had noticed him and cornered him, and it had led to this.

Perhaps it was my pride. Wanting to be so good as an aviator. Wanting to show off to Lyyndaya last summer. Wanting to outsmart the pilots that jumped me at the July picnic. Suppose I had let them win? Suppose I had deliberately flown poorly and let them trounce me? Then they would have flown away happy and left me alone. They would have considered me a mediocre pilot and left me to myself. The army would never have come to call or schemed how to pressure me into enlisting. My Amish friends would never have been put in harm's way. I would never have had to intervene to save them by giving the army what it wanted. My pride has been my undoing.

Jude groaned and lay back on his bed. He felt trapped. *God, I am so sorry,* he prayed. *I don't know how to do anything that is not my best, whether I'm at the forge or at the controls of a Curtiss Jenny or a Nieuport 28. I don't know how to be less of what I am, less of what has been created in me. I'm sorry I'm not more humble. I'm sorry I didn't perform more poorly when the occasion warranted it. Yet here I am, Lord — here I am in the middle of this terrible war. What shall I do? Is it possible, is it in any way possible, that in my small life, here and now, blemished and sinful though I might be, you can make all things work together for good? Can you? Will you?*

SIXTEEN

Lyyndaya stepped down from the buggy and walked into the post office. She could never avert her eyes from newspaper headlines these days and now she noticed one in a rack that said *Doughboys Push Germans Back at Chateau Thierry and Belleau Wood.* Nearby was an article in smaller print about a flu outbreak in Kansas that she promptly ignored upon reading a line of type with the words *American Aero Squadrons Score Victories.* She waited a few minutes for another woman to finish her business and then approached the window with, "Good morning, Edward," handing him an envelope and some coins.

"Tuesday, June eleventh, and here you are, just like a grandfather clock," announced the clerk, taking the envelope and money.

"I hope not like a grandfather clock, Edward."

"Well, they don't make princess clocks, d they?"

She lowered her eyes. "You are quite ga lant today. What's the occasion?"

"Our boys are putting a licking on th Huns land, sea, and air. You'll see. With o army over there it'll all be done within matter of months. Which means you'll s your beau again before you know it."

Lyyndaya considered the thin, baldi man's cheerful face. "Are you going to ma a prediction, Edward?"

"Sure. Why not? It's the eleventh tod right? Three, four —" He paused to cou on his fingers. Then looked up. "All do by October. Or maybe November or D cember. On the eleventh. Not the tenth twelfth. Right on the eleventh."

"Surely you can't be that precise, E ward."

"Care to make a wager?"

Lyyndaya smiled and shook her hea "You're well aware of the answer to tha Only God knows the future, Edward. If has imparted that information to you v shall soon find out. Please recall that tho who got their predictions wrong in biblic times were stoned to death as false prop ets."

"Ha!" Edward drew back in mock terr

"I'll be sure to wear a suit of armor. But, somehow, I believe my hunch is right. Home for Christmas!"

Lyyndaya was turning to leave, when she paused and looked back at the clerk. "Edward, would there be anything wrong with you telling me if I have any letters from Jude?"

"Not as far as I know. You've got two. One from May and one from a week ago."

Edward watched her eyes turn a brilliant green and thought, not for the first time, what a fine-looking woman Lyyndaya Kurtz was.

"Thank you," she said.

To keep her in the post office a little longer, Edward blurted, "Miss Zook had two from Jude Whetstone as well, but she told me to throw them out."

Lyyndaya stopped and returned to the clerk's wicket, her eyes large. "What did you say?"

"I didn't want to do it, but she insisted. Had me show them to her and then had me rip them up right in front of her eyes."

"Why?"

"She didn't say why. Had me hand over the letters to him she'd posted with us as well. Six or seven of them. Took them all and walked out."

"And when was this?"

"Last Friday."

Lyyndaya went out the door quickly and into her buggy, snapping the traces and putting Trillium into a fast trot. *What was Emma doing? What sort of thoughts could be running through her head to make her destroy Jude's letters?* When she pulled up in front of the Zook home she saw Emma in a sunbonnet working at a large flowerbed of roses. Once she had climbed down and walked over, Emma looked up, read her face, and tugged off her white gardening gloves.

"Hello, sister," Emma greeted her, but she didn't smile and her green eyes were a dark jade.

Lyyndaya didn't waste any time with the usual pleasantries. "They told me at the post office you had destroyed the letters Jude sent you."

Emma met her eyes. "Edward or Henry Jacobs had no business saying so. But it doesn't matter. I would have told you."

"They also said you asked for the return of the letters you've written, the ones they have been setting aside since April."

"Yes." Her face was defiant.

"Why, Emma? Why are you turning your back on Jude right now, when he needs our

257

friendship the most?"

Emma's eyes softened slightly. "Come, Lyyndy, walk with me a few minutes."

They had scarcely started down the lane to the road before Emma began to talk nonstop, like a green summer stream spilling over its banks. "It's like a game, you know, Lyyndy, just as we played games when we were children. Jude writes us letters, but we never see them. We mail him letters back, but they never leave Paradise. In our hearts we say, ah, he will read them someday, and after he does, he shall choose one of us for a bride. But it's a game. He will never read them, never see them, never know about them unless we get a chance to tell him we wrote them and he goes to the post office to pick them up. And if, God forbid, he doesn't come back from Europe, it will have made no difference at all."

"But, Emma," Lyyndaya protested, "when you write them, you think about him, don't you? And once you are thinking about him, do you also not start praying for him? This is what happens with me."

"Oh, I suppose, but mostly it's all a fantasy, Lyyndy. Something that goes on in our heads. He doesn't hear us, we don't hear him. He's been gone now for how long? If you count the army camp as well as

England and France? Eight, nine months? And how much longer will it go on? Another year? Two? What if he never comes home? Or what if he comes home and never confesses and repents?"

"Of course he will confess and repent!"

"Then why did he enlist in the first place? He could be here right now, walking beside us, teasing us, choosing me or choosing you to be his bride. But no — he chooses his aeroplanes and the war over us. What makes you think he will come back and repent? Why, he may even decide not to return at all. If the war ended next week he might not show up here. Why wouldn't he stay in the army and keep flying their planes for them? He has already done it once and turned his back on you and me and on his faith, on his father, on the church. What makes you think he will give up flying just to be back in Paradise? He didn't care about us in 1917. Why should he care about us in 1918 or 19 or 20?"

"I believe there's more to the story than what we know. Something else happened to make him enlist and go overseas. He didn't leave us on purpose."

Emma stopped and looked at her in exasperation. "You're always saying that. Your father is always saying that. My papa tells me it's just wishful thinking. No one twisted Jude's arm, he says. No one put a bayonet in his back. You simply won't accept that he up and did this of his own free will. Instead, you insist that we believe in his innocence and goodness despite the fact he is now flying planes in a war and shooting at other men."

"We don't know that," Lyyndaya shot back.

"Of course we know it. Remember how he defeated three or four planes here last summer, right over the Stoltzfus hay field? Do you imagine they have him peeling potatoes in an army kitchen in Paris? A newsman came to Papa last week, yes, a reporter from a big New York paper, can you imagine? He told Papa that Jude Whetstone was showing up in military dispatches more and more often. Why? Because he's rescuing other pilots by chasing Germans all over the sky, shooting their wings off, knocking their planes to the ground. Yes, that is what he said. Papa didn't have much to tell him, only that Jude had always been a good boy and had embraced the teachings of the Amish faith. He said to the reporter he didn't understand why Jude had decided to fight in the war. 'Oh, but it is an important war for America,' this man tells Papa.

Papa says to him, 'I do not see that America is threatened or less free that we should fight in a war thousands of miles away.' "

They were standing by the side of the road in the bright June light. Emma's eyes had grown darker and darker as they talked. Now she took one of Lyyndaya's hands in her own. "I'm sorry, Lyyndy. I can no longer pretend to understand Jude. I can't understand why he left us to kill people. Even if he came back tomorrow I could not . . . marry such a person. If you wish to keep waiting and hoping, if you believe there is some great secret that will be revealed one day and absolve him of his sins — well, I can't stop you, can I, sister? But I myself, I must move on. I have invited other men to visit me, men from Intercourse and Bird-in-Hand, even from here in Paradise. No need to give you a list of names. You shall find out soon enough when the tongues start to wag." She leaned over and kissed Lyyndaya on the cheek. "It's not as if I'll stop praying for him. And I do wish he would come home and say he's been wrong to do what he's done. But even if he did, that wouldn't be enough for me. I want a man, a true Amish man, who is more . . . pure."

They walked back to the Zook house in silence. Lyyndaya climbed into the buggy and clicked her tongue, and Trillium began to walk. When she glanced back from the road Emma's tall frame was bent over among the red and pink roses once more. Her heart heavy as rock, Lyyndaya let Trillium take her time, in no hurry to get home and start on laundry or baking. Emma's words had put darkness and a doubt into her. She noticed that though there wasn't a cloud in the sky, in herself they covered her mind and her soul.

Lord, have I been mistaken all along? Am I foolish to believe that somehow Jude has been wronged? But even if he were wronged, why should he take it out on others, on strangers he's never met, on other human beings, and shoot their planes out of the sky? Why should he take brothers and sons and husbands away from their families? What if Emma is right about all this? It simply can't be.

She noticed two buggies coming toward her on the other side of the road. The first carried Mrs. Stoltzfus, who smiled and waved and called something Lyyndaya didn't catch. The second carriage was driven by her father, who was holding the traces to Old Oak. They stopped opposite each other.

"Good morning, Papa."

He smiled. "It's almost lunch. Where have you been?"

"I was at the post office, then I went to Emma Zook's. Where are you off to?"

"I will break bread with Jude's father."

"Of course." Her father had been visiting Mr. Whetstone several times a week.

He took off his straw hat and mopped his face with a turquoise bandana from his pocket. "Like a stove, eh? But we may yet get some rain today."

She looked at the perfect blue dome over their heads. "But Papa, there isn't a cloud in the sky. Not even on the horizon."

"I was thinking of the clouds there in the buggy with you."

She dropped her eyes.

"So what did Emma say to you?"

She looked at her father in surprise. "What makes you think it was Emma? I could have spoken with someone at the post office about the war."

He tucked the bandana away. "Sure, sure, but it was Emma. What does she say to you?"

"She will not wait for Jude anymore," she blurted. "She doesn't think he's coming back and even if he does, even if he confesses and repents and the shunning is lifted, Emma doesn't believe he's worthy to be her husband."

Her father's dark eyebrows slashed downward in a frown. "Why?"

"She says he's tainted because he joined the army and is flying a plane in the war. A newspaper reporter from New York told Bishop Zook that Jude was getting a name for himself because he had shot German planes down — and killed —"

She couldn't speak any further. Brushing her fingers against her cheeks she stared at the stained brown leather of the reins in her hands.

"All right, listen to me," she heard her father say. "Are you listening?"

"Yes, Papa."

"Emma may do as she wishes regarding her choice for a husband. But she may not speak as she wishes regarding another of God's children. I thought it would be enough for me to sit down with the pastors and bishop and Mr. Whetstone. I see now it's important I give my news to you as well."

Lyyndaya lifted her head. "What news?"

Her father sat hunched forward with the traces to Old Oak steady in his grasp, his eyes on hers. "I've heard from my former colleagues in Philadelphia, in the state office. I have made inquiries about our young man. I know there have been statements about our fliers and our Aero Squadrons in the New York and Philadelphia newspapers. So here is what I know for certain from those who know for certain. When they write about Lt. Whetstone, they cannot say he is an ace — no, because he has never shot anyone down. You understand what is an ace? A pilot who has shot down five enemy planes. Jude has not shot down one. *Not one.* Are you listening?"

What he was telling her was too good to be true. Would her father make this up just so he could help her feel better? No, her father was not the sort of man who would do that, even for his children.

"I'm listening, Papa," she said.

"So why all the fuss about this Jude Whetstone? It's because they reckon he's saved six or seven of his friends from death, yes, death from the guns of the German planes. How has he done this? By chasing the German aircraft away. And how does this Amish boy chase them away? He fires over their heads. He fires under their wings. Knocks the tails off the backs of their planes and forces them to run for home and a safe place to land. All this he has done and killed no one. All this he has done and saved German and American lives." He leaned over and gripped his daughter's arm. "Never mind what Emma Zook does. It's important you do what is right in the eyes of God."

He flicked the reins and moved quickly along the road, Old Oak's hooves and the buggy wheels raising small spurts of dust.

Lyyndaya could hardly bring herself to tell Trillium to move ahead. She was crying again, but this time it was out of relief. Jude was being honored not for taking lives, but for giving them back to God to make something more out of them. Perhaps some of these men, in America or in Germany, would survive the war, marry, raise children, grandchildren, even great-grandchildren, and bless the earth. All because the man Emma had fallen out of love with had chosen to fight to save and not to destroy. Lyyndaya suddenly snapped the traces in her hands with a new determination.

Well, Emma Zook, you may have changed your mind, but I have not changed mine. I will write the letters, I will take them to the post office, I will pray for him, body and soul, I will every day thank God I have met him. For something is going on here that is greater than you or me, and I shall, by the grace of our Lord Jesus Christ, continue to remain a part of it — until the war is done and God's will is done, and whatever light is supposed to shine out of the darkness gleams brighter and brighter until absolutely no one in Paradise or

266

Pennsylvania or America can ignore the hand of God in Jude Whetstone's life.

SEVENTEEN

Monday, July 8, 1918

Dear Lyyndy,
I have the last letter you sent, which I received, I think, in May. I know it sounds crazy, but I read it over every night before I turn in, right after I've read a chapter from the Bible. I guess there won't be any more, it's been months now, I don't suppose the church lets you mail anything to me. They probably won't let you have my letters either so I don't know why I bother writing. Won't they all end up in some dusty bin in Henry Jacobs' post office? But I can't help myself. I talk to you in the plane, I talk to you when I'm over France or German territory, I talk to you after I talk to God in the evenings. Crazy. And writing you letter after letter that you can't read is even crazier. What can I do?

I need to talk everything over with you. So I do it. But what I wouldn't give for one real look from your eyes, one real touch from your hand, a laugh, a smile.

There was a knock on the door and a man with a large mustache and strong body poked his head in.

"Whetstone. Guess what?"

Jude smiled up from his bed where he was writing Lyyndaya a letter on the flat top of a book. The wooden model of the *Flyer* — "Kitty Hawk" his father had carved was resting on a nearby table. "What, Zed?"

"The new commanding officer's been here —" he glanced at his watch. "Not even two hours? And he wants to see you."

Jude made a face. "I heard his speech in the mess."

"Yeah. Pretty speech. Wonder how pretty the one he's got for you will be?"

"So you're not joking? He wants to see me?"

"I'm not the joker in this squadron. If Flapjack was standing here instead of me then you could have your doubts."

"When does the old man want to see me?"

"Five minutes ago."

Jude groaned and set his book and pen down.

"What's the matter? Writing your girl?" asked Zed.

"The fog is a foot off the ground, they won't let us go up, so I thought I could —"

"When are we ever going to see a picture of this gal of yours?"

"Just a friend, Zed."

"This friend. Where do you hide her pictures?"

Jude began walking with him down the hall. "There is no picture."

"Come on."

"No, really, there is no picture. She is — I am — the Amish don't believe in having their pictures taken."

"Why not?"

"There's a verse in the Bible, one of the Ten Commandments, that says not to make graven images. The Amish feel a photograph is a graven image."

The squadron was billeted in a large French farmhouse built before the Revolution. Zed stopped when they reached the tiled foyer just by the front doors and the commanding officer's room. The ceiling was high over their heads. He put one hand on Jude's shoulder and began to reel off a long quotation that seemed to echo in the cavernous space.

"Thou shalt not make unto thee any graven

image, or any likeness of any thing that is in heaven above, or that is in the earth beneath, or that is in the water under the earth: Thou shalt not bow down thyself to them, nor serve them: for I the Lord thy God am a jealous God."

Jude was astonished, and his face reflected that astonishment until Zed laughed. "What? You think only the Amish know the Bible? I was in Sunday school until I was fourteen."

"I'm sorry, Zed, it's just that since I left Lancaster County I've only heard the Bible quoted out loud by the padre at church parade."

Zed put his arm around Jude's slender shoulders. "My granddaddy that got wounded at Gettysburg? He was a preacher. I got it all drilled into me from the time I was no bigger'n a wood tick. But this is what I don't understand, Whetstone. The way I read it, this verse is about making idols, you know, to bow down and worship, like wooden gods with buggy eyes or devils carved out of rock with ugly grins. I'm sure your girlfriend looks as sweet as sunshine, but do you pray to her? Bow down and worship her? Think she's good God Almighty?"

"Of course not."

"Then you probably wouldn't do any of

271

that with a picture of her either. Do yourself a favor. Do the whole squadron a favor. Ask for a photograph. Get one of your non-Amish friends to sneak in and take one and mail it to you." He smiled and shoved Jude toward the commanding officer's door. "Don't worry. I catch you burning candles to it or kneeling in front of it, I'll give you such a clout on the ear you'll wake up in Yuma, Arizona. And speaking of Arizona, you're late."

Jude knocked twice and entered when he heard a "Come in."

Major Jackson was standing behind his desk, his uniform buttoned from top to bottom. Jude saluted. Jackson saluted back. He left Jude standing at attention.

The officer was still lean, still had his tan that never seemed to fade regardless of the wet weather. There were a number of papers on his desk. He picked one up at random, it seemed to Jude, and read from it silently.

"Do you speak any French, Whetstone?" Jackson asked.

"Enough to ask directions, sir, or give instructions to waiters."

"I have a letter here saying the government of France wants to give you some sort of medal."

Jude had heard about this from the squadron leader, Frank Sharples, but he said nothing.

"Not the Croix de Guerre, but still," said Jackson, half to himself. He looked over his tabletop and selected a newspaper clipping. "Look at this. An article about the American Aero Squadrons. You're in it along with Billy Skipp. You brought down two Pfalzes by shooting away their rudders. Both pilots taken prisoner."

"Yes, sir, I —"

But Jackson wasn't listening. He had another clipping in his hand. "This one's from London. You forced down a Fokker. Doesn't say how. Doughboys picked the pilot up at gunpoint. Some Baron Ritter, they use two different spellings for his name. This Hun refers to you as a knight-errant. Do you know what a knight-errant is?"

"I have an idea, sir."

"How about *hosti acie nominati?* Do you know what that means? Named by the enemy." Jackson scanned the sheets on his desk. He began to read out loud: " 'One of the knights of the air. Embodies the true spirit of the winged warrior. Gallant. Chivalrous. Respected and honored on both sides of the battle line. Clad in shining armor he jousts in the skies of France and

Lorraine. Unhorsing his foe he graciously permits him to live as a prisoner of war. The angel with the sword of steel and the heart of Christ.' Can you believe this?" He glared up at Jude as if daring him to believe it.

"I am not comfortable being compared to Christ, sir —"

"I should hope not!" Jackson barked.

"Nor do I think of myself as a knight of the skies."

"I didn't say you were." Jackson swept his hand in the air over his desk. "They did." He snatched up a small piece of paper. "We've even got a cable from the White House, for heaven's sakes. From Vice President Marshall. Congratulating you on the distinction your gallant combat has bestowed upon American arms." The major came around from behind his desk. "In truth, I ought to court-martial you, Whetstone. For cowardice in the face of the enemy." Jude could see anger working through the major's face. "But I can't. Because you're untouchable now, you're America's white knight. The chivalrous fighter who wins the field and spares his enemy's life. Everybody's on your side — the French, the British, America, the Canadians — why, I expect to get a telegram from the Kaiser any day now telling me you're up for their Iron Cross or Blue Max. Have you ever seen anything like it?"

"No, sir."

"I'm not talking to you, Whetstone. Keep your mouth shut."

Wisely, Jude did not respond.

Seething, Jackson paced the room. "It would have made my life easier if you had turned tail and run the first time you saw a German plane. Then I could have thrown you in jail as soon as I set foot on this base. But now they have credited you with every plane you forced down — two Pfalzes, Ritter's Fokker, and a twin-seater observation plane, a Rumpler. You are one victory away from being an ace and you haven't shed a drop of blood. It's outrageous. You even have your squadron on your side. Well, why not? You've saved half of them from getting shot down."

Jackson stopped pacing and leaned into Jude's face. "Why didn't you run the first time you saw a Hun plane, Amish boy?"

Jude looked straight ahead and said nothing.

"Answer me, runt!"

"I — wasn't afraid, sir."

"The Amish are not supposed to fight, they are not supposed to kill."

"I haven't killed, sir."

"I *know* you haven't killed! This is war and you make it seem like a schoolyard picnic. Who brings the potato salad? Who brings the fried chicken? Who brings the lemonade and the mushy peas? Who brings the *bratwurst?*" He began to pace again. "It's all right with everyone else, but it's not all right with me. The object is to *defeat* the enemy. Not to ask, *I'm terribly sorry, have I hurt you at all?*"

"Isn't forcing planes down and putting the pilots in prison camps defeating the enemy?"

"Are you speaking, Whetstone?"

"No, sir."

The major sat down at his desk. "There's nothing I can do with you. I'd transfer you out of my squadron, but the men would probably revolt and I'd get sent back to England's rain and bogs to sharpen pencils for colonels and generals. If I hitch my wagon to your star, as reprehensible as I find that to be, I just may wind up with a few stars of my own before this war is over." His gray eyes burned across the room. "All right, Whetstone — you've dazzled the Western Front. Made Huns land on our side of the line, made them pancake in muddy fields, made them throw in the towel while you saved your men's lives. You're even second in command of the squadron, and I'm not going to change that. But here's what you *will* do. You're going to up the ante, Whetstone. Do something even more spectacular. Bigger than anything you've done before. And you will not shed one drop of blood. That's an order. Not one drop. But you'll outdo anything you have done up to now. You understand?"

"I — think so —" Jude had no idea what Jackson meant, amazed that the request wasn't that he no longer spare the lives of his targets.

"I want someone bigger than Baron Ritter. I want more than another Pfalz landing on a wheel and a prayer by our trenches. I'd ask for von Richthofen, except he was killed in April. But you get the general idea. In short, I'm giving you permission to be Amish. I'm giving you permission to keep them alive. But make it spectacular, Whetstone. Bring me the Pegasus. That's what I want. The Pegasus."

With that, the major stood up flagpole straight and saluted. Jude returned the salute, turned, and began to walk out of the office.

"Whetstone!"

Jude stopped as he was opening the door

and looked back. "Sir?"

"I do respect your bravery, Whetstone — your bravery. Yes, I do respect that. I just didn't expect it to come from Lancaster County, Pennsylvania."

"Thank you, sir."

"Oh, and . . . God bless you."

Jude left the office, only to find a dozen men scatter as he appeared, including Zed, Billy Skipp, and Sharples. Only Ram Peterson, whom the squadron had nicknamed Flapjack, stood his ground.

"What's this?" asked Jude.

Peterson grinned. "Everyone wanted to hear the old man take a strip out of your hide. Not that any of us agree with him, because we like how you fight. You always get the German and you always save one or two of us in the bargain. We admire your style."

"So I was a dull afternoon's entertainment?"

"You could say that."

"Well," mumbled Jude as he began to walk toward to his room, "I'm glad someone got something out of the afternoon's exercise."

Peterson walked beside him. "You don't know what a Pegasus is, do you?"

"No."

"It's Greek mythology, Whetstone. A

winged horse."

"He wants me to find a winged horse?" Jude stopped and stared at him.

"Well, not literally, old boy, because, quite frankly, the Pegasus doesn't exist. The thing is that old Ironwood wants you to do something absolutely brilliant. Something that will astonish the press, astound the enemy, rally the Allies, and make Jackson a four-star general overnight — and you the toast of the Republic."

Jude smiled. "I see. And what might I do that would accomplish all of that?"

"I know the very thing." His comrade leaned over and whispered in Jude's ear. "Secret mission. Capture the Kaiser. Stuff him in your cockpit like a sausage and bring him here in irons. Right to the old man's office. You'll win the day if you can do that."

Jude laughed and pushed him to the side. "Think of something hard and I might pay attention, Flapjack." He walked on to his room.

"The courage of the early morning!" called Peterson. "Get up early and you'll catch the Kaiser napping!"

"What do the meteorology boys say?" Jude called back over his shoulder.

"Fair stood the wind for France! Clear sky at morning! Fokkers and Albatros at two for a penny, a clutch of Pfalzes at six for a pound!"

"See you at supper, Flapjack!"

"Remember me to your wife!"

Lyyndy, we have such a wonderful bunch of guys in our squadron, I really think you'd enjoy them, Amish or not, but you'd have to put up with their teasing, especially from Flapjack, who is half Brit and half American. I'm going up in the morning and I'm supposed to do something wonderful that doesn't hurt a soul, but wins the war and sends the boys home by Christmas. Or so I was ordered by my commanding officer, the one from Arizona they call "Ironwood," and so I was told by my mates at the supper table tonight, right after I read out loud from the squadron's Bible as we do every day. Now what is this thing I need to do? I have no idea. But you will be surprised to hear that the old boy has said I must not shed a drop of blood, that I must continue being the gallant knight and spare my foe's life while still bringing him down for a stay at our version of the best hotel in New York (I mean a prisoner-of-war camp).

Jude woke early the next day — Tuesday, July ninth — pulled aside the curtain, and looked out the window. It was almost dawn and he could see white stars in the navy blue sky. He read a chapter from the Gospel of Luke, prayed, then dressed quickly, and headed for the mess. No one else was there except the new boy, Jack Zatt, who Flapjack called Jack Sprat because he was so skinny. They ate pancakes and bacon and eggs together and then Jude clapped him on the back and said he'd take him up later in the day.

"Would you read a verse or two from the Squadron Bible?" asked Jack.

Jude looked at the boy and saw the fear hidden behind the shyness and smile. "Why not?"

The Bible was kept on a podium at the front of the mess. It was not a tradition Jude had started. Sharples had begun it. Sometimes they read it in the evenings, sometimes at breakfast. Usually most of the crew was present when it was opened. Jude felt the boy's anxiety was important enough to add a new wrinkle to the tradition. He flipped the thick pages of the massive old Bible and read from Psalm 23.

" 'The Lord is my shepherd; I shall not want. He maketh me to lie down in green pastures:

he leadeth me beside the still waters. He restoreth my soul: he leadeth me in the paths of righteousness for his name's sake. Yea, though I walk through the valley of the shadow of death, I will fear no evil: for thou art with me; thy rod and thy staff they comfort me. Thou preparest a table before me in the presence of mine enemies: thou anointest my head with oil; my cup runneth over. Surely goodness and mercy shall follow me all the days of my life: and I will dwell in the house of the Lord forever.' "

Jude slowly closed the Bible.

"Thank you, sir," the boy said.

"God bless you, Jack."

As Jude left the mess, Flapjack, Zed, Billy Skipp, and Sharples tumbled in, saw he was already on his way to his plane, bolted down their breakfasts, and got to the field just as Jude's mechanics were pulling the chocks away from the front of the wheels and his Nieuport 28 was beginning to head down the strip and turn into the breeze.

"We're coming up!" shouted Sharples.

"I'm headed toward Ponte-à-Moussan!" Jude yelled back. "I want to get to twenty thousand feet if I can in this old girl!"

"Right! We'll look for you!"

For the better part of half an hour Jude egged on his Nieuport, higher and higher, but couldn't nudge it above nineteen thousand feet. So there he stayed, his eyes on Metz and Marieulles on the German side of the lines. There was not that much activity this early. Jude twisted his neck this way and that, his white silk scarf keeping his skin from getting rubbed raw on the collar of his uniform. No one was up and about, neither friend nor foe. Warm and snug in his Teddy bear flight suit, he cruised back and forth and settled in to wait for his friends. It was, he knew, about minus fifteen degrees Celsius at that height, or five above zero Fahrenheit, and without his gear he would have been turning blue. As it was, he kept rubbing his gloved hands over his face every few minutes to drive out the sting and bite of the cold.

He saw them about fifteen minutes later — Sharples, Zed, Billy, Flapjack — and someone else. Who had they brought up with them? He was finally able to read the number on the fuselage or body of the plane — nineteen — the new pilot from Nebraska he'd had breakfast with, Flapjack's Jack Sprat. Well, he supposed there was no time like a quiet morning over the front to get the young man acquainted with the French sky. Sunlight was falling copper-gold over the engine and propeller of his craft and he said, *Lyyndy, isn't that beautiful?*

Then from nowhere it seemed, there was a rush of wind above his head and the scream of an engine. A blue aircraft with black crosses swept over him in a steep dive, guns blazing at his companions only a thousand feet below.

In shock, Jude watched for several long seconds as the plane seemed to hang motionless above the Nieuports, blasting away parts of their wings, never stalling or collapsing into a spin. Then he thrust his joystick forward and went after the German, throwing his plane into the kind of sharp, fast dive that could rip the fabric off a Nieuport's wings. But the German was faster and had already raced past Jude's friends, hammering away at them the entire time, then swooped down into German territory, heading for Mars-La-Tour. Both Billy Skipp and the new boy, Jack Zatt, were spinning out of control, trailing black smoke and flame.

Frantically, Jude followed them down, hoping that one or both might level out or that the wind would snuff out their flames. From the corner of his eye he could see that the blue German aeroplane had returned just close enough to watch the fall of his victims and ensure he could claim them as victories. Billy was able to pancake his plane onto a muddy field near a string of French trenches. The nose went right into the ground and the rear of the Nieuport flipped up in the air. Jude could see Billy scramble free and sprint for the closest trench while a German machine gun fired at him. Thankfully, he made it, even waving up at Jude and indicating he was in one piece.

A mile away Jude saw Flapjack and Sharples circling the spot where Nieuport Number 19 had crashed and exploded. French troops ran toward the wreck, hoping to save the pilot. But their efforts were in vain. The young man was done for.

Zed was off after the blue German aircraft that had brought down two of his friends, but once the Nieuports had crashed, the German skipped back over the border, where a snarl of heavy antiaircraft bursts forced Zed back. Jude felt numb and cold with shock. The four of them slowly came into formation and headed for Nancy and their aerodrome, Sharples glumly leading the way. Once they had landed he led the men to the dining hall.

As they sat down in silence, Jude retuned to the Squadron Bible he had read from at breakfast. This time he chose another Psalm — the ninety-first. The men looked up at

Jude as the words came out slowly, but powerfully.

" 'He that dwelleth in the secret place of the Most High shall abide under the shadow of the Almighty. I will say of the Lord, He is my refuge and my fortress: my God; in him will I trust . . .' "

When he finished, he sat down with the other men.

Sharples said, "Whetstone, would you say a few words at the service they'll have for the boy?"

Jude found himself swiping at the corner of his eye as he said, "I'd be honored."

Sharples made sure everyone stayed put for an hour, talking, having coffee, just being together.

They waited until an army vehicle brought Billy Skipp in, and after they had welcomed the young man, seen for themselves that his wounds were superficial, and fed him until he protested he could take no more, each of the pilots quietly went off to their private rooms one after another.

Tuesday, July 9, 1918

Dear Lyyndy,
I shouldn't even be writing. I'm sick to my stomach. We're supposed to harden

ourselves to these things, but I doubt I will ever be able to do that. I need to talk to someone about what happened today, and even though you may never hold this page in your hand, it helps just to think about you, to imagine you sitting here and listening to me.

We lost two men today. I suppose I shouldn't put it like that. One of them will be all right. In fact, they picked him up in an army truck and he's in his own bed tonight — though he'll likely be sent home. But there was another casualty and he is not back in his room like Billy. A young boy from Nebraska named Jack. He was killed when his plane exploded on the ground.

It happened so fast. A German came out of the sun above and behind me and went at our planes while they were still rising to my altitude of nineteen thousand feet. For him, it was like shooting fish in a barrel. In seconds he had put scores of bullets into all five of them, even Sharples and Flapjack had holes in their wings and fuselage. But Billy Skipp and Jack Zatt, the young boy, got the worst of it, and they caught fire and crashed. Billy got out of his wreck. The French finally pulled young Jack from his plane, stone dead. We will be holding a military funeral for him tomorrow.

Sometimes I feel nothing writing you about this. Then suddenly, like now, I feel like breaking down and weeping. I could do nothing to help my friends, do you understand? I was helpless. By the time I reacted, the German had done most of his damage. Do you see what a fool I've been? Dashing about the sky thinking I could rescue everyone, that I could create a war in which no one on either side ever got killed? No wonder my commander was disgusted with me. What a fairy tale! Where did I think I was? The July picnic in Paradise? I am in a war zone, Lyyndy, I have placed myself in a war zone, and now people are dying and falling from the sky like leaves.

There is something else I wanted to tell you. I am ashamed to mention it, but I feel I must. I suppose you will think the less of me for it. There is a scalding hot anger within me. Prayer has not yet put it out. Or reading God's Word. I doubt sleep will either, or a meal, for I have no appetite for food or rest. This rage is directed toward the pilot who killed Jack. I know his name, because Sharples and Zed recognized the aircraft. Blue Number 9. He is a German ace with something like sixty or sixty-five kills, Captain Heinrich Schleiermacher, and he is flying one of the new Fokker D.VIIs.

I cannot get him out of my head, Lyyndy. How would you counsel me if you were here? What words would you pray over me? What would you tell me to do? For the first time, I want to find someone, use my guns, and shoot him to the ground. I don't know how to get rid of the feeling. It's three in the morning and I've been sitting here in my room going over those twenty or thirty seconds of his attack again and again. To tell you the truth, right now I believe the only thing that will give me peace is to see this Schleiermacher crashed and burning and never crawling free of his wreckage. Then something inside of me would be satisfied. I wish I could say otherwise. But this minute, this hour, God help me, I can't.

Eighteen

The Millers had cleaned out their barn, and Lyyndaya sat on one of the benches set up for Sunday morning worship. Her mother was on one side of her, Ruth on the other. The fresh straw Pastor Miller and his son Samuel had spread over the barn floor smelled sweet, but it tickled Lyyndaya's nose so that she sneezed several times in a row, quite loudly, drawing attention from others seated and waiting for the service to begin.

"Here's a handkerchief," her mother said. "Cover your mouth."

"It's just the hay, Mama, I'll be all right."

"Maybe so, but next time sneeze into the handkerchief. People will feel better if you do."

Lyyndaya took the pale blue handkerchief and, sure enough, there was one more sneeze in her and she quickly put the cloth to her mouth and nose.

She felt annoyed at the look others gave her. She wanted to stand up and say, *Listen, it is the fresh straw, all right? It's the dust, I do not have the flu that's going around, I do not have the sickness.* But then she calmed herself. Philadelphia and other cities had a growing number of influenza victims. There seemed to be no cure, and many people who contracted the disease passed away swiftly, gasping for breath and drowning as their lungs filled with fluid. It was a horrible death. How then could she blame her Amish neighbors for looking concerned when she sneezed again and again, almost uncontrollably? No one wanted the flu bug to find its way into Paradise.

For an instant she remembered her fear of Jude being killed in combat and thought, *But that is a better death than those who collapse on the streets of Philadelphia and suffocate.* Then she chided herself — *You would not think so if you were the mother of a son shot down in flames. You would not think it was a better way to die if an army person came to your door and told you Jude's plane had crashed and he was buried in a graveyard in France.*

The pastors had picked straws to see who would preach that Sunday and Lyyndaya inwardly groaned when she saw it was

Pastor Miller and Pastor King, the two men most angry at Jude. Just as she feared, Pastor Miller began a long sermon in High German based on the verse found in Isaiah and Micah about beating swords into plowshares. He went on for ninety minutes.

All she could think of was that he was using the message to point the finger at Jude. When he sat down, a man started singing a hymn and the rest joined in, including herself, each of them taking different parts, some low, some high.

After several hymns had been sung, Pastor King stood in front of them and read from the Bible. It was the words of Jesus about loving enemies and offering them the other cheek. Again, Lyyndaya couldn't help but feel the sermon was less about forgiveness and more about Pastor King's inability to forgive Jude.

After the church noonday meal together, Lyyndaya and her family returned home.

"Can we take a walk?" Lyyndaya asked Ruth before they went in.

Ruth agreed and they took a path through the fields, opening and closing gates behind them as they went.

Once they were on their way, Lyyndy said, "Ruth, is it just me or were the sermons today aimed against Jude? Condemning him?"

Ruthie waited before answering. Finally she said, "It's natural that you would think so. That you would feel it so more than the rest of us. It's been weeks since those two chose the short straws. We've heard from the bishop and the other pastor more than enough. It was past time for King and Miller to speak."

Lyyndaya grew exasperated. "That's not what I am asking you."

Her sister stopped and looked at her as they came into the shade of a cluster of large beech trees. "All right. Yes. I think Jude was on their minds. I think he's on everyone's mind."

"Did you find them harsh?"

"Harsh? Not especially. They were only trying to reinforce the truth that the decision Jude made was wrong."

Lyyndaya sat down on a large rock. "If I felt they were condemning him, how did his poor father feel?"

" 'Condemning' is perhaps too strong a word."

Lyyndaya looked up. "And what word would you use to describe messages about peace and forgiveness that offer no peace or forgiveness for Jude?"

Ruth sighed and sat beside Lyyndaya on the rock. She took one of her sister's hands in both of hers. "An Amish boy fighting in such a terrible war makes no sense to our people. It frightens them — suppose their boys go off and enlist too? They thought they knew Jude, and now they feel as if perhaps they didn't know him at all."

"Papa thinks there's more to the story than we are being told."

"Yes, you both go on about that."

Lyyndaya pulled away her hand. "So you think he is dyed black through and through just as everyone else does?"

"No human is dyed black through and through, Lyyndy. I just think that it has been almost a year now since you have seen him — a year! — and that he may be a different person than the one you knew last summer and last October. I change, you change — why wouldn't he change?"

"He flies a plane, Ruth, but he doesn't kill anyone. The Lapp Amish should be proud of that."

"Lyyndy, the Lapp Amish are never going to be proud of one of their own while he's a soldier — *never*. It doesn't matter what he does or doesn't do."

"The newspapers —"

Ruth interrupted. "The newpapers! Yes,

all right, the newspapers of Philadelphia and Boston and Chicago and Detroit are proud of him. I suppose America is proud of him. The gallant young knight of the air! But the Amish will never feel that way."

Lyyndaya stood up. "Americans are proud of him because he wins without shedding blood. They know there's plenty of it already soaking into the ground. They know there will be more. It's a blessing for them to see an American boy fighting and overcoming the Germans without adding another measure of destruction and death to an awful war."

"Lyyndy —"

"At least he's doing something to speed the conflict to its end. We who point fingers, what do we do? Are we rescuing lives as he does? How many of us are doctors and nurses and bringing the wounded back to life? What do we do to help anyone get through this war except go on our merry way plowing our fields and filling our bellies with Sunday lunches?"

"Lyyndy! The Amish pray!"

"Well, Jude Whetstone prays too — and then he does something! He does more than this entire colony does. Papa showed me a clipping where they said Jude was second in command of his squadron and that he felt a personal responsibility to get every one of his pilots back home safely to America. And he has been doing it! How many Americans have the Amish saved lately?"

Ruth got to her feet. "I can't listen to this. You're not sleeping well. You're not eating well. And now you're not thinking well. Your words are wild and — and — ungodly, not the language of a Christian. It's one thing to say them to me. I can forgive you easily enough and forget I ever heard them. But if you talk like this where others hear you — well, beware, my sister, or you may be the next one in the church to be placed under the *Meidung.* Then what will we do? Please, think about your family a little bit, not just Jude. Think about Mama and Papa. And about me too. What will I do if I can't speak or sit at a table with my sister? What will happen to the two of us?"

Lyyndaya stretched out her hands. "I'm sorry," she began, but Ruth waved her away, tears in the corners of her eyes.

The two young women stood and headed back along the path to their house, stumbling every third or fourth step. Lyyndaya thought more about what she had said. Yes, she had been forceful. Perhaps too much so. But that was how she felt. Why shouldn't Amish be using their skills with teams of horses and driving ambulances at the front? Why shouldn't they train as nurses and physicians and bring healing to the badly wounded? What right did they have to sit back so smugly in Pennsylvania and say they were untainted, while all the time men were dying?

"Ruth, you go on," Lyyndaya said. "I want to be alone for a while. I'll take the path by the railroad home."

"Are you sure?"

"I'm sure."

The path she took would come out on a road that wound around back to Paradise. It was longer and would give her more time alone. Back at the house, Mama would go on about all the handsome young men swarming about Emma Zook at church, how lovely all the boys who had come back from the terrible army camp had turned out, that Jude could have been one of them if he hadn't taken it into his head to run off and join the war just so he could fly a plane. And how Lyyndaya could have a dozen young men at her feet, even steal a few from Emma Zook, if only she would let it be known she was available and had chosen to turn her back on Jude and what he had done, like everyone else had.

No, she was not ready to listen to that

again. She would, however, listen to her father. He had objected to Jude when he first began to fly and now it seemed he went out of his way to show kindness to her and Jude's father.

Oh, there is a restlessness in me, Lord. I know it could just be from my own heart and, yes, my own sin, but what if it is not? What if it is from you? How do I know you are not telling me to do something, to try to make a difference when this world is at war? I'm sorry I hurt my sister, but I'm not sorry I said what I said. Why aren't the Lapp Amish driving ambulances on the front? Why aren't they putting bandages on wounds? At least Jude is trying to bring some boys back to their mothers. Who are the Amish bringing back to their mothers and fathers and families?

A whistle blew and brought her out of her prayer. The man driving the locomotive that was hauling freight through the summer fields was sitting on the edge of the open window and waving, a red bandana tied around his throat.

She smiled and waved back. Mr. Clements — "Cannonball" everyone called him — was in his seventies, but looked no older than fifty. On the few trips she had taken to Philadelphia he had twice been the engineer. One time he had sat and spoken with her at a stop where the locomotive needed to take on water. Mr. Clements had delighted her with the story of how he had driven his first steam engine back in 1869 when he was twenty-three, and supplied her with tales of the Old West and running locomotives through places like Montana, Nebraska, New Mexico, and even Dodge City, Kansas.

She watched now as the train steamed east for Philadelphia and then New York. As she stood still in the August sun, new ideas tumbled into her head just as bright orange butterflies tumbled past to touch down on purple, pink, and crimson flowers. A light breeze brought smoke and cinders her way, but it didn't bother her. In her mind, she was on the train traveling toward the Atlantic.

All right, my dear Jude, I am going to do as you are doing. Save lives from death. We will both be in it together, you on your side of the ocean, I on mine.

She reached the road and began to march along it with the fast stride of someone who has made up their mind about a matter and is determined to do something about it.

As she walked along lost in her plans, a buggy came along at a good clip, stirring dust and causing birds hunting insects in the ditches to rise in clusters of grey and brown. As it came alongside her the driver reined in the horse.

"Why, Miss Kurtz," Pastor Stoltzfus greeted her, actually raising his straw hat from his head, something Lyyndaya had seen few Amish men do. She felt she ought to curtsy in response, as an old-fashioned *English* girl might, but only inclined her head.

"Good afternoon, Pastor."

"It's a hot time of the day to be walking."

"I was out in the fields and under some shade trees most of the time."

"Perhaps you have had your full measure of steps for the day."

She laughed. "Perhaps."

"May I drop you off anywhere, hm?"

"Well —" Lyyndaya hesitated. "I thought I might stop by Bishop Zook's."

"I must go past there." He extended a hand. "Climb up."

Lyyndaya knew the Zook farm was not on Pastor Stoltzfus's way, but she stepped up into the seat beside him just the same.

"Thank you," she said.

"I am happy to rescue you."

After a few minutes of quiet, the horse trotting at a steady pace, the pastor asked, "You are going to see Emma, maybe? I know it is none of my business."

"Actually, I want to speak with the bishop."

"*Ja?*"

Lyyndaya smiled at his gentle prodding. "You are one of the pastors. It will come before you soon enough. I would like permission to travel to Philadelphia and offer my services as a volunteer with one of the hospitals to aid those stricken with the influenza. What would you say to that?"

Pastor Stoltzfus gave a low whistle.

When he didn't immediately respond, Lyyndaya decided to practice the short version of her speech on him. "Think how hard the doctors and nurses are working during this influenza epidemic. They must be run off their feet. And think how the poor people are suffering — men and women and children. What would Jesus have us do, Pastor Stoltzfus? Watch from a safe distance? Or express the love of God in real, practical ways? How do you read the Scriptures on this?"

They traveled another minute before he cleared his throat. "The people will say, *How do we know she does not bring this terrible disease to us?*"

"I've thought of that. They require people to have certificates of good health from a physician before they can travel on passenger trains now. I could not move back and forth between Philadelphia without such a piece of paper. Dr. Morgan in Paradise could provide it. Wouldn't that be sufficient to guarantee my good health?"

He grunted. "Still, you could carry the bug in you."

"So could anyone. So could you."

"I am not back and forth to the big city."

"But the people you sell your grain to are. Didn't one of your buyers come in from New York just last Monday?"

The pastor let out another low whistle. "I argue with you and the head aches."

She leaned forward and looked into his face. "But truly, Pastor, isn't the question a simple one? How do we live out the love of God in the midst of this crisis?"

"I think you are not asking. I think you know and want to tell everyone in Paradise what it is God wants them to do — this work for Philadelphia."

Their eyes met and they both burst out laughing.

"I'm sorry," she said.

He shrugged. "For what? It is the question the Lapp Amish need to ask."

The horse turned up the Zooks' drive at the pastor's urging. As Lyyndaya stepped down, Pastor Stoltzfus said, "I will wait a moment and say hello."

"Of course. Thank you again."

"Bitte."

She knocked several times before she heard a man's footsteps coming slowly to answer the door. *Had he been napping? Have I gotten him out of bed?* She panicked a little, wondering if this was going to create a difficult environment in which to ask her question. Perhaps it would be best if she just up and stated her business without any of the customary small talk and then he could go lie down again and think about it. He might appreciate that if he was weary.

The door opened and the usually cheerful bishop did look weary. There were bags under his eyes and a sunken look to his face. She was a bit startled by his appearance, but smiled and inclined her head regardless.

"Good afternoon, Bishop Zook. I'm sorry, I think I have disturbed you."

"I was up," he said in a quiet voice. "Have you come to see Emma?"

"I would like to see Emma, but my reason for dropping by was actually to speak with you. Very quickly."

"Very quickly?" Despite his haggard features, Lyyndaya saw a breath of a smile form.

"Well, I will just out with it and you can . . . pray . . . and tell me what you think."

"All right."

"I've been wondering how we — or *I* — might best show the love of God to the people who are suffering from that terrible disease in Philadelphia. I had a mind to ask the leadership if I might be allowed to travel to the city and volunteer to help the nurses and physicians. They must be exhausted, wouldn't you think, Bishop Zook? This is something I believe Jesus would have me do. There is so much illness. We must try to help. Dr. Morgan would ensure I was healthy, I could ask him to examine me every week so that everyone might be sure I was not sick or carrying the germs into Paradise or into the church —"

The bishop glanced beyond her. "Is that Pastor Stoltzfus with you?"

She turned and looked at the buggy. "*Ja.* I was walking and he offered me a ride."

Pastor Stoltzfus waved and began to flick the reins to move on.

"You should wait," the bishop called, but his voice was not strong. At first the pastor did not hear him. "Please, you should wait, I wish to speak with you."

Finally the pastor brought his horse to a stop.

The bishop nodded and then turned his eyes back to Lyyndaya. "You wish to help the sick and dying. As Jesus would."

"*Ja.*"

"There is no need to worry about carrying the disease into Paradise. It is already here. And there is no need to go to the city to nurse the sick. We have the sick here now who you can take care of."

Lyyndaya's mind was in a whirl. "What — what are you saying?"

The bishop opened the door wide. "If you mean what you have said, then please make yourself a mask, or whatever it is you need, and come in and help me. They are all sick, Lyyndaya. The papers say the disease can come to you in just a few hours and take your life. My whole family has become ill since church this morning. And Emma — Emma —" He swayed and leaned his hands against the doorframe for support. "I think my daughter is dying."

NINETEEN

Knowing it was the last letter he would receive from Lyyndy, Jude kept the one dated April 1918 on him at all times. He would be embarrassed to admit that it had become almost as Scripture to him, so precious it was.

And yet as he read it yet again, its message took root in his heart.

My dear Jude,
You surely won't be surprised when I say that people in the colony are still sorry that you have, in their eyes, left the faith to be a part of the war effort, just so you can continue to fly. Not all believe that, but many do. But as for me, I hope you know that I trust you. I think that one day it will be made clear to me and everyone else why you have done what you have done. Until then, I will pray for you, think of you, and hope for

you — yes, even hope for us. I have no idea what plans God has for you and me, but if they include marriage, as I believe they might, then I know he shall bring you safely home.

I ask only this one thing — whatever you do, whatever you feel you must do, do not let it include taking another human's life. Yes, I know you are in a war, I know men are killing other men every minute of the day, but God forbid you should be one of those who snuff out a soul as easily as I snuff out a candle. Promise me, Jude, promise me you will not shed innocent blood — no, that you will not shed anyone's blood, no matter what the circumstances. Please keep your heart pure. Do not succumb to the temptation to kill another man in a fit of rage, or in the act of combat, or out of a desire to avenge a companion's death. Be different than the others, Jude — even different from the other Christians. Protect life, but do not destroy it.

Jude sat in his cockpit high over France and the German lines, mulling over Lyyndy's words. He knew they were true, but his own burning desire to avenge the deaths caused by Heinrich Schleiermacher tore at him daily.

Now he waited, looked, even prayed, as he had every day since young Jack Zatt's death, that he would have a chance to fight the Fokker D.VII flown by Schleiermacher and end his reign of terror. For the killing of members of Jude's squadron had not ended with Jack. Another new recruit had been shot down by Schleiermacher only a few days after Zatt's death, and then he had brought down Flapjack, who was now in a German prison camp. Worst of all, and still hard for Jude to bear, only the day before on August twenty-second, the Blue 9 had tangled with Frank Sharples over St. Mihiel, and the squadron leader's Nieuport had exploded in mid-air, killing him instantly. Now Jude ached all the more for a moment of reckoning with the Hun. He had no intention of sparing the man. In his imagination, he could see himself coming at the Fokker head on. He could see his bullets tear the murderer apart before the blue aircraft erupted in flames and fell into its death spin.

Jude fully understood why Lyyndy had written what she had. But she wasn't in his shoes. She hadn't lost anyone dear to her, she didn't feel the responsibility he felt for failing to keep so many of his men alive.

Now, with Sharples' death, he had been promoted to squadron leader, and he had no intention of losing another good man. Nor did he have any intention of letting Schleiermacher live to fight another day. No torn wings or broken rudder. He would not be satisfied with the blue Fokker landing inside Allied lines and Schleiermacher being captured and afforded every mark of honor and respect by the French or British. Death was what Jude wanted for the German pilot. Death at his hands.

I'm sorry, Lyyndy. This is the way it has to be. If you were here and if you could see what I saw in these grim summer skies you might find yourself feeling as I do about taking this man's life.

Some days Jude flew in formation with two or three others. There had been dogfights. Billy Skipp had wreaked havoc on the German Albatros and Fokker triplanes and was now a double ace credited with 12 victories. Jude had chased and intimidated and harried whatever enemy fighters came his way and had kept his squadron alive and intact. Yet he was always scanning the sky for the Fokker biplane with the nine of diamonds on one side of its fuselage and the number 9 painted big and black on the other.

He had only spotted Schleiermacher twice, both times from far away. One evening Jude saw the Blue 9 gliding down from a high elevation toward Metz. He knew he could never catch it. Still, he made an effort, racing through tall banks of cloud tinged purple and bronze by the lowering sun. Another morning, Jude was flying solo through puffs of cloud white as his silk scarf and saw the distinctive blue-and-black camouflage splotches of Schleiermacher's wings above him. Jude was already at nineteen thousand feet and could not attain the German's height of twenty thousand no matter how he coaxed his Nieuport. The other pilot didn't descend and attack him; he continued on his way, looking for different prey, shadowed by Jude a thousand feet below until the Blue 9 vanished in a tower of snow-white cumulus.

David fought. Gideon fought. No doubt the Roman centurion whose servant Jesus healed had fought in many campaigns. Had God condemned any of these persons? Had Jesus confronted the centurion and commanded him to stop being a soldier? Had he ever pointed out the error of taking up arms in the defense of the nation of Israel? I have a better reason than most to fight, Lyyndy. If I stop Schleiermacher then more boys live and go home to

the families that love them. The world is a bet-
ter place without a man like him.

The very day Frank Sharples went down, Major Jackson had told him, "Whetstone, I'm making you captain in his place and promoting you to squadron leader."

"Yes, sir," Jude responded.

Jackson had stood looking at him while Jude remained at attention. "No doubt you're feeling a lot of things inside, Captain, things you never felt in Lancaster County. In a way I'm sorry. Yes, you needed to see how ugly and unromantic war can be, but nevertheless I'm sorry."

"Yes, sir."

"I still want you to bring me the Pegasus, Captain. But I will release you from one restriction — I don't care how you do it. If you must bring the winged horse down in black smoke and fire, then do it. I know the newspapers want you to remain the white knight until this brutal war comes to an end. I know you're a symbol of purity and hope to America in the middle of a conflict that oozes blood and hate. If you can maintain your integrity in the face of the death of your men and the enemy's guns, guns that have none of your pity, do so. But if not, you are no longer bound by my command. Instead, my order now is for you to do what you must to save your squadron and the victims of the Kaiser's tyranny in Belgium and France." With a final salute exchanged between them, the major said, "Dismissed!"

Jude looked down on a formation of Fokker D.VIIs just like Schleiermacher's aeroplane. None of them had the blue paint scheme he was so familiar with. He let them pass on their way back to the German lines. Checking his gas gauge he realized it was time he returned to his own aerodrome. He banked right and began to drop slowly from nineteen thousand feet to sixteen thousand, then ten thousand.

Soon he saw the buildings and houses and chimneys of Nancy.

Circling the landing strip he noticed six new planes lined up at one end of the runway. Each of them had distinctive markings of green and brown camouflage as well as red, white, and blue roundels on top of their wings. A group of mechanics was swarming over one of the planes, painting a number. Jude decided to circle again to take a better look. Three number ones in a row were being placed on the right wing. He came down for a landing nearby and hopped out as his ground crew ran up.

"What's up?" he asked.

"We got our first batch of SPADs," they

told him. "The new ones that Eddie Rick-enbacker and the guys at the 94th Aero Squadron are using."

He smiled for the first time in days. "These are the S.XIIIs?"

"Right."

Jude began striding toward the six aircraft. "Talk to me about them."

Mickey, his chief mechanic, chided him. "You remember the briefing about the XIII, Skipper."

"Tell me again."

"Well, top speed is 135, engine is an eight-cylinder Hispano-Suiza, so now you have 220 horses to rein in."

"Quite the Lancaster buggy," Jude responded. "What about ceiling?"

"At least twenty-two thousand feet. You can probably coax another thousand out of it, who knows?"

"Twenty-two thousand! What about rate of climb?"

"Six feet per second."

He came up to the plane the men were painting with the white number 111 on the top right wing and both sides of the fuse-lage. Jude could almost feel the strength and energy bristling in its struts and engines.

"What's this?" he asked them.

They grinned down at him. "Your plane,

Captain. We decided to make you Triple One. Now the Heinies will know who's chasing their tails back to the Rhine."

Jude ran his hand over the fuselage and examined the engine, the strip of blue paint that made a circle around it, and the two Vickers machine guns. "Did you pick me out a good one?"

"Yes, I did." Major Jackson appeared from the behind the long row of aircraft. Jude and the others sprang to attention, but he waved them down. "Stand easy. Keep at your work. I looked them over and this seems to be the one for you, Captain."

"Thank you, sir."

"How was your sortie?"

"Nothing to report."

"It may be that the extra height the SPAD will give you can change that."

"I think it might, sir."

"You can get above the D.VII now. I looked into it."

"That's good news." Jude looked up at the men finishing the paint job. "Is it ready to go?"

"What? Now?" one of them asked in surprise. "You just landed."

"It's only ten in the morning." He turned to Mickey. "Can you make sure she's in the pink?"

"Yes, sir, but —"

"They were flown here, weren't they?"

"Of course."

"Then they're ready to go. Gas 'em up." He put his hand on his armorer's shoulder. "Stan, check the guns out, will you?"

"You bet."

"Have you assigned the other planes yet, sir?" he asked Jackson. "Will we be getting any more of them?"

Jackson nodded. "The whole squadron will be flying them within the week. For now I made sure your second in command, Zedediah, had one, and of course, Billy."

"Where are they?"

"Still up with a few recruits."

Jude looked around at his mechanics. "I'm going to freshen up, grab a coffee and a roll, and then I'll be ready to head out. Twenty minutes. All right?"

Mickey laughed and shook his head. "Whatever you say, sir."

Jude drank his coffee in the dining room alone. Then, chewing on a freshly baked bun, he wandered over and looked at the Squadron Bible, still deliberately left open to the last verse from Isaiah that Frank Sharples had read from the day before he went down.

But they that wait upon the Lord shall renew

*their strength; they shall mount up with wings
as eagles; they shall run, and not be weary;
and they shall walk, and not faint.*

"Amen," he whispered to the empty room.

In less than half an hour Jude was back winging his way toward Pont-à-Moussan and the front. He felt an odd sense of elation. It came not only from flying a stronger and better plane than the Nieuport. It also came from a sense of destiny — that now, soon, God would deliver Schleiermacher into his hands, and the deaths of his men would be avenged.

"I must put you through your paces, Lucille," he said out loud.

He was not sure why he suddenly decided to name the plane that. He had not named the Nieuport. But this aircraft seemed to beg for a way to address it beyond the terms "aircraft" and "aeroplane" and "SPAD." *Why not Lyyndy?* he wondered. Because, he realized, he did not think Lyyndaya would wish to have a warplane named after her.

Now I have two women in my life. But when I am back in the States, God willing, if I can ever get my hands on my own aeroplane, that will be the day to put LYYNDY on the fuselage in bright yellow paint.

He shoved the joystick forward and thrust the SPAD into a fast dive. *They said you*

316

*were good when it came to dives. This morn-
ing we will see how good.* Jude imagined
himself closing in on the Blue 9 and fired
several quick bursts from his guns into the
empty air. Then he continued to dive as
steeply as possible. At three thousand feet
he pulled up sharply. The wings and struts
held firm despite the enormous forces being
exerted on them.

"Good girl," he said and patted the left
side of the plane with a gloved hand.

Next he climbed as swiftly as he could —
eighteen thousand, nineteen, twenty, twenty-
one — and finally leveled the SPAD out at
twenty-two thousand, four hundred. Cold
stung his nose and cheeks, but he felt
wonderful at that height, all the battlefields
spread out under his feet, locations in German territory like Metz and Mars-la-Tour
recognizable. He listened carefully to the
pitch of the engine. The roar was steady and
consistent. Perhaps a bit of a tune-up by
Mickey to bring it up to snuff was in order,
but otherwise everything seemed right as
rain. Time for a barrel roll.

Are you ready? he asked.

Ready for what? Lyyndaya responded.

A barrel roll.

Without waiting for an answer he threw
the SPAD over on its left side and then had

317

it flying upside down. He went like that for one long minute before flipping it right side up in one long smooth movement. It was easy to imagine Lyyndaya shrieking or biting her finger.

How was that, Barrel Roll Kurtz?

I loved it. Are you going to do it again?

Why not?

Oh, Jude, can't we just leave the war behind? Can't you stop thinking about this Heinrich Schleiermacher for an hour or two? The sky is empty and as perfect as — as perfect as —

Your eyes? he suggested.

She laughed. *Can't we just fly for the rest of the morning? Can't you give yourself time to get used to this new plane and act like it was July of last year again and neither of us had a care in the world?*

What do you want to do?

Drop into a spin. Do loops. Dive. Try three barrel rolls in a row. I don't know. Go fast. Oh, yes, please — go as fast as you can.

It will be twice as fast as you've ever flown before.

I don't care. Open her up, as you like to say. And never mind if you hear me screaming. It means I'm happy.

So, imagining Lyyndaya shrieking with delight beside him, her golden hair streaming behind her in the wind, Jude threw the plane about the sky as if it were a brand-new toy he couldn't keep his hands from. He dove down to eight thousand feet and opened the throttle, watching the speed dart forward from 100 to 110 to 125 to 137 miles per hour. Then he climbed as quickly as a skylark. Dove. Barrel-rolled. Straightened out and loop-de-looped. Dove again. Climbed. Fell into a spin so that the ground hurtled at him in faster and tighter circles of green and brown. Waited till the last minute and then pulled up, the engine howling and, Jude was sure, an imaginary Lyyndaya howling right along with it.

Watching their squadron leader from a distance as they took off and rose toward him in their SPADs, Zed and Billy Skipp — as well as a recruit everyone called Tex for reasons that became obvious once he opened his mouth — were amazed by the stunts and maneuvers Jude was pulling off at high speed in front of their eyes. They had never known he had those kinds of acrobatics in him — though Billy and Zed had seen him twist about in the air like a flying corkscrew often enough during aerial combat. Not able to match him turn for turn, all three nevertheless decided to join in, spiraling and diving and climbing as if thousands of people below had paid good money to see the four of them at their very best.

"The greatest show on earth!" shouted Tex in his distinctive drawl, but no one could hear him as they ripped past one another, heading in every possible direction on the face of the compass. Yet every moment they played they still kept flicking their eyes up and down, glancing over their shoulders, squinting up at the sun, scanning the sky for enemy planes. But none appeared.

Finally they ran low on fuel and headed back toward Nancy and the field.

Exhilarated, the whole gang sat down to lunch at the aerodrome and devoured chicken and green beans and ice cream as if they hadn't touched food all week. Zed summed it up for them when he said, "Remember why you fell in love with flying in the first place? Eh? Remember what made your heart go faster and how the sky and sun filled you to the top with strength? That's what we had today. That last hour was better than all the others we've had since they brought us to France."

Billy, the ace, nodded. "Combat flying is pretty exciting stuff. But doing the stunts, the flips, the rolls — that's what I love. Do you think, after the war, there'll be air shows, that they'll let us do all kinds of wild things in the sky for paying customers at state fairs and exhibitions and things?"

"I'd bet on it," responded Zed.

"At rodeos?" asked Tex hopefully.

"Why not?"

"Well — it'd spook the horses and rodeo stock."

Zed shrugged and sat back, poking a toothpick about in his mouth. "Just use a field far enough away. And don't buzz the stadium."

Billy ran his hands through his red hair and grinned. "Won't those be fine times? Just have to get there first. In one piece."

Jude sipped at his coffee. "Just have to end the war. Just have to finish the job."

He wasn't thinking of fairs or rodeos or July Fourth celebrations. For a moment, he wasn't even thinking of getting back to Paradise and to Lyyndaya. Only one thing was on his mind, only one plane, only one man. When Lyyndaya returned to his thoughts, smiling, full of life and God, her hair shining in the Pennsylvania sun, he whispered, *I'm sorry. I pray the day will come when you can understand.*

Zed was standing over the Squadron Bible. He marked Sharples' page with a

321

thumb and then turned the tall pages slowly and carefully until he found what he wanted.

"Frank opened to this psalm the day Jack Zatt was killed," he told them without looking up. "But he didn't get to one part. So this is for us. This is for now — today, tomorrow, and the day after — all the days after." He read the words out loud with a certain measured cadence no one else used, as if they were seated in a cathedral for a time of worship. When he was done he turned back to Frank's last reading from Isaiah. Then he walked from the room. The others got up, but Jude remained sitting until he was by himself, turning an empty coffee cup over in his hands.

Surely he shall deliver thee from the snare of the fowler, and from the noisome pestilence.

He shall cover thee with his feathers, and under his wings shalt thou trust: his truth shall be thy shield and buckler.

Thou shalt not be afraid for the terror by night; nor the arrow that flieth by day;

nor for the pestilence that walketh in darkness;

Nor for the destruction that wasteth at noonday.

A thousand shall fall at thy side, and ten

thousand at thy right hand; but it shall not come nigh thee.

Only with thine eyes shalt thou behold and see the reward of the wicked.

Because thou hast made the Lord, which is my refuge, even the most High, thy habitation;

There shall no evil befall thee, neither shall any plague come nigh thy dwelling.

For he shall give his angels charge over thee, to keep thee in all thy ways.

They shall bear thee up in their hands, lest thou dash thy foot against a stone.

Thou shall tread upon the lion and adder: the young lion and the dragon shalt thou trample under feet.

Because he hath set his love upon me, therefore will I deliver him: I will set him on high, because he hath known my name.

He shall call upon me, and I will answer him: I will be with him in trouble; I will deliver him, and honour him.

With long life will I satisfy him, and shew him my salvation.

TWENTY

From the window of the Zooks' house, Lyyndy watched the buggies move like shadows in the soft rain. Three or four turned up the drive. The bishop stepped down from the first and then walked around it and took his wife's hand. The pastors emerged from the other buggies and came up to the couple. Dr. Morgan strode firmly to the porch from the final carriage.

"Are they back from the funeral?" came a faint voice from behind Lyyndaya.

"Yes. The doctor is on his way in to see you."

Emma Zook smiled as much as she could. "I feel better."

"You look better."

"But such a sad day."

"Yes," agreed Lyyndaya.

"Except they are with Jesus."

Lyyndaya walked over to the bed where Emma had the covers pulled up to her neck and held one of her pale hands gently. "You're right, sister."

There was a knock on the door. She crossed the room and opened it.

"Dr. Morgan," she greeted the tall, broad-shouldered physician.

He took off his black hat and raindrops fell on the carpet. The hat had less of a brim and a different crown than the Amish men's hats. Lyyndaya took it and helped him off with his long dark overcoat. He went immediately to the bed.

"How is my Emma?" he asked, lifting her wrist and checking her pulse.

"I think I'm stronger. I walked around the room twice — with Lyyndy's help."

"Did you?" He warmed the end of his stethoscope in his hand and then placed it on her chest. "Take a deep breath for me and hold it. Now let it out slowly. Good. Once more. And cough. Again." He smiled at her. "No crackling. No congestion. I believe you've turned the corner, young lady." He glanced over at Lyyndaya. "Thanks in no small part to your friend here."

"I know," said Emma. "She's been wonderful."

Lyyndaya had draped the doctor's coat over a chair and was holding on to his hat for him. "Feeding her broth? Mopping her brow? That hardly amounts to a cure."

"Day and night," the doctor said, putting his stethoscope back in his bag. "You stood on the line between life and death. If I had a nurse like you for every patient, we'd stop this biblical plague."

Lyyndaya dropped her eyes. "Thank you."

There was another knock on the door and it opened a crack. Emma's father peered in.

"May we?" he asked.

"Of course," Dr. Morgan replied. "I'll just take her temperature."

Emma's mother and father stepped into the room, bringing with them the scent of rain on grass. Her mother sat on the edge of the bed and smoothed back her daughter's long dark hair that was spread over the pillow.

"You have some color," she said.

"How was the funeral, Mother?"

"It went very well. Hosea and little Annie and John are not suffering anymore. Heaven is their home now. Your father and I thank God. They were in so much pain, Emma. You know how it was. They could not . . . they could not . . ." Her mother struggled with her voice and to control her tears, ". . . even get a breath at the end."

Emma placed one thin hand on her mother's. "Yes, but now — they breathe freely."

Her mother nodded, her eyes glistening.

Dr. Morgan gestured to Lyyndaya. "Let's step into the room across the hall. I must be sure you have no symptoms. Excuse us, please."

The room across the hall had been Annie's. It was neatly made up and seemed to be waiting for her as if she was expected back from a trip at any moment. Dr. Morgan placed his stethoscope on Lyyndaya's back and chest and listened carefully.

"Do you feel feverish at all?"

"No."

"Are there any chills that come and go?"

"None."

"Do you feel up to doing some more nursing for me?"

She caught his eyes. "Why? Who is sick now?"

"I'm not sure what I'm dealing with. But I would feel better if someone like you, who is experienced with how the disease manifests itself, could spend some time at their side."

"Of course."

"I don't want you to get upset when I tell you their name —"

Her green eyes widened and she caught his arm. "Doctor — is it my family?"

"Yes. It's Ruth."

"Ruth!"

"Calm yourself. I do not see all the symptoms, but —"

"We must go now, then!"

"Yes, yes. Emma's parents can see to her needs now. Gather up your things."

Lyyndaya flew from the room. She didn't wish to disturb the three surviving members of the Zook family as they spent a few quiet moments together, but most of her items were in Emma's room. She hesitated at the door and suddenly heard the three begin to sing a hymn, deep and slow, yet somehow with a strength that sent a quick chill up her spine. Feeling compelled to pray, she bowed her head a moment. Then, as they continued to sing, she recalled that her long coat and an extra pair of boots were in a closet near the front door, and she made her way downstairs.

The pastors were sitting at the table in the parlor off the hallway. All of them murmured their greetings as she passed by the doorway and opened the closet. When she turned around, coat and boots in hand, Pastor King was standing in the hall waiting for her.

"We wish to thank you for all the work you did for our bishop's family," he said.

Lyyndaya felt flustered, wanting to go back upstairs and fetch her clothing, anxious to join Dr. Morgan who had already come down the stairs and was out in the buggy, beginning to feel a slight panic about what was happening to her sister. But she forced herself to slow down.

"It was something I believe the Lord wanted me to do," she replied.

"They tell us Hosea and John passed away in less than two days."

She nodded.

"And the little girl?"

Lyyndaya did not want to say. "Didn't Dr. Morgan mention this to the church leadership?"

"No, but we wish to hear it from you."

"From the time of the first symptoms that Mrs. Zook noticed after lunch on Sunday, to the time of Annie's death — it was not three hours."

The color in the pastor's eyes seemed to pale as she spoke.

"And what are these symptoms, Miss Kurtz?"

"But you have been told, haven't you? It can look like ague. Or a person feels the usual things a person with flu feels — headaches, pain in their shoulders and elbows and knees — there's a fever, they grow very tired and have no energy."

"I have heard that sometimes . . . a patient . . . can turn blue —"

"That did not happen here. But Dr. Morgan told me it has happened in Boston."

"Will it spread?" he asked her abruptly.

"The doctor had this house quarantined all week," she responded quickly, "but Emma is better now."

"No, but will it spread?"

Lyyndaya wanted to say she didn't know. But she felt that would be a lie. "Yes, Pastor King, it will spread."

His gaze was steady, but troubled. "The doctor tells us we shouldn't gather for worship until this is past. And that we should consider wearing masks as they do in the city."

"It might be something for the leadership to discuss, something that might be done for a month or two," Lyyndaya said, trying to be careful not to speak out of turn. This was, after all, more fitting if it came from Dr. Morgan.

"A month? Two months?" Pastor King grew agitated and his dark eyes gleamed. "How will people be encouraged if they cannot meet together for prayer and worship? If they cannot break bread together? Who will shepherd them?"

"Lyyndaya." Bishop Zook was coming down the hall from the staircase with her black overnight bag. "These are your things. I think my wife found all of your items. If there is something missing, please let us know."

"Thank you."

"No, no, I thank you," he said, putting the bag in her hands. "And I thank God for his mercy in leaving us one of our children to bless us."

Lyyndaya saw his struggle to control himself and a dampness came to her own eyes as she saw his pain. "It is a great mercy. And for myself also, for Emma is a friend and — like a sister —" She stopped, thinking of Ruth and how swiftly the illness could affect someone. "I must leave. The doctor is waiting."

The bishop gently took her by arm. "Is there someone else?"

Lyyndaya looked away. "There may be, I don't know."

"Who?"

"In my own house . . . Ruth . . ."

"I am so sorry. We will pray. Perhaps it is something else." He didn't let go of her arm. "Of course you are in a hurry to get out the door. I do not wish to detain you any further, only . . ." Lyyndaya watched him try to form the words he wanted several times. Eventually he blurted, "Hosea said some things before he went to be with the Lord. Some things I need to tell you. I do not understand completely. But I shall come by your house."

Despite her urge to rush out the door and into the buggy, Lyyndaya held back. "What things? What did Hosea tell you?"

The bishop shook his head. "It is not easily said. I shall come by your house." He released her arm. "Please go to your family. It was not my wish to upset you further. I promise you we will talk. Go to your family now — and may Christ be with you."

Lyyndaya was torn. Something told her that Hosea's words had been important and that she needed to know them, but right now the image of Ruth perhaps hovering between life and death compelled her to leave.

Dr. Morgan drove his two-horse team and carriage almost at a gallop through the rain that was now coming down heavily and beating against the roof. His carriage wasn't built after the Amish style — it was brown in color with brass accents and could travel much faster. As they neared the Kurtz home, lightning tore at the sky a few miles south, followed by a sharp crack of thunder.

Minutes later Lyyndaya's father and mother were waiting at the door as she and the doctor hurried up the steps. Her mother was crying.

"Has something happened?" asked Lyyndaya. "Is she in her room?"

Mrs. Kurtz waved her hand, unable to speak. Dr. Morgan looked at Lyyndaya's father. "What is it?"

Lyyndaya's father cleared his throat and tried to speak twice before he found his voice. "She is . . . coughing so much, so violently . . . and there is now a blue color . . . in her face and on her . . ." But he could not finish and looked away.

Lyyndaya and Dr. Morgan were quickly up the staircase and into Ruth's room. She was sitting in bed, leaning back against pillows piled against the headboard. Lyyndaya put her hand to her sister's forehead while Dr. Morgan pulled his stethoscope out of his bag.

"She's burning up!" Lyyndaya said.

Ruth opened her mouth and whispered, "So we have not spoken all week — not since we quarreled — and that is the first thing you say to me?"

The doctor was warming his stethoscope in his hand. "Your parents said you had been coughing."

"Not for . . . the last half hour." She opened her hand and showed them a bloody cloth. "I am glad because . . . it hurt my stomach . . . so much . . ."

The blue on her face and arms was unmistakable, but not as dark as Lyyndaya had feared. There was a basin and wet cloth on the bedside table, and she began to gently touch the cloth to Ruth's face and throat.

"That feels so good — thank you — I just didn't have the strength to lift my arm anymore."

Dr. Morgan held up a finger for quiet while he listened to Ruth's chest. Lyyndaya mouthed the words *Ich liebe dich* in German and Ruth smiled slightly and mouthed *I love you* back in English.

The doctor straightened. "There are some beneficial teas I will have your mother brew. Lyyndaya, as you know well, it is important your sister drink as much as possible. And a mustard plaster for the chest. You remember the ingredients we used with Emma?"

"Mustard powder and seed mixed with the white of eggs and flour," recited Lyyndaya. "Placed within flannel cloth."

"Exactly. Remove it every thirty to forty-five minutes, wait a quarter hour, then apply it again. Exchange the ingredients for fresh ones every couple of hours."

"Yes. I know."

"You might want to feed her my recipe of garlic, chives, and red onions. Do you like chives, Ruth?"

"I like chives . . . I am not so sure . . . about garlic."

"It may very well help you. Also steam. This can open up the lungs and airways." He was looking down at Ruth. "We will use everything we know to help you."

"Do I . . . have it?"

"Yes."

"Why do they call it . . . the Spanish influenza, the Spanish flu?"

"Because there was so much of it in Spain this past spring," Dr. Morgan explained.

"What started it? What caused . . . it?"

"We don't know."

"Can you cure me . . . sister?" She weakly reached a hand out to Lyyndaya, who took it in both of hers and squeezed gently.

"We healed Emma," she responded. "With God's help."

Dr. Morgan patted Ruth on the arm. "Leave the cure to us and to divine providence. I will go and ask your mother to make up a tea for you. Lyyndaya, we will require the mustard poultice."

"Of course."

"But let me have five minutes alone with

your father and mother first." He slipped out the door, shutting it softly.

"Such a silly argument we had last Sunday," murmured Ruth.

"It was the heat." Lyyndaya smiled.

"You think so?"

"I do. We shouldn't have been out in the sun for so long."

She continued to hold one of Ruth's bluish hands between the two of hers.

"What do you hear . . . about your knight in shining armor?" Ruth asked.

There was a chair by the bed and she sat down in it. "Jude is a captain now. Commanding an entire squadron."

"He has not been hurt?"

"No."

"And he has not hurt another . . . ?"

Lyyndaya smiled. "No, he has not, and he never will."

"But he fights — to keep his men fighting."

"He fights to keep his men alive."

Ruth sighed and looked up at the ceiling. "Such faith you . . . have. In this boy. In the God . . . you pray to for this boy. I wish we all had your trust . . . your innocence."

"But I don't think of it as innocence," Lyyndaya responded softly. "I think I have seen too much this past year to call myself an innocent. I prefer to think of myself as hopeful."

"Like — Christian's companion in *Pilgrim's Progress*." She turned her pale eyes on her sister. "Lyyndy, do you think — I'm going to die?"

"No."

"Will you give me a kiss on the cheek? My Hopeful? But . . . I will understand if you are afraid . . ."

Lyyndaya leaned forward across the bed. "I'm not afraid. I was in Emma's room for a week. Perhaps I'm immune." She kissed her sister on one side of her face, then gently kissed her on the other.

Ruth managed to get her arms around Lyyndaya's neck. "Why would you be immune . . . and no one else?"

"I don't know. Is it because God wants me to nurse others that are precious to him back to health?"

Ruth laughed quietly. The pain of the laughter made her wince, but she couldn't stop herself from laughing a second time. "I am precious. Emma is precious. You don't think you are precious? You don't think God cares about you . . . as much as he does for those who are sick?"

Lyyndaya shrugged.

Ruth patted her on the cheek. "My sweet

sister. I know one person who thinks you are precious — who counts you as more precious than even I do."

Lyyndaya kissed her sister a final time on her brow and then sat back, amused, a smile playing about her lips. "*Ja,* and who is that? Mama? Papa? Edward at the post office?"

"You know who it is. He adores you. Every time I saw . . . the two of you together it was in his eyes. Even when Emma was hovering around and flirting."

"Oh, stop, Ruth — you exaggerate, he could never make up his mind between Emma and me."

Ruth made a small flicking motion with her hand. "That's what you thought . . . and Emma thought. Maybe he thought it too sometimes. But I never believed it. When my eyes looked, I knew. When I prayed, I knew. Sick and dying, I still know."

"You're not dying."

Ruth closed her eyes. "I know what you do not know . . . because in this one thing you would not permit yourself to hope . . . or to believe. Jude, your Jude, your crazy boy . . . he would gladly give his life for you."

TWENTY-ONE

The sky was a flat blue calm. It reminded Jude of lakes he'd seen in Minnesota when he was eight or nine and his father had taken him to visit an uncle who lived in the north of the state.

He rubbed his gloved hands roughly up and down over his nose.

Lucille was cruising at twenty-two thousand feet and the September air was sharp and clear with a good bite to it.

He checked his watch. His men were late. They were supposed to be flying formation below him by now. Jude glanced toward Nancy. There was a cluster of black dots rising from the green and brown earth. That would be them.

A look toward Metz revealed nothing. Visibility from the cockpit of a SPAD was not all Jude could have wished, but he was certain no German plane was in that vicinity. Still, he hoped his squadron might pique some interest as they moved closer to enemy lines. Perhaps a *Jagdstaff el* might appear and challenge them. Then perhaps even Schleier macher might show up with the German fighters. Or, as was his preference, haunt the edges of any ensuing air battle, hoping to catch a solitary target off his guard.

He drifted over into German territory. "Archie" — antiaircraft fire — burst angrily in red and black far below him. When his squadron finally arrived and crossed over, the shots were above and below and all around them. They ignored the bursts and carried on at sixteen thousand feet. Jude counted the squadron craft, recognizing each different camouflage scheme of light greens and forest greens and earth browns, knowing each number by heart, connecting each plane with a face and a man he realized he loved dearly — Zed, Billy, Tex, Sam Baker from Wisconsin, Timmy Erwin from Louisiana, Jack Ross from Nevada — even Ram Peterson, Flapjack, who'd escaped from the German camp where he'd been held. He had spent a harrowing week crawling through no-man's-land hoping he wouldn't be shot by French, British, or American troops. In the end, it was the Canadians who'd rescued him and driven him to Nancy and the aerodrome, fed, cleaned up, and in a fresh set of clothes, the red flannel shirt making the flyer complain the Canucks had dressed him up like a lumberjack.

"You're Swedish, aren't you?" Billy Skipp had pointed out.

"Everyone should have a go at no-man's-land," Flapjack had responded. "It'll put red blood in your veins and hair on your chest. You know, I imagine our northern neighbors recognized these qualities and decided to dress me suitably as a symbol of North American manhood."

"How long were you mucking about in the barbed wire and rats?" Jude had asked.

"The Canucks found me on day six."

"It must have given you a different perspective on the war and life."

"You mean that I ought to be thankful to God I fly an aeroplane?"

Jude had smiled. "I wasn't preaching a sermon, Peterson."

Flapjack had been busy cleaning the bean sauce up from his plate with a thick slice of bread while they talked. "It'll do wonders for your Christian faith and prayer life. I highly recommend it." Then he'd pointed his hunk of bread at Jude. "Though I would suggest traveling only by night and bearing south by west rather than north. The Heinies notice movement in the daylight, for some reason. And the heaviest concentrations of their troops are in the north."

"That's a spiritual lesson I think I'll skip," Jude had replied, pushing away from the lunch table.

"If God wills," Flapjack had quipped.

Now, as he sat in his SPAD, Jude suddenly noticed movement from the direction of Metz. He began to count — four, five, six, seven. It was a *Jagdstaffel*. And they were flying Schleiermacher's kind of plane, the Fokker D.VII. But as they rose to meet the threat from Jude's squadron and their colors and markings became clear, he couldn't spot the nine of diamonds or the blue paint that would spell Heinrich Schleiermacher to any Allied aviator. But then, as Jude reminded himself, it was rarely the German ace's style to fly with a group. If he was around, he'd show up somewhere else and by himself.

Minutes before the two squadrons were about to engage, that was exactly what happened. Jude had his eyes on his men and, as was his custom before a fight, was praying for each of them one at a time, watching as they prepared to dive down into the German planes, which were already beginning to fire. Out of a white cloud directly below him, at twenty thousand feet, a blue aircraft with black Brunswick crosses on its wings appeared. It shadowed Jude's squadron, waiting for the right moment and the right opportunity to strike. When it banked slightly to follow Billy Skipp, the nine of diamonds on its fuselage was obvious.

Jude knew why the German hadn't seen him and was leaving himself open to attack. Jude had positioned himself carefully so anyone looking upward for him would catch only the glare of the sun. He was also passing in and out of the same intermittent cloud cover as Schleiermacher — sometimes visible, sometimes not. And the other pilot wasn't used to having aircraft hover over him at twenty-two or twenty-three thousand feet. He wasn't used to the SPAD and its capabilities. The German ace was sure of himself and thinking only of his next victory.

"The Lord," Jude whispered, "has delivered you into my hands."

He began to edge his plane, Triple One, slowly downward so he would be within striking distance in a few minutes.

The dogfight was already swirling all over the sky below him, Fokkers chasing SPADs and SPADs hunting Fokkers. Tracers zipped yellow and white from one aeroplane to another. A Fokker began to corkscrew, flames pouring out of its tail and fuselage. Then it fell from the sky and Billy Skipp broke away to follow it down. Schleiermacher banked and stayed on top of the redheaded boy. When he felt Billy was least on his guard and far from the protection of his comrades, Jude knew the Blue 9 would leap and tear him to pieces with his guns. But Jude wouldn't give the German even another instant to decide when to go after Billy. He pushed his joystick forward and Lucille screamed into a sharp dive. In seconds Jude was in range and opened fire.

The German twisted his head and looked back in shock and fear. Jude kept firing. The Blue 9 went into a dive of its own. Both the Fokker and the SPAD shrieked past Billy, who was startled to see not only Schleiermacher, but Jude as well, race past him. If the German went left, so did Jude. If he steepened his dive, so did Jude. When he pulled up and tried to loop around on Jude's tail, Jude pulled the same stunt and kept his sights on the German's rudder. Less than a minute after Jude had attacked, the Fokker seemed to lose control and drop into a lazy spin.

"I'm not that stupid," Jude hissed.

He followed Schleiermacher down and, to let the German pilot know he was wise to the ploy, fired a burst into the fuselage. Suddenly the Fokker pulled out of its spin and began to flick back and forth to get out of the SPAD's sights. Jude stayed with him, firing again and again. The Blue 9 steered a course for Metz. Jude roared up on him and aimed his guns. Words came into his head — *And Agag said, Surely the bitterness of death is past. And Samuel said, As thy sword hath made women childless, so shall thy mother be childless among women. And Samuel hewed Agag in pieces before the Lord in Gilgal.*

His shots took out the Fokker's rudder, and the blue fighter began to swerve from side to side. He crept closer and this time put the back of Schleiermacher's seat in his sights.

Suddenly more words rushed into his mind — *Dearly beloved, avenge not yourselves, but rather give place unto wrath: for it is written, Vengeance is mine, I will repay, saith the Lord.*

Jude hesitated before making the killing shot. It was not only the words that disturbed him, it was the voice that had spoken them. Not his voice or Bishop Zook's or some other preacher's. It was Lyyndaya's.

Therefore if thine enemy hunger, feed him; if he thirst, give him drink: for in so doing thou shalt heap coals of fire on his head. Be not overcome of evil, but overcome evil with good.

It seemed as if the old game of pretending that Lyyndaya was in the cockpit had taken on a new twist. Her green eyes touched upon him with an intensity he couldn't ignore. It seemed to him she took his hand and squeezed it and her face was only inches from his own when she spoke — *Love your enemies, Jude, bless them that curse you, do good to them which hate you, and pray for them which despitefully use you.*

It wasn't only that he felt the presence of the woman he loved in his aeroplane. He could not deny he had a strong sense of the presence of God as well. He closed his eyes, in the briefest of moments prayed one of the most important prayers of his life, then threw his joystick to the left and roared up on Schleiermacher's side. The German stared over at him and saw the three ones on the fuselage. Jude, using unmistakable hand movements, pointed at the enemy pilot, then pointed back behind them to the Allied lines. He did this several times until the German pilot nodded and began to turn his plane, which was sluggish due to the loss of most of the rudder and a large section of fabric from one wing.

Jude followed him closely as they flew west. Once Schleiermacher attempted to descend and bank left, but Jude fired a burst over his head. When the German glanced back, he pointed again to the Allied lines. After that, his Fokker responding heavily to his hands, Schleiermacher made no further attempts to escape his captor.

Suddenly they were surrounded by an escort of SPADs, one after another forming up on the left and right. Jude counted them. His whole squadron had returned from the vicious dogfight with the *Jagdstaffel.* He saw holes in wings and fuselages, as well as scorch marks where fires had flared up and died, and Zed was leaking oil as if writing in the sky with a thin line of India ink, but they were all there.

Thank God, he thought to himself. *Thank God.*

There was no Archie when they crossed the lines from east to west. The German antiaircraft gunners recognized the blue Fokker, and the British and French gunners recognized the SPADs. Zed and Billy, in the lead on Schleiermacher's right and left, began to turn south for Nancy and their aerodrome. The German ace didn't need more direction than that. His D.VII wob-

347

bling, he banked left and dropped in elevation.

Jude couldn't honestly say that his spiritual experience in the skies over the German Empire had brought him to the point where he loved his enemy. But he did know he no longer desired Heinrich Schleiermacher to crash and die.

He drew up alongside the German aviator again and pointed down. Schleiermacher nodded and, likely relieved to be landing an aeroplane that was pitching from side to side more and more violently, immediately began to lose altitude. Jude stayed with him so that, when they touched down, they did it simultaneously and side by side. The German made a perfect landing with a plane that seemed ready to fall apart, and Jude couldn't help but admire him for his flying skills.

All the SPADs landed and the men came running toward Jude and Schleiermacher. The ground crew and "Ironwood" Jackson were already there — as well as a reporter from the *Boston Globe* who had been hanging around for days, hoping for a dramatic story that would get him "above the fold" when he wired it back to America. He asked the German to pose for a shot, then Jude, then he wanted the whole squadron to stand for a picture until Jackson pushed him aside. His eyes locked with Jude's.

"What do we have here, Captain?" he asked.

Jude had pulled off his leather helmet and goggles. "I've brought you the Pegasus, sir."

Jackson turned to the German ace, who was standing by his plane. There was blood running from the sleeve of the German's flying jacket onto his hand. Nevertheless, he had accepted an American cigarette from Jude's head mechanic, Mickey, and was smoking it, ignoring his wound.

"You're hit," Jackson said to the captured pilot, indicating his injured hand.

The German came to attention and saluted Jackson. Jackson returned the salute. Schleiermacher lifted the hand with the blood on it. The other held the cigarette. "It is — small thing." He looked at Jude as the young man came toward him. "I must — thank you — for — my life."

"Liebe deine Feinde," Jude responded. *Love your enemies.*

Schleiermacher was startled. *"Sprechen Sie Deutsch?"*

Jude nodded.

The German pilot asked, *"Sie sind religiös?"* *Are you religious?*

Jude replied, *"Ich glaube an Jesus Chris-*

349

tus." I believe in Jesus Christ.

"My father is — pastor — yet we are still — at war," said Schleiermacher.

Jude nodded. *"Möge Gott uns verzeihen."* *May God forgive us.*

Astonishing himself, he extended his hand. The German put the cigarette in his mouth and gripped Jude's hand with his good one. *"Es freut mich, dass ich Sie nicht umgebracht habe,"* Jude told him. *I am glad I did not kill you.*

Schleiermacher smiled. *"Ich auch." I am too.*

The others, listening to this German flying back and forth, were surprised when the two men began to laugh.

"His wound needs to be tended to," Jackson broke in gruffly. "You Krauts can chitchat later. Before we send him to prison camp, where he'll get better care than our boys in their graves received from his murderous hand."

Two guards stepped forward to take Schleiermacher for treatment. As they led the captive away past the knot of American pilots and ground crew, with the reporter from the *Boston Globe* trailing after them, Jude called, *"Wieviele Männer haben Sie verloren?" How many men have you lost?*

Schleiermacher looked back at him as he walked away. *"Genau wie Sie, Weisse Ritter. Gar zu viele, dass die Mütter in Frieden wären." Just like you, White Knight. Far too many for the mothers to be at peace.*

Zed was at Jude's side. "He's no older than you or Flapjack."

"No," Jude agreed.

"And not a bad-looking chap for a Hun," tossed out Flapjack.

"Yeah," Billy said. "Almost as good-looking as you."

Flapjack snorted. "Tell that to Kaiser William's batman. He's not even close."

"You're an ace now, Triple One," said Tex. "And your hands are still clean."

Jude shook his head, his eyes remaining on Schleiermacher. "No one's hands are clean. Not on their side or ours. Not in war or peace."

Dear Lyyndy,
I thought I would kill him. I swear before God, I wanted to kill him. The verses came to mind about Samuel hewing Agag to pieces. But before I could administer the coup de grace, I heard you quoting the Bible to me. All the good Amish verses about mercy and forgiveness and loving your enemies.

This was all in my imagination, but it was like getting hit in the head by the rock from a slingshot when I was a boy. The verses stunned me. For some soldiers it is given to kill and defend, I don't know. The Bible never condemns them and never says you can't be a good soldier and a good Christian. But for those he calls to be Amish, those he tells to be peacemakers, those he says cannot be the ones who shed blood, who are set aside to bring only mercy and peace — well, for them it is a different matter. These Amish and Mennonite and Quaker boys are not permitted to be the killers. That is not why God has given them the breath of life. They are on this earth to be a different kind of soldier.

I don't know if I've succeeded to God's satisfaction. I haven't succeeded to my own. God must be the judge. But at least Schleiermacher's mother doesn't have to get a telegram or see an officer at her door tonight. And the mother of the one he would have killed, Billy Skipp, does not have to see an Army Air Service captain at her door either. That is something, isn't it?

Love, Jude

Schleiermacher dined with them at six that night. His wound, which had been caused by a wood fragment high up on his shoulder, had been cleaned and dressed and he wore his right arm in a sling. He jabbed at his food, finding it awkward to cut the meat, but wouldn't accept any help. The squadron had many questions for him so Jude was kept busy translating back and forth. The men began to call him Heinrich or, as he said he was referred to at his own squadron or *Jagdstaffel,* Rich. He had been born and raised in Madgeburg, a beautiful medieval city west of Berlin. Yes, he had sisters as beautiful as the city. No, he was not a natural flier. He had been a very poor pilot during training, but finally managed to pass and was given a Pfalz to fly in 1915. His first victory was over a French flier who had survived his crash landing and been taken prisoner. When Tex asked him if he had any brothers flying, Heinrich shook his head.

"No, only one brother, in the army, on the ground."

"Where is he?"

"He died two years ago. Pneumonia in the trenches."

There was an awkward pause in the conversation when Jude translated this. Then

Heinrich said in German, *If pilots flew in trenches none of us would wish to be pilots and none of us would still be alive.* But Jude let the conversation pick up again with questions about Heinrich's *Jagdstaffel* and whether or not he had known von Richthofen, and he never translated Schleiermacher's bitter sentiment.

At one point Timmy Erwin asked if Jude was able to read from the Squadron Bible in both English and German. Jude said that he could and went to the front of the hall. He announced that the evening's reading was from Acts. First he read in English and then in German.

" 'And hath made of one blood all nations of men for to dwell on all the face of the earth, and hath determined the times before appointed, and the bounds of their habitation; that they should seek the Lord, if haply they might feel after him, and find him, though he be not far from every one of us: for in him we live, and move, and have our being; as certain also of your own poets have said, For we are also his offspring.' "

Jude glanced up from time to time as he read. A few of the pilots had given Schleiermacher dark looks on the airfield and had refused to eat with him, pushing their plates aside and never lifting knife or fork. They continued to glare at the German even as words from the Bible filled the room. But Jude could also see that most of his men accepted the code of the air warrior — what happened in the skies was war but it was not personal. If Schleiermacher had killed several of their friends they had also shot down several of his. Had they been the captured pilot sitting in a German mess, Jude knew most of them hoped they would be treated with the same courtesy and respect they were showing their prisoner.

Now, in the quiet following the reading from the Bible, the sound of the German aviator getting up from his seat made everyone look his way. He was standing at attention. Then he bowed his head. Out loud, he began slowly to recite the Lord's Prayer, beginning with the German — *Vater unser im Himmel, geheiligt werde dein Name* — but then switching to English, struggling along as best he could recall.

"Thy kingdom come," he said. "Thy will . . . be done . . . on earth . . . as it is in heaven."

He struggled for the words of the next phrase. The silence was broken as Zed suddenly spoke the German for "give us this day our daily bread" — *Unser tägliches Brot gib uns heute.*

Then Tex: "And forgive us our debts."

The German nodded, his head still bowed. *"Wie auch wir vergeben unsern Schuldigern."*

Flapjack took up the next line of the prayer: "And lead us not into temptation."

Schleiermacher spoke the following verse in English and, as far as Jude could see, the whole squadron joined in, even the pilots who had made it clear they detested him: "But deliver us from evil."

The combined voices made the walls of the French farmhouse ring with an ancient strength as Schleiermacher and the men of the squadron completed the prayer. "For thine is the kingdom, and the power, and the glory, for ever."

Then a sudden quiet.

The German looked around him, his eyes soft. "Amen," he said. "*Danke,* my fellow aviators."

At eleven, Jackson had Heinrich placed in an empty room with a bed and dresser and put an armed guard at the door. Jude remained with him and they talked in German throughout the night. Now it was not about squadrons and planes and Madgeburg and von Richthofen. Instead, they discussed and debated the Christian faith — how it should be lived or how it should not be lived — the Bible, Martin Luther, the Reformation, the Anabaptists, the Swiss Mennonite Jacob Ammann who had founded the Amish movement, why the German soldiers had the phrase *Gott mit uns* inscribed on their helmets.

"Don't you Americans also believe God is with you?" asked Heinrich.

"I'm sure many Americans do. But at home in Paradise, among the Lapp Amish, my church prays for peace for both sides in this conflict. I have heard our pastors pray for Germany as well as France and Britain. Not for someone to win. But for all of them not to keep losing so many of those men they love."

Heinrich didn't know what to think, and the puzzlement on his face reflected this. "You are a member of a strange church, White Knight. I don't know what my papa would do with you. He is such a patriot. God and country." Then he smiled. "Be careful, Judah." It was the name he used instead of Jude. "If your church keeps this up they could be mistaken for Jesus Christ. And you recall what happened to him."

At four in the morning a car came for Heinrich. Jude saw there was another German flier in the vehicle after he had walked outside with Schleiermacher. Heinrich

357

recognized him and leaned in at the open window.

"Schmidt! *Was machst du hier?*"

Schmidt had a sour expression on his face and a guard on either side of him. "My guns jammed."

"Ah. Bad luck."

"Then my engine jammed."

"Ah. Worse luck."

"Then I practically landed in an American trench and in minutes they were all over me. Someone stole my sidearm."

"Ah. Your luck improves. American food. No mushy peas and cock-a-leekie soup. No frog legs or *escargots.*"

"I prefer sauerkraut and *bratwurst.*"

Heinrich smiled. "Judah, if the food is no good, Schmidt here and I will have to make our escape."

"Good luck. I think they are sending you over the Channel. If you manage to get away you will have to survive on British food for weeks."

"Perhaps we will stay put then if they can find us a German cook." He put out his good hand. "*Auf wiedersehen,* Judah. If the war ever ends, and we have both survived, look me up in Madgeburg. Ask for my father, the Reverend Schleiermacher. People will direct you."

"*Danke*. And I extend the same invitation. If you are in America make your way to Paradise, Pennsylvania. Whetstone the blacksmith. People will direct you."

"*Bitte, Judah.*"

"*Gott segne dich, Heinrich.*" God bless you.

The American soldiers gave Jude long, suspicious looks and then climbed back into the motorcar and drove off with their prisoners. He went to bed. He had less than four hours sleep before his batman, Spencer Wilcox of Indiana, woke him.

"Ironwood wants to see you."

"What for?" he groaned.

"Search me."

The commanding officer was leaning against his desk sipping a cup of coffee. He picked another cup off his desk and offered it to his captain.

"Thank you, sir." Jude took it gratefully, the sides of the cup warm on his fingers.

"Stand easy, Captain. I hear you were up half the night."

"Yes, sir. Heinrich and I were discussing theology — among other things."

Jackson barked a laugh. "Heinrich. Theology. I'd like to know what an Amish boy like you has in common with a fighter ace of the German Empire."

"Well, we —"

Jackson put up a hand. "On second thought, I don't want to know. You're an ace yourself, Whetstone. The press corps has been ringing my phone off the hook. No one else has ever brought in an enemy pilot alive and landed them right at their own aerodrome. The White Knight is about to achieve something of a celebrity status."

"That was not my intention," Jude responded.

"I know it wasn't your intention. Your intention was to bring him in alive and to not kill him. I doubt you ever gave a moment's thought to how it would look to the rest of the world." Jackson checked his watch. "You and I have a press conference in fifteen minutes. But that's not why I hauled you out of the sack."

"I'm ready to take the squadron up at any time, sir."

"I'm sure you are." Jackson looked at him over his cup rim. "Did — the German — ever tell you what his fellow pilots thought of you?"

"Well," Jude thought back to the night before. "He said they had great respect for me. That it was obvious I could — fly a plane. They felt my tendency to mercy was — naïve — in modern warfare. Of course, they wanted to bring me down. Heinrich said they were aware of my number — Triple One — and the propaganda value of my bloodless victories that made the Germans look like ruthless barbarians and — Americans appear like Sir Galahads in white hats with silver six guns."

Jackson nodded. "Saving women and children from the black villain. Doing it with an easy grace and magnanimity. You're the true man, and the foes you vanquish and permit to live are something less. A number of the Germans take your mercy as a slap in the face, you know."

"It is not my intention to insult them."

"Doesn't matter. That's how they see it. Our intelligence reports indicate that taking you out of the skies isn't the only thing that matters to the Germans. They'd like to get Rickenbacker and Frank Luke and the Canadians' Billy Bishop as much or more. But you — you they don't want to just shoot down. They want to provoke you to kill one of their own and *then* shoot you down. That way they can tarnish your reputation and make you look as bad as anyone else. No American Sir Galahad. No White Knight."

"Yes, sir," Jude admitted, finishing his coffee. "Heinrich did mention that in passing."

"In passing." Jackson stood up and paced the room with his hands in his pockets.

"What you did yesterday, bringing in one of their greatest aces and forcing him to land at an American aerodrome, will be seen as the ultimate insult. They'll be scouring the skies for you, setting out bait, pushing you to kill, then knocking you out of the air. I used to think they'd be happy enough to take you prisoner. Now I no longer think that. Have you any idea what your mechanic, Mickey, has been up to while you slept?"

Jude frowned. "No. What's the problem?"

"It's not my problem. I think it's a good idea. But it could make you even more of a target. He's painted a white knight on horseback on both sides of your fuselage. The knight is charging ahead with his lance at the ready."

"So you're worried it's putting even more of a bull's-eye on my plane than the Triple One already does?"

"Initially I felt that. Then I got Mickey and his crew to paint the figure on *all* the squadron's aircraft. Like Rickenbacker's 94th outfit has that hat in the ring symbol." Jackson stopped pacing and stared at him. "This is my thinking. If the Huns get you, the squadron lives on and the spirit in which you fought for America lives on. You may kill the man, but you can't kill a squadron.

Does that sound rough?"

Jude turned the empty coffee cup over and over in his hand. "If it's God's will I go down, I go down. But it would be nice if some of the boys really did carry on in — the same spirit — and took Germans out of the sky by putting them in prison camps — and not in their graves."

"That's up to them. They're not Amish."

Jude smiled. "No, sir. Not yet."

Jackson barked his laugh. "You never give up, do you, Whetstone? I shouldn't like you, but I do." He came over and put a hand on his shoulder. "You watch your back, young man. I'd like to invite you to a roundup at my ranch in Cochise, Arizona, after the war. It would please me if you were around to honor the invitation."

"Yes, sir."

Jackson extended his hand and Jude shook it.

"Now let's go meet with those pesky reporters," Jackson growled, opening the door. "We must get our propaganda value out of you before someone signs an armistice and this show is all over."

Lack of sleep and the questions from the press corps weighed Jude down, but after lunch, Lucille and the rest of the squadron's SPADs, all sporting the galloping knight with the lance on their fuselages, took to the sharp autumn air. The bite of the cold at twenty-two thousand feet brought him back to life. Zed forced a Fokker D.VII to crash-land by a British trench, where the pilot was quickly scooped up at gunpoint, but that was it for the sortie, and they returned to an early supper and a celebration meal the cooks had planned for Schleiermacher's capture and Jude making ace.

The next day was dark and heavy with rain, and no one flew. Jude spent a good part of it helping Tex and Billy write letters home to their sweethearts.

"Why do you think I'm some sort of expert on this?" he asked them.

"You've had a gal forever," Tex replied. "And your batman says you mail a letter almost every week. So you must know something."

"What I say to my — gal — and you say to yours, they're two completely different matters."

"Come on, Captain," Billy prodded as the three of them sat in the empty dining room together. "Just a few ideas. Just a few golden opening lines."

Jude sat thinking as the rain banged

against the windows.

"All right," he finally said. "Have you talked about moonlight? And starlight?"

"What?" Tex exclaimed. "In the sky?"

"In — her hair, her eyes. On her skin. Have you mentioned whether the color in her eyes is like . . . a sunset, or dawn, or the sea? What about her voice? Does it remind you of a creek — whispering — as it runs past a grove of cottonwoods near some of your Texas hills? Billy, do her words make you think of, uh, soft summer breezes and . . . the way butterflies move from flower to flower?"

Both of the men gaped at Jude, then began scribbling ideas down on paper.

"Thanks a lot, sir," Tex said as he wrote. "You sure are cookin' with gas."

The next day was full of sun. Jude held Kitty up to the window and turned the model just like a plane flying across the sky. Then he prayed, read his Bible, and dashed off a note to Lyyndaya.

I guess you will read about me in the papers, or someone will tell you, or someone will tell Bishop Zook and he will tell you. I have no idea what our people will think about my bringing in the Blue 9 instead of shooting him down. I'm sure nothing I do will warm their hearts while I'm a military man. Well, you and God are my inspiration. I had no intention of becoming a hero. I just wanted to fight a war and end a war without taking anyone's life. I pray every day I will be able to stick to that. Now that Schleiermacher is out of the picture I hope it will be easier to do.

You know, I really do love you. Whenever you get this, whenever you read this, please take it to heart as one of the truest things I have ever said. You mean the world to me. Now I am heading into the sky and wish you were in that crazy small cockpit with me. Christ bless you forever, Lyyndy.

He placed the note in an envelope, sealed and addressed it, and gave it to his batman. "Spencer, see if you can get this out today."

The young man grinned. "I'll do the best I can, sir. After me and the boys have had a chance to read it first, of course."

Jude laughed and punched him on the arm. "Here's a tip — Billy's and Tex's letters are juicier."

At breakfast it was Flapjack who stood up and read from the Bible — the first time in his life he had done so, he admitted in a rare moment of self-disclosure. A verse had caught his eye when he had been leafing through the tome the evening before. He had one hand in his pocket, the other holding the page, and was slouching a little at the podium — nevertheless his voice was strong and steady and even dramatic.

"'If I take the wings of the morning, and dwell in the uttermost parts of the sea; even there shall thy hand lead me, and thy right hand shall hold me.' "

After everyone had eaten, the White Knight squadron took off as one and flew toward Pont-à-Moussan and Metz. They cruised at twenty thousand feet, looking for German fighter formations or reconnaissance aircraft.

For a long time the blue and white sky was quiet. Jude kept turning his head, looking in every direction, but nothing appeared. Part of his mind began to drift toward Pennsylvania and Lyyndaya, while another part dwelt on reports of food riots in Germany and demonstrations against the war. Could it be possible the German Empire might collapse from within? Could the conflict be over as soon as November or December? He saw himself disembarking from the train in Paradise and Lyyndaya waiting for him in a black carriage. Bishop Zook and the pastors sat nearby in a different carriage. What could he say to the leadership of the church that would convince them to welcome him back? What words could he speak to Lyyndaya to convey all he felt for her after a year's separation? Mulling over these things preoccupied him more and more as the squadron held formation for no-man's-land and Metz.

So he did not realize the Albatros fighters were there until he and his men were under attack, the Germans dropping out of the sun one after another like fireflies, their guns winking and glittering, the bullets tearing into wood and fabric, smoke and flame erupting from his engine, Lucille hurtling through the sky as if she had a mind of her own, Jude with no time left to think, hardly any time left to pray.

TWENTY-TWO

Swallows were rolling across the October fields in dark clouds as Lyyndaya and her sister walked slowly along the road, Ruth leaning heavily on Lyyndaya's arm. The sun was still warm on their faces and there was green in many of the trees, although leaves the color of pumpkins skittered across their path. Their house was only a few hundred yards in front of them and they could see their mother sitting on the porch watching her daughters while pretending to sew a torn pair of pants.

"She's been working on Papa's trousers for more than an hour," said Ruth.

"It must have been a large rip. Perhaps Papa caught it on a nail."

"If only she would relax."

"We almost lost you. I suspect it will be months before she believes you're completely well."

"But the epidemic is over, isn't it? She

knows that?"

"It's not entirely over," Lyyndaya said. "There are still plenty of cases, especially in the cities, and especially in Philadelphia. It's true that things have quieted down, but that can change in a few days or weeks. No one knows when this influenza will die out to the point that the doctors can actually stand up and say to the public there's no longer a reason to fear it."

"No one is sick here that I know of. Are you still thinking of volunteering in a hospital in the city?"

"I don't know. Not until you're stronger."

"I *am* stronger."

"Not strong enough."

"What is that?" Ruth suddenly asked, looking ahead.

"Where?"

"Up the road. It is a motorcar, isn't it?"

Lyyndaya squinted. "Yes."

"We hardly ever see them here."

They watched the vehicle come along the road toward them, then slow and turn in at their house. Their mother stood up and they could see her open the front door and call to someone, probably their father. Sure enough, he came out and stood on the porch with Mama just as the sound of slamming metal doors reached the sisters' ears.

"That's Bishop Zook," said Ruth.

"Yes."

"And soldiers. Officers."

Lyyndaya felt a coldness in her arms and stomach. "Why would they be here?"

"There's no reason for them to be here unless it's about Jude." Ruth looked at her sister's face. "Lyyndy, don't think the worst. They're probably going to give him a medal for bringing in that German pilot you told me about."

"Schleiermacher."

"Who has ever heard of such a thing in a time of war? Why else would they be here?"

As they drew closer the sisters could distinguish more easily between one person and another.

"There's Jude's father," said Lyyndaya.

"You see? It is all right. It's about an honor they're going to bestow."

Yet as they turned into their lane, Ruth determinedly putting one booted foot in front of another, Lyyndaya could almost taste the feeling of dread that rose up in her throat. It seemed that a touch of darkness was drifting toward her from the cluster of people. None of them were laughing or smiling, no one was shaking hands, no one looked relaxed or at ease. It was not a picture of joy.

What has happened? Please, Lord, brace me.

Jude's father stepped down from the porch and came to them, his hands outstretched. "Lyyndaya," he said softly.

She stopped, Ruth leaning against her.

"The men from the army have come to tell us —"

An officer left the larger group by the porch and walked over to them. "Miss Kurtz?"

Lyyndaya hesitated. "We are both Miss Kurtz. We are sisters."

"Miss Lyyndaya Kurtz?"

"Yes."

"Major Robert Trenton. Your bishop told me you have been in something of an intimate relationship with Captain Jude Whetstone for some time. Captain Whetstone's father has said the same thing."

"I would not use the word 'intimate' — but we have been good friends . . ." Lyyndaya stumbled, feeling the blood coming to her face.

"It's important that I tell you what I have already informed the others of. Captain Whetstone was shot down over the German lines about five days ago. I'm very sorry to have to be the one to tell you this."

"Shot down?" Lyyndaya felt her mind going numb and could only keep hearing those words. "Do you have him . . . in the hospital?"

The officer's blue eyes were firm, but not without gentleness. "Officially, he is missing in action. Our doughboys got to the crash site as soon as they could, but it took some time as the position was under German sniper fire. Captain Whetstone was not in the cockpit."

Lyyndaya didn't know what to ask or say. She felt Ruth squeeze her hand with a strength she didn't know she had in her.

"Is he a prisoner of war, Major?" Lyyndaya heard Ruth ask without a trace of illness or weakness in her voice.

"Both sides exchange this sort of information regularly as a courtesy. The Germans do not have him. They assured us that if they did they would be telling everyone about it."

"Then where is he?" Ruth persisted, seeming to gain strength with each question she asked on Lyyndaya's behalf.

Major Trenton was reluctant to voice his opinion, but finally said, "He may have fallen out of the cockpit before his aircraft hit the ground."

Again, Lyyndaya felt Ruth's hand tighten on hers.

"But you have found no body?" Ruth demanded.

"No."

"So he could have escaped from the aeroplane's wreckage after the crash?"

The major looked away. "He might have. However, German troops were concentrated in the vicinity. It's doubtful he could have eluded them. Especially if he had sustained injuries."

"You said he was officially missing in action."

The officer glanced back at them. His face and eyes were rock. "Yes. Missing in action and presumed dead. I'm sorry."

From a great distance, it seemed to Lyyndaya, she heard Major Trenton apologize again, say that it was a great blow to America as well, Captain Whetstone was a genuine hero, even the Germans and Austrians had sent condolences and tributes through official channels, a combat pilot who had never taken a life, who had fought with honor, a man who had brought down one of the German Empire's greatest aces without killing him. A true Christian officer and a gentleman.

"There are some other things I need to tell you," she heard him say. "I feel they would be an encouragement at such a difficult time. But we should go somewhere and sit down, perhaps?"

"Thank you, Major," she heard Ruth say. "Our kitchen would be best for that."

Now Lyyndaya felt her sister guiding her up the porch steps and then through the door into the kitchen. She sat down across from Bishop Zook, whose eyes were dark and kind as they rested on her. Her mother was with her and Ruth. Her father sat on one side of Major Trenton, and Mr. Whetstone on the other. The officers who had accompanied the major elected to stand.

"I should make coffee," Lyyndaya heard her mother say.

"There is already some that our young Sarah has brewed," Lyyndaya's father spoke up. "Let me get a few cups and pour."

"Some water for our daughters, Father."

"Ja, ja."

When a glass of cool well water was placed by Lyyndaya's hand her mother urged her, "Drink, it will help."

Lyyndaya felt as if everyone was sitting farther away from her than they should and the sensation disturbed her. "I can't, Mama."

The major stirred cream and sugar into his coffee. It was so quiet the clicking of his spoon against the sides of his cup sounded like a harsh ringing of bells in Lyyndaya's ears. Finally he put the cup to his lips, drank some, then set it down and looked around the table.

"Captain Whetstone was not alone when this happened. He was with his squadron, so there are several witnesses to what occurred. It seems pretty clear that the captain was hit when he put his plane between one of his men and a German attacker. The Hun had the other American pilot dead to rights and was about to fire directly into him, when the captain hurled his plane in the way of the guns and took the bullets. It set his engine on fire, but he would not leave the fight. His men report that he continued to harass and fly circles around the enemy, as was his custom, in order to throw off their aim and separate them from the planes they were attempting to shoot down. Finally he was hit by a burst of machine-gun fire and his craft went into a spin he couldn't pull out of until the last. He managed to level out just above a field, and then the plane struck the mud and barbed wire and broke up. The other men of the squadron say his craft was smoking badly, but there never was an explosion."

No one responded. Bishop Zook, as was his habit, began to drum on the table with his fingers.

"So, at the end," the bishop said, "he gave life back, he did not take it."

The major cleared his throat. "Well, from what I understand, the way Captain Whetstone went out was the manner in which he usually conducted himself throughout the war." He reached into a pocket of his uniform and read from a small piece of white paper. "I am directed to express to you the regrets of the United States Army Air Service and to convey the personal condolences of the Vice President of the United States, as well as those of President Wilson. Captain Whetstone is posthumously promoted to the rank of major and awarded the Distinguished Flying Cross. A posthumous Congressional Medal of Honor is under consideration. From France, he is awarded the Croix de Guerre."

The major handed the paper to Jude's father and murmured something Lyyndaya couldn't make out. Mr. Whetstone nodded and held the slip of paper tightly in his hand. Then Major Trenton looked directly at her.

"His men mentioned you, Miss Kurtz. Apparently not a week went by that he didn't have his orderly mail something to you. I trust you have received the majority of his letters despite the inevitable delay in postal services during a time of war and when great distances are involved."

Lyyndaya said nothing.

"I am instructed to inform you, in conclusion, that Captain Whetstone served his country, his allies, and — in the words of Vice President Marshall — 'the human race' in the best traditions of the United States Army, and in doing so represented the best the people of the United States of America have to offer the world. He gave his life for the life and liberty of others. *Greater love hath no man than this, that a man lay down his life for his friends.* God rest his soul, and God bless his memory to us and the American Republic."

Lyyndaya remained in her chair while the three men left. Her sister stayed with her while the others accompanied the officers to the door and to their car. She listened to the engine start up and slowly fade in the distance.

"I don't feel anything," she said.

Ruth put a hand on her arm. "That's all right."

"No, it is not all right. Jude meant a lot to me. Why don't I feel anything?"

"Because it's too much, you can't take it in."

"God help me, I want to feel something!"

"Shh, shh. In time you will. In time all you feel will come out of you."

Bishop Zook and the girls' parents returned and sat back down at the table. Lyyndaya's mother looked at her daughter with deep and troubled eyes and rested a hand over hers. The bishop ran large fingers through his dark beard and stared at the wall.

"God's ways are past finding out," he finally said in a low, unhurried voice. "That an Amish boy should be in the army and fly an aeroplane in a war — and then be honored by his country for fighting in that war and never taking a human life. Who can plumb the depths of these things? Who can comprehend the mysteries and wisdom of God?"

He looked at Lyyndaya. "You will remember that I spoke with you a few days after my son's funeral, hm? I asked you not to share what I said."

Lyyndaya nodded, still feeling everyone was sitting far from her and she from them.

"So now I will tell your family." He looked around him from one person to another as he spoke. "Before Hosea died, once he knew . . . he was going to die . . . he takes my shirtfront in his hand, in his fist, and he pulls, you would not think he had such strength left, but it was the strength of a man that drowns. *Jude,* he says to me with what voice he has left, *Jude.* Over and over again. His eyes are desperate for me to understand, but he cannot form all his words, his tongue will no longer help him, and he does not have the breath. *Us,* he says, *us,* and he looks around the room even though we are alone. *All of us, Papa,* he tells me, *all of us.* Then he collapses on his bed and is only able to whisper — *Jude. All of us.*

"Nothing more comes out of him about this again. He dies the next day. Yes, he speaks a few more times, says he loves his mother, asks us to pray for his soul, wants to see Emma, but of course Emma is fighting for her own life and cannot come. What did he mean about Jude, hm? What was it my son wished to convey? I have talked with the pastors, we have prayed and thought and read the Word of God. This is what we understand — that he speaks about the army camp where they were all imprisoned, and that something happened that affected Jude and all of them, something very important. But what? What? The other boys do not know. We do not know. Something needs to be understood, something needs to be revealed. But I myself think that Jude may have been forced to fly. That the others were released on the condition that Jude fly for the army."

He shook his head. "It may be we will never come to an understanding. In any case, Jude is gone and my Hosea is gone. Perhaps it does not matter now." He reached inside his black jacket and brought out a packet of letters bound in twine. "These are yours, my dear." He placed them by her hand. "Jude now faces the Righteous Judge who understands all. The *Meidung* is no longer in force. His words for you belong to you. God bless, my sister. Let me pray."

His hat already hung from a hook by the door. He bowed his head and prayed in High German for five or six minutes. Lyyndaya bent her head along with everyone else, but later she couldn't recall much of what the bishop said to God. Then he looked up.

"There is also this, which the major told me when he first came to my house. Jude's squadron has sworn to avenge him. But how will they do this? As our world would do such a thing, and kill as many Germans as possible? No, they wish to make every effort to honor him by taking German planes from the sky and putting the pilots in prisoner-of-war camps. That is what they intend. The major told me they realize they do not share all of Jude's convictions, and that many times the only thing they will be able to do is shoot the enemy down in flames. Yet, they want to try to win the bloodless victories Jude won and see their enemies behind walls of wire, not under mounds of earth. So that also is something. That also is the hand of God."

He finished speaking. Slowly he got to his feet and left, taking his hat and placing it on his head. Slowly Lyyndaya went up the staircase with Ruth, both of them leaning on one another.

In their room, they each sat down on their bed.

Slowly, Lyyndaya untied the twine and opened a letter.

It was dated July seventeenth. She started to read out loud — *"My dear, sweet Lyyndy, how I wish we were up in the air together every day, how I hate flying alone . . ."* but then she couldn't continue, and the pain she hadn't felt, and the tears that wouldn't come, suddenly swept through her body like a wind and came out of her mouth in a loud cry. Ruth threw her arms around her and rocked her while she wept.

"Oh, Jude, oh, Jude, oh, my friend . . . I

thought . . . my Lord, I thought . . . you had promised him to me as a husband —"

Their mother rushed into the room and put her arms around Lyyndaya along with Ruth. They cried out together, heads and bodies touching. In the doorway stood her father, his eyes glistening with tears, watching them. After some time the weeping stopped, and Lyyndaya asked her mother and father to stay in the room and hear some of Jude's letters. They sat on her bed and sometimes Ruth read out loud, sometimes Mother, and then when Lyyndaya had enough strength and composure, she read the letters to the others herself, though not without tears or sharp stabs of anguish. Even the most intimate dreams Jude shared she read to the others because she wanted them to know who he really was and how real their love had grown until a war had ended it.

There were nineteen letters. After they were done Lyyndaya lay down in the dark alone while her mother and father and Ruth went downstairs to eat supper with the rest of the family. For the longest time she could not close her eyes or sleep. The window faced east, and she watched a small moon rise and scatter drops of silver on the walls and across her bed. She thought of Naomi in the Bible telling others to call her by the name Mara, because God had made her life bitter, but she realized she didn't feel that way. Millions had lost their sons and husbands and fiancés to the war. Millions had lost their families to the Spanish flu. She was just one among many who were grieving. The letters had filled her to the brim with his love for her. Thank God she had known him, thank God he had written, thank God he had said the things he had said.

Before the moon slipped out of the window frame she prayed a prayer of thanks, despite the ache that went through her whole being. She committed Jude's soul into the hands of the loving and merciful God. Softly, under her breath, she sang a hymn the English liked, one the Lapp Amish never sang at church, the one called "Amazing Grace." The non-German words sounded strange on her tongue, but the thoughts the writer expressed, and the melody, comforted her. When there were only stars in the window she finally closed her eyes and slept, the letters carefully folded under her pillow.

TWENTY-THREE

"May I see your health certificate, please?"

Lyyndaya presented the conductor with the document Dr. Morgan had signed. He nodded and stepped aside to let her board the train. Behind her, a woman protested.

"What's this? The Spanish flu ended months ago."

"No, ma'am," responded the conductor. "We have another outbreak this January and it's particularly bad in Philadelphia."

"How can that be?"

"I expect it's the soldiers returning home now the war's over. A lot of them could be bringing it with them from Europe. May I see your certificate?"

The woman grew more indignant. She put her hands on her hips and her face reddened in anger. "I need no certificate! My husband has been home for well over a week now, thank you very much. He has no symptoms and neither do I!"

"That's wonderful. Now if you'll get a licensed physician to attest to that in writing and fill out one of those medical slips —"

"I'll do no such thing. Anyone can see I'm fit as a horse. You let me on board, sir. I have important business in Philadelphia."

"Sorry, ma'am. It wouldn't be fair to the other travelers. You could be fit at the depot here and be dead on us by lunch."

The woman's voice rose. "I have no intention of dropping dead on anyone by lunch. I have too much to do. If you won't let me on board I'll find a police officer or introduce you to my attorney, Mr. Eldon Snikkitt . . ."

Lyyndaya found a seat and settled in. She watched two men shovel snow off the platform, their breath coming in puffs of white. Near them a man and wife and four children were making no effort to board. They must have been waiting for the train that went to Pittsburgh or some other connection. All of them wore white medical masks over their noses and mouths.

I don't think it will help. But you might as well try.

Ever since the news about Jude, she had been spending each week volunteering at one of the large hospitals in Philadelphia, with the blessing of the Amish leadership. Every Monday she took the train into the city and on Friday night she returned to her family in Paradise. Now and then the influenza reasserted itself in Lancaster County, but the cases were infrequent and Dr. Morgan didn't require her assistance. In fact, Ruth was working closely with the doctor now and that was the only nursing help he seemed to need.

Philadelphia was another story. One outbreak of the flu would scarcely die out before another would take its place. The conductor may have been right. Since soldiers had begun returning to Pennsylvania in late November and December, Lyyndaya had noticed a surge in the number of cases. There had been weeks when there were so many dead that volunteers had been forced to stack them like logs in the hallway outside of the hospital's morgue. There was nowhere to put them but in the ground, and she had been witness to more than one mass burial. Many times she had said to herself, *This is what I read in the newspapers about the war. These are the deaths beyond counting in the trenches.*

The whistle blew. The woman who had argued with the conductor had not made it on board. Lyyndaya glanced back through the window and saw that she had managed to find a policeman, but the officer, who was wearing one of the medical masks, was leading her away rather than insisting she be allowed to board. They pulled out of the station and were soon lumbering through the January countryside of snow and brown grass. Lyyndaya closed her eyes and leaned her head for a moment against the ice-cold of her window.

Everything is stiff and dead. Just like me.

Near the end of December an army car had brought a box of Jude's personal items to his father — a Bible, pens and paper, socks and shoes and clothing, a spare uniform, a toothbrush, the wooden model of the *Flyer.* Mr. Whetstone had found the letters his son had received from Lynndaya and had passed them on to her, along with a leather flying jacket. She never wore the jacket, but she kept it in the closet in her room. Around the same time a letter had come from an Amish woman who lived at Bird-in-Hand. She told Lyyndaya that Jude had written her a nice note after locating her brother Matt at an aerodrome in France. She knew Lyyndaya couldn't receive letters from Jude, just as she couldn't receive them from Matt, but she wanted to tell her that Jude had sounded cheerful and had lifted a stone from her heart with his good news about her brother who, thank God, had survived the war.

A final letter from Jude had shown up at the post office January fourth. Edward, who had taken every opportunity to remind her about his prophetic abilities since the war had ended on November eleventh, handed it to her in silence. Lyyndaya asked Ruth to sit with her while she read it through, something that was far from easy. The letter was short and had been written the day his plane went down. The ending broke her heart.

You know, I really do love you. Whenever you get this, whenever you read this, please take it to heart as one of the truest things I have ever said. You mean the world to me. Now I am heading into the sky and wish you were in that crazy small cockpit with me. Christ bless you forever, Lyyndy.

In Philadelphia, a horse-drawn cab took her to the home of Mrs. Henrietta Thorndike, who billeted several of the young women from out of town who were volunteering at the hospital during the crisis. A wealthy widow whose husband had invested in the Pennsylvania railroads but had died in the summer during the first flu outbreak, Mrs. Thorndike wouldn't accept any payment for food or rent. It was her way, she told Lyyndaya, of helping others work against the disease that had taken her husband's life.

"It's my Christian duty," she said. "You, an Amish woman, must appreciate that."

"Of course I do," Lyyndaya had replied. "I suppose, Mrs. Thorndike, you could say the same thing about me."

The older woman's eyes softened. "Did you lose someone to this pestilence, my dear?"

"I — lost someone I cared about very much — to the war." Lyyndaya still found it difficult to talk about. "Perhaps, like you, I wish to save as many lives as I can. Whether they are civilians or soldiers. There has already been enough death."

Several times over the fall and winter Mrs. Thorndike had sat down and patiently drawn out of Lyyndaya the story of herself and Jude. The shunning had angered her, Jude's self-sacrifice in France for the life of one of his pilots had caused her to weep, a China teacup trembling in her fingers. Now and then both women would, by common consent, agree to pray together. Lyyndaya admitted to herself that their moments of prayer were one of the few things that gave her any lasting comfort.

"I am a good Episcopalian," Mrs. Thorndike had pointed out, "and you have been raised Amish in Lancaster County. But our Lord God takes no note of such things when it comes to prayer and worship. We are the same in his eyes. And he treats us the same."

At the Thorndike house Lyyndaya changed into her work clothing — a dark dress and apron that wouldn't show the blood, a black prayer covering, her most comfortable shoes. Then a cab took her to the hospital. Sometimes she shared the ride with one or more of the other young women staying at Mrs. Thorndike's. They were never charged cab fee from the train station or to and from the hospital. One young cabbie with a small black mustache spoke for his fellows — "We knows what you're doin' for our people and we thank you for it. One day it could be one of us or one of our own loved ones we're countin' on you to save. This we're doin' for you here is a small thing, a very small thing."

Mondays were difficult. Patients Lyyndaya had been caring for and had left regaining their health on a Friday were often dead and buried by the time she returned. This Monday was no different. Old faces had vanished and new ones had taken their place. Shar Hayden, one of the young women who boarded at Mrs. Thorndike's, handed her a basin of cool water and a stack of clean cloths as she appeared at her usual ward.

"Here, Fritzie," she greeted Lyyndaya. "There are some new soldier boys at the end of the hall. You like soldier boys, don't you? So this is right up your alley."

Lyyndaya had long ago learned to ignore Shar's jibes at her German accent. "Who are they?"

"I don't know." She tugged a folded sheet of paper from a dress pocket. "Timmy Cameron. Ross Campbell. Jules Witsun. Sam Irving. Sorry. None of your German boys to fuss over."

"Do they have battle wounds?"

"I really don't know. Maybe the Kaiser missed these ones. Dr. Levy thought they might be exhibiting some symptoms. The last room. All crammed in together."

"But the last room is so tiny!"

Shar shrugged and hurried off. "All crammed in together. No mattresses. Guess they aren't war heroes."

"Every man who suffered through that

terrible war in Europe is a hero," Lyyndaya said to Shar's retreating back.

"Especially the Huns?"

Lyyndaya made her way in the opposite direction, passing nurses and orderlies and two men in masks who were carrying a dead soldier, still in uniform, out a side door. A gust of January air made her take in her breath sharply. She glanced through the doorway and saw a pile of bodies that had been stacked in the snow. One of the men coming back in saw the look on her face and snapped, "It's as good as a morgue. Don't worry, they don't feel anything."

Lyyndaya prayed for the man, who looked exhausted and ill himself, then went to the end of the hall to what had once been a storage room for buckets and mops and such. The four men were shoulder to shoulder, head to head, each with only a woolen blanket beneath them and the cold bare floor, and another on top. A couple of them looked up when she opened the door. One man grinned.

"Hey, boys. Wake up. This nurse is pretty. Not like the other."

Another man craned his neck. "Yeah, but she looks religious."

"She ain't religious. You ain't religious, are you, honey?"

Lyyndaya smiled and knelt by him. "I'm a Christian. Just like you. Yes?"

The man stared at her as she felt his forehead. "Yeah, I guess so."

"You're pretty warm. Sam?"

"Ross."

"I'm Sam," said the man lying next to Ross.

Lyyndaya began to wipe Ross's face and neck. "How does that feel?"

"Very nice." Ross had suddenly become polite.

"All of you could use shaves."

"It was such a shambles crossing the Channel," grumbled Ross, "and no better when we got back to England. I started getting the aches and chills and my unit embarked for the States while I was laid up. Lost my shaving kit. The four of us here are some of the odds and ends that got packed into the same steamer. I kept telling them I was better, but they drove me here anyway. Under guard."

"Where's home, Ross?"

"Idaho."

"Well, you'll need to be fit for a long train ride like that. Better let us keep an eye on you for a few days."

"In a few days we'll probably be dead. There're more sick people in Philadelphia than there were in the trenches. Excuse me for saying so, but this hospital of yours is like a graveyard."

"That's why you are isolated here in one of our finest rooms. To keep the germs far away." She wrung out her cloth and turned to the other man. "How about you, Sam? Any aches? Trouble breathing? Do you have a cough?"

"You sound like a doctor."

She laughed. "Oh, I can't help that. I spend so much time with them." She felt the side of his face. "You don't seem to have a fever."

"I'm okay. Like Ross says, I was feelin' real lousy in France so they left me behind. That was weeks ago. If I'd had the flu I'd be dead by now, wouldn't I?"

Lyyndaya didn't answer him. "What about the other two?"

"Don't know them," said Ross.

Lyyndaya glanced over at the sleeping men. Their backs were to her. She shook her head. "I can't stand the sight of your beards. Heaven knows what is living in them. Will you let me take them off?"

"Fine with me," said Ross. "I haven't had a woman shave my face in my entire life."

Lyyndaya patted him on the arm and stood up. "So then this will be a late Christmas present. Let me fetch a razor and some shaving soap."

How strange that an Amish woman should be in this setting. But you would have me here, wouldn't you, Lord? I do this for you, I do it for these poor men and for their families who wait for them at home — I do it for you, Jude, for you were one of them, you suffered, and you tried to give lives back, not take them away.

She returned bearing a mug, a cake of soap, scissors, and a brush in one hand, and a razor in the other. When she walked in, one of the men who had been sleeping was up on his feet facing her. It was heartbreaking to see him like that, so thin, barely standing really, almost ready to fall over, hair straggling over his face and in his eyes.

"Oh," she said. "I don't think you're quite well enough to be up and around."

But the man remained on his feet and didn't speak. Lyyndaya looked for help from the others.

"Why is he on his feet? He could hurt himself."

Ross was propped up on an elbow. "I don't know. He stood up right after you left the room. Then he started using your name. I guess it's your name."

She was startled. "How could he know

my name?"

Ross shrugged. "He keeps saying something. Maybe it's another word. Maybe it's another person. Maybe he's got the fever."

"Len— Lin— La," tried Sam. "Something like that."

For the first time Lyyndaya looked closely at the man standing in front of her. Past the bushy beard and long hair his eyes pulled her in. The mug dropped from her fingers and broke.

"No!" she said.

The man tried to take a step, but almost collapsed. He steadied himself. He didn't take his eyes off her.

"Lyyn . . . daya," he said in a voice hardly stronger than a whisper.

"Oh, mein Gott!" she cried out. *"Oh, mein Gott in Himmel!"*

Everything else tumbled from her hands. She rushed to the man and held him tightly in her arms so he couldn't fall. Her hands were pushing the beard back from his face and brushing the hair out of his eyes in a frantic way, as if both were on fire. Then she began to cry and laugh and kiss his cheeks, his eyebrows, his forehead, holding him with so much strength she thought she might be hurting him, but she couldn't hold back, couldn't stop herself, all the time calling out to God in Pennsylvania Dutch.

The other three men looked at one another. Finally Ross shook his head and raised his eyebrows.

"I guess one of us should have tried to stand up," he said.

TWENTY-FOUR

Take me home, he had said to her. *Take me home to my father, to my people.* After three more days under observation he was declared symptom-free and safe to travel by one of the doctors. Lyyndaya shaved off his beard, cut his hair, and had one of the orderlies give him a thorough bath. Then she dressed him in new clothes, plain clothes, which she had purchased at one of the downtown shops. She had health certificates for both of them and white masks she insisted they wear.

"I feel like a train robber," he mumbled.

"There is nothing on a train to Lancaster County to steal," she said with a smile, her arm through his.

"You're not acting very Amish."

"Why? Because I'm touching you?" She hugged him until his back popped. "I'm never going to let you go again. God does not often give a person miracles like this more than once in a lifetime."

More than once before he was released from the hospital she had told him, *I do not understand, I do not understand.*

And every time he had patiently told her his story again, sometimes adding new details or dropping old ones.

"I got out of the wreckage. No matter what they tell you, the German soldiers did not shoot at me. I know some of them saw me climb free and crawl away and yet they didn't raise their rifles. My head was throbbing and my mouth was full of blood and I was disoriented. Which way was east? Which west? I was certain I was making my way toward the Allied lines, but I kept running into heavier and heavier concentrations of German troops. Finally I was worn out, and I found an abandoned trench, where I kept out of sight. There were dead men near me, and I slept among them so I would look dead too. But few troops were near as night fell and I doubt anyone looked while I slept.

"The next day I didn't move. But that night I crawled toward a cluster of farmhouses and hid in a barn. The owners found me, but you must have been praying a great deal. This family had no love for the Kaiser and his army. They fed me, cleaned my wounds, put me in

a spare bed, and it was there I remained until the Armistice. Of course everything on the German side of the lines was in chaos by then. Soldiers were even more trigger-happy. So I stayed put another week and then said goodbye — not easily done, they had saved my life — and made my way back the few miles to the lines. I wanted to get to my aerodrome, but the French picked me up and took me to Toul. I wound up all the way north at the Marne and Chateau Thierry. They dropped me off with the Americans there.

"The wound in my mouth had broken open again and made it difficult for me to speak clearly, so they put me down as Jules Witsun. I didn't find this out for a long time. I think it was in England an officer kept bellowing for Captain Jules Witsun, U.S. Army Air Service, and I ignored him until someone said, 'That's him over there,' and he was pointing at me. I tried to correct the error, but it just made the spit-and-polish military types suspicious so I let it go and stayed Jules Witsun. I knew that if I could just get someone to believe me, the news would reach you and my father and the church. But I never had the chance and then I came down with a bad fever.

"I didn't have the Spanish flu. How could I? I was still alive three weeks later. But they wouldn't put me on a steamer until late Janu-

ary. Lost my appetite on those winter seas —
how I wish they would have let me try to fly a
plane across the Atlantic! With almost no food
I lost the strength I'd built up and I was as
weak as a kitten when we disembarked in
New York. They sorted us out and of course
anyone from Pennsylvania or further south
got shunted by rail to Philadelphia. Doctors
examined me and decided I might be showing
symptoms so into the hospital I went. Still
Jules Witsun. I made one final effort to get it
straightened out, I tried to tell them my serial
number, but no one was interested. They all
thought I was off my head."

"And then what?" Lyyndaya always asked,
knowing the answer.

He smiled at her. "Then I heard the voice
of *der Engel* and woke up. I looked over and
saw that, *ja,* it was the angel with golden
hair and eyes green as sunlight on emeralds.
You left, but I was certain you would be
back. So I pushed myself to my feet. I knew
you had no idea I was in the room, no idea
I was behind all that hair. I had just enough
strength to hold on until you noticed me.
Then — I was in heaven — oh yes, heaven,
for the angel was holding me and kissing
me, something this angel had never done.
And it was better than all the daydreams
that had sustained me for so long. Much

402

better." He sighed. "I thank God the epidemic is over."

"Ah, no." Lyyndaya stroked his face. "How I wish that were true, my love. The disease has come and gone many times and I'm certain we'll see more of it before it's finished with us." Then she hugged him. "But the war is over, that is true, and for that I'm very grateful."

Jude's father and Lyyndaya's father both met them at the station in Paradise. Jude had sent a telegram ahead. Mr. Whetstone was standing by his horse and buggy. When Jude and Lyyndaya stepped off the train he did something he had not done for twenty years or more. He ran.

Pulling the mask off his son he kissed him and hugged him with a strength that shouldn't have been possible. Tears poured down his cheeks. He kept murmuring praise to God in Pennsylvania Dutch. Then he held his son at arm's length.

"Jude," he said.

Quietly waiting his turn, Mr. Kurtz also took Jude in his arms and held him a long time. "Welcome. Welcome home."

They took the buggy back to the Whetstone house. It was a crisp, bright January day with snow glistening on the fields and the sky a deep luminous blue over their heads. Jude had not thought he would experience any strong emotions other than what he knew he would feel upon seeing his father. But once he stepped down from the carriage and walked around back to look at the smithy he found it difficult to control himself. He placed a hand on his father's face and another on Lyyndaya's and said, "I was certain I would never see either of you again — or you, Mr. Kurtz. When the plane was going down, never, never did I think I would survive."

At the kitchen table Jude and his father and Mr. Kurtz had coffee while Lyyndaya sipped a cup of hot cocoa. Jude told the two men what it had been like in England and France and talked about his Aero Squadron, things he had already told Lyyndaya in greater detail. He didn't go into what had happened on various sorties or dogfights, but the men did want to know about the plane crash so Jude explained how he had pulled himself from the wreckage and evaded capture.

Knowing he would be telling all this many times over, he sketched out what happened with the family that had taken him in and how he had wound up back across the Channel and eventually on a steamer bound for New York.

"You come out of a war alive," his father said, "yet this terrible influenza, this little germ, could have taken you from me as easily as a bullet."

Lyynadya nodded. "That's what is so sad. A boy makes it home from the trenches and dies in Boston or Philadelphia. It doesn't seem right."

"No, no," murmured Mr. Kurtz, "all is not as it should be until Christ returns."

Sunlight drenched the room and made Lyyndaya's hair sparkle like the snow. Jude found he couldn't take his eyes off of her. It seemed to him he was seeing her for the first time — not on a train, not in a hospital setting, not as a girl of eighteen but a young woman now almost twenty who had grown up a great deal in his absence, whose beauty was fuller and richer and more dazzling.

Lyyndaya was acutely aware of his gaze. She kept on quietly drinking her cocoa, but let the sensation of his undisguised attraction for her run like warm water through her body. At one point, as they sat making conversation, she decided they had been through too much, including almost losing one another forever, for her to play the modest Amish woman who pretends the man's eyes are not upon her. So she met his gaze, her green eyes colored with the light from the windows, held it, and smiled with all the love for him she had within her. He didn't break eye contact and they sat smiling and staring at one another, leaving Mr. Whetstone and her father to toy with their coffee cups, glance out the windows, and finally clear their throats almost in unison.

"Perhaps, my boy, you are wondering why we two were the only ones at the station?" asked Jude's father.

Jude broke his gaze with Lyyndaya and looked at his father like a man who has just woken up. "I did expect to see the bishop or pastors. And all of Lyyndaya's family."

His father nodded. "They will be here. The leadership first. Then anyone from the church who wishes. It was arranged this way so that we might have time alone together."

"That's very kind of them."

"It was our good bishop's idea. If it were up to Pastor Miller or Pastor King they'd have been here an hour ago."

Jude raised his eyebrows. "Lyyndy told me the *Meidung* had been lifted."

"Only because they thought you were dead. Now it is a different matter."

"So they will want me to confess and repent?"

"I think so, *ja*."

Jude sighed and leaned back in his chair with his coffee, looking at the three of them. "It's the big mystery, isn't it? Why did a good Amish boy go to war? Even my commanding officer didn't understand it. Well, I can't explain it beyond this: it was necessary that I enlist. That's all I can say. I did it to save lives. There is no more to it than that."

His father was listening closely to his son's words. He half-smiled. "It is enough for me. It will not be enough for Pastor Miller."

Lyyndaya leaned forward. "But why not, Papa?" She had taken to calling him that since Jude had been arrested and taken from them in September of 1917. "Everyone knows the news stories. Even Pastor Miller. How Jude did not kill. How he took Germans prisoner and didn't shoot them. How —"

Mr. Whetstone put up a hand. "It doesn't matter. He put on a uniform and went to fight. That's all they will see."

"If he had not put on the uniform and gone to fight," Lyynadya argued, "he would not have been able to save the lives he saved. Men would be dead who now shall live."

Mr. Whetstone shook his head and stood up. "Your fight is not with me, my dear. It's with the leadership. And they are here now.

407

I will fetch more cups."

Lyyndaya craned her neck to look out a window. "All four of them at the same time?"

"They were already meeting together and praying at the bishop's." He stopped a moment and watched them climb down from their buggies.

The bishop was first through the door. He swept Jude into his massive embrace and laughed. "My boy, my boy, praise God, *Gelobt sei Gott,* such miracles he bestows. You look well, very well."

"The longer I'm here in Paradise," Jude replied, "the better I feel."

"Wonderful, this is wonderful, how good is our God."

"Danke," said Jude. "I'm sorry, truly sorry, for your loss of Hosea and John and Annie."

A shadow flitted in and out of the bishop's eyes. "Thank God, they are both safe in the arms of Jesus."

Pastor Stoltzfus hugged him as well. *"Alle Dinge sind möglich bei Gott.* All things are possible with God, huh? Welcome home. *Willkommen.* God bless you."

Pastor King shook his hand warmly. "Such a blessing, such a surprise, God continues to astonish us all. It is good to see you, Jude."

Pastor Miller shook Jude's hand briefly and nodded. "God is beyond our comprehension. That is why we honor Him."

"Yes," Jude responded.

At the table Bishop Zook and Pastor Stoltzfus asked Jude all sorts of questions about his health and his journey back from Europe. In time, Jude recounted what had happened on his final flight; how he had crashed, crawled free, and made it to the farmhouse in Lorraine. Pastor King listened attentively, but Pastor Miller sat stiffly in his chair, looking past Jude to the wall and windows. When Jude brought the story to Philadelphia and Lyyndaya and how she had found him, Bishop Zook nodded and drummed his fingers on the table.

"What was meant to be, God has brought to pass," he said. "Clearly, you two will be together." He smiled at Lyyndaya and Jude. "So you and your father may remain in the room, Lyyndaya." He looked at Mr. Whetstone. "You must also stay." He sat up. "There are important things to discuss. We should pray. Pastor Stoltzfus?"

Pastor Stoltzfus got to his feet and prayed for several minutes. Then he sat down and before anyone else could say a word Pastor

Miller pointed at Jude with his finger. "You told us once you would never use a plane in war. That you would never bear arms. Was this not a lie?"

"Gently, gently," said Bishop Zook in a reproving tone. "Remember he is only this day out of the hospital."

But Pastor Miller appeared not to have heard the bishop. "My Samuel didn't feel he had to enlist to get out of that army camp. And his trust in God was rewarded for he was released only hours after you made a decision that flew in the face of everything you said you believed, *ja,* and in the face of the Lord Jesus Christ and the Amish people. Think if you have waited, think if you had relied on Him who alone can move heaven and earth. You would not have had to put on a uniform. Or go into combat. Or kill others."

"He did not kill others," Mr. Whetsone spoke up softly. There was iron underneath his words.

Pastor Miller ignored him and raced on. "All of our boys were released. God did not overlook one of them. They returned to Paradise and their church. You were meant to return with them. Why did you not wait on God, Jude Whetstone?"

Jude paused before speaking, then said,

"Certainly I prayed before I did what I did, Pastor Miller. You can believe that."

"*Ja?* And what kind of prayer was it? The other boys pray and they come home and live in peace. You pray and leave us to make war thousands of miles away. What kind of prayer leads you to do this?"

"I felt . . . I must do it."

"Why?"

"Lives were at stake — souls were at stake."

"So you pick up a gun and bombs and suddenly you have saved these souls? Our Lord dies on the cross, but you wield a gun and bring salvation?"

Bishop Zook raised a large hand. "Excuse me. I have some thoughts on this. Jude, tell me, tell us — did the army force you to fly? Is that what happened?"

Jude met the bishop's gaze. "I can't answer that."

"Why? Why can you not answer?"

"I'm sorry, Bishop Zook."

"Then I will ask one of your friends who was there." The bishop looked up and gestured to Samuel Miller who he had spotted through a window. The young man hesitated, looking at his father, and finally entered the house and came to the table.

"Hello, Sam," smiled Jude, getting up and

extending his hand.

Sam gave Jude a small smile and shook his hand. "Welcome back. I'm glad you're safe and well."

"For months some thoughts have been turning over and over in my head, Samuel," the bishop spoke up. "I wonder if you cannot help me clear up some matters concerning Jude?"

Sam stood stiffly as all their eyes fell upon him. "Of course. If I can help."

"It is a simple question. At the camp where you were all detained was Jude approached by the army and ordered to enlist? Was your release based on whether or not he complied with the army's demand?"

Sam stumbled. "I — I —"

"Come, my son," his father, Pastor Miller, said. "You have nothing to fear. Before God and before us, speak the truth. Was Jude ordered to fly a warplane as a condition of your release and the release of the others?"

Sam stared down at his father. "No. Jude was not ordered to join the army. It was what he wanted to do."

"Are you certain?" pressed Bishop Zook. "Speak freely."

"I am certain. Our release had nothing to do with Jude. He joined the army and fought in the war because it was what he desired. That is what he told me."

"Enough." Pastor Miller glared at the men seated at the table and at Jude. "It is not my son who is on trial here. We have heard all we need to hear. It is just as we thought all along."

"Pastor Miller, if I may," intervened Pastor Stoltzfus. "Jude, this need not be drawn-out, huh? You did what you did for reasons I don't think any of us will ever understand. So, all right, but here is what I want to know — do you see what you have done as a sin? Is this something you wish you had never said yes to, this soldier thing? Do you repent of your actions in joining the United States military? Tell us."

Jude drew a circle in some spilled sugar near his hand. "I wish I had not had to do what I did. I wish there had never been a war. If I'd had the choice, I would have returned to Paradise and never put on a uniform."

"Of course you had the choice!" snapped Pastor Miller. "Just like the others did!"

"Shh," admonished Bishop Zook, putting a finger to his lips.

"But joining the army felt like the right choice before God," Jude said. He took a breath, then added, "If I had to do it again I would not change a thing."

The room was silent at Jude's words. There would be no repentance.

"Before God!" Pastor Miller finally snarled, slapping his hand loudly on the table.

Jude looked at him. "You must think I like war. You must think I wanted to be an ace. That I desired the glory of it all. Nothing is further from the truth. I did not want attention and I did not ask for acclaim. But I wasn't wrong to follow the course of action I did."

"Not wrong?" repeated Pastor King. "War is not wrong? You, an Amish boy, taking up arms and violence, this is not wrong? Conflict between nations — this is a great thing?"

Jude shook his head. "War, combat, burning aircraft — no, it is not right. I felt led to go into something bad, very bad, in order to do something good. That is as simply as I can put it."

"Do you mean this?" demanded Pastor King. "You felt you should step into the carnage of human warfare and act as some sort of redeemer?"

"I only wished to obey God and follow in the footsteps of Jesus, as the Scripture commands us. He went about doing good and healing all who were oppressed by the devil.

So I thought I could bring some light, some holiness, into what was bleak and godless and destructive —"

"You dare." Pastor Miller had risen to his feet, face dark, his hat in his hand. "You dare to call upon Jesus as an example to justify your wicked deeds? He comes in peace and dies for us. You come clothed in war that kills. You dare!" He pushed his hat firmly on his head and looked at Bishop Zook. "You know what my feelings are about this. I'm glad young Jude has survived to return to his father. But I will not tolerate his presence in our church until he is made pure. The *Meidung* must be reinstated until he confesses and repents. I have nothing more to say. Nor do I wish to be here when the other families come to welcome him back. Good day."

He didn't slam the door as he left, but closed it with a firmness that continued to express his anger. Sam left with him. Lyyndaya sat in a stupor, upset by Pastor Miller's obvious dislike of Jude, but also turning Jude's answers over in her head. Could she agree with him? If he didn't repent and was not permitted to live freely among them again, would she be willing to leave her family and her people to go with him wherever the Lord led? Did she believe that God was

415

at work in Jude's life despite his having gone to war? Did she honestly think he was a good Christian man?

"So, so, so," murmured Bishop Zook. "We discussed this possibility before we came to the Whetstones', hm? Did we not say that if Jude did not immediately repent we would wait fourteen days and ask him again? We came to this decision due to the fact he is only recently returned from the grimness of war and a dreadful disease. We wanted to give him more time to think matters over." He looked at the two remaining pastors. "Shall we abide by that decision?"

Pastor Stoltzfus grunted. Pastor King ran his fingers over his beard and finally nodded.

"Recall that this decision to allow Jude the space of fourteen days to repent was made after much prayer." The bishop stood up. "Is this all right with you, young man? We do not welcome one of our people back one minute only to shun them the next. You must have time."

"Thank you," responded Jude.

"But also you must bear in mind who we are, the kind of people you have been part of for ten years. You have put us in a difficult position. We love you. We are grateful for the kind of man you were in the war. Yet

416

still it was a war, hm? You fought in it. You were a soldier. We Amish — we do not fight in wars. We do not engage in violence. We do not put on the uniform."

"I know."

He placed a hand on Jude's shoulder. "It does not sound to me as if you are going to change your mind. We shall certainly not change ours. But — who knows? Perhaps you will view things differently in a few days."

He walked toward the window that overlooked the drive. "I will remind Pastor Miller of this fourteen-day period we agreed upon. Now, I see our first families are arriving. You will stay, Pastor Stoltzfus? Pastor King?"

"We are pastors to all the people," replied Pastor King.

Lyyndaya's father poured more coffee into Bishop Zook's cup. "I'm not satisfied with Samuel's response or Jude's silence. Someone in the army knows the truth of the matter. With your permission, I will write an old friend who has been transferred to the War Department in Washington. His mother is Amish and lives at Bird-in-Hand so even though Nicholas has become English he knows us and understands us."

Bishop Zook nodded and walked back to

the table to take up his cup of coffee. "Why not? Truth is truth regardless of where it comes from, hm?"

Mr. Kurtz looked at Jude. "I'm sorry to interfere. But there is something you are not telling us that we need to know. That *I* need to know."

Jude shrugged. "Do what you think you must."

"It is not my wish to violate what you believe you must keep within, but —"

"Mr. Kurtz, I would rather you did nothing. Yet if you feel compelled to act, that this is God's will for you, then you should go ahead, *nicht wahr?*"

Mr. Kurtz stared at Jude and nodded, his face set. "I do feel it is God's will, yes."

The first person through the door was Lyyndaya's mother, surprising Jude by throwing her arms around him and kissing him on the cheek, her eyes glimmering with tears.

"So God blesses you and blesses us," she said. "Welcome home, oh, thank God, look at you, how strong you look."

"I have had good nursing," Jude replied, hugging Mrs. Kurtz back.

"Oh, yes," laughed Lyyndaya, "I did everything."

Then the kitchen filled. Daniel and Harley

418

Kurtz were asking if he had come by aeroplane and where it might be parked, Benjamin Kauffman was slapping him on the shoulder, Peter King and Luke Kurtz wanted to know if he had left the army and whether he would still fly whether he was in the army or not. Emma Zook came up to him towing Samuel Miller by the hand.

"Jude, it is so very good to see you again," she gushed.

"Thank you, Emma. I'm glad you're looking so well after your illness."

"That was months ago. I'm as strong as a Percheron. Just not so big, I hope."

"You look like the same perfect Emma."

"Do I? Why, thank you." She tugged Sam forward and hugged his arm briefly. "Did Lyyndaya tell you we're engaged?"

Jude nodded. "Yes, she did mention that when we were back in Philadelphia. Great news. I'm happy for both of you."

"Of course we can't get married until November," pouted Emma. "That's the Amish way, you know."

"A long wait."

"But worth the wait." Emma hugged Sam's arm again.

The families had brought food, and the welcome turned into a meal that lasted several hours. Afterwards, once everything had been cleaned up and the buggies were rattling down the lane toward the road, Mr. Kurtz leaving with the rest of his family, Lyyndaya took Jude's hand in hers.

"How was that?" she asked him.

He smiled. "It was fine, Lyyndy. Thank goodness everyone was friendly and not barking at me like Pastor Miller."

"They all love you."

"It certainly felt that way. Well, perhaps not so much from Sam Miller."

"The apple doesn't fall too far from the tree. Are you going to let his words stand?"

"Yes."

"Even with me?"

"Yes."

"I don't believe him. I don't believe Sam. I think the bishop has a hold of something."

They were looking out the window at the line of buggies moving along slowly in the evening winter light.

"So I am to accept that Sam feels you let the Lapp Amish down by enlisting?" Lyyndaya said, leaning her head against his arm. "Or maybe his harshness is because he's worried that Emma will get drawn to you again?"

"Sam Miller has nothing to worry about from me," he said.

"No?"

"No."

"Why is that?" she teased.

"Must I spell it out?"

"Ja." Lyyndaya held onto her bright grin. "I would like you to spell it out."

"Can I say it in *English?*"

She nodded. "You have picked up a lot of quaint expressions from the *English,* yes."

He shrugged. "Sometimes I feel I have to use them to say what I really mean. The German doesn't always convey what I wish to say. Especially when I'm in the pink."

She made a face. "This pink is a good thing?"

"A very good thing."

"And why are you in it?"

He gripped both her hands. "Because I love you, Lyyndy, that's why."

She smiled and said, "I don't think you need *English* words to say that."

Mr. Whetstone coughed as he came into the kitchen from the parlor. "Someone else is coming."

Headlights glimmered over the snow and windows.

"It's an army staff car," said Jude, peering through the glass into the semi-darkness. "Well, I telegrammed them where I'd be and here they are." He gave Lyyndaya, who looked worried, a crooked smile. "Now we'll see what they think of the Amish uniform you have me decked out in, won't we?"

Twenty-Five

Two officers spoke with Jude for half an hour in the parlor while Lyyndaya and Mr. Whetstone both had hot cocoa in the kitchen. When they emerged, Lyyndaya offered them a cup, and they sat down at the table for ten minutes and chatted. Then they were gone into the night, the staff car's engine rumbling in the distance.

"They're local boys," Jude explained. "Stationed near Harrisburg. I have to report to a base by Philadelphia in forty-eight hours. I can muster out then."

"Is that all?" Lyyndaya prodded, her hands wrapped around a third cup of cocoa. "Just muster out?"

"Well." Jude sipped at his. "Whew. That's hot."

"What else, Jude Whetstone?"

He looked at his father and at Lyyndaya. "I can stay in. As a flight instructor."

Lyyndaya stared at him. "And you would

consider it?"

"Well —"

"Of course you would or you wouldn't be hesitating. We just have you home safe and sound and now —"

"I don't have to leave the country, Lyyndy."

"The Lapp Amish will never accept that. A military flight instructor?" Lyyndaya felt the heat in her hands and forehead. "Never."

"You're forgetting they do not accept me now," Jude responded in a quiet voice.

"How can you say that after the way they just welcomed you?"

He sat back. "I know they care for me. I know they love the aeroplanes and the flying. But they're warm toward me today because they're free to be warm. In two weeks, when I'm shunned, it will be a different story."

Lyyndaya glanced away from his dark brown eyes. "They believe you will repent and that there will be no *Meidung*."

"But Bishop Zook and I both know there will be a *Meidung*. You also know this. And you, Papa."

His father nodded.

Lyyndaya grew agitated, biting her lower lip and twisting a spoon about in her hand. "Why? Why must it be so?"

Jude sighed and rubbed a hand over his eyes. "I've told you, Lyyndy. I can say the war was wrong. I can say *all* wars are wrong. I can say all killing is wrong. But I can't say what they want me to say — that I should never have gone to war. There is no use asking me to confess and repent. I had to go, it was right for me to go, I can't repent of something I believe God wanted me to do."

She got to her feet and began to clear up the cups.

"Lyyndy, please sit back down," Jude asked.

"No, there's nothing more to say, is there?"

He saw the dampness in her eyes as she turned to the sink and continued.

"You are finished with the Lapp Amish and will be a flight instructor for the army. After ten years, your life in this part of the world is over. Jude Whetstone the blacksmith is packing up and moving on."

"Lyyndy —"

"I will quickly wash these up and then I would appreciate a ride home. With you or your father. Whoever is less busy."

Jude's father cleared his throat and made his way to the door. "I will put Grit in the harness. But then I have to tend to the other horses." He slipped on his dark winter coat and went out.

Lyyndaya was pouring hot water into the sink from a kettle she had lifted from the top of the woodstove.

"Of course I'll take you," Jude said to her. "You know that."

"I get you back only to lose you again. It's not right!"

At first they didn't speak as Grit jogged along the road. The stars were spread out before them, and several times Jude wanted to say something about their beauty, but every time he glanced at Lyyndaya her face was granite. He began to whistle, something he hadn't done before the war. Nor was it something he had begun in France. As he whistled several melodies he recalled the man named Pierce in a hospital bed in England. Lying next to him, Jude had listened to him whistle morning, noon, and night. Pierce had said whistling kept his mind off the pain of his wounds.

"What song is that?" Lyyndaya suddenly asked.

Jude stopped whistling. "I'm not sure."

"How did you learn it?"

"A soldier in the hospital in England."

"Well, can you do a tune you can tell me the name of?"

"Ja." He blew out a few notes. Then he

426

sang, "Pack up your troubles in your old kit bag and smile, smile, smile."

"That's a funny song for a war."

He shrugged. "You try to cheer one another up any way you can."

She rested a gloved hand on his arm. "Aren't the stars lovely?"

"Ja."

"I like the whistling. I can't think of too many men who whistle among the Amish."

"Maybe they whistle out in the fields and you just never hear it."

"I don't think so. Sing me something else."

"All right." He saw Flapjack sitting in his plane and waiting for the order to take off. What was that song that was always on his lips?

"Sometimes when I feel bad and things
    look blue
I wish a pal I had — say one like you.
Someone within my heart to build a
    throne
Someone who'd never part, to call my
    own

"If you were the only girl in the world,
And I were the only boy,
Nothing else would matter in the world
    today,

We would go on loving in the same old
   way.

"A garden of Eden, just made for two,
With nothing to mar our joy.
I would say such wonderful things to you,
There would be such wonderful things to
   do,

"If you were the only girl in the world,
And I were the only boy."

"Oh, my goodness, now you're going to
make me cry." Lyyndaya put a gloved hand
to her eyes. "Please stop the buggy."
"Whoa, Grit, steady."
Jude had scarcely reined in the horse and
turned to look at her before she had taken
his head in her hands and begun to kiss
him, first on his eyes and cheeks and then
on his mouth. He was so startled he almost
fell backward out of the carriage. Finally he
put his arms around her and drew her
closer. They kissed for several minutes
before she gently pulled away and then
tucked her head on his chest.
"That's enough for tonight," she said.
"Can't I kiss the top of your head?"
"I won't stop you." She laughed softly.
"See what winter stars and whistling do to

an Amish girl?"

"I was a million miles away, Lyyndy. And now I can smell the scent of your hair and feel the warmth of your face. It's a miracle."

"Shh. Sing me one more tune. Whistle it and then sing it to me."

He peeled back her bonnet and put his lips against the part in her hair. "You're very *English* tonight."

"Well, hymns are not good for romance. Perhaps that's why God also gave us the Song of Solomon."

"Am I to quote that to you?"

"No."

"But it's the Bible."

"Just sing. Whistle and sing."

Jude leaned his head against hers and closed his eyes. "I could fall asleep right here. You are the perfect pillow."

"Please."

Was it Flapjack who liked the song about the wedding? Or was that Zed? He heard the deep voice. The person was taking a bath and singing at the top of their lungs. Always dropping the bar of soap on the floor. Yes, Zed.

He whistled the melody into her ear so quietly he could scarcely hear it himself. Then he hummed, trying to bring the verses to mind.

"The bells are ringing for me and my gal,
The birds are singing for me and my gal,
Everybody's been knowing to a wedding
    they're going,
And for weeks they've been sewing,
Ev'ry Susie and Sal.

"They're congregating for me and my gal,
The parson's waiting for me and my gal,
And sometime, I'm going to build a little
    home for two,
For three or four, or more,
In Loveland,
For me and my gal."

She put her head in his lap and looked up
at him, smiling in a very tiny way that she
sometimes had. She traced his cheek with
her gloved fingers. "Is that what you wish?"

"Wedding bells? For you and me? Yes. I
want so badly for you to be my bride."

"Is this your proposal then?"

"Oh, no, no, I can do better than that."

"How long will you keep me waiting?"

"I would be asking you to leave your home
— your father, your mother — Ruth —"

"I know."

"The Amish people. Lancaster County. It
seems too much . . . who am I to ask that
of you?"

She didn't take her hand from his face. "I've been thinking about all this since before I was told you were missing and presumed dead. And hardly anything else since you came back to life only days ago."

Jude shook his head. "It's not something I can ask of you. Look how beautiful you are. Look how perfect you are. It's this place that made you the way you are. This place, your family, the Lapp Amish, God —"

"*You.*"

"No." He played with a loose strand of her hair. "I'm not a man who moves such mountains. I enjoyed watching you grow up, though."

"*Ja?*"

"Sure. I've been in love with you since we were eight."

Her smile widened. "You have not."

"Deeply and painfully."

Lyyndaya was surprised. "And you never told me."

"Told the tomboy? How could I tell you? Instead I pushed you in the mud."

"Many times. And got in trouble with Mrs. Beachy."

"*Ja*, I did a lot of extra chores on account of you and your gleaming gold hair."

"I suppose you will tell me it was worth it."

"More than worth it. I just wish I'd kissed you once or twice and then pushed you in the mud. All the extra chores Mrs. Beachy would have loaded me down with would have felt as light as air."

Lyyndaya curled one hand behind his neck. "I think I will break some of my rules tonight. I think I will take a few more kisses home with me, please." She brought his head down to hers.

"You smell wonderful, you know," he murmured.

"I didn't know. It's just ordinary soap."

"How could anything you touch ever be ordinary again?"

She laughed. "My, you know how to win the extra kisses, don't you, my brown-eyed Amish boy? Keep it up and we'll never get home."

"I don't mind. I don't feel the cold."

"Neither do I."

After another kiss, Lyyndaya put her fingers on his lips. "Mama and Papa will start to worry."

She faced him and held his hands tightly. "Jude, before we go back, it's important to me that you know that the reason I began to volunteer at the hospital was because of you. The reason I was prepared to help Dr. Morgan was also because of you. There you were in Europe trying to keep your men alive, trying to defeat the Germans without killing their pilots. You wanted men to come home to their families. All the Amish here were doing about the war was criticizing it, but they were saving no one. So I decided to do as you were doing. Get my hands dirty and work hard to rescue people from the valley of the shadow of death."

He watched her eyes. "You are not just saying this, are you?"

"I don't just say things. I mean them or I don't speak."

"There were Mennonites over there, you know, driving ambulances, motor ones and horse-drawn ones, some were bringing in the wounded on their backs, it wasn't just me. I even met a few Amish. I suppose they would be shunned for doing it, wouldn't they? Binding up wounds, cleaning out bullet holes. I know they were doing this for the men in the trenches."

"But you were my inspiration, Jude. Now let me pray for us and then we had better get going lest Papa's worry brings him out looking for me."

When they arrived at the Kurtz home, Jude pulled the buggy to a halt. Lyyndaya turned and kissed Jude one more time on the cheek.

"How long will you be in Philadelphia?" she asked.

"I'm not sure. A week. Maybe a bit longer."

"It is not just about mustering out or deciding whether or not to be a flight instructor, is it?"

"You've always read my mind. No, they have medals to give out, honors to bestow."

"I suspected as much. They told us you would be receiving the Distinguished Flying Cross and the Congressional Medal of Honor."

"The DFC, yes, not the Medal of Honor anymore. If I'd died they would have still given it to me. Not that it matters, Lyyndy, because honestly it doesn't. What gives me joy is thinking of my men. I'm not sure how many of them made it through, but I have a sense that most of them did — Billy Skipp, Zed, Tex. The officers didn't know much about my squadron, but God does."

She brushed one or two stray hairs away from his eyes. "When you come back, you ask me what you want to ask me. Once you do that, I will tell you what I want to tell you. Please don't stay away too long."

"I won't," he said.

The first week Jude was gone Lyyndaya was

434

so full of hopes and dreams that the days she spent with her family in Paradise rushed past. She had decided to wait for him to return before making any further plans for volunteering at the hospital in Philadelphia.

The second week, with no word from Jude, the days seemed to drag on as if she were pulling a heavy weight, especially as the deadline for the final decision about the *Meidung* loomed closer. She prayed, read the Bible and her great-grandmother's red book, and spoke with Ruth about everything. Yet still the week felt gloomy and ominous.

"Nothing will change," Ruth said to her. "You know that. I think this is the reason you feel so much dread."

"Perhaps the leadership will extend the deadline."

"With Pastor Miller circling like a red-tailed hawk? In any case, an extension would change nothing. Your young man is set in his ways. And we Amish have been set in ours for hundreds of years."

The two sisters were sitting on the edges of their beds. Lyyndaya ran her hands back through her hair and knocked the *kapp* from her head. When she bent over to pick it up Ruth interjected, "Why bother? In a day or two you won't be needing it anymore."

Lyyndaya looked at her in surprise. "Why do you say that?"

Ruth shrugged. "Because you'll go with him."

Her eyes glistened with tears and Ruth reached over and took her hand. "I can't blame you, Lyyndy. Not at all. Of course it hurts me. But the manner in which God gave him back to you is a miracle. I would never turn my back on such a miracle. You must be his companion, you must be his wife. And I must get used to being without you. But perhaps not forever. I pray not forever."

Lyyndaya continued to hold the prayer covering in her hands, her eyes still glistening. "It's so hard to decide, so hard to understand. But when he came back from the dead, when he stood before me in the hospital room like that, just as if he had dropped from the sky . . ."

Her sister took her into her arms, her own eyes shining now. "Hush, hush, we all understand. It's your destiny. God will work everything out in time, you'll see."

"But there's Mama to think about — Papa — Sarah and Luke are getting so tall — even Harley and Daniel are growing up so fast —"

"Shh. You mustn't go on as if you'll never

436

see us again. Where is it written we may not look you in the face? Oh, so we can't eat together or hug each other, but where does the *Ordnung* command us to never look one another in the eyes and say *I love you*? And how long can the shunning last? Is it supposed to go on forever? Is that what Paul had in mind in Corinthians? Is that what Jesus would have us do? Never forgive? Never begin anew? *'If ye forgive not men their trespasses, neither will your Father forgive your trespasses.'*"

The night before the final day of the two-week period, Jude had still not arrived, and Lyyndaya tossed and turned in her bed while Ruth slept. She had been hoping she could leave with him while she still had the freedom to talk to others and say goodbye properly, but if the shunning took force first — and the shunning would be directed toward the two of them, not just Jude — how would she be able to take leave of her family?

The grandfather clock struck one, a sound she normally never heard. Doubts rose in her mind, the same doubts that had been picking at her all week with their sharp black beaks — what if all this time she had been simply imagining the hand of God in their relationship, what if his return was simply a coincidence, a marvel, but didn't mean they were supposed to be husband and wife? What if she wasn't meant to leave the Amish church, but remain in Paradise and marry someone who wouldn't desert the faith of her father and mother and family?

She didn't hear the clock sound two, for by then her body and mind had simply given in to exhaustion and she was deep in a murky and troubled sleep.

Until a hand shook her shoulder far from gently and she sat bolt upright, confused about where she was, blackness all around her.

"Lyyndy! Lyyndy!"

The voice was a harsh whisper.

"Who is it? What's going on?" she asked.

"Dr. Morgan needs both of us. There has been an outbreak. Several families — the Kauffmans, the Fishers, even Pastor Miller's children."

She finally was able to focus on Ruth's face. "Is Jude all right?" she asked.

"This has nothing to do with Jude. Quickly, sister, they need us."

"Where is Dr. Morgan?"

"Waiting in the kitchen with Papa. He will take us to the homes that are hardest hit. No more talk. We must get dressed as swiftly as we can."

"How fast is it moving?" asked Lyyndaya as she threw back the covers and jumped to her feet.

Ruth's face was a pale white in the early morning darkness.

"Sam Miller has already died," she said.

TWENTY-SIX

The only one of Jacob and Rachel Miller's children who had not contracted the illness was the eighteen-month-old. That was typical, it seemed to Lyyndaya. Mostly it ignored the very young and the very old and struck the healthiest persons — in their teens, twenties, and thirties.

While neighbors brought extra kettles so Rachel could heat and reheat water and keep a kettle in each room so there was steam to loosen congestion, Lyyndaya prepared mustard poultices for Jonathan and Paul, who were thirteen and fourteen, and the Millers' one girl, Naomi, who had just turned seventeen.

After the poultices had been placed on their chests, she went to the kitchen to chop up garlic and red onions while Pastor Miller brewed tea nearby and Mrs. Miller rushed up the staircase with a steaming cast-iron kettle for her daughter's room. Samuel Miller lay silently in his bedroom with his hands crossed on his chest and a clean white cloth tied under his jaw so that his mouth would remain tightly closed. Lyyndaya offered a prayer for poor Emma Zook at her loss in Samuel's death.

The clock in the parlor had only struck noon when Mrs. Miller began to cry out that the baby, Joshua Caleb, was turning blue. Dr. Morgan had just come through the door on his circuit between the houses and he examined the boy without removing his hat or coat. He instructed the Millers to place a kettle in the child's room and told Lyyndaya he required a mustard plaster as soon as possible. Then he pulled her aside once the parents had rushed downstairs and said the flu rarely affected infants or toddlers, but when it did, death occurred within hours, just as it did in the worst adult cases.

"What can we do for him?" asked Lyyndaya, feeling a tightness in her chest.

"We can do nothing. There is a physician in Harrisburg who has had some success with babies and newborns who have contracted the Spanish flu, but it would be impossible to get Joshua to him in time." Dr. Morgan consulted a pocket watch. "No, it's pointless to even mention it to Rachel and Jacob. There isn't another train west for three or four hours. We can't get him to Harrisburg. If the poor boy is still alive an hour from now that will be a miracle in itself."

He left her with Joshua, who was squirming and crying and struggling to breathe. Lyyndaya stood over his crib in an agony she had never experienced with any of the other flu victims she had nursed. *Oh God, will you let this pestilence take away the infants now too? Will you take away our colony's offspring? Can you not help us? Can you not help this family?*

She came down the staircase at the same time Mrs. Miller was running up with a kettle trailing white steam.

In the kitchen Pastor Miller and Dr. Morgan appeared to have stopped in their tracks to listen to something. She picked up a tin of mustard powder and began making the poultice for Joshua and when she dropped a large spoon with a clang the doctor frowned and asked her to be quiet. Hurt, she snapped back, "What is the problem? How can I work without making a sound?"

"Do you hear that?" Dr. Morgan asked.

"Hear what?"

He took her by the arm. "A plane has landed. It can only be Jude Whetstone. He

442

has put down east of here, in a field by your house or his father's." Then he looked at Pastor Miller. "Jacob, there's a physician in Harrisburg who may be able to save Joshua's life. He's a specialist with infants who have this disease. We can do nothing for him here. His case is as grave as Samuel's. Jude's aeroplane may be able to get him to the city in time to save him."

Pastor Miller's face lost what little color it had left. "Jude Whetstone? Take my child in his aeroplane? Never. If we must get to Harrisburg we will board a train."

"There's no time for that! There will be no train for hours."

"Then we will pray."

Dr. Morgan narrowed his eyes. "Jacob Miller, God has heard your prayers and placed Jude here at the right time! Now if you choose to spurn God's answer to your prayers out of anger, who will you blame for the loss of your baby?"

Mrs. Miller ran into the kitchen. "Jacob, have you taken leave of your senses? An aeroplane can get to Harrisburg in minutes. This stubbornness is because of your hatred for Lyyndaya's young man and nothing more."

"I do not hate him."

She turned to Lyyndaya. "Please. I will

bundle him up. Jude's plane will have two places to sit, *ja?* You can hold him while Jude flies?"

"No." Pastor Miller stood in front of his wife. "No."

Mrs. Miller pleaded. "He could live, Jacob, he could live!"

"No."

She put her head against his chest and began to cry. "We have lost Samuel this very day. We could lose Naomi and Jonathan and Paul. What if we lose our baby too? Then there is no one, no one." She looked up into her husband's stern face. "When I put the kettle in his room just now . . . he was not moving . . . and the color of the blue in his face . . . had deepened . . ."

Dr. Morgan was already heading up the staircase.

Fresh pain and dismay filled Pastor Miller's eyes.

Amidst her sobs, he gently removed his wife's hands and rushed up to the baby's room. Lyyndaya took the woman into her arms and let her weep.

Only minutes later, Pastor Miller came down with Joshua wrapped in blankets and a woolen hat and a sheepskin, the doctor trailing him. Mrs. Miller cried out to God, looked over how the baby was bundled up, then took him from her husband and gave the child to Lyyndaya.

"Please," she said. "Hurry!"

Lyyndaya took Joshua and cradled him. Then she looked at Pastor Miller. He lifted one hand as if in a blessing. "Go with God."

Dr. Morgan raced his carriage out to the road. It was a clear day, and mild, the middle of February. He stood up and looked toward the east. Then he sat back down and called out to his horses. They broke into a gallop.

"Where is the plane?" asked Lyyndaya.

"I can't see it. But we must go by the Whetstones on the way to your house in any case."

The carriage bounced along the frozen road. The aeroplane wasn't at the Whetstone house or in any of the nearby fields, so they thundered past.

"How is the baby?" asked the doctor.

"He is breathing."

When they were two or three hundred yards from her home Lyyndaya saw the aircraft. It was in the same field of stubble where Jude had first landed in the summer of 1917, and it was a Curtiss Jenny with stars on its wings.

The horses pounded up the Kurtzes' lane to the house and the door swung open before they had pulled to a stop. Jude stepped out in his leather flying suit, followed by Lyyndaya's father in his black hat and jacket.

"What is it?" called Jude from the porch. "What's going on?"

"Do you have fuel to get to Harrisburg?" shouted Dr. Morgan.

"Harrisburg? That's less than fifty miles by air. I have more than enough."

"We have a sick baby. There is a doctor there who may be able to save him. Can you fly him to the city with Lyyndaya holding him?"

Jude came down the steps quickly. "Who is it?"

"Joshua Miller."

"Joshua? He's not even two." Jude came up to the buggy and looked at the child in Lyyndaya's arms. Jude touched his hand where it poked out from under the sheepskin. "He's so young. The oxygen gets thinner the higher we go. And the air gets colder." He hesitated, looking at Lyyndaya. "We will have to fly very close to the ground. Take off a few rooftops. Frighten a few cows. People with telephones will be calling in complaints to the police from now until we land." Then he smiled, and said, "Let's go."

Dr. Morgan held little Joshua while Lyyn-daya pulled on a flying suit Jude had brought that covered her from foot to neck. Once she had put on a leather helmet and goggles, climbed into the front cockpit, and tightened her harness, she took the baby again. Jude got into the pilot's seat, behind her.

"Keep Josh as warm as you can," he said. "Keep him close to your heart."

She put the child inside her flying suit and let his head peep out at her throat, sheepskin all around him like a shield.

Lyyndaya's father placed a hand on her arm. "God bless you in this, daughter. I will speak quickly. I have just received a letter from my friend Nicholas in Washington, the one in the War Department. They have taken a particular interest in Jude's case because he is a war hero. Several generals have looked into the matter of his enlistment. They do not want anything to cloud his name or record."

"But what can they do to sway people like Pastor Miller?"

"These generals will be able to tell us whether Jude was coerced or enlisted willingly. From what Nicholas writes in his letter it looks very favorable for Jude. So I have asked them to come to the spring communion service. Bishop Zook has promised me the entire issue surrounding Jude will be settled there once and for all. A delegation from Washington bearing proof that Jude was forced to fight would make all the difference."

"Will they come, Papa?"

"It is my hope."

"What does Jude say about all this?"

Mr. Kurtz patted his daughter's arm and smiled. "What do you think? He says nothing."

Lyyndaya twisted her head around to look at Jude. He was busy checking the gauges on his instrument panel. Feeling her eyes on him he glanced up.

"What is it?" he asked.

"Papa was talking to me about Washington sending a delegation to clear your name."

He went back to his instrument panel. "I know. He told me."

"And you still have nothing to say about all that?"

He played with a dial. "No, my love. I don't."

Dr. Morgan suddenly stepped over and handed Jude a slip of paper. "The man you want is Leif Peterson, Dr. Leif Peterson. He is at the large hospital in downtown Harrisburg. I will get a telegram to him immediately so he knows to expect you. God-speed, my boy."

Jude pulled his goggles down over his eyes. Around his throat was his white silk scarf from the war.

"Can you spin the prop?" he asked Lyyndy's father.

"*Ja.* I will try my best."

When Jude gave him the signal, Mr. Kurtz yanked down sharply on the propeller blade, but the engine didn't catch. He did it again and still there was nothing. A third time brought a look of fierce determination to his face and he swung down with all his might. The engine sputtered, coughed, and roared. Jude gave him a thumbs-up and started forward, turning into the wind. In moments they were lifting off the ground and swiftly climbing to five hundred feet, where he leveled out.

"We'll see how far we can get at this altitude!" he shouted to Lyyndaya. "How is the baby?"

"Breathing!"

"You keep breathing too and we'll be all right! This is a JN-4H! It has a more powerful engine, a Hispano-Suiza 8! We can go like the wind — up to ninety-three miles an hour! Our last Jenny could only do seventy-three!"

"How did you get it?"

"It was a gift! The army is selling them off to civilians!"

"A gift? From who?"

But the shriek of engine and airstream combined to deafen his reply. They were streaking over brown and white farm fields and she could see horses running away from them and one vaulting a fence. People came out of their homes and pointed as they roared overhead. Cattle were running too, and crows scattered at their approach. Roads, carts, barns, cars, and smoke from chimneys flashed past. Always there were men and women and children darting out to look at a plane that was flying lower than any aircraft they'd seen over their houses and yards before.

The plane whistles like Jude whistles.

Joshua was warm when she put her face against his. Fever or not, she was glad. If he had felt like ice she would have been more worried than she already was. He wasn't crying, but neither was he sleeping. His lovely brown eyes were open and he was taking everything in. The boy's breathing was still troubled yet he seemed to be in less distress than he had been on the ground.

But she knew not to trust the illness. It

had a mind of its own, and that mind was sinister and treacherous. A patient could look like they were improving one minute and the next go into a sudden and irreversible decline. She prayed and rocked the child and willed the Jenny to go faster and faster. Finally she blurted out, "Push it!"

"What did you say?" called Jude from behind her.

She twisted her head around as far as she could. "Push it!"

He laughed. "Where are you picking up all these English expressions? Were you a pursuit aircraft pilot in France and never bothered to tell me about it?"

"*Ja!* I was just one aerodrome over! You thought I was the odd little man with a mustache the color of your girlfriend's hair! But please, go faster, go faster!"

"We are doing almost ninety miles an hour!"

"You said we could do ninety-three, didn't you? The boy has to make it, Jude, he has to!" Then a verse from the Bible flashed into her mind. " *'They shall mount up with wings as eagles!' *"

"I'll see if I can coax ninety-five out of her!"

She checked the baby again and his skin was cooling off though his eyes were still active. "He's cold, Jude!"

"I'll drop down!"

Jude swooped so low over a road that Lyyndaya could clearly see the expression of a woman who was a passenger in a black Ford. Her mouth was open and her eyes were popping. The car went off the road and into a bank of snow and stopped dead.

Electricity poles pelted past. She thought she could reach down and skim the tops of them with her hands. A group of boys were sledding on a snow-covered hill and she smiled to see their mouths move in shouts and cheers. One little girl standing off to the side unwound the red scarf from her neck and began to wave it like a flag.

A verse popped into her head, a verse her great-grandmother had written about in the red book the day before — *Thou shalt not be afraid for the terror by night; nor the arrow that flieth by day; nor for the pestilence that walketh in darkness; nor for the destruction that wasteth at noonday.*

"How is he?" Jude yelled.

"Warmer!"

"Warm enough?"

"I'm not sure!"

"Hang on!"

How could he possibly fly lower? Lyyndaya wondered. But he did, now swerving left and right to avoid flocks of birds that could damage the engine or wings, or wound them with a bullet-like impact against their bodies, and send their aeroplane crashing to the ground. Fear fought with excitement as they screamed over haystacks and leafless orchards and frozen ponds with boys and girls skating in circles and then raising their arms as the Jenny ripped past — almost, it seemed to Lyyndaya, capable of pulling the skaters' caps and toques from their heads with the prop wash. She hardly ever saw American flags in Lancaster County, but here they were unfurling from flagpoles in backyards and porches and schoolhouses. She found them beautiful, so much lively color and pattern against a landscape gray and white and brown.

The baby closed and opened his eyes and then closed them once again. She put her ear to his mouth. Yes, there was breath, but it crackled. She exhaled over his mouth and nose, trying to imitate in some small way the effect steam would have. A worry about catching the disease came and went. It was more important to her that the little boy survive than that she avoid close contact. She continued to breathe warm air into his nose. The landscape hurried past.

So this is how you flew in France, didn't

you? This is how you outflew the Germans and your own men as well. It's the kind of skill that made you an ace without killing a single person so that even your enemies admired the way you handled an aircraft, though they could not comprehend your mercy. Such tributes poured in from the Germans and Austrians when they thought you had perished! In that war you fought to preserve life as well as end the conflict. Now you are flying with all the ability you possess to preserve life in a different kind of fight. And you are my man. Thank God, you are my man.

"Here we are!"

The large brick buildings of the city swept rapidly toward them. Jude banked right to a field, where Lyyndaya could see other Jennys lined up on the grass and ice and half a dozen flags snapping in the breeze. They didn't have far to descend. She saw soldiers running out of huts as the plane circled once and touched down. A car came racing out to them as Jude pulled off his leather helmet and sprang to the ground. She could hear an officer shouting, "Who are you and what do you think you're doing buzzing a U.S. Army aerodrome? Do you want to get yourself shot?" And Jude replied calmly, "Major Jude Whetstone, U.S. Army Air Service, lately returned from France. Captain, I'm flying a mercy mission. I have a sick child here and I require immediate transport to a hospital."

"Whetstone? Whetstone?" The captain gaped. "You're the ace who brought in Schleiermacher. I attended your award ceremony in Philadelphia last week." He snapped to attention and saluted. "It's an honor, sir."

She smiled to see Jude return a salute.

"Thank you, Captain. Now I really could use a car —"

"This is my personal staff car, Major. It's at your disposal along with my driver. What hospital do you need to get to?"

"The large one. Downtown. A Dr. Leif Peterson is on staff there."

"Corporal Samson knows it. Bring the child and we'll get you on your way at once."

Lyyndaya handed Jude the boy while she climbed down from the plane. The captain saluted her as well as she stood there in her bulky suit and goggles and helmet. She decided to leave them on for the time being so as not to embarrass him and she gave an awkward salute in return. In the car, as the driver whisked them off the base and into Harrisburg traffic, she tugged off the goggles and helmet. Her prayer covering came off along with the helmet and she found that many of the pins had fallen out of her hair. As the corporal roared through the streets in the same way Jude had roared through the sky, she took Joshua back into her arms. His eyes were open and he seemed to be able to breathe through his nose again, though she could still detect a great deal of congestion.

When they told the receptionist at the hospital who they were she ran off down a corridor, returning in moments with a doctor in a white lab coat. Dr. Peterson had received Dr. Morgan's cable and he scooped the baby from Lyyndaya's arms and vanished. The receptionist asked them to take a seat and offered them two white masks.

"You're not wearing one," Lyyndaya pointed out.

"I'm tired of them. They make it hard for me to get my breath."

Jude and Lyyndaya sat down on the hard wooden bench in their leather-and-sheepskin flight gear. His arm went around her and she snuggled up against his chest. The masks remained in her hand.

"You look a little tired," he said.

"I've been up since three. Nursing. And I didn't get much sleep before that."

"Well, you can rest now. We're sticking around till we know Josh is okay."

" 'Okay'? More English."

"No, it comes from Pennsylvania Dutch."

"It does not."

"Yes, from *oll korrect,* which comes from *alles in Ordnung.*"

Lyyndaya laughed. "So you are a language professor now? I'll just close my eyes for a little bit. Once we find out about the baby we must head back to Paradise. There are so many who are sick. They need our help."

"Of course."

"And, I must tell you, the answer is yes."

Jude looked down at her as she grew drowsier. "Yes to what?"

"I will marry you."

"But I haven't even asked."

"You have asked with your eyes. Many times."

"What if I'm still in the army? What if I'm a flight instructor? What if we're both turned out of the colony?"

She smiled with her eyes shut and murmured, "When I told you it was Pastor Miller's son you didn't blink an eye or miss a step. I saw the concern in your face. I watched how you flew for that boy — I could have plucked cones from a spruce tree. If you flew any better in France it's no wonder you didn't need to shoot anyone down. The poor Germans probably got dizzy just watching you. You are my man. And the answer is still yes."

She drifted off. Jude kissed the top of her head, savoring the texture of the soft blonde hair that fell loose over her face and shoulders. He prayed for Josh, prayed for the sick in Paradise, prayed for the woman he was going to marry.

In time, he also fell asleep, leaning his head against hers. The receptionist watched and tapped her fingernails against her desk.

"Bill," she said to an orderly that was rushing past. "That guy remind you of anyone?"

He paused and glanced over. "Where've they been? The North Pole?"

"Dr. Peterson said they flew in. But that face. I've seen it before. In the paper, maybe?"

He shrugged. "I gotta go."

"That's Whetstone," said a nurse behind her. "You know? The ace? Like Rickenbacker. They called him White Knight, the pilot who always brought 'em back alive."

"Brought who back alive?" asked the receptionist. "The enemy?"

"The enemy and his own men too."

At half past six Dr. Peterson shook Jude's shoulder. "Major Whetstone."

458

Jude's eyes flicked open. "What is it?"

Peterson was smiling. "Joshua Miller has recovered rapidly. You did well to bring him in as swiftly as you did. It saved him. We had plenty of time to work."

Lyyndaya's head came up suddenly. "The little boy's alive?"

"Very much so," said Peterson.

"Oh, thank God."

"Yes, God. And the pair of you. I must get back. But I wanted you to know." He started to walk off down the hallway. "I have telegrammed Dr. Morgan. He will tell the family. It is good to save a life during times when so many have been lost."

"Ah," sighed Lyyndaya and kissed Jude on the cheek. "My hero." Then she sat up. "But we must get back. Can we fly this late?"

"Probably not a good idea."

"But I must help. Ruth can't nurse them all."

Jude got to his feet. "Come on. We'll put you on a train. Get a cab to the station and get you rolling east. I'll cable my father to pick you up."

She took his hand and he helped her get up from the bench. "What about you? What about the plane?"

"I'll come down first thing in the morning," he said.

"But where will you spend the night?"

"Probably at the army base."

"So you still are in the military?"

"It's like the Amish. The army gave me another month to think about it. At first I told them no."

Lyyndaya stopped walking and looked up into his face. "You told them no?"

"I told them no."

She hugged his arm as they went out onto the street. "You don't need to worry about the Amish. Or Jacob Miller. Not after this. You will be able to stay."

"I hope so, Lyyndy. But what about flying? What about aeroplanes? Will they ban them like the telephone and the motorcar?"

"I can't answer that today and neither can the Amish. They still haven't made up their minds about electricity poles. So we will let it sit. We have no choice."

Lyyndaya always carried a health certificate in a pocket in her dress. Dr. Morgan had renewed it that very day, checking her and Ruth over before they began helping him with the sick. The conductor let her board a train for Lancaster City and Paradise and asked her to put on a mask. She still had the two from the hospital.

"Now you look like Jesse James," teased Jude as she leaned out the window to talk with him, the lower half of her face covered.

"And what does she look like?"

He laughed and said, "Please tell Papa I will land by the smithy tomorrow so long as there isn't a snowstorm."

"I wonder what he will think when I tell him about our wild ride?"

"What wild ride? Treetop flying? It worked, didn't it? You can tell Josh all about it on his fourteenth birthday and embarrass him."

"*We* can tell Joshua Caleb all about it on his fourteenth birthday and embarrass him together. My almost-husband."

The whistle blew twice and the train began to move. Jude reached up and gave her hand a strong squeeze. "Love you," he said.

"Really love you," she said back.

Then the train moved forward into the black.

Lyyndaya rested her head against the seat. She thought of the welcome Jude would receive once he returned, and she even indulged in a daydream about Pastor Miller hugging him and shaking his hand in gratitude and Christian love. Ideas about what color she would choose for a wedding dress drifted through her sunny thoughts — blue, lavender, green? Whatever it was it needed to be right because someday they would bury her in the same dress.

"Sometimes your eyes are *celadon*," Emma had told her once, showing off. "Do you know what color that is?"

"No," Lyyndaya had replied.

"A beautiful light green. You should think about wearing that color."

"I don't want to draw attention to myself."

Emma had ignored her. "In certain moods your eyes are so bright. Then they're chartreuse. That's such a lively green. That would be good for your wedding dress."

"Chartreuse?"

"Or turquoise. There are few colors richer or more beautiful than that. Turquoise is a gemstone, you know. That is your best color."

Lyyndaya watched the lamplight from farm windows as the train steamed east. They had probably flown over some of those houses. She wondered if neighbors were still talking about it or if anyone had actually telephoned the police like Jude was sure they would. It didn't matter. She was certain it had thrilled and delighted many, just as it would have at an airshow. And the stunt flying had saved a human life.

Thank you, Father, for the word you gave me so long ago — "Perhaps he therefore departed for a season, that thou shouldest receive him forever" — a promise I feel you are now bringing to pass. You have done so many marvelous, inexplicable things because of Jude's flying and because of the war, who could have guessed it? Even Bishop Zook is amazed and sees your hand in it. I pray that all the people in the church will see what he sees and what I see. Please open their eyes, my Father. And thank you again for preserving Joshua's life.

Jude's father was friendly, but quieter than she had expected him to be considering what his son had done to save Joshua Miller. She tried to liven him up with stories about the Jenny flying over flagpoles and tall spruce trees and running cars off the road, but the old man only grunted or smiled slightly and kept his eyes on the dark road and the plodding horse. Finally, exasperated at the cold water he was throwing on all her good cheer, she said, "Honestly, I don't understand your lack of cheer. Your son flew like an angel of God today. He saved a child's life. It's a miracle, and you act as if I'm talking about him cleaning mud off his boots."

Mr. Whetstone looked at her with sorrow in his face. "I'm sorry, my dear. Truly. My mind is elsewhere, I'm afraid."

She felt a chill. "It's the disease, isn't it? Other people have died, and here I am going on about the baby and the aeroplane flight as if that's all that matters."

"No, no, it's not that. The sick are doing better than expected. No one else is in real danger right now, according to Dr. Morgan. *Ach,* no, do not berate yourself. Your sister Ruth is doing marvels. And Emma is now helping the doctor as well. Yes, Emma Zook has stepped up and made a difference for our people today."

"But then — thank God — that's wonderful."

"*Ja, Gott sei Dank.* No, my dear, it is something else that weighs me down, forgive me."

Lyyndaya put her hand on his arm. "What is wrong, then? What can have happened to steal your joy? Yes, we lost Samuel, but he is with Jesus now, and that's a mercy. Still, the Lord gave us the little boy back and, as you say, all the Millers and Kauffmans and Fishers as well —"

"It is the *Meidung,* Lyyndaya," he blurted. "They are going to enact the *Meidung.* They are going to ban my son."

464

"What?" She felt as if she had swallowed a lump of ice. "That can't be, not after what he's done today, something none of them could do, something God has blessed."

Mr. Whetstone was back to staring straight ahead into a darkness lit only by a few lamps and now and then candles in small square windows. "The leadership assembled this evening and took the vote as scheduled. I heard that one of them even suggested the community was being punished with the sickness because of Jude's sin in going to war, a sin the church has tolerated. The ban will be made official at the communion service."

"No!" Lyyndaya's thoughts spun in a circle like floodwater swirling in a swollen creek. "They can't all have voted for this. Not Bishop Zook. Not Pastor Miller. Jude saved the life of Pastor Miller's little boy today."

Mr. Whetstone turned his head and glanced at her in the nighttime darkness. "Why, it was Pastor Miller who said that God had afflicted us with the disease because we had turned a blind eye to Jude's transgressions. It was he who cast the first vote for the *Meidung.* It was he who insisted all the others vote with him in order to put an end to God's curse."

TWENTY-SEVEN

Lyyndaya was certain she heard a lark, the distinctive song that to her was a distillation of pure sunshine and clear skies. Perhaps it was a sign that God would have His way and that darkness would be turned into light this day. She hoped so. She prayed so. Yet often the ways of men could, at least for a time, appear to obscure and obstruct the purposes of God.

They were in Bishop Zook's barn. It was Sunday, March sixteenth, in 1919, and the fields were greening while snowmelt and rain showers left puddles everywhere. Light had been gleaming like silver on the early hay when she had come to the church meeting with her family in the large buggy. Jude and his father were already seated on the other side of the barn. She kept her eyes on Jude until he felt it and looked up, and they both smiled at one another.

The bishop came and stood in front of

them all. "You know, twice a year we meet for communion, in the spring and in the fall. And each time we meet we examine our hearts and our lives as we prepare to renew our commitment to Jesus Christ and to our Amish faith. Always before we take communion we talk about matters that have arisen in our church. We want to make sure everything has been laid to rest at the feet of Jesus before we take his cup and his bread together. So today, we have asked Jude Whetstone to join us, even though he is under the *Meidung,* because many of you have said he was not treated fairly by the leadership and you desire to hear him speak for himself. You are free to converse with him this Sunday, to listen to his words, shake his hand, to pray with him if you wish. Who knows? Perhaps our Lord will bring about reconciliation between young Jude and our church as he did between Paul and Barnabas and Paul and John Mark."

He cleared his throat and paused to look out over the congregation. "You know also that two families have said they feel God is telling them to leave our colony if justice is not done for Jude Whetstone this day. I, as your bishop, grieve that matters have come to this. We would rather Adam Whetstone, Jude's father, remain among us, but we must respect his decision before God, even if it means he is severed from our fellowship forever.

"In the same way, I grieve that the Kurtz family has also indicated their desire to part ways with our church. I would rather they made peace today and that Amos and his good wife Rebecca and their beautiful children would remain among us to farm and to worship and to follow the teachings of Jesus Christ. But again, we can only respect the decisions they make and place their family in the hands of God, as they must also respect the decisions we make before the Lord. So, here is this day that the Lord has made, we will rejoice and be glad in it. Let me pray and then the talking can begin, hm?"

Bishop Zook prayed for almost ten minutes. Then he sat down. Lyyndaya's father was the first one on his feet though she had noticed Pastor Miller beginning to rise. It was a warm day and her father held a straw hat in his hands as he spoke.

"I was never one for the flying," he began. "I did not want my daughter to spend too much time with young Jude. I thought, suppose he wants to court her in an aeroplane? Then, if he takes off into the air and flies away like a duck, how will I ever catch up to them in my horse and buggy?"

Everyone laughed. *Everyone,* Lyyndaya thought, *but Pastor Miller.*

"The flying is something the Amish people are going to figure out. Maybe this year, maybe next year. There is no rush. The aeroplane is not going anywhere but up and the same is true of the Amish."

Again there was laughter.

"But I saw how Jude brought honor to God with his flying, *ja,* even in the middle of an awful war. We all know how he acted, we all know how the English and German people have praised his mercy, we all know how he deliberately avoided killing and sought to help end the conflict at the same time as he sought to hold human life sacred. And for all of this we do what? We ban him? We shun him? Just because one of our pastors bears a grudge against him and leads you all about by the nose to do his will instead of God's? No, this is not right. This too we all know."

Her father sat down, his face dark, knowing Pastor Miller would be on his feet immediately to refute him.

"I bear no grudge against any man," protested Pastor Miller before he was even standing straight. "I only hold to the teachings of the Amish people, the ancient teachings based on the Word of God, for which our forefathers were persecuted and martyred. I do not wish to see these teachings set aside for any man, no matter how honorable some may think that man's actions to be. Never mind that Jude Whetstone did not take human life. Others in his squadron did. He had no business being there in the first place, he had no business assisting them in *their* killing of other men."

"For shame, Jacob Miller." Benjamin Kauffman was on his feet. "Jude Whetstone saved your child's life and you treat him like *Schmutz.*" *Like dung.*

"It was God who saved my child's life!" retorted Jacob Miller.

Benjamin remained standing. "Yes, and he used Jude and Miss Kurtz and a doctor of the *English* to do it. You could not fly the plane, Jacob. You could not save your son. God worked through others and now you spit in his eye."

"I honor God!"

"You honor your opinion. I would hate now to do you a favor, Jacob, if how you have treated Jude Whetstone is how you thank those who help you. It is better I pass you by like the Levite or you might have me shunned for lifting a hand to give you some sort of assistance." Benjamin sat down, his lips still forming words, but silently.

The bishop was in front of them again. "Calmly, brothers and sisters, calmly and gently, as Jesus was before the cross. Let us remember whose children we are. Yes, I know you wish to speak what you believe is the truth, but truth must be spoken in love, as the Word says."

Jude's father was up. His voice was quiet and Lyyndaya had to strain to make out what he was saying.

"I do not wish to leave. I have no desire to leave. Is my wife not buried here in holy ground? Have my son and I not made your tools and wheel rims and plowshares? Has our work not helped you till the soil and travel about by horse and buggy? When you enacted the first *Meidung* against my son I bore it. I could not send him letters and I could not read the letters he sent to me. Every day he was in grave danger, but you would not even let me speak to him with the pen. I respected the *Ordnung* above my own flesh and blood, believing I did the will of God.

"Then we find he has gone into the war to cleanse it, to bring Christ's presence into it, to save human life from it, as a man goes into a filthy well to clear it of rubbish so that the water may be sweet again and nourish both the body and the soul. But how do we treat him for cleansing the well of blood and corruption? Hours after he risks his life flying low to the ground so that a sick boy has air and warmth, hours after he and Miss Kurtz get this boy safely to a hospital none of us could reach in time by horse or by train — we shun him again. *This* is the Amish faith? *This* is the Lord Jesus Christ? Then I must take my forge and my anvil and I must find, I think, another Amish people, another Jesus Christ — yes, a Jesus who we find in the holy Scriptures, not in our imaginations and traditions of men."

"But Adam," pleaded Bartholomew Fisher, "you know what Jacob is saying is true. We are the people of peace. We do not put on the uniform, we do not wave the flag, we do not go to the wars. This others do, it is not for the Amish. We are to be salt and light in our nation, not more of the guns and bombs and killings. It is good your son saved Jacob's son. But we must not reject our faith and the teachings of Jesus Christ because of that. I say let Jude repent of going to war. Let him ask forgiveness for taking a plane into combat. We will welcome him back with open arms, yes, Jacob will as well, and we shall break bread together this day and be one people under God again."

Lyyndaya prayed as the speaking continued. Now and then she glanced out a small window on one side of the barn. There had been no more letters from Washington but she still hoped officials from the U.S. Army might arrive and stand up for Jude. Yet the situation was beginning to look hopeless. She hung her head. Suddenly a woman's voice made her look up in surprise. It was Rachel Miller and she stood with young Joshua asleep in her arms.

"Perhaps I should not speak among the men, Bishop Zook," said Rachel. "Perhaps it is not my place. Perhaps I should remain silent and let God speak among those he has ordained. But it was my child Jude Whetstone flew to the hospital that terrible day in February, that day when we lost our precious Samuel — that day, Bartholomew Fisher, when you could have lost members of your own family as well, but for the grace of God."

She stopped, but did not sit down. Bishop Zook said nothing. Then voices rose from all corners of the barn — *sprechen, sprechen — speak, speak.* Her husband sat with his head down and his arms folded across his chest.

Rachel looked directly at Jude. "I do not understand what made you think you must

473

go to war to end a war. None of us do. But you saved my Joshua's life. Have I thanked you enough for it? No, I can never thank you enough. I never stop thanking God and I can never stop thanking you. For suppose you did not know how to fly? Suppose you had never learned how to fly a plane that fast and that low without crashing into a tree or a house or an electricity pole? Suppose there was no one at hand for God to use — for we know our Lord works through the creatures He has made? Would my Joshua be in my arms today?"

Jacob Miller was back on his feet. "I, like my wife, am not ungrateful to Jude Whetstone. I know God had his hand in this. But how do we know Jude did not bring the calamity down upon us in the first place? How do I know if my child ever would have been sick if Jude had not sinned by breaking the *Ordnung?*" He turned and pointed at Jude. "You wished to hear him speak for himself? All right, you tell them, young man, so that everyone can hear, you tell them what you think of war."

"I hate war," Jude said quietly.

"Yet you went to war," pressed Pastor Miller.

"I did."

"So — do you repent? Do you repent that

474

you went and fought in the war you say you hate?"

"No, I do not. I had to go to war. It was the only way I could save the lives of those I love."

People began to murmur. Jacob Miller flung his arms wide. "There. You see? That is how he talks. That is how he always talks. He had to go to war to save people's lives. He had to sin to do the will of God. Now you hear for yourselves what his heart is like. Now you hear for yourselves that he will not repent. That is why the leadership have called for *Streng Meidung* and, if that does not bring this young man to the cross, excommunication from the church."

"No, that is too harsh," Lyyndaya heard one man call out.

"Our leadership are right to do this," said a woman. "Listen to them. God speaks through them."

"Too far, the *Streng Meidung* takes things too far. We act as if he killed someone. There was no killing. He did the exact opposite. So we punish him for having mercy on others?"

"The Amish are a peaceful people. That is our gift from God and our gift to America. We cannot go back on that because of one headstrong boy with his head in the clouds."

"You are not listening to him."

"He is not listening to God."

My goodness, thought Lyyndaya as more voices sounded from all parts of the barn, *the church sounds as if it has split in two over this.*

Bishop Zook was waving his hands and asking people to wait their turn, not to shout, to let others speak, but the meeting was getting out of his control. Lyyndaya imagined the church breaking apart, with some leaving to support Jude while the others remained faithful to the leadership. It had happened to other Amish colonies. Could it not happen here also?

"Genug!" David Hostetler was on his feet, his voice booming. *"Genug!"* Enough!

The talking and shouting died out quickly. David still stood, even when silence was restored. He looked around the barn. Lyyndaya saw him lock eyes with Jacob Beiler and give a short, sharp nod of his head. Jacob stood up, but kept looking at the ground. David found Jonathan Harshberger as well, his eyes, she thought, like blue flame, and Jonathan got up, staring straight ahead. David continued to look over the congregation.

"Scham," he whispered, but everyone

could hear him. *"Scham, Scham."* Shame, shame.

He walked to the front and faced the people on the benches. "How quick we are to condemn. How quick to find fault. To point the finger. To blame. To cast the stone. Eh? Each of us eager to become an accuser of the brethren. But it is *we* who must confess, not Jude Whetstone. Oh yes, Mother, Father, I, your son David. Mr. and Mrs. Beiler, your son Jacob. And Mr. and Mrs. Harshberger, your son, yes, your only son, Jonathan. We have fallen short of the righteousness of God. We have fallen far." He looked at Pastor Miller. "Even Sam." Then he went to his knees as tears began to come.

"Forgive us our sins. Forgive us our trespasses."

Jacob and Jonathan came to the front and slowly went to their knees alongside David, their faces deeply flushed as they did so. Their voices joined his, weakly at first, then gradually growing stronger as they repeated the phrases four times — "Forgive us our sins. Forgive us our trespasses."

"Bishop Zook," David said, his cheeks glistening, "we should have come to you long ago, months ago, but we were afraid. We should have given our fear to the One who casts out fear, but instead we held onto it and it poisoned us. Now we will tell you. We *must* tell you. We must save our souls. We must confess publicly before the whole church while there still is a church to confess to." He hesitated, as if he wanted to change his mind, then shook his head. *"Nein,"* he said aloud to himself. "I will speak."

He looked at the faces before him. "All of us visited Hosea before he died. The first day he took sick — you will remember, Bishop Zook — all of us came to see him and pray for him — Jonathan, Jacob, myself, Samuel too. And Hosea told us — told us — that Jude had been *ordered* to enlist. At the camp where we were all imprisoned. Jude had been told if he did not join up, if he did not fly for the army, they would keep us in the camp until the war ended or until we were all dead.

"The rest of us were too far away to hear this conversation. But Hosea approached Jude after he had spoken with a general and that is when Jude said he had decided to join up. Hosea suspected he had been coerced because he could not believe he would ever do this thing willingly. He confronted Jude about joining the army and tried to get the truth out of him, but he kept evading Hosea's questions. Then this general came over and said Jude was doing this of his own free will and that if it ever got out that he had been forced to enlist it could go hard on us, and not only us, our parents, our families, the whole colony. We might be arrested and beaten again. Hosea was warned that Hutterites had been killed and Mennonite meeting houses burned to the ground. English neighbors would do nothing to protect those who spoke German, they would not stand up for those who did not fight or salute the flag. Did we not pray about just such things when we met for worship during the first summer of the war?

"So Hosea took the threats seriously. Then and there, he chose to believe Jude had wanted to go to war, had wanted to fly in France, had wanted to fight. He told us it was what he made himself believe because he was afraid the Amish in Paradise would be persecuted if he didn't. But in his heart, all along, he knew the truth. Jude enlisted not only to save the three of us here, and Hosea and Sam, but to save all of you, to save the whole community. He went to war so that war would not be made upon us."

Lyyndaya could scarcely breathe. *Oh, Jude, my poor man, I knew there was something — my father knew, Bishop Zook knew, but still, this is too much, it is far beyond what we thought.* The silence in the barn had weight and it was pressing down upon her, upon them all, taking away their air. But David wasn't finished. He found Jude with his eyes.

"I'm sorry, my brother. Hosea made us promise we would tell the church what you had been forced to do. But after his death, when we talked among ourselves, we grew worried that what Hosea had feared could still come upon us. After all, the war showed no signs of stopping. What if the truck and the corporal came for us again? What if they came for our fathers? What if they made sure no one would buy our milk or our barley or wheat? Sam — God have mercy — Sam led the way in this and talked us into going along. *Better Jude than the rest of the colony,* he argued. So we said nothing. God forgive us, we said nothing. My brother, we left you to this . . . disgrace."

Jude stood up. Lyyndaya saw Pastor Miller briefly before others blocked her view with their heads and backs. He was so pale she thought he was going to collapse.

"No, David," said Jude. "I should be asking your forgiveness. You mustn't torment yourself like this. I could have told the truth. I could have told the whole story at any

480

time. But, like you, I was afraid that certain people in certain places would take matters into their own hands if I spoke out and that there would be repercussions. I, like you, was afraid our people would be persecuted, that more persons would be hurt just as we had been hurt in that camp. So I said nothing. I decided to make the best of it. I thought, *If Jesus had been forced to do what I am forced to do, how would he have handled it, how would he have flown, how would he have tried to alter a war from the inside out?* I suspect he would have done a much better job. I'm sorry I have made such a hash of things."

Then he walked toward Pastor Miller, and stopped in front of the man. "Pastor, I am sorry for the heartache I've caused. I didn't know what else to do. I, like David, wish I had given my fear to the One who casts out all fear. But, as much as I hated war, I could never repent of enlisting, I could not in good conscience say I should never have joined up, because that would have meant I repented of trying to save my brothers in that camp, that I repented of trying to save the people of this colony, that I repented of trying to save your son Joshua — and I couldn't say that. Before God I could not say that. Nevertheless, I ask you to forgive me. I ask you all to forgive me."

Pastor Miller stood. "You ask for forgiveness. It is swiftly and freely given. But it is all of us you must forgive, my son. It is I, this foolish man, you must forgive." Then he took Jude into his arms and broke down.

There were few people who were not groaning or shedding tears. Half of the church was on its feet, moving toward Jude to hug him and speak with him and ask his forgiveness, while at the same time he was asking forgiveness of all who came to him. Lyyndaya had never seen anything like it. A few minutes before she had been certain the church was splitting in two. Now she realized how strong it really was. How the confession of the young men had turned the weakness of the colony into a strength.

I am standing on holy ground.

Only a few people saw the barn door open, and only a few heard Lyyndaya's brother Daniel, now eleven, say to Bishop Zook, "Sir, the whole yard is full of soldiers."

A few heads turned in shock and sudden fear even as men and women farther from the door gathered around Jude with tears and prayers. The bishop put his large hand on Daniel's shoulder and said, "I know, my boy. I have been watching them gather for the past ten minutes from that window there."

His face was grim. "Open the door, Daniel. We will not be afraid of what man may do to us. Our hope is in the Lord God who made heaven and earth. Yes, go ahead, open it wide, let them in, there has been enough fear and trembling among our people for the past two years. It is time to put it to rest once and for all. There are many ways of fighting for your country, Daniel. Today we will show the soldiers our way."

Twenty-Eight

Lyyndaya watched with apprehension as dozens of men in brown uniforms entered the barn. They fanned out and filled the space at the front, where the bishop was standing and David Hostetler, Jacob Beiler, and Jonathan Harshberger were still kneeling. Behind them came a tall lean man with a dark tan and sharp features. A gold star glittered on each side of his collar.

"Which one of you is Bishop Zook?" he asked.

The bishop stepped forward. "I am."

"Bishop, I fear we are interrupting your religious ceremonies."

"That is so."

"However, I was given to understand you had meetings to deal with church issues twice a year and this is one of those days."

"That is also true."

"Then I ask permission to speak at this meeting. Does it by any chance have to do with Jude Whetstone and whether or not Amish boys should serve their country in a combat role during a time of war?"

"Among other things, yes."

The man removed his large, broad-brimmed hat. "I'm General Omar Jackson, U.S. Army Air Service. I've been ordered to bear a message to you and your people from the government of the United States of America."

All the crying and talking in the barn had stopped and every head was turned toward the officer and his men. He tugged a folded sheet of paper from a breast pocket and began to read. But, after only a few seconds, he raised his eyes to his listeners and never returned them to the paper. Lyyndaya realized he had the document memorized. Or perhaps he was simply saying what he felt must be said.

"Some of your young men were refused the religious exemption from military service guaranteed the Amish people by act of Congress and the President of the United States. It was your constitutional right, one of the reasons our men fought in Europe in 1917 and 1918. Yet it was violated and your young men were harmed. The command to arrest your young men was undertaken without the authority or knowledge of the highest branches of the United States Army or the White House or the Congress of the United States. Nevertheless —"

The general paused, his eyes running over the Amish people clustered in front of him, the children, the women, the men. Then he folded up the paper and tucked it away in his pocket again. His eyes remain fixed on the faces before him, young and old.

"Nevertheless," he resumed, "it happened on our watch. It happened on my watch. Major Whetstone!"

Jude came forward and stood at attention in front of the general. He saluted and the salute was returned.

"Stand easy, Whetstone."

"Yes, sir."

"It was so arranged by various officers in the United States Army that your friends and neighbors, other young men your age, be arrested and detained at a military base until such time as you agreed to fly in a combat role for the United States and her allies. To that end you and your friends were denied food and proper clothing, and were beaten and subjected to abuse until you turned your back on your religious convictions to save your men's lives. No man willingly goes against what makes him tick, Whetstone — no man easily goes against what he believes in his heart and soul."

"No, sir."

"You and your men were then threatened that if word of this act of coercion on the part of certain officers in the United States Army became common knowledge, your families and community would be at risk. Taking the bit in your teeth, Whetstone, you said nothing, but chose to serve in France and take to the skies to fight the German Empire.

"You were an Amish boy and you had no business being there. Frankly, I didn't think you could cut it. I thought you would turn tail and run. Then I could have court-martialed you and sent you home in disgrace. But you fooled me, Whetstone. Me, America, and the whole German Empire. You flew like the wind and you fought in your own fashion and in so doing you proved not only the courage and faith of the Amish people, but brought a peculiar distinction to American arms they had scarcely known before — bloodless victories. For a second time, you saved the lives of men you had with you. You made me into a believer, Whetstone. And a general."

Jude smiled a quiet smile at this.

"You people," the general said, looking out over the church again. "Your courage is one of the reasons for the greatness of America. I know you don't care for the military man or his duties. Nevertheless I salute you. Whether you believe it or not, every time our army fights it fights so you can say no to warfare on behalf of America."

General Jackson came to attention and held a salute, Lyyndaya estimated, for a full minute. She knew the Amish should feel nothing at being saluted by an American soldier, certainly not excitement or pride, yet she felt both.

Still holding the salute, the general continued, "I apologize for the way your boys were treated. I apologize for the threat leveled against your community's religious freedoms and right to life, liberty, and the pursuit of happiness. I apologize for the coercion of one of your finest men, Jude Whetstone. On behalf of the army and government of the United States of America — I am sorry." He dropped his salute smartly, and Lyyndaya finally took in a big breath of air.

"One more thing, Bishop Zook, before we go, if I may," the general said.

The bishop, Lyyndaya could see, was as stunned by the way events had unfolded as everyone else in the barn. "Of course."

Jackson turned around and nodded. "Invite them in, Sergeant."

In a moment more men in uniform came into the barn, but along with them were women and children. These persons were no sooner inside where Jude could see their faces clearly than she heard him utter a cry and watched him fight to resist an impulse to rush forward. The general saw this. A smile flickered over his lips.

"Go to your men, Major," he said.

And Jude ran. Immediately the men in uniform clustered around him, hugging him, thumping him on the back, pumping his hand, laughing, shouting. Lyyndaya felt the tears come, put a hand to her mouth, and stopped breathing again. *Oh, my goodness. It is his men. The men from his squadron. I know it is.*

In a minute, Jude confirmed this. His face flushed, smiling as broadly as she had ever seen him smile, he turned to the church and announced, "These are the men who flew with me. These are the men who saved my life."

"What?" One of his men stepped forward. "We are here to set something straight today — who saved who." The men cheered.

"The guys call me Flapjack. I'm always the joker, but right now I don't have any jokes to pull out of my hat. I just want to thank you for Jude." Then an impish grin came onto his young face. "Thank you for Lover Boy." The men in the squadron laughed. "Can we finally see the gal you fought the whole German Empire for, Jude? Which one is she?" Then his roving eyes rested on Lyyndaya. "I'll bet it's you. Am I right? Am I right, Jude?" He smiled at her. She felt her face burning up as all the men in the squadron gawked at her and two of them gave low whistles. "It is you, isn't it, honey? You're the one he wrote a million letters to."

Lyyndaya dropped her eyes. *"Ja."*

"Wow. What a beauty. Now I know why Jude stayed up half the night with his pen and paper."

The men laughed again and began to come forward one after another. "I'm Billy Skipp," said a boy hardly older than Luke. "Thank you for Jude Whetstone. He really did save my life."

Another with a strong body and dark mustache brought a woman up with him and two children, both girls with black hair like their father. "I'm Zed. This is my wife, Charlotte, and my girls, Betty and Sal. The gals have got a husband and father today because of Jude Whetstone. Thank you."

A tall man walked to the front, holding a

pretty blonde woman's hand. "I won't bother with my other name," he drawled in his distinctive accent. "The boys call me Tex and I guess that's my real one. This is my fiancée, Peg. We're getting married in April. In Austin. Y'all are welcome to come." Then his long face grew serious. "I'm alive today because I had a squadron leader by the name of Jude Whetstone. Thanks a million."

Every man in Jude's squadron stood before them and expressed his thanks, often with a wife or girlfriend or one or both parents in tow — a few, like Zed, with their children. The depth of emotion was so great Lyyndaya found she was constantly having to tell herself to take a breath, she was holding it so much without realizing it. Muffled sobs made her glance back to see Pastor Miller seated on a bench with his hands over his face. He kept groaning, "Ah, God, ah, God."

When the men had finished expressing their thanks to the community, Flapjack stepped forward with a huge black book in his hands. He offered it to Jude. "This is the Squadron Bible. Lord knows we got strength from it often enough. The boys wanted you to have it. They've signed their names in the flyleaf."

Now, Lyyndaya knew, *my man will not be able to hold back his own tears.*

And she was right. His eyes glistening, Jude thanked Flapjack and took the heavy book from him and held it to his chest like the precious thing it was. Then Zed came with a large and weathered American flag folded into the military triangle.

"We know the Amish don't fly the flag," Zed began. "But we know they love America as much as we do. It's the squadron flag, Jude. We saved it when they closed the aerodrome and we hauled the Stars and Stripes down for the last time. We don't expect you to fly it. But we want you to keep it safe somewhere in that house your little lady and you will be making a home in. Just to remind you of us and the months in France. And that God sometimes moves in mysterious ways his wonders to perform."

Jude took the flag. "It's an honor. A great honor."

Lyyndaya heard Bishop Zook murmur *Amen.*

"Squadron, ten-hut!" The men formed up behind Zed, stood at attention, and saluted Jude. He came to attention and returned the salute.

"God bless you . . . God bless all of you," Jude said, his voice tight with feeling. "I thank God no more of you were lost . . . after I left you so unexpectedly."

"That is a story we would like to hear, sir," Flapjack said.

"Some other time," General Jackson cut in. "We have to let these people get back to their service. Their prayers make a better America, I think we can all agree on that."

"Yes, sir," said Flapjack.

"Wait." The bishop stepped toward the general. "It is true we have other things to say and do, other prayers to pray, as you say. But I think it is time to eat a bit, hm?" He looked at his congregation. "Shall we not have lunch with our friends? Shall we not ask them to stay? Is their coming not the hand of God?"

Lyyndaya heard the people voice their consent.

"You will not have enough food for my men and myself," General Jackson protested. "Just host Jude's squadron. The rest of us will head back to base."

"But that will be army food at the base, General," the bishop pointed out.

"Yes."

"So unless the army has changed a great deal because you had an Amish pilot, I think it is better your men have some, what you *English* call, *home cooking.* Yes?"

"We have plenty of food." Rachel Miller was on her feet and smiling. "It will only make us fat if we try to eat it by ourselves. There is plenty to share. Please remain with us, General."

"Well —"

The bishop, towering over General Jackson, placed a hand on his shoulder. "I look at your men and their faces say *home cooking.*"

The soldiers and the Amish laughed. Even, to Jude's astonishment, General Jackson.

"Very well," the general said. "Just tell us where to line up." He turned to his men. "Fall out for chow!" he barked.

So they ate together, Amish and soldiers and pilots side by side, men in uniform and men in Amish jackets and shirts setting up wooden tables in the barn together. One after another Jude's men found an excuse to sit with Lyyndaya and chat, plates of potatoes and meat and fresh bread in their hands.

To her surprise, many of the young men clustered around her older sister, Ruth, and kept her talking so much she hardly ate. How her sister was laughing! And Billy Skipp was obviously fascinated by her younger sister's sandy brown hair and red lips and was doing all he could to engage Sarah and get her to laugh as well. He seemed to be succeeding. *Well,* thought Lyyndaya with a shrug as she glanced their way now and then, *why not?* There couldn't be more than a year between them. Looking around she saw that a number of the soldiers had found their way to a smiling, jade-eyed Emma Zook. That was no surprise at all.

I am glad for you, Emma. You have suffered enough and lost enough. It is good to see your green eyes dance again.

The goodbyes were long. But Lyyndaya had the strongest sense she would see many of the men from Jude's squadron again so she didn't feel she was saying farewell for all eternity. The whole community waited outside in the warm March afternoon to see the soldiers and pilots off. General Jackson was the last one to leave. Climbing into his Dodge Brothers staff car he looked back at Jude.

"How are you feeling, Major?"

"You made my day, sir."

"Did I? I don't think I've heard too many of my men say that during my military career. It took a lot of work getting that crew of yours together again. Half of them had mustered out."

"I appreciate the effort you put into it, sir."

"I could see that you did. The work was my pleasure, Whetstone. And my duty. It was necessary that an apology be extended toward your people for what the army did. But it was also necessary that the Amish not reject and exclude you because you fought for your country. It was important to me that I make it clear to them the manner in which you fought and who it was you saved because you bit the bullet and enlisted and flew into harm's way."

He put out his hand. "It's been an honor, Whetstone. If you're ever out Pima County way I'd like your help working my cattle. You can even bring your Appaloosa. I think I noticed him on the way in."

Jude shook his hand. "Thank you, sir. That was Grit, all right. The only Appie in Paradise. Perhaps if I fly into your ranch you can rustle another one up for me."

"An Appie? Among my paints?" He barked a laugh. "Don't hold your breath."

"I won't, sir. It would be a privilege to ride one of your paints, sir."

The car began to drive off, following the convoy of trucks and vehicles ahead of it. The general gave a quick salute. "Stand easy, Whetstone."

Then the church returned to the barn and sang hymns. Bishop Zook gave a short message about Christ's sacrifice on the cross for the human race. After that the leadership drew straws to see who would preach the second and longer sermon. The lot fell to Pastor Miller. Lyyndaya had never heard him speak with more gentleness, love, and depth. Everything that had happened that day went into his message, everything that had happened since Jude had returned from the dead, everything that had happened over the past two years.

When he was done, the bishop said more time would now be granted to those who felt they needed to make things right with Jude or with anyone else. Another hour was spent with people grouped around Jude, praying and hugging and weeping. Then Pastor Stoltzfus and Pastor King brought out a large round loaf of white bread, cut it up, and gave pieces to the bishop and Pastor Miller as well as taking portions for themselves. Following this, they brought the bread to everyone. Lyyndaya took her piece when they made their way to the women. Standing when she received it, she sat to eat, praying to Jesus. A large pewter cup of red wine was then brought to the congregation and she stood with the others once more, took a sip when it came to her, and sat down.

The women began to wash each other's feet among each other and the men did the same among themselves. Lyyndaya bent and removed her shoes and socks. Glancing over, she saw Bishop Zook wash Pastor King's feet and Pastor King wash the bishop's. "The Lord be with us," they said to one another and kissed each other on the cheek.

It was expected that Pastor Miller would then wash Pastor Stoltzfus's feet, but he made his way to Jude instead. Pastor Stoltzfus nodded at the gesture. After the pastor had dried Jude's feet, Jude asked him to sit down. Jude then washed and dried Pastor Miller's feet and the two embraced, kissing one another and murmuring, "The Lord be with us. Amen." Lyyndaya felt a great peace settling down over the Lapp Amish of Paradise, as if a dove had descended on soft white wings from the sky above the town.

"Please. Let me wash your feet, sister." It was Rachel Miller. "I can never forget that you held my child tightly in your arms as you flew over the earth. Christ be with you." She slowly washed Lyyndaya's feet, wringing out the cloth in a wooden bucket. Then she dried each foot carefully, even between the toes, as if Lyyndaya were one of her own children. Lyyndaya then knelt and did the same for her. When they embraced, Rachel whispered, "Marry that boy. And do not take forever."

Once the foot washing was finished and a final hymn sung, once there had been the last hugs and handshakes and kisses, it was Lyyndaya Kurtz and Jude Whetstone who stood alone in front of the Zook barn amid the mud and wheel ruts.

Lyyndaya smiled. "You had yourself quite a day, Master Whetstone."

"Everyone had quite a day. Thanks be to God."

"Amen. So what's next? Your father left us Grit and a buggy. Will you give me a ride home — the long way around?"

He laughed. "If you mean doing a long loop by way of Pittsburgh and Chicago and Omaha in order to avoid the worst puddles, my answer is yes." He took her hand. "But first, please come around to the back of the barn."

"The back of the barn? What are your intentions?" teased Lyyndaya.

"Come." He tugged her around to the other side of the large red building.

"But people will be watching."

"Who?" He stood with her and looked out

over the empty brown and green fields. "Who do you see? Ah, there is a flock of crows — is that who you meant? The old crows are watching?"

She grinned and punched his shoulder. "Stop."

"Bishop Zook said I should marry you quickly. That I shouldn't wait until the fall, but wed you early, in the summer, like the Amish do in Ohio. Pastor Miller told me the same thing."

"His wife told me that as well."

"Did she?" Jude tipped his straw hat back on his head. "What do you think, Lyyndy? Should we charge ahead?"

"Charge ahead? You and your *English* expressions. All right, let's charge ahead. Is that what you dragged me around to the back of the barn to tell me?"

"Not exactly." He put his hands in his pockets. "You know, out there in Philadelphia and Pittsburgh and Boston a boy gives a girl an engagement ring when they say they want to marry one another."

She arched her eyebrows. "But this is not so among the Amish. Now what are you up to?"

"No, you are right, it is not so among the Amish. I'm supposed to give you a practical and plain gift — like china. Or a clock." He made a face. "That does not suit me."

Her eyes gleamed and narrowed and became her cat's eyes. She took both his hands in hers and squeezed them until he winced. "No? What does suit you — Lover Boy?"

They both laughed. Then he tugged a hand free. "If you haven't broken all the bones in my fingers I'll show you." He brought a white scarf out of his back pocket. "There. A plain, practical Amish engagement gift from a man to his beauty."

Her eyes brightened as she unfolded the scarf and let it run through her hands. "This can only be pure silk. It's wonderful." Then her lips curved upward. "But how is this a plain and practical Amish engagement gift I can explain to my mother?"

Jude took the scarf and gently wound it about Lyyndaya's throat. "In the war we always had to have eyes at the back of our heads. Since God did not put any there we were forced to twist our neck in every direction imaginable to try to spot enemy planes before they jumped us. Without this scarf a pilot's skin would be worn raw in a few days. It had to be silk. Cotton wouldn't work and certainly not wool."

"Ah," she smiled. "So I shall tell Mama when I go up in my plane to fight the German Empire this silk scarf will keep the skin on my throat from chafing."

"Exactly. Though I really do have something more practical in mind." He pulled her to himself. "Fly with me across America, Lyyndy. Before too many years the sky will be full of planes, and there will be so many rules about where we can go and what we can do that it will feel like the Amish have written a flight *Ordnung.* Fly with me now while the air is still clear and free. Then you can look up and down, east and west, for the most beautiful sights in God's creation, point them out to me one after another, and never have to worry about rubbing the skin raw on your pretty little neck."

She ran her fingers over his face, her eyes getting greener by the minute. "And you? What will you use your silk scarf for?"

"Not much. Staring straight ahead. You see, the most beautiful sight in God's creation will be right in front of me."

She reddened. "Ah, my brown-eyed Amish boy. You still know how to win the extra kisses."

"And behind the barn too."

"*Ja,* behind the barn with the old crows." Laughing, she brought his head down and put her lips warmly against his.

TWENTY-NINE

Bishop Zook let his horse take its time plodding down the hot, dusty road toward the Stoltzfus meadow. The laughter of children reached his ears, giving him both joy and a sharp pang of sorrow.

"But my John and my Annie do not grieve as I do, Lord," he said out loud so that his horse twisted its left ear back toward him. "They run and play with you and are like the angels in heaven. And I do not grieve as one without hope."

The Curtiss Jenny became obvious as the buggy rolled around the last turn in the road. Along its fuselage, in bright white paint against the yellow paint of the plane, was the name LYYNDY. The bishop bit into the toothpick in his mouth. The plane cost around four thousand dollars, even as army surplus. It had been a gift that Jude could not refuse, but he had never discovered who had purchased it for him until the Communion Sunday. Then Flapjack and Zed admitted the boys in the squadron had chipped in and raised the money. General Jackson himself had contributed half the sum. The bishop shook his head. When God was on the move in people's hearts, anything was possible.

The pie table was set up under the tall shade trees again, his daughter and wife serving up slices. There had even been ice cream for the first two hours. Many families had spread their blankets nearby, but few of them were occupied. Almost everyone stood around the aircraft that rested in the freshly cut hay field. Jude and Lyyndaya were smiling and chatting, but they had already tugged their leather helmets down over their heads, pulled on their flying jackets, and wrapped white silk scarves around their necks. They were ready to lift off.

"Here he is!"

"He finally made it!"

"Are all the cows milked so quickly, Jeremiah? It's only just noon."

He waved his free hand as the people laughed and clapped. "I would not miss the chance of giving that propeller a turn one more time," he called.

Stepping down from the buggy, he wiped his hands on his pants and extended his hand to Jude. "Congratulations to you, young man."

"Thank you, Bishop Zook."

Then he leaned down and planted a brief kiss on Lyyndaya's cheek. "Is that your wedding dress I see peeking out from under your flight jacket, my dear?"

"*Ja.* It's too beautiful to take off. Your daughter is a wonderful seamstress."

Emma laughed. "Don't make my Amish head swell. Turquoise is your color. That's why you like the dress so much. Not because of the stitching."

"No, it's more than the color. It falls from my shoulders just right. I know you spent a lot of time on the dress. It's perfection." Lyyndaya kissed Emma on the cheek. "Thank you again, sister."

Emma kissed her back. *"Bitte."*

Bishop Zook put his hands on his hips. "So you get married in July instead of December. You go on a honeymoon instead of helping with the haying. The aeroplane is something you own, not one you have borrowed. Are there any more Amish traditions you wish to break this summer?"

As the people laughed, Jude reached up to the bishop's height and put a hand on his shoulder. "The Amish have said no to the telephone and now to the electricity poles.

They may be a passenger in a car, but not drive or own one. However, nothing has yet been finalized about the aeroplane."

The bishop smiled. "Go quickly then, before a messenger comes and tells me every time an Amish plane goes up an Amish bishop must be in it to be sure it comes down safely and in the right place. Then where will your bride sit?"

Lyyndaya grinned her green-eyed tomboy grin. "On the wing." Then she became quiet and everyone saw her eyes brimming. "Thank you for everything. All of you. Mama, Papa. Ruth, Sarah — my young beauty. Harley, Daniel, Luke, my handsome men. Pastor Miller. Rachel."

"Jacob," Pastor Miller corrected her.

"Jacob."

Jude was shaking hands and giving hugs. "Papa. Mr. Kurtz. Mrs. Kurtz. Ruth. God bless you." Then Jude turned and saw Pastor Miller waiting. The two men stood for a few seconds and then they embraced as tears formed in the pastor's eyes. "Godspeed, my boy."

"Thank you, my friend," Jude said as the two men released their embrace.

Jude turned and helped Lyyndaya into the front cockpit, then clambered into his own. Bishop Zook rested one large hand on the side of the Jenny.

"Where is your first stop?" the bishop asked.

"I hope I can get past Pittsburgh to an army base for refueling," replied Jude. "After that, we keep heading west until we fly over the Grand Canyon. They say it is one of the great wonders of God."

"A military base? But you are no longer in the army."

Jude shrugged. "They still do me favors."

"Well, as God opens the doors so we should walk through. You will write us all? *Ja?*"

"Once we're in Pima County in Arizona," Lyyndaya promised. "If we try to go over the Grand Canyon and head to California to see Zed without stopping at the Jackson Ranch, that crazy general of Jude's will probably have us shot down."

Jude's father handed him the wooden aeroplane. "Here's 'Kitty.' She's been everywhere else with you. Might as well join you across America."

"Thanks, Papa."

"Christ be with you, my son." He held Lyyndaya's hand a moment. "And with you, my daughter."

"Amen, Papa. God's peace."

People began to step back from the plane

and mothers shooed their children toward the fence. Bishop Zook stepped to the front of the plane.

"I'm sorry, Adam," he said to Jude's father. "Bishop's rights."

Adam Whetstone laughed. "It's all right, Jeremiah. At least I won't lose my hat."

Jude reached forward to touch his bride. "Are you ready, Barrel Roll Kurtz?"

"Why? Are we going to do one?"

"As soon as I reach a thousand feet. That's how I want them to remember us."

"I'm strapped in."

"You could take your helmet off too."

She laughed. "So my nicely brushed hair can fly all over the sky?"

"Something like that," he grinned.

"We'll see."

"Here we go. Love you."

"Really love you."

He gave the thumbs up. Bishop Zook pulled down on a propeller blade with a burst of strength. The engine roared and Jude turned the Jenny into the wind while the bishop chased after his straw hat.

The people watched as LYYNDY raced over the stubble and rose into the blue sky. No one was interested in pies or games or lemonade. Their eyes were fastened on the aircraft as it lifted higher and higher.

"If only he would do a stunt," Lyyndaya's father whispered.

A minute later and the Curtiss Jenny turned over on its side, hung upside down for several long seconds, then flipped right side up again. Everyone shouted. Amos Kurtz gave a very un-Amish cheer.

"I saw her hair!" squealed Sarah.

Emma announced that she had fresh lemon and cherry pies and even one last batch of freshly churned ice cream that would soon turn into colored water if it was not eaten. Boys and girls ran for the shade trees and the pie table while Emma ran after them. Families returned to their blankets, and even the Kurtzes and Adam Whetstone turned away, walking and talking together.

But Bishop Zook lingered, straw hat back firmly on his head. He stood in the empty hay field until the plane was only a dot and indistinguishable from a swallow or robin. Finally he whispered a prayer for their safe journey and safe return. Only then did he decide that a large slice of cherry pie from his daughter's hand, a scoop of ice cream, and a tall glass of lemonade sounded like a good idea. Turning away and walking back across the field a cluster of verses came to mind, and he thanked God, smiled, and began to whistle.

When the Lord turned again the
captivity of Zion,
we were like them that dream.
Then was our mouth filled with
laughter,
and our tongue with singing:
then said they among the heathen,
The Lord hath done great things for
them.
The Lord hath done great things for us;
whereof we are glad.

ABOUT THE AUTHOR

Murray Pura earned his Master of Divinity degree from Acadia University in Wolfville, Nova Scotia, and his ThM degree in theology and interdisciplinary studies from Regent College in Vancouver, British Columbia. For more than twenty-five years, in addition to his writing, he has pastored churches in Nova Scotia, British Columbia, and Alberta. Murray's writings have been shortlisted for the Dartmouth Book Award, the John Spencer Hill Literary Award, the Paraclete Fiction Award, and Toronto's Kobzar Literary Award. Murray pastors and writes in southern Alberta near the Rocky Mountains. He and his wife, Linda, have a son and a daughter.

Visit Murray's website at
www.MurrayPura.com